THE
GENTLEMAN'S
GENTLEMAN

SAMANTHA SORELLE

His Lordship's Realm

Balcarres Books LLC

ISBN-13: 978-1-952789-19-9

ISBN-10: 1-952789-19-2

Cover design by: Samantha SoRelle

To Mutiny, my constant companion.

CONTENTS

CHAPTER 1

Kilconquhar, Scotland

March 1819

"To the cats being away."

Jarrett raised his tankard in salute. It would be a better toast if he had someone to share it with, but he didn't, so he tapped his drink against the scarred wood of the bar and took a swig. The ale was only passable, but he wasn't going to waste his own coin on better when he had an employer who was blessed with both a fine collection of spirits and a poor memory when it came to how full the bottles had been before his valet tidied the room.

Not that Jarrett was keen to take advantage of the earl any time soon. He seemed fair enough as far as that sort went. Besides, the Right Honourable Alfred Pennington the Earl of Crawford and Balcarres or Some Such came part-and-parcel with his handsome companion, Dominick, no title given. The two were absolutely besotted with each other so Jarrett didn't have a chance with either man, but still, he could look. Although he wouldn't even have the opportunity to do that any time soon.

He'd seen the pair off in their carriage yesterday as they'd headed towards Edinburgh to catch the mail coach to London on some urgent errand. They hadn't said much to Jarrett other than they'd be gone for some time and that his services wouldn't be required.

He hadn't argued. He barely had skills enough to make the earl presentable for local society, which was mostly sheep. He'd be woefully out of place in London. Still, he'd have liked the chance to see Tattersall's. The horses sold there were said to be some of the finest in the world. He probably couldn't afford even a single shoe for horseflesh like that, but again, he could look.

He frowned into his drink. Hopefully, the earl wasn't looking for a real valet while he was in London. Occasional tipple aside, Jarrett was working hard to learn his new duties since working his way up through the ranks. Aside from that, he'd gotten used to sleeping indoors in a real bed and a room with actual walls, not just in the loft over stables. There'd be worse things than going back to being a footman, or even all the way back down to stable lad, but it wasn't nearly as fine as being able to say he was a *valet*.

A valet with nothing to do until the earl returned except hope he'd still have a job.

He shook his head to dislodge the thought. He might have more experience with real horses than the horses' arses that made up the nobility, but the earl was a good man. If worse came to worse, Jarrett would at least be walking away from Balcarres House with a good reference and full pockets. Either way, life was far too short to worry about the future. The cats were away and this mouse wasn't going to miss his chance to play. Now if only he could find someone to play with...

He let his eyes roam the room. The Kinneuchar Inn was doing a brisk trade tonight with a fair mix of those just passing through and locals filling its whitewashed walls. The locals all had their usual spots, and God help the outsider that claimed one of those. They clustered around the fire, warming gnarled hands and having the same conversations about the weather they had every night. Jarrett was bored just looking at them.

If he was going to tup a farmer, he wanted a great strapping lad, not one old enough to be his grandfather—or great-grandfather. And if he was to go after a shopkeeper, it'd be one with soft hands and a smooth voice, not a phlegmy cough and a wife at home with the bairns. Beggars might not be choosers, but Jarrett liked to think he had *some* standards.

Besides, for the type of play he was looking for, he'd be safer finding a man who was only staying a single night, or even better, only an hour or so while his horses were changed for the next leg of his journey. A handful of minutes in a secluded spot and they could both go away content, never having to worry about seeing each other again.

The villages around Balcarres House were wee more than clusters of homes, most too small for even a kirk or a decent pub so his options for local companionship were few. That Kilconquhar had both, and right across the lane from each other, made it the largest town for miles and was certainly convenient on a Sunday morning. When he'd first arrived in town, he'd looked for signs of interest among the locals gathered for a pint after Sunday services, but gotten none back. As far as he could tell, the only other men of his sort were Lord Crawford and Dominick and while it was fun to flirt because he could, they'd made it clear that they were firmly unavailable.

It was all right. He did well enough by the men just passing through. Besides, not counting the two out of reach, he could count on a single hand the number of local men he had any interest in. Well, a single finger really. Unfortunately, all the flirting in the world couldn't turn a gentleman who preferred the contents of petticoats to breeches. And from the giggled gossip he overheard near daily, that single gentleman liked the contents of many, *many* petticoats.

So that left Jarrett to catch what few minutes of pleasure he could from like-minded men passing through. Not that it'd ever been otherwise for him.

He thought back to Lord Crawford and Dominick. *What must it be like to wake up next to the same man every morning? To wake up next to him at all instead of just shrugging your trousers back on after and calling it a night?*

He drained his tankard. Aye, that had better be his last for the night, clearly ale turned him into a right soppy bastard.

"Another of those?" asked Marta from behind the bar, testing his better judgement.

Before he could answer, a great mass of woollen coat heaved its way beside him.

"I'll take one."

Jarrett slid a glance over at the stranger. Over... and up. And up. Lord, the man was tall. Big, too. The path he'd shouldered through the crowd was wide enough for two or three Jarretts to walk abreast, and if that greatcoat hid as muscular a body as those broad shoulders suggested, then Jarrett might be in for a real treat.

The greatcoat suggested other things too. Long and heavy with a great flapping cape, it was the sort worn by those expecting to spend hours in foul weather, coachmen and night watchmen in particular. The latter was reason enough to give him pause, making this a worse idea than usual. But if the man was a coachman just passing through, it would be cruel of Jarrett to deprive him of everything the county had to offer...

Besides, the odds were on his side. It was a common enough sort of coat. In fact, if he checked the kitchens at Balcarres now, he'd find a rack of the same waiting for use by any servant who had to go out when the weather was miserable, which being Scotland, was often. Add to that, if Magistrate Carnbee had added a new night watchman he'd have been strutting around crowing about it.

But if Jarrett had a pound for every coach driver he'd seen in the inn wearing that exact coat with its cape about the shoulders and hem splattered with mud, he'd have a stable of his own horses by now and a fine house to go with it. Perhaps even a fine gentleman to keep him company. Jarrett would never be as well-turned-out as the earl, but surely all those imaginary pounds could tempt someone to stay with him for more than just a night.

Perhaps even a fine gentleman with coal-black hair, flashing eyes behind golden spectacles, and mouth that always seemed half-curled in a grin...

He shook his head. No use wishing for things—and men—he couldn't have. Better to stay in the here-and-now. As the stranger accepted his drink from Marta with a nod, Jarrett gave him a thorough looking over.

It was a dangerous game, this part, with high stakes. If Jarrett made a mistake he might end up with a black eye. If he *really* made a mistake he might wind up before the magistrate. Still, there were signs and codes he'd picked up over the years that sounded innocent enough to ordinary men, but held special meaning for men like himself.

He leaned his elbows on the bar, bending at the waist and straightening his legs so his arse might be displayed to the best effect if the man cared to look. He'd be the first to admit he didn't have the plumpest rump in the world nor the longest legs—a less confident man might even consider himself a wee bit bony and more than a wee bit short. But he had a lean figure that many men appreciated. Being rather vain about his high cheekbones as well, he turned his head to just the right angle, long practice letting him know how to accentuate them in the lamplight.

"Just come in off the road?" Jarrett asked.

The stranger gave him a quick glance then went back to his drink. "Aye."

Not the most promising start, but Jarrett had had worse. "In town for long?"

"No."

Still only one-word answers, but when the stranger spoke, he looked at Jarrett again, a little longer this time. It wasn't quite, *Meet you round back,* but it was something. Jarrett risked pressing a little further.

"Would be a shame to miss the sights before you left. I know a lovely, quiet spot for stargazing."

This time, the stranger's gaze didn't leave Jarrett at all. Well, that was more promising. Unless he was simply sizing Jarrett up to see whether it would take one blow to fell the molly making advances on him or two.

The slightest prickle of wariness chose that moment to make itself known. The stranger didn't seem inclined to violence yet, which was just as well because he likely wouldn't even have to spill his ale to knock Jarrett senseless.

Big and tall—Jarrett had already noticed that—the man had a flat mouth which didn't seem inclined to smile, at least not at him, and a long straight nose, which looked never to have been broken. That hopefully meant he wasn't the sort to solve his disagreements with his fists. Promising, unless he was too damned good a fighter to get struck, which was worrying.

There was little else to give away where the stranger's inclinations lay, nothing pinned to his lapel or affixed to the band of his hat. The only thing that marked him at all was his unexpectedly garish trousers which were mostly concealed by the swirl of the greatcoat. Jarrett caught a flash of red and green plaid.

Definitely a city man then. Edinburgh, most likely, as it was closest. City fashions took a long time to make it out into the countryside, but if that's what they were wearing there now, Jarrett wasn't looking forward to their arrival in County Fife. The single strand of yellow that cut through the plaid made the pattern hideous enough to hurt his eyes from just a single glance. If the earl returned with a trunk full of them, Jarrett might have to resign or risk going blind.

At least Edinburgh trousers meant that if this went to hell, Jarrett would never see the stranger again, one way or the other. He decided to make one last attempt before admitting defeat.

"Ah aye," he continued, "the stars are quite lovely when it's not raining."

"Too bad it's Scotland then," the man snorted, but he raised his fingers at Marta to signal fresh drinks for himself and Jarrett. *Promising.*

"There is that," Jarrett all but purred. "But it's not raining now. Would you like me to show you? I find it a very *inspiring* place, especially at night. Secluded too. Few people are inclined to wander after dark in these parts, especially not to the chapel ruins."

In an instant, the stranger was in Jarrett's face, the bulk of him that had seemed so enticing a moment before now nothing but a threat.

"What did you say?" the stranger snarled.

Jarrett shrank down as best he could. He barely noticed the clank as Marta set two fresh tankards down in front of them, no doubt already reaching for the cudgel she kept beneath the bar.

Jarrett raised his hands. "Easy now, it was just a suggestion. I didn't mean to cause offence if you're a religious sort. The chapel hasn't been used in years. It's just ruins, like I said."

"I'm not fucking going to any fucking chapel ruins." The stranger spit. "And you'd best not either if you know what's good for you."

"Fine, aye. I meant no harm."

"Good." The stranger eased back a fraction of an inch. Still intimidating, but with enough space for Jarrett to slip away. He did just that, casting a longing glance at the fresh tankard meant for him, but he'd pressed his luck enough for one night.

With mumbled goodbyes, he exited the inn, feeling very much like a dog with its tail between its legs. He pointedly did *not* look back at the stranger in the greatcoat. Whatever his business was, it was none of Jarrett's. From some men, a display like that might mean the just opposite. Sometimes, "I'm not going somewhere to have it off with you!" meant, "Meet me there instead." But he didn't want to find out if that was the case. If that giant bugger somehow found his way to the chapel and waited for Jarrett to show up, then let him. Jarrett hoped he froze a bollock off.

That thought was enough to cheer him on the walk back to Balcarres. It wasn't the way he'd wanted to end the night, but at least with the house understaffed at the best of times and its master away, the earl's spirits would be unguarded. For that matter, so would his stables.

Jarrett let out a low whistle. The stablemaster had taken his young son with him to act as carriage footman when he drove off with the earl and his companion this morning. They'd be back as early as possible tomorrow, but he could go for a ride tonight without anyone noticing. What would be the harm? In fact, if it wasn't as late as he thought, he might just have time to ride to Kirkcaldy.

There was a pub there where three roads met, the main road from St. Andrews, the coastal road, and the one coming down from Perth. He'd found out about it through rumours and asking the right sorts of questions. The Cross Keys looked like a normal pub, and was for the most part. But if a certain type of man knew the right words to get him into the rear room, he might find all sorts of like-minded other men to share a drink with, or even a room upstairs.

He picked up his pace, determined not to waste a moment more. He'd have to stop in the kitchens as well, grab himself his own damned greatcoat if he was going to be out riding all night—and hopefully *riding* all night. But how often was he going to have a chance like this? It would be a long ride each way, barely doable in a night, but he wasn't going to let his new freedom be wasted.

It was time for this mouse to play.

CHAPTER 2

As Gil Charleton stepped into The Cross Keys, he was momentarily blinded. Cursing, he removed his spectacles. It hadn't begun to rain just yet, but going from the cold damp air into the hot press of too many bodies in too small a space was enough to fog the glass.

He wiped the lenses with his handkerchief before sliding the gold frames up his nose. As the room came into focus, he couldn't help but grin. The back room of The Cross Keys was filled to bursting tonight; for once he'd be spoiled for choice. In fairness, it wasn't a large room and it wasn't—by most standards—a large crowd, but he was used to being the only one of his sort, so to see at least thirty, perhaps even forty men all with the same interest in other men? It might as well have main street on market day.

He hung up his coat and made his way towards the bar, nodding at a few familiar faces. A man he didn't know cocked his head towards the stairs with a raised eyebrow, but Gil shook his head. If the man was still free later, Gil wouldn't be opposed to seeing where a bit of conversation led—although he doubted someone that brazen would be willing to wait for Gil to determine if he was worth the risk when there were easier pickings available—but such was the price of circumspection. For now, Gil simply wanted to enjoy a few drinks in like-minded company before considering more intimate relations.

Whistles and shouts rose from the rear of the pub as some brave couple he couldn't see amongst the crowd made clear why they were headed out the back, threatening weather or no. Easier pickings indeed.

He could practically feel the tension sliding off his shoulders with each step further into the pub. He resisted the urge to shake himself like a wet dog, letting his worry fly off him in droplets. Even for The Cross Keys, that sort of behaviour would be considered peculiar. By the time he'd gotten his pint and claimed one of the few free tables, he felt like a new man. One who didn't have to worry about business, or investments, or his bloody family never giving him a moment's peace.

Gil cursed again. He'd promised himself he wouldn't let any of them spoil his night. He should be at home catching up on paperwork. As Lord Crawford's estate manager, he'd been run off his feet getting everything arranged for the earl's departure and had been fully planning on spending the evening curled up with a stack of ledgers when his lout of an older brother had started in on him again over supper and Gil couldn't take another moment. It was a more impulsive decision than he preferred to make, but he only got the chance to come to The Cross Keys every few months and now that he was here, he'd be damned if he let yet another argument with Robert ruin it. On the ride back tomorrow, he'd have to think up a good lie about where he'd spent the night as the snapped, "Business!" he'd shouted at his father as he stormed out was only going to lead to further prying and a lecture. But that was a problem for the future.

A small glass of something clear and potent was set down on the table in front of him.

"Y'could use something stronger."

Gil recognised the voice immediately.

"Daniel! How've you been?" he asked, leaping to his feet and embracing the other man. "And how long has it been? Last April, was it? Or no, the trees were still bare, my God, don't tell me it's been a full year!"

He and "Daniel" had met at the pub several years back when Gil was just a twig of a thing, blinking and terrified. Daniel had taken Gil under his wing, steering him away from the wolves and introducing him to a few fellows who'd be kind to an inexperienced young man without eating him alive. It was a kindness Gil would never be able to repay.

They'd spent a few nights together themselves, even though Gil got the feeling he wasn't quite what Daniel was looking for. But that was all right as Daniel, while kind, wasn't quite what Gil was looking for either. Daniel didn't say much and they'd never spoken about it, just as they'd never told each other their real names, but from his long absences and the scores of tattoos that littered his body, Gil assumed he was a sailor. Gil respected that calling, but he was too tied to the earth, to the land that bore his family name, even if it would never be his.

"I think you're right," Gil said, picking up the glass and knocking its contents back in one. He winced at the burn. No one came to The Cross Keys because of the quality of the liquor, that was for certain.

Daniel took the other chair and let Gil talk at him for the next hour about nothing in particular, adding nods and a few comments of his own here and there, but never choosing two words when one would do and even that one was often hard to hear over raucous party at the rear of the pub. But Daniel seemed content to listen until he spotted an unattended cribbage board and Gil let himself be dragged into a game. They played for no stakes, only bragging rights, and he couldn't remember the last time he'd had this much fun. The foot bumping his under the table was the only distraction, but one he hardly minded.

He slit his eyes the next time Daniel did it again. Daniel was handsome in a windburned way, laugh lines carved deep around his eyes, his fair hair lightened even further by the same sun that had darkened his skin. They were of the same height, neither too tall nor too short, but that was where the similarities between them ended. Instead of short fair hair, Gil's was black as ink,

and he let it grow unfashionably long, finding it easier to tie it
back with a ribbon than continuously remember to trim it. He
might not be as pale as most Scotsmen with all the hours he
spent outdoors managing the earl's lands, but the Scottish sun
would never allow him to bronze as deeply as Daniel. Daniel was
built like a blacksmith, all arms and shoulders, while a lifetime
of tramping up hills and over crags had left Gil with a trim build
and legs like iron. Not to mention a most shapely backside, as
more than one previous lover had been inclined to comment.

The foot nudged his again.

Daniel was a friend, nothing more, and there was no
understanding between them. Gil had planned to seek out
someone new tonight, hoping that perhaps this time... but it
didn't matter. It was getting late and whoever it was he was
looking for wouldn't be walking into The Cross Keys tonight.
How could he, when Gil wasn't even certain himself what it was
he wanted?

Daniel was easy, and safe. Really, what more could he ask for?
He'd invite Daniel to join him in one of the rooms upstairs,
spend a pleasant night together, then in the morning Gil could
ride back home, satisfied in body if not in spirit.

He leaned over to ask, but Daniel cut him off with a nod,
setting his cards down and heading towards the stairs. Gil had
a quick word with the publican to arrange payment for a room
above before following. As he reached the top of the staircase,
he couldn't help but look back over the crowd of men to soak
up the sounds of their merriment. He smiled, filled with joy at
their joy.

Then the back door was flung open to another round of
cheers and two men stumbled back in, looking more than a
wee bit worse for wear. One seemed annoyed by the attention,
scowling and melting back into the crowd, but the other threw
back his head in delight, grinning from ear to ear.

It couldn't be.

Gil crouched down, hiding behind the banister like a child
trying to spy on his parents' dinner party.

There was nothing in particular that stood out about the man he was looking at, there were a dozen other thin men with medium-brown hair in the room, but there was no mistaking that flash of sharp features over a dangerously shapely mouth.

It was Jarrett Welch. God*damn* it, it was Jarrett Welch. Valet to the Earl of Crawford, phenomenal rider, and the one person who had ever made Gil lose his words.

Gil had had teachers quite literally gag him just to get through a lesson without interruption, was always happy to pass the time with every farmer who wanted to lean against a fence post for a yarn, and had fostered a reputation as a silver tongue who could talk his way into any woman's affections, although if they compared notes, they'd realise that no woman could actually claim to have bedded him. Yet around Jarrett, his words simply dried up. He'd start to say something, then the light would catch the knife blade of Jarrett's jaw, or the curl of his fingers, so fine and yet so strong, and Gil would find himself making excuses. Or even worse, commenting on the weather.

His heart beat loudly in his chest. He'd suspected, from things that Jarrett had said that might mean something innocent or might mean something far too interesting, and noted the way he always stared a little too long after the earl's companion, Dominick. But he'd been too afraid he was only seeing what he wanted to see.

Now he knew for certain. Jarrett was like him. Jarrett enjoyed the company of men. Would Jarrett enjoy the company of Gil?

The thought was enough to take his breath away. Not just because Jarrett was attractive, but because he was someone near, someone Gil could see more than once every few months, every few years even. By Gil's standards, Charleton House wasn't much of a walk from Balcarres House where Jarrett worked. If they wanted to, they could see each other every day. All he had to do was go talk to him and see if he was interested.

But what if he wasn't interested?

And that was the rub, wasn't it? As it was, he knew about Jarrett, but Jarrett didn't know about him. Nobody knew about him, except for Dominick, who Gil had entrusted with the truth in a moment of peril. Was it worth the risk?

He was, by nature, a very careful man. His greatest risk was his infrequent visits to The Cross Keys, but he never used his real name, never said what he did for a living, and if the pub hadn't been several hours' ride away, he probably wouldn't come at all.

He was safe that way, treating his half-truths the same way he treated his money—with deliberate precision, letting them grow piece by piece into something that would give him long-term security. Telling Jarrett would be like gambling it all on a single turn of a card.

He peered between the slats of the banister, calculating his odds.

Below, Jarrett was winding his way from man to man, letting his hands linger in places they shouldn't. Gil couldn't hear what he was saying, but he could see the effect it was having on the other men downstairs. Then one man pulled Jarrett down into his lap, and Jarrett let out a peal of laughter that caught the attention of the whole room.

Gil turned away with a heavy heart. He'd seen enough. He'd always been too flustered to speak to Jarrett properly, but it was clear that was just as well. He wasn't worth the risk.

Daniel had already removed his shirt when Gil entered the room, and was seated on the edge of the bed, working off his shoes. His tattoos danced across his bare back, but all Gil could think about was Jarrett waltzing his way through the crowd, laughing and flaunting himself for anyone who cared to look. God help him, Gil cared to look, but he couldn't trust such reckless behaviour with the truth about himself. He'd already caught Jarrett being careless with his words and looks before. What if someone else did, especially if next time those words and looks were aimed at Gil?

He shivered at the very thought, but there was a thread of pleasure amongst the fear.

He cut it short.

"Cold?" Daniel asked.

He had a gentle smile and for a moment, Gil wished with all his heart that this could be enough for him, a soft bed and a night with someone more than a stranger but less than a friend. A few fleeting encounters a year, pleasurable but ultimately meaningless. If that was all he wanted, he could be happy.

Daniel frowned slightly. "Not tonight?"

"I'm sorry," Gil whispered. From downstairs came a roar of laughter, and he couldn't help but wonder if Jarrett was the cause. "It isn't you, it's just, I saw someone downstairs and he got me thinking. And then there's my whole family, which believe me, you don't want to hear the half of, and now I'm in an absolutely repugnant mood. I apologise."

Daniel shrugged his shoulders. "Pity."

It was enough to startle a laugh out of Gil. He crossed to the bed and kissed Daniel, relishing the feel of strong fingers tangling in his hair. He supposed he could try. Something was better than nothing after all and Daniel really was most pleasant. Perhaps he didn't move like quicksilver, or have eyes greener than the fields on spring morning, or a perfect cupid's bow of a mouth.

God, that mouth.

It took him a moment to realise they were no longer kissing. Instead, he was hanging awkwardly over Daniel, mouth half open. Daniel was giving him a bemused look but said nothing.

Gil sighed. "Apologies again. The room's already paid for, I'm sure you won't have a problem finding someone else."

Dread filled him as the image of Daniel and *Jarrett* together flashed before his eyes. Thick arms encircling that narrow waist, tanned hands pushing down on a pale chest, pinning him to the bed as Jarrett looked up at him, eyes blazing with lust.

He shook his head. He had no right to let the idea bother him so. Soon Daniel would be far away again, wherever it was he went, and Jarrett... Jarrett could do what he wanted, with who he wanted. Just as long as it wasn't Gil.

It was the right decision all around, but that didn't mean he had to like it.

"I'm sorry," he said again.

Daniel patted him on the cheek. "Won't be back for a while."

Gil nodded. "I wish you the best then, in all things. And I hope we'll meet again."

He dropped another quick kiss of farewell on Daniel's lips and turned to leave. His hand was on the door when he stopped.

"Daniel?" He shouldn't do this. He had no right. "There's a man downstairs. He's slim and, well, looks rather like a fox if I'm honest. You'll know what I mean. Just... please not him?"

He didn't wait for Daniel's reaction, if any, before he was out the door and down the stairs. He hunched his shoulders to hide his face as best he could without being obvious, but risked a quick glance to make sure he hadn't been spotted.

He needn't have bothered. Jarrett was in one of the far corners of the room, his back to Gil and his front pressed against a man he didn't recognise. The lamplight didn't reach that far, so Gil couldn't see exactly what they were doing, but he could see the way the man's hand clenched Jarrett's arse.

Gil gritted his teeth and with a curse, swept up his coat and headed out into the night, more miserable and unfulfilled than when he arrived.

The rain chose that moment to begin, freezing cold and quickly turning the roads to mud, but Gil couldn't bear the thought of spending one more minute under that roof. As bad as it was, the rain couldn't last much longer. He'd start for home and surely it would let up at any moment.

It didn't.

He spent the entire wretched ride back cursing Jarrett's name. If it was up to him, he'd never see that fox-faced little trollop ever again.

CHAPTER 3

J arrett shivered himself awake the next day with a sore head and a suspicion something had died in his mouth. Then he tried to sit up and it seemed likely that what had died had actually been him.

"Christ alive," he croaked, clawing his way to the edge of the bed. Apparently an evening of celebration involving meaningless fucks and endless drinks shouldn't be followed by a several-hour horse ride in the freezing rain. Lesson learned. Well, likely not, but it was a lesson that would take several months to unlearn. At the very least several weeks.

Wincing, he pulled himself somewhat vertical. At least he'd been sober enough to find his way home. Or perhaps he had Thistle to thank for that. After all, she was a very intelligent horse.

He might be feeling better if he'd actually made it back into the main house the night before, where he'd now have a warm room and a pitcher of water by his bedside, assuming he'd been able to hobble up the many, many flights of stairs to reach them. But by the time he'd gotten Thistle back into her stall and given a good brushing and handful of oats for her trouble, the eastern sky had been lightening and he simply couldn't bear to go any further than he had to. Besides, if he'd awoken any of the household coming in, he'd have had to come up with a lie for where he'd been when he was in no fit state to try.

Fortunate then, that he'd been gifted with this shed to make his own. Lord Crawford's lover was an understanding man and had handed Jarrett the keys to the shed at Christmas, wishing him fond use of it and allowing Jarrett leave to invite any companionship he wanted to join him there, as long as he didn't try to invite the earl or Dominick himself.

It was a kind gesture, even kinder when he'd helped Jarrett move in some old furniture. More likely an outbuilding set for a specific purpose some decades ago, the one-room structure was large as sheds went, and now sported a table large enough for one, a single chair, and a bed fit for two. It didn't matter that the table wobbled or the ropes holding up the mattress creaked, it was the first time Jarrett ever had a place that truly felt like his own.

He barely remembered his childhood before he entered service, but ever since he'd been stuck up in the hayloft with all the other stable lads and grooms. When he'd come to Balcarres House, he'd marvelled at being given his own room in the servants' quarters, even if it was so high up that he'd worried he'd be sharing it with the attic bats. But even that room, as wonderful as it was, didn't feel like his own. The rug on the floor was worn bare by the feet of generations of servants before him, and the mattress still curved to accommodate the shape of its previous owner.

But the shed, cramped as it was, was his own kingdom. He could come and go as he liked and do with it whatever he wanted. He'd scrubbed the small windows until he could see out, then hung curtains over them so no one else could see in. He'd bought the fabric for the curtains himself in town, rather than take any from the house, and even bought a matching quilt to go on the bed. He'd been adding a few other wee trinkets, and brought in a small chest for necessities. Even as sore as he was, the sight of all these things chosen by him and placed precisely where he wanted them brought a smile to his face.

If only it had a fireplace. Ah well. It didn't do much for heat, but at least he could leave his candle burning on the table all night without worrying he'd take the whole household with him if it caught.

Gingerly making his way over to the chest, he removed a set of fresh clothes and wrapped himself in his still-damp greatcoat, preparing to face the walk between his shed and Balcarres House proper. He hadn't acquired a pitcher and basin yet, so he couldn't shave, and even if he had, the water in them would have likely frozen over anyway.

Hissing as the even colder air outdoors struck him, he locked the door behind him and made his way towards the kitchens with their warmth and hopefully, breakfast. As he tucked the shed's key into his pocket with the utmost care, he thought back on the night before. It really was a shame The Cross Keys was so far away. Although that was still better than the nothing he'd have otherwise. He certainly hadn't been making any progress with that great lout earlier in the night. And Jarrett had been at his most enticing too! Clearly some men didn't know a good thing when they saw it.

Fortunately, that gentleman at The Cross Keys had. Or was it two gentlemen? It was all a bit of a blur. Regardless, Jarrett could have been spared quite a lot of long miles with a sore arse if that first bugger had just taken him up on his offer to "stargaze" at the chapel.

Another gust of wind struck him, but the kitchen door was in sight. In fairness, even if that first stranger had been obliging, the unprotected ruins of the chapel would've been a damned cold place to get off, even before it started to rain.

You could've invited him to your shed.

The thought made Jarrett pull open the kitchen door with more force than was necessary. Immediately he was struck by the warmth from the ovens and the smell of burnt bread. It would be nice to have a well-cooked meal for once, but his rumbling stomach didn't care and enough honey and fresh butter could cover even the most charred of breakfasts.

He tried to forget the stranger the night before and look forward to the meal ahead, but that wee thought still nagged him. Why hadn't he invited him to the shed instead of the chapel? Sure, he'd have had to come up with a better lie than "stargazing", but he'd have found something. Perhaps it was because he'd only had the shed a few months, it'd completely slipped his mind as an option.

That had to be it. He'd merely forgotten it was a safe place he could invite company. It certainly wasn't that the shed was *his* and he wasn't ready to share it with some stranger he'd never see again. The man might even have made fun of it. Sure, it was special to Jarrett, but that didn't mean anyone else was going to look at it and see anything other than a place to store broken tools.

"Penny for your thoughts?" asked a voice as Jarrett hung up his coat with the others beside the door.

Jarrett gave the best smile possible without tea or coffee in him.

"Morning, Mrs. Finley. Just contemplating breakfast."

Mrs. Finley, a plump woman in her sixties who'd been the housekeeper at Balcarres long before Jarrett came to work there, bobbed her head in easy acceptance of his answer. The motion reminded him of a partridge ducking its head as it made its way through the tall grass. She looked rather like a partridge herself, fussing through the household as she tidied, her smock grey with the endless dust. He'd never share that observation with her, however. While she'd likely take it with her perpetual good humour, she might enlist him to clean out the worst of the cobwebs in the east wing, despite him being a valet and not hers to command. The worst part was, he'd do it too.

"Bit late for breakfast," she said with a twinkle in her eye. "I reckon it's because you spent the morn double checking that His Lordship didn't leave anything important behind, eh?"

"That's me, Mrs. Finley. Too dedicated for my own good."

She laughed. "You'll want a better lie for Mr. Howe. Don't think he didn't notice you missing from supper last night. But for now..." She gave a quick glance around the kitchen, ensuring they were alone. "The bacon's edible today, but avoid the eggs."

Jarrett nodded gratefully and went to put a kettle on for them both. As he did, the sound of tripping feet coming from the direction of the storeroom was all the warning he had before a flurry of red curls collided with him.

"Oh, Jarrett! I apologise! I haven't hurt you, have I?"

Jarrett hid his wince as he set Janie back to rights. The wisp of a girl hardly came up to his shoulder. If he hadn't been damaged goods already, the idea of her hurting anyone was laughable. Except for possibly poisoning them all with her cooking, although if she ever did, it would be an accident and only because she was trying to "improve" a recipe.

"No harm done," he said. "What've you got there?"

She held up the jar proudly. "Potted shrimps. I thought while His Lordship was gone, I could try some new recipes. He'll be so impressed when he returns! But those dratted cats must have smelled them and near knocked me over!"

Jarrett's already uneasy stomach roiled at the thought of potted shrimp, especially after Janie had her way with them. He shared a glance with Mrs. Finley, who gave him a nod. She'd warn the rest of the household, but it'd be up to Jarrett to rescue the kitchen cats.

"Well, don't give any shrimps to the creatures then, as punishment for being so ill-mannered. And guard the pot, lest the beasts swipe any."

Janie giggled. "What a clever idea! I'll be sure not to."

Cat poisoning averted, Jarrett went to try his luck with a bit of cold toast and bacon, leaving the two women to chat while he ate. At some point, the butler, Mr. Howe joined them, pouring himself a cup of tea.

Aside from Graham and his son, Davey, in the stables, that made up the entirety of their wee household. It was barely a fraction of the number of servants needed to run such a grand house as Balcarres, but they made do. Before the earl's return the previous autumn, the house had been left empty for years, with only the most necessary of upkeep. The garden ran riot and the entire east wing was uninhabitable, but the house itself was still in good nick, owing mostly to the careful eye of Gil Charleton, the earl's overseer or *grieve,* as the job had been called at Jarrett's last, less noble house.

The man was a wonder. Jarrett had trouble just keeping Lord Crawford and Dominick in fresh linens, but Gil was only a handful of years older than him, and handled the entire estate, as well as all the tenants and their troubles. Many a time Jarrett had looked out one of the high windows of Balcarres to see his figure in the distance, striding purposefully across the heath to sort out one problem or another. If the sun was right, Jarrett might even be able to make out the shine of his long dark hair pulled back in a tail, or a glint of light off his golden spectacles. The spectacles, old-fashioned hairstyle, and the practical brown coat he always wore should make him look like a clerk who'd been locked behind a desk until he withered, but with the charming smile he seemed to have for just about everyone, Jarrett thought Charleton more resembled a dashing highwayman, some charming rogue who wore his stolen treasures on his face for all to see and concealed his fineness behind plain dress.

"And where were you last night?" asked Mr. Howe, interrupting a lovely daydream in which Jarrett had just been told to stand and deliver.

"Minding my own business," Jarrett replied, more sharply than he'd meant. Even though he was no longer a footman under the butler's direct control, the man still outranked him in the order of servants. Mr. Howe didn't deserve to be spoken to that way either. For all the man looked like the caricature of an undertaker with his long bony features, he'd always been kinder to Jarrett than he probably deserved.

"Sorry," Jarrett apologised. He tried for a half truth. "I may have celebrated not having to iron any more blasted cravats a bit too hard."

The butler shook his head, but his expression was forgiving. "Ah, youth. I remember when I was a young valet myself, there was one instance where—"

Mr. Howe's youthful indiscretions were cut off by the kitchen door slamming open, followed immediately by Davey, the stable lad. This was not an uncommon occurrence. As the young boy had both boundless energy and an iron stomach, he was often in and out of the kitchen begging Janie for treats.

The boy's eyes were wide with excitement. "You won't believe it!"

"Glad to see you home, Davey," said Mrs. Finley. "Did you enjoy your trip to the city?"

"What? Oh aye, it was a marvel! There was more buildings than I'd ever seen at once, and you should've seen all the people with their funny clothes! I even saw the regent, himself! Da said it weren't, he's in England, but I know what I saw!"

"I'm sure you did, dear. Did you help your father put up the horses?"

"Aye, and exercised the rest so they wouldn't feel put out, but that's what—"

Mrs. Finley gave him a pat on the head. "Then go wash up and you can tell us all about your adventures once you're clean."

"No, but—"

"You heard Mrs. Finley," said Mr. Howe. "After you're clean."

Davey continued on in defiance of his elders, his words rushing out in a single breath. "No, but I was exercising the horses just now as I said and Liquorice was having none of it and broke away, so I had to go get him and—" He took an enormous breath. "—I found a dead body!"

Mrs. Finley gasped. Janie dropped the jar of potted shrimps.

"What did you say?" Mr. Howe asked firmly.

"I found a dead body!" Davey was all but bouncing on his toes in excitement. He didn't seem frightened but instead delighted at this ghastly finish to his adventure. However, based on his tale about the regent, Jarrett wasn't sure this wasn't just another fancy.

"Do you mean you saw a body in Edinburgh and remembered it while you were exercising the horses? A hanging or some such?"

"It weren't a hanging," Davey said firmly. "And it weren't in Edinburgh, but here. I found it while I was exercising the horses here. There's a dead body in the chapel!"

After Davey's pronouncement, Mr. Howe had leapt into action, ordering the women to stay in the kitchen to console Davey. It seemed more likely that Davey would be consoling them as Janie had immediately burst into tears and Mrs. Finley started muttering a prayer that sounded suspiciously papist. Mr. Howe was going to ride into town with Graham to find the magistrate, leaving Jarrett with instructions to guard the house. It was likely that the body was just some poor farmer who'd collapsed, but Balcarres had seen enough tragedy in the past, so it was his duty to stay behind and keep watch.

To Hell with that.

As he strode up the hill to the chapel, Jarrett told himself it was just a coincidence. Despite what he'd told the stranger in the inn, people went there all the time. That he'd invited a man up to the ruins last night and this morning there was a body there was one of those odd twists of fate. Likely, there was no more a dead body in the chapel than there was the Prince Regent in Edinburgh.

The chapel was located a short hike from Balcarres at the base of a crag that overlooked the entire countryside. It was a lovely place, and not just for illicit meetings. It sat in a small glade, the woods surrounding it bringing a sense of protection to the spot. The trees drew their branches over where the roof had long since fallen away, as if even they knew it had once been hallowed ground.

It would be a terrible spot for actual stargazing.

Tall weeds and gorse grew thick across the clearing, bright yellow flowers glowing after the gloom of the forest path. As lovely as the flowers were, they couldn't fully hide the graves the gorse had overgrown, the carved tombstones still visible through the thorns.

Above the doorway that led into the chapel itself was carved the crest of the Crawford earldom with a winged face below, staring down at him as he approached. Two empty windows to either side of the hollow doorway gave it the appearance of a great mouth waiting to swallow him up.

As he climbed the crumbing steps, Jarrett let his eyes fix on the far wall of the ruins, holding off the horror for as long as he could. Finally, he didn't have a choice.

Davey was right. In the middle of the chapel lay a body.

His heart pounded as he stepped closer. The body was clearly a man's, completely naked and staring up sightlessly at the sky.

Like he's stargazing.

Jarrett's stomach, only recently soothed by tea and toast, roiled again. Grass had long since grown up between the church pavers, making the pallid corpse look even more lurid against the dark green. But there was a worse colour than green. There was a rock beside the man's head, most likely a broken piece of gravestone, and both the stone and the man's face were covered in red.

Jarrett didn't want to go any closer, but he had to know.

He gritted his teeth to keep the bile back as he took in the shattered mess of the man's face. With how badly it had been beaten, he couldn't be sure, but between what remained and the man's size and build...

His foot nudged something in the grass. It was a bundle of dark fabric. He picked it up and cold certainty gripped him, dread digging in its icy fingers. The body was the stranger from the pub.

It had to be, because in his hands Jarrett held a black greatcoat, its cape fluttering softly in the wind.

CHAPTER 4

"Gilleasbuig Ailean Charleton! Where do you think you're going?"

Gil sighed and dropped his boots to the floor. He'd hoped that by sneaking out one of the lesser used corridors, he'd be able to avoid the horror that was a Charleton family breakfast, but once again his mother had outsmarted him.

"And put those on," his mother continued. "Skulking through the house like that. It's a wonder you weren't shot for a burglar!"

Gil couldn't help smiling. "Are there many burglars who come calling for breakfast?"

She swatted him gently on the cheek. "I'll have no more of that from you. Are you joining us?"

As it wasn't really a question, his mother didn't wait for a response. Gil watched her disappear down the hall in a bustle of skirts and her sense of accomplishment at foiling her youngest once again. Bernice Charleton lived to continually redecorate her home and vex her children, in that order. Gil sometimes wondered if he'd have better luck escaping her well-meant but frequently unwanted attention if he threw a bolt of upholstery fabric her way and legged it in the opposite direction. It was worth a try.

Lacking anything appropriately damasked this morning however, he carried his boots to a nearby chair and steeled himself to face the rest of the Charletons. His family was trying at the best of times, but on barely any sleep he'd rather go hungry than face them over a plate of eggs. He'd lay even odds he wouldn't even get the chance to add sugar to his tea before they interrogated him where he'd been the night before.

He'd felt badly waking a stableboy when he'd returned home, but he didn't know enough about horses to ensure the one he'd ridden to The Cross Keys and back was put away properly. He'd pay for his ignorance this morning. His mother's lady's maid was an even greater busybody than her mistress, and if there was gossip to be had, between the two of them it was only a matter of time before the entire household, both upstairs and down, knew about it.

He turned his boots over and shook them, one by one. Satisfied when nothing fell out, he pulled them on and prepared to face the lot of them.

"Aunt Bernice caught you again, eh?"

Gil sighed. It looked like he wasn't even going to make it to the breakfast room, never mind the sugar bowl.

"Good morning, Charles."

While his entire family was unbearable, Gil's cousin Charles was perhaps the least unbearable, possibly because he was the only Charleton with a worse name than Gil's own.

Charles Charleton and Gil had often played together as children, two younger sons left to their own devices while their older brothers plotted against them. Many was the time Charles had hauled Gil up a tree after him, the two of them climbing to the very treetops to escape their older—and heavier—brothers. Charles had been a short wisp of a thing until about his thirteenth year, after which he'd grown up and out, winning every local footrace and wrestling match.

He'd grown into himself as well, developing the confident air befitting a baron's son. A true corinthian, he wasn't only as tall as a damned pillar, but now nearly as broad across the shoulders. After his older brother's death, however, he'd become far less adventurous, although whether it was grief or the mantle of responsibility that came with becoming the heir of a barony, Gil wasn't certain.

"I only mention it because I'd laid odds on you making it at least until luncheon before she cornered you. Clearly, underestimating your mother is a costly mistake."

Charles smiled down at him, Gil having inherited his mother's more reasonable height than the towering reaches all the other Charleton men had obtained. Still, Gil couldn't help but think of how forced Charles' smile seemed now compared to the gap-toothed grin he'd had as a boy.

"You're only gloating because *your* mother isn't around to harass you," said Gil as they made their way towards the stairs.

"She does her best by post," Charles replied. "Which reminds me, if you see any letters from her, feel free to accidentally drop them in the fire without opening them. I've taken care of as many as I can and the damn things still keep turning up. She sends her love, by the way."

"You're not worried they might be urgent?"

Charles waved a flippant hand. "Ach, you know Mother. It's always something urgent."

He wasn't wrong. After her last year's debacle, Doctor Mills had refused to return to Charleton House while she was visiting after their disagreement over which was more important, a cartwright with a severe leg fracture or a baroness with a slight cough.

"She's on to me though," Charles continued. "Her friends are now sending letters on her behalf. I've been burning anything that comes from the city, just to be safe."

Gil froze with one foot on the bottom step. Well, that explained why he hadn't heard back from his Edinburgh solicitor lately. He'd have to send the man an apology for the tone in his last missive. And just when Gil had almost been enjoying Charles' company too. He'd almost forgotten that while Charles had always been the one to get them to the tops of the trees, he'd never once had a plan on how they'd get back down.

Gil started going through the list of people in Edinburgh he was expecting letters from. Solicitors, investors, merchants, land traders—it was an extensive list. Charles nudged him aside and made blithely his way down the hall following the enticing smell of ham, toast, and tea.

Tea. That was what Gil needed if he was going to make it through the rest of the day. Strong tea. Although if Charles' thoughtlessness had cost him that land deal in Dumfries, for the sake of the continued Charleton line his cousin had better hope the pot had gone cold.

Upon reaching the dining room, he wasn't surprised to see his mother and father sitting side-by-side, sharing a paper. Bernard and Bernice Charleton were as well-matched as their names would imply. Aside from his mother's lack of height, it was hard to say which of them Gil got his looks from, as they were both fair-skinned, hazel-eyed, and near-sighted. Their formerly black hair was now liberally shot through with grey and they'd somewhat run to fat in their later years, something Gil would have to watch out for as time went on. The job of a *grieve* being too hard on the knees was the reason his father had handed down the earl's estate management work in the first place, or so he claimed. Gil had his own suspicions.

At his mother's nod, his father turned the page and they read on.

One of those suspicions was currently sitting at one end of the breakfast table, the other suspicion at the other. He didn't like that his uncle sat himself at the head of the table in his parents' house, but he was the eldest brother, and the right to sit wherever he liked was his by birth, as was the Charleton title.

The Charleton line stretched so far back that the name and title had become one and the same, making his uncle's full title Andrew Charleton, The Baron Charleton.

Lord Charleton wasn't a bad sort, but after four months, Gil was beginning to wonder when he'd stop "taking the sea air" and return to his own estate. For one, despite the sea being less than three miles away, the Scottish coast in winter was hardly likely to improve anyone's health. Besides, despite his appearance, Uncle Andrew was hardly an invalid.

Unlike Gil's father, the baron had decreased rather than increased as time went on, shrinking a little more every year. If he did try to take the sea air, a strong breeze off the Firth of Forth might be enough to carry him off. But even though his body had diminished in size, it hadn't in strength. He was barely sixty after all, and even keener on *stravaiging* around the countryside than Gil. The few times they'd gone rambling together, Gil had resigned himself to following in his uncle's footsteps after a few miles as the man disappeared over some distant *beinn*.

The baron kept a fine kennel at one of his other estates, more for the prestige of his collection than any interest in either the animals themselves or the poor creatures they hunted, and when he'd visited as a child, Gil could remember seeing his uncle crest some hillock like some god of the hunt, the whole pack of hounds baying and snapping at each other but following him with blind devotion. His eldest son, Patrick, had been equally devoted, save for his inability to provide another generation of heirs to the barony before being thrown from his horse and dying.

Due to his position as the baron's remaining son and future heir, Charles was just now settling in at foot of the table—the second highest seat.

Beside Charles sat his lovely wife Catriona, because at some point the Charleton men had apparently decided to only seek out women with matching names. Charles and Catriona, Bernard and Bernice, even Uncle Andrew's conspicuously absent wife was Aunt Anne when she didn't have to be Lady Charleton. That she'd chosen to go to their modern and fashionable townhouse in Edinburgh at the end of the Autumn hunting season when her husband and son had come here instead was a topic of much discussion between Gil's mother and her maid.

To keep with the naming device, if Gil was inclined towards women, he'd probably be forced to take up with a Grace if he was lucky, a Griselda if he was not. At least his older brother Robert could find himself a perfectly matching Roberta, although Gil didn't blame any Roberta who closed the curtains and locked the doors when he came calling.

The last Charleton at the table, Robert was as unpleasant as he was unappealing. He'd been a hideous bully to Gil their entire childhoods, but once he'd been old enough to piece together how to get the cork out of a wine bottle, he'd devoted himself to ensuring no bottle ever remained corked in his presence again, only tormenting his younger brother while his glass was being refilled. He even had a glass of something red beside his breakfast plate. Gil didn't know what wine paired with kippers and ham, but he trusted his brother's expertise in the matter.

"Morning all," Gil said, as he fixed himself a plate.

He was just reaching for the sugar bowl when his brother said, "Out late, were we?"

"Oh, well done," Charles added, "I almost forgot to ask."

"Charles," Catriona said, shaking her head fondly at her husband.

"What?" Charles gave Gil a wink. "Gil's reputation precedes him. Who was it last night Gil? A lonely widow or a comely maid?"

"*Charles.*" Uncle Andrew's voice was stern. "There are ladies present."

Gil sent up a silent prayer of thanks for his uncle's prudery, then gave his cousin a wink back. "For the sake of the ladie, I shall have to keep my whereabouts—and my exploits—to myself."

In truth, his mother likely didn't care what alleged women Gil was tupping, unless they were of marriable quality. And several orders of books with no titles on the covers had arrived for Catriona, so Gil suspected she might actually enjoy any tales he had to tell. At least if they featured some women as well instead of men exclusively. Unfortunately for her, despite his deliberately calculated reputation as a seducer of the fairer sex, Gil had had a grand total of one experience with a woman, which had ended in disappointment for them both.

At least his record with men was exemplary. Well, except for his dismal showing last night.

Gil shook away the image of broad hands spanning Jarrett's narrow waist and the pity in Daniel's eyes. Unfortunately, his breakfast wasn't much of a distraction, so he was forced to listen to his brother's monologue yet again on how there were no women worth his time in this county anyway, which is why he remained unmarried, although at least he wasn't going about disgracing the family name as Gil was.

If only he knew.

Robert had just about reached the climax of his tirade, "But then, if I was set up with a townhouse in the New Town in Edinburgh or perhaps even London—with a proper allowance, of course..." when the butler came in and announced the magistrate was here to see the baron on an urgent matter.

As it turned out, Magistrate Carnbee hadn't called to bemoan the lack of a proper courthouse or invite himself to a social engagement—not that either Gil's father or uncle ever held any—but to announce that a body had been found.

Much as Gil suspected, his mother only made the expected protests and appeals for the poor man's soul before turning back to an article on the latest developments in wallpaper while Catriona's eyes lit up with excitement, which she did her best to hide with several ladylike dabs with her napkin that fooled no one.

Following much discussion about whether seeing a dead body so soon after eating would ruin the baron's digestion, it was decided Gil would be dispatched as a representative of the family in his place.

"What an honour," Gil grumbled to himself, shrugging on his coat. He immediately hissed and pulled his arm out of his sleeve. His middle finger was bleeding from underneath the nail bed. Cursing, he stuck the injured digit in his mouth, sucking to relieve the pain before awkwardly turning coat around with one hand and shaking it firmly.

A sprig of dried lavender fell from the sleeve, its cut end disturbingly sharp. He stamped the damn thing with his boot, spilling tiny purple flowers across the floor. It didn't do any good, but it made him feel a wee bit better.

He was twenty-five years old; at some point he'd learn to always check his clothes before putting them on. The Charleton House laundry maids had been stuffing lavender into everything they possibly could since before he was born, which was all right in summer when the blooms were fresh and the stems supple, but he'd nearly put his eye out the week before by collapsing onto his pillow without checking for dangers in his bed linens first. At least they used lavender and not gorse. If Gil had to inspect his underthings for thorns each morning, he might actually go mad.

The magistrate had ridden on ahead, but after the hours spent on a horse the night before, Gil elected to walk the distance. So it was no surprise that when he reached the chapel there was a small crowd gathered there already. The presence of the magistrate and the doctor made sense, as did the minister, but Gil was pulled up short by the fourth figure.

Jarrett.

Christ, Jarrett had only been beginning his debauchery when Gil left last night. He must have ridden like the hounds of Hell were after him to make it back from The Cross Keys by morning. The bastard didn't even have the good grace to look appropriately bedraggled either. From what Gil had seen before leaving, Jarrett had been on his way to having *quite* the eventful evening, yet here he was, looking only a wee bit underslept.

A swell of hope rose in Gil's chest. Perhaps Jarrett hadn't actually been with anyone at The Cross Keys at all.

Enough of that. I've no claim over him. If the wee bugger fucked half of Fife before riding for hours and is still standing, my hat's off to him.

Gil repeated that to himself several times. It was true, Jarrett was free to do as he wished. And from his behaviour at the pub, flaunting himself for everyone to see, he was far too free with what he wished for the likes of Gil. Theirs was a dangerous indulgence and if Jarrett didn't learn a bit of discretion, he'd hang for it. Gil refused to risk being on the scaffold next to him.

"Who's this then?" Gil asked, joining the others inside the chapel.

Doctor Mill was digging through his medicine bag, but nodded at Gil as he approached. "I can't say I'm able to recognise him, but you're free to look."

If Doctor Mills didn't recognise the body, it was unlikely Gil would. The doctor had been present at a good number of the births in the county, even more of the deaths, and was on a first-name basis with all of the farmers and most of their livestock. Still, another pair of eyes couldn't hurt.

The body was covered with a large black cloth, which upon closer examination turned out to be a greatcoat. It was pulled down to the man's bare shoulders, leaving his face exposed. At least, what was left of it.

Gil turned away in shock. Would a warning have been too much to ask? Doctor Mills might be used to looking at gruesome injuries all day, but Gil certainly wasn't.

He took a deep breath and forced himself to look at the body again. The blood-covered rock beside the man's head had obviously caused the damage, the shattering of bone all but destroying his features and a dark coating of congealed blood covering what remained. Dark hair, although that may have just been more blood, possibly unshaved, that was about all that was left. Gil couldn't bring himself to look closely enough to determine the man's eye colour, assuming they were still...

He was going to be sick.

He leapt back and walked out of the chapel, not far, but far enough that the wind didn't carry the sour tang of blood. Tilting his head back, he took several deep breaths, but the shifting patterns of leaves above only made things worse. He closed his eyes and a few moments later felt a swift pat on his shoulder.

"There, there, lad," said Doctor Mills. "Bit of a shock, wasn't it."

"A wee bit." Gil attempted a grin, but he could feel the edges of it crumbling.

Doctor Mills patted his shoulder again, a rapid tattoo that matched his rabbit-like nature. The quick touch was nevertheless comforting, and after a moment or two, Gil felt ready to return.

"Apologies," he nodded to the other men as he stepped back into the chapel. The minister and magistrate both nodded, but Gil couldn't bear to look at Jarrett to see his reaction. It was likely pity.

"No, I don't recognise him." Gil looked over the body again, his eyes shying away from the face. "Large fellow, though. I'm sure if he was local I'd have seen him coming down the lane at least a time or two."

"My thoughts were the same, of course," blustered Magistrate Carnbee. Very little he said wasn't bluster. "Most likely a bandit if you ask me, from a team of them. Fell out over their spoils and this one got knocked on the head for it. Good riddance, I say."

Jarrett started and opened his mouth as if to speak, then decided better of it. Gil understood completely. The magistrate would see bandits if a platter of cream went missing, ignoring the cat licking its paws beside the empty plate. God help them all the day actual bandits arrived in town.

"If that's the case, why is he unclothed?" The minister, a fresh-faced man by the name of MacLennan, had only arrived at his post a few months back and clearly hadn't learned yet that it was pointless to question Carnbee's opinions. But Minister MacLennan was young for a man in his position, perhaps that wisdom would come with age.

Magistrate Carnbee harrumphed. "The heavenly realm may be your area of expertise, but the earthly realm is mine. These criminal sorts will take anything that isn't nailed down. Mark my word, this man's clothes will be finding their way to a new owner before the day is through. Likely already have, and for a pretty profit."

"Then why leave his coat?" Jarrett's voice was soft.

That seemed to stump the magistrate. "That's not yours?"

Jarrett shook his head. "It was beside him when I found him. I thought he should be covered."

There was an odd tone to Jarrett's voice, almost wistful.

"That was quite right of you," Minister MacLennan said soothingly. "Did you say a prayer for him as well?"

Jarrett shook his head again, but rather than look disappointed, the minister looked pleased to take on the duty himself. Gil bowed his head as he said a few words, the whole time aware of Doctor Mills next to him, his hands twitching to get back to work.

Finally, the doctor got his chance, whisking the coat off the body to examine it further. It was caught by a shocked Jarrett who looked right at Gil in surprise.

Until that moment, Gil hadn't realised Jarrett had been avoiding his gaze just as much as he'd been avoiding Jarrett's.

His heart began to thunder. Had Jarrett seen him at The Cross Keys? Surely not, Gil had kept to the shadows and Jarrett had been far too busy to have noticed him anyway. But if that wasn't it, what was it?

The doctor interrupted his thoughts before they could spiral further.

"Naught else wrong with the front of him. One of you help me turn him over to look at the back."

Neither the magistrate, the minister, nor Jarrett stepped forward, but in fairness, neither did Gil. After it was clear the stalemate wasn't going to end any time soon, Gil sighed. At least he might be able to redeem himself a bit for his cowardice before.

The corpse's skin was cold under his hands and clammy with dew. It didn't feel like a person at all, but something both more natural and more unnatural at once, as if the body was a giant mushroom that had grown out of the earth after the rain.

The unpleasant thought caused him to push too hard, rolling the man over gracelessly and nearly sending Gil tumbling after him. He put his hand on the grass where the body had been to steady himself.

"Good you didn't do that an inch or two to the left," said Doctor Mills.

Beside Gil's hand, an inch or two to the left, the grass was red with blood.

The minister let out a gasp. While the front of the body had only been bloodied about the head, his entire back was soaked in it, the blood still fresh enough to flow in slow rivulets, dripping onto the ground.

"Perhaps there's more than just a head wound," Doctor Mills said, sounding far too eager to investigate.

Gil dug his fingers into the dirt, once again fighting the urge to be sick. While he waited for the urge to subside, he tried to focus on anything else to take his mind off it. There were no sounds save for the wind in the trees and Doctor Mills' muttering to himself as he examined the body, so Gil focused on sensations instead. The grit of earth underneath his fingernails, and the grass crushed under his palm. The bite of the cold air against his cheeks. The wet chill spreading upwards from where he was kneeling in the still-sodden grass.

He frowned. That wasn't right. He twisted the hand fisted in the dirt, ripping up the grass as he did. Careful not to touch the blood, he slid both hands over the grass where the body had lain.

It was dry. Whereas the ground around the body was still soaked from the rain the night before. That meant the man had been there since before the rain started. As Gil had spent the entire ride back from The Cross Keys cursing it, he had a pretty good idea of the exact time the rain had started. That might be a valuable clue in finding the man's killer.

"There's no blood on the coat."

All eyes turned to Jarrett. Even the doctor stopped his prodding.

"Pardon?"

"At least, not anything like *that*." Jarrett nodded towards the pool on the ground. He held the coat out at arm's length, turning it so they could all see both sides. He had to hold it a good ways above his head to keep the ends from brushing the grass. There were a few stains on the hems and sleeves that could as easily be mud or blood, but the back of it was completely unmarred.

Magistrate Carnbee cleared his throat. "It's as I said. The killer—another thief—wanted to sell his clothes. He must have forced the dead man to disrobe before he killed him, rather than do it after. Clean clothes would fetch a higher price than bloody ones, after all."

Gil was worried to find himself agreeing with the magistrate. But convincing a man to undress on a cold night, even before it started raining, must have taken some doing. Perhaps his killer had a weapon other than the rock to coerce him.

Unless it hadn't been coercion at all. Had the dead man come to the chapel for a rendezvous, only to be killed when he was at his most vulnerable? There was only one sort of rendezvous that required the removal of garments in secluded locations. Their killer could still be a man, of course, but this opened the possibility it could be a woman too, or at least, a woman as an accomplice. Could a woman have taken down such a big man on her own, or done *that* to his head?

Gil shuddered. The idea that their killer was a man was equally unsettling, for much more personal reasons. He was careful when finding other men to be with, but his concern was always in being seen. If the killer lured his victim to a hidden place before killing him, then all the steps Gil took to protect himself would play right into his hands.

The idea was a horrifying one.

"Is there a hole in the coat?" asked Doctor Mills. He was leaning so close to the body, his nose was almost brushing the dead man's shoulder. Heedless of the blood, he had one hand on the corpse's back, his fingers disappearing into a hole in the flesh with a squelching sound.

"No hole," Jarrett confirmed, looking several shades paler.

Minister McLeannan swallowed a few times before speaking. "I suppose you're right, magistrate. His clothing was removed first."

The magistrate looked smug enough to make his moustache curl all on its own. "You know these things when you're as experienced as I am. Is there anything else you can tell us, doctor?"

Doctor Mills wiped his fingers on a handkerchief. He stopped himself from putting the stained fabric back into his coat pocket and dropped it into his bag instead.

"There's an injury here, possibly several, but it's hard to tell with all the blood. We need to get him somewhere we can get him washed up and take a better look. My home is unavailable, I'm afraid. My wife's sister is visiting and we've put her up in the sickroom. She's complained enough as it is, I doubt she'd agree to sharing with a corpse!"

Sometime later, after a cart had been arranged and suitable accommodations for the body were found, Gil found himself leading the doctor, the magistrate, and the body into the Kinneuchar Inn.

None of the patrons had been willing to give up their spots by the fireplace to help bring the body in, so that job had fallen to the minister and Jarrett, leaving Gil to carry in the piece of broken stone, now wrapped in a greatcoat that was bloodier than it'd been before. He cursed as he heaved the foul parcel onto the bar and eyed the men seated by the fire where they could watch the proceedings but still keep warm. Hopefully Minister MacLennan had a nice sermon prepared on following the example of the good Samaritan or risk spending eternity a bit too close to the fire.

"What in God's name is this?"

Marta, the pub's owner, was standing in the doorway that led to the cellar, a small cask of ale under either arm and a sour look on her face.

"My dear lady—" began Magistrate Carnbee.

Marta's face soured even further. She'd been hounded one too many times about the source of some of her better spirits for her to want anything to do with a representative of the law.

"I am sorry, Marta," Gil said, stepping in before she could get to her cudgel and there'd be two men with bashed-in heads in the inn. "It's not the roses you deserve, but they aren't in season this time of year. Will you accept this more... singular token instead? I promise no other girl in Kilconquhar has one. At least, I hope they don't."

He winked at her over the rim of his spectacles for good measure. While he was practised at working his charms on the fairer sex to keep them from suspecting his tastes lay elsewhere, getting a woman to agree to keep a naked corpse in her place of business might be a stretch even for him. Marta certainly appeared unconvinced.

"We need your cellar, I'm afraid," said Doctor Mills. "There will be plenty of room to work down there, and the cold will keep the body fresh until we can deliver him to his relatives for burial."

Marta wavered, but didn't fall. Gil tried again, leaning as close to her as he dared and lowering his voice. "I would consider it a personal favour."

Marta let out a heavy breath. "Fine, but get him off my bar before he mars the finish."

Gil gave her a quick peck on the cheek. "Thank you."

"Well," she said, more than a little flustered. "It's as much as I can do. To help the doctor and all."

Gil grinned and took one of the ale casks from her, setting it where directed.

Magistrate Carnbee, clearly unhappy with not being the central authority for once, tried to take control of the conversation once again.

"My dear lady, I don't suppose you recognise this fellow?"

"The one without a face? Wee bit tricky that. Though from the size of him, it could be he's the great big one who was in here last night. But if that's the case, I don't know why you're asking me when he's about."

The magistrate frowned. "When who's about?"

"That one." Marta pointed. "You should be asking Jarrett. After all, he's the one I heard invite the man up to the chapel."

CHAPTER 5

All eyes turned to Jarrett.

"Well, that's not exactly..." He stammered to a halt. But it was. It was exactly what happened.

As soon as he'd realised who the body at the chapel had to be, he'd wanted to turn and run, but the damned doctor had come haring up the hill before he'd had the chance. After that, he couldn't see a way to leave that wouldn't look suspicious, especially after the magistrate arrived. So Jarrett had watched Doctor Mills poke and prod the body, had loaded it onto the cart, and had helped carry it into the pub, praying all the while that no one who'd seen him talking to the dead stranger would remember it.

But Marta had.

Of course she had. And overheard their conversation to boot.

"Is this true?" Magistrate Carnbee asked, looking like he wished he'd thought to bring some constables.

"Not exactly," Jarrett lied. "We were both in here last night and he struck up a bit of conversation. Asked about the area. I said when it's not raining, the chapel's a nice bit of scenery. He must have taken the suggestion."

Heads swivelled from him back to Marta.

She narrowed her eyes at him. "He also said something about stargazing."

Curse the woman. Did she have the ears of a hound? Jarrett had barely been able to hear himself think over the chatter in the inn the night before. Was there anything else she wanted to share while she was at it? Perhaps the way Jarrett had been making a fool of himself trying to get into the man's garish plaid trousers?

He shrugged. "If she says so. We didn't talk for more than a minute. I barely remembered it myself."

Despite his outward calm, his heart was pounding wildly in his chest.

"So you did remember it and didn't say anything?"

Curse old Carnbee too. It wasn't as if Jarrett killed the man. He'd had his drink, made a fool of himself, and left. Whoever had done the fellow in, Jarrett had nothing to do with it. He'd been far too busy getting his prick sucked at The Cross Keys to be murdering folks here.

Oh God. Oh God. Oh *Christ*! He couldn't tell them where he'd been when the man was killed. He'd be taking the noose from his neck for one crime and tightening it for another. A good half dozen things he'd done the night before were hanging offences, and those were just the ones he could remember.

"I-I didn't think it was important." He could barely get the words out. "I didn't recognise him. And a minute's idle talk with a stranger didn't seem worth a mention."

The magistrate hummed. The mood in the room had gone from morbidly curious to something just a step below hostile.

Jarrett took a slow breath, trying to appear as innocent as he was. Well, innocent of murder at least.

Surely, it was nothing to worry about. They'd find the one that did it and everything would be all right. They'd all go back to ignoring Jarrett just like they'd done before. Some of the attention was off him already. The doctor had returned to his poking and prodding of the body. The minister was protesting that such a thing was inappropriate with a lady in the room and Marta was saying to damn the lady and get that filthy thing off her bar.

But Charleton was still looking at him. In other circumstances, Jarrett would be thrilled to be the focus of the gorgeous eyes his spectacles did nothing to hide. But now all he wanted was to be ignored long enough to slink away, go back to bed, and wake again when everything was put back to rights.

The look on Charleton's face was an odd one, considering almost. He couldn't truly think Jarrett was the killer, could he? Of all the men here, he seemed the one to have sense enough to know Jarrett would never do such a thing.

Although perhaps not. It wasn't as if Charleton really knew him. Their paths had crossed a few times at Balcarres—it was impossible for them not to with Jarrett running about the house as valet and Charleton handling all of the earl's property, and a good bit of his money too, if what Jarrett overheard while topping up the whisky decanter in the study was anything to go by.

He had a tendency to do that more often when Charleton was visiting. It wasn't really his job, but he was always happy to help if it meant getting a chance to see that handsome face smile as Jarrett handed him a glass, and hear the soft, "Thank you, Jarrett," in the man's warm voice.

It was enough to make a poor valet's knees weak. With any other man, Jarrett would've long since asked Charleton to join him in a storeroom or bend him over the kitchen table, Janie and all her cats be damned. But every time he tried to work up the courage, his words never came out right. Charleton likely thought him a bumbling idiot, but it wasn't as if he did anything to keep their conversations going either. Unlike the easy charm Jarrett had seen him have with everyone else, their conversations were awkward and short. Those treasured thank yous were about as much the man seemed inclined to speak to him.

Well, let him look then. Charleton hadn't said a word to him all day, even as they lifted the corpse together to get it on the cart. If he wanted to start talking now, there was nothing Jarrett could do about it.

In the meantime, a bucket and rag had been produced and Doctor Mills was wiping the blood off the body. Marta didn't look any happier about the filthy thing on her bar being slightly less filthy. The doctor hummed and made all sorts of interested noises as he cleaned the man's ruined face, but didn't say anything except request help in turning him over. This time Jarrett didn't move. Let them all do it their damned selves, he was done helping.

A few of the inn's patrons got to their feet with a groan and did the gruesome work. After repeating the whole process to the man's back, the doctor let out a crow of triumph.

"Have you found something?" asked Minister MacLennan, sounding a wee bit more excited by a murder than a clergyman should be.

"See here," replied the doctor, "the man was stabbed in the back, at least once, perhaps twice. I thought as much from the amount of blood on the soil. I'll need time to do a proper examination to be sure, but if you look closely, you'll see that the blade pierced a tattoo. Impossible to see before with all the blood, but it might help with identification.

"Tattoo?" Charleton rushed over to the body, his attention finally not on Jarrett. He squinted at the lines of ink.

"Do you recognise it?" asked the doctor.

After a long moment, Charleton shook his head.

"No. No, I don't. Thank God. For a moment, I worried..." His voice was shaky but relieved. "I worried it was someone else. But no, it couldn't have been. I don't recognise this."

Jarrett wondered how many tattooed men a county lad like Charleton could possibly know, but he didn't have much time to wonder.

"Pity," said the magistrate. "Mrs... Marta, I don't suppose there's anything else you remember about the victim?"

She pursed her lips. "Now, let me see. Big strapping fellow, ordered a few ales. Was in here most the night. Don't remember precisely when he got in, but he stayed 'til nearly midnight. Wore a bloody large greatcoat when he came in, but took it off after a bit. Don't remember much else save he was wearing the most awful trousers I ever saw. Plaid they were, but you wouldn't soon forget a clan with that as a tartan!"

"Expensive looking?"

Marta snorted. "I wouldn't've paid a tinker's cuss for 'em, but they might've been. I don't know what some coves would pay for such colours running every which way. Homespun's good enough for me."

"Ah, but looks such as yours don't require any enhancement. Not all of us are so lucky." Charleton said to her, all but leaning over the corpse to pay her the compliment. Marta tittered in a way that would be too much from a woman half her age.

Jarrett rolled his eyes.

"And you, Mr. Welch? Anything else we should know?"

The tone in Magistrate Carnbee's voice when he spoke to Jarrett was much different from when he spoke to Marta.

"I've told you all I know," said Jarrett, praying it would be enough. "Besides, she said the fellow didn't leave 'til midnight. I'd left hours before that! She should be able to tell you that since she remembers so much!"

"That's true, weren't here much longer after they spoke," Marta admitted, and Jarrett was inclined to take back all the unkind things he'd thought about her. "He stormed out after he and the dead man got into an awful row."

Oh, for Christ's sake.

Jarrett began to shout, "That's not—"

But Magistrate Carnbee interrupted. "Let me see if I understand. You were heard inviting this man to the very place where he turned up dead, before getting into an altercation with him—"

"It wasn't an altercation! He started yelling at me and I left."

"Of course," Carnbee continued, folding his hands over his straining waistcoat. "And where did you go?"

Jarrett snapped his mouth shut. He couldn't tell them the truth. Even if he did, no man at The Cross Keys would admit to having seen him there for fear of their own lives. Telling the truth would be worse than a lie, but he couldn't think up a good one of those either.

"I don't remember."

"Of course not." The magistrate was sneering now and a few of the larger men by the fire were looking between themselves. Then one of them took a few steps towards Jarrett. The others followed.

"And there's the missing man's clothes!" added Minister MacLennan, who should keep his nose out of it. "You said yourself, magistrate, that they were likely sold and now we find out they were flash. Could that be part of the motive?"

"I did say that, didn't I?" Carnbee said, sounding as surprised as anyone he might be right, but far more pleased. "And I suppose a footman's salary isn't much."

Jarrett straightened his shoulders. "I'm not a footman. I'm His Lordship's valet."

But the magistrate just waved a hand. "Aye, a servant's wages are a mere pittance. I see it all now. After you two argued, you laid in wait for this man to leave, then either following or coercing him up to the chapel, forced him to undress at knifepoint, stabbed him, and took his clothes, missing the greatcoat in the dark."

"Perhaps he fought back, so Jarrett hit him with the rock," added the minister breathlessly.

Carnbee scowled at the distraction from his grand moment. "I was just getting to that. Aye, finding his victim not quite dead, he used the nearest thing at hand to finish him off."

Jarrett gaped. It wasn't true. None of it. All he'd been doing was trying to get his end away and somehow it'd all turned into this. He looked around for help but there was none to be had. The magistrate was ready to hang him then and there, and most of the inn's patrons looked ready to provide the rope. The one or two that didn't were fixed firmly on the fire, not wanting to get involved. Surely a man of God would be on his side, but the minister looked delighted, as if this was the most entertainment he'd had in his life. The doctor and Marta were ignoring them all, pointing at the body and arguing.

Jarrett turned to his last hope. Charleton was frowning, but there was no malice on his face, which made him slightly a more hopeful prospect than anyone else.

"Charleton?" Jarrett said softly.

Charleton's head snapped up at the sound of his name, but his frown only deepened. For a moment, their eyes met.

Jarrett didn't know what else he could say. "I didn't do this."

"Enough of that," huffed Carnbee. "You'll get your chance to have your say at the inquest. Or more likely, the trial."

The magistrate nodded. At once, Jarrett's arms were seized by the larger men who'd been eyeing him since he came in. The blood rushed in his ears, drowning out whatever else Carnbee was saying. *Inquest? Trial?* No, that didn't make any sense. He didn't do anything. This couldn't be happening.

His sense of hearing slowly returned, but he felt dazed. It was as if everything was being said through water. Perhaps it was. He couldn't breathe; was he drowning? He began to panic.

"Marta has agreed on a price to keep the body in her cellar," Doctor Mills said, although none of his words held any meaning. "The cold will keep the body fresh enough until I can examine it further and his family can be found to provide a burial."

"Very good." The magistrate motioned to the men still sitting by the fire. "You there, help the doctor. And you men..."

He nodded at Jarrett, which was confusing, until someone squeezed his arm painfully and Jarrett remembered the men holding onto him.

"...take Mr. Welch outside. Use the cart to take him to Crail. Tell them to keep him in the tolbooth until we can get this sorted out. Or until the assizes. Whichever comes first."

The assizes. They really were going to try him for this, for *murder.* There'd be no sorting it out. Carnbee had made up his mind that Jarrett was guilty. He wasn't going to waste a moment more searching for the real killer, nor would he lose a moment's sleep when an innocent man was hanged.

When Jarrett was hanged.

The panic that had been building and building snapped. The tolbooth served as the nearest gaol. If they got him there, he was as good as dead. Jarrett howled, and wrenched his arm from his captor's hand. The man loosened his grip in shock at the sound and Jarrett was able to pull free. But the man holding his other arm was stronger, and Jarrett found himself dragged to the floor before he could break away.

He thrashed—dignity be damned, his life was at stake—but it was to no use. He was pinned down, making him struggle harder, his only thought to get away, get free, get somewhere safe. The minister was saying something, his tone soothing, but Jarrett didn't care.

"Please," he begged, trying to reach for the minister but instead getting his arm nearly yanked out of its socket. "Please, help me! I didn't do this! Help me!"

Then he was hauled roughly to his feet. He kicked out, connecting with one of his captors, who fell to his knees swearing, but two more took his place.

Jarrett screamed. "I didn't do this!"

In one last burst of strength, he got a hand free, reaching out for any lifeline he could grab. Miraculously, his fingers grabbed soft wool and Jarrett clenched his fingers into the coat before looking to see who it belonged to.

Charleton blinked at him, his eyes huge with surprise behind his golden spectacles, his nose only inches from Jarrett's own. He could feel Charleton's shocked exhale against his lips.

"Help me," Jarrett pleaded, gripping tighter to his last hope. "I didn't do this. Please, Charleton, help me!"

The last thing Jarrett saw as he was dragged away was Charleton turning his back on him.

CHAPTER 6

The wind rustled the leaves overhead, their increased urgency promising a storm to come, but Gil couldn't tear his eyes away from the flattened patch of grass, the stain at the centre no longer red, but dried to a brown so deep it was nearly black.

He hadn't been able to return home after the scene in the inn. Instead he'd walked, too lost in thought to notice where his feet carried him, until he heard the crashing of waves and realised he'd made it all the way to the coastal path. He'd followed that for a bit, allowing the familiar sound of the sea beating against the cliffs to soothe his tattered nerves. A seabird dove past him, its cry so similar to Jarrett's anguished scream as he'd been carted away that Gil had to sit down heavily on a nearby rock, the memory robbing him of all strength.

The coastal path wasn't quite so soothing after that. He left it and tried to tell himself he didn't know where he was heading, but he ended up at the chapel all the same. Now clouds were rolling in, heavy and dark with rain.

Would the blood be washed away with the coming storm, diluting as it spread, losing its colour, trickling out between the stones and running in rivulets through the forest until it made its way back to the sea? Or would it seep deep into the ground, forever marking the spot where a man had lost his life?

"You may be many things, Gil Charleton, but a poet isn't one of them," he whispered.

He'd been surprised to find the chapel not filled with curious souvenir seekers, but he likely had the weather to thank for that. By tomorrow, the story would have spread across half the county. Any loose stones that could be lifted would be carried off and the story told that each was the one that Jarrett had used to deal the fatal blow.

Except Jarrett hadn't done it. It was absolutely impossible. The ground under the body had been dry, and it had started to rain as Gil left The Cross Keys. Even if he'd ridden out immediately after Gil, Jarrett would've been hard pressed to make it back to the chapel much before dawn, and the ground would have been thoroughly soaked by that time. So if he'd killed the man after visiting The Cross Keys, the ground under the body would be just as drenched as the ground surrounding it.

It was possible Jarrett had killed the man before riding to The Keys, but it was a good fifteen miles from the chapel to there. Gil usually rode the distance in a little over three hours, taking care to mind his horse and the state of the roads. A better horseman could cover the distance in less than that. Two and a half hours, perhaps only two if he pushed his horse to the limit.

But even then, Jarrett had been at the pub before he arrived. He wasn't sure exactly when that had been, but he'd dined with his family before heading out, so with a three-hour ride, no later than eleven o'clock. According to Marta, the dead man had still been alive and drinking at the pub then, while Jarrett had been hours away getting up to—whatever he wanted, as was his right.

So, it was impossible for Jarrett to have killed the man before he went to The Cross Keys and it was impossible for him to have killed him after. He was completely innocent and Gil knew it.

But he couldn't say a damned thing. If he did, he and Jarrett might as well share a noose and save the executioner some time. He could tell the magistrate he'd seen Jarrett at The Cross Keys, but that risked getting them both hanged for sodomy instead of murder. Even if by some stroke of luck the reason for their visit to that particular pub remained secret, the authorities would want to confirm Gil's story by speaking to other men who were there. Gil wouldn't risk any more lives by naming names. Even if he did, all those men would disavow any knowledge of Jarrett, Gil, and The Cross Keys itself to save their own skins. Gil couldn't blame them. It wasn't their fault Jarrett was in this mess.

Stupid, unthinking, reckless Jarrett. Gil had a good idea what he'd been up to when he'd invited the dead man to join him here at the chapel and it had damned all to do with stargazing.

He looked up at the branches overhead and sent up a quick prayer that no one else figured out the same thing. Although it was unlikely Jarrett could be in any more trouble than he already was, the brash idiot. What had he even been thinking, approaching an ordinary man in an ordinary pub? Didn't the fool have any idea how dangerous that was? Or was he too led by his cock to care?

The breeze picked up and Gil pulled his coat tighter around himself.

And all that risk just to bring someone *here*, the tumbled ruins of an old chapel, with neither roof nor doors, never mind a soft bed and a basin to wash up with after.

Gil kicked a clod of earth in disgust then let out a heavy sigh. *Disgust* really wasn't the word for what he was feeling, was it? No, it was *pity*. Pity for Jarrett, and pity for any man he invited to this forlorn spot when there were plenty of nice safe rooms if you knew how to inquire discreetly.

Perhaps that was the problem, perhaps Jarrett didn't know. He was young, likely only twenty or so to Gil's twenty-five, but there was a lifetime of learning to be had in those four or five years. Clearly, Jarrett had found his way to The Cross Keys somehow, but so had Gil, and he'd still been completely clueless about how to go about things until Daniel had taken him under his wing.

For a horrible moment when Doctor Mills had discovered the corpse's tattoo, Gil had been terrified the dead man was Daniel, despite the impossibility. The idea that someone he cared about could face such a horrible death was too much to bear. But whoever the dead man was, he wasn't Daniel, thank God. Cleaned of blood, his back had borne only a single, slightly mangled star instead of the familiar riot of anchors, ships, and mermaids that swam across Daniel's back. His friend still lived. Gil prayed he'd live well.

If Jarrett hadn't had his own Daniel, a friend to teach him how to look after himself, then it was no wonder things had turned out this way. Perhaps not with a murder charge, but certainly some kind of serious trouble. Jarrett was lucky he wasn't the one found in some out-of-the-way spot with his head bashed in. At least he was still alive for now. There was still some hope, even if Gil couldn't see it.

That moment in the inn when Jarrett had grabbed his coat would be etched into his mind for the rest of his life. The absolute terror he'd seen on Jarrett's face was unforgettable. He'd wanted to grab Jarrett just as tightly, to tell him that he knew he was innocent, that it would all be all right. But he hadn't, he'd frozen, and like a coward he'd let Jarrett be dragged to his fate. There would be no saving him.

Unless Gil did it.

"Oh, for fuck's sake!" Gil swore, his shout startling a bird from its branch. He couldn't, he *wouldn't* risk his own life trying to save someone so reckless he'd probably find his way back onto the scaffold within a few years anyway. It wasn't Gil's fault Jarrett had ended up in this mess.

But if I don't say anything, it will be my fault if he swings because of it.

Gil swore again and kicked at the earth a few more times for good measure, splattering his boots with mud. Goddamn Jarrett. Goddamn himself. Goddamn the dead man and the fucking magistrate and the law and this whole goddamned situation.

His kicking unearthed something small and hard, sending it bouncing against the chapel wall with a metallic clatter. Momentarily distracted from his fury, Gil went after it. Wiping the clotted dirt away revealed a small button. Not much in and of itself, but it might be something. He pocketed it and began looking for more.

Half an hour later he had a pocket full of small treasures: two more buttons, assorted scraps of fabric, what looked like an old belt buckle, and numerous other small items that would need a good cleaning to thoroughly identify. He'd also found three pennies and a tuppence, so he'd even been paid for his time.

He ran a small scrap of lace through his fingers. It'd been caught on a nearby gorse bush. If nothing else, all these bits and pieces proved Jarrett wasn't the only one to use the chapel as a meeting spot. The thought made him even sadder but it might prove to be Jarrett's salvation. If Gil could find enough proof someone else was at the chapel the night of the murder, it wouldn't matter where Jarrett had actually been. A good barrister could argue that this mysterious other person had been the one to kill the victim. That might create enough doubt to render a verdict of "Not Guilty" or at the very least "Not Proven". Who knew, perhaps Gil would even uncover the identity of the real killer and see him brought to justice. He wasn't willing to risk his life to save Jarrett, but at least he could do this much.

He squared his shoulders, ready to start the hunt again, when a drop of rain struck his spectacles, blurring his vision. Then another. And another. The hunt would have to wait for another day.

He turned and headed for home, praying that nothing important would be washed away in the rain. By the time he made it back to Charleton house, the heavens had opened, making twice in as many days that Gil had found himself soaked to the bone because of Jarrett fucking Welch.

Gil stared into the fire, slowly rolling a glass of the local, highly illegal scotch back and forth between his palms. He'd arrived home despairing and drenched only to be told he looked a disgrace and to clean up before supper. As he was a grown man and not an errant child, he was already well aware, but his mother meant well, even if she was extraordinarily overbearing.

Her warning had been somewhat premature, as he was now as refreshed and respectable as he was likely to get, but still had an hour until the dinner bell.

"Ah, so this is where you've run off to. We were wondering. Don't mind if we do."

Gil heard the distinct sounds of the whisky decanter being unstopped and two more glasses poured before his brother and his cousin's wife seated themselves on the settee beside his chair.

He nodded in greeting. "Robert. Catriona. Where's Charles?"

Catriona waved a hand. "Oh, he's in with his father discussing all sorts of baronly things, I suspect. You won't mention this to him, will you? Charlie thinks it's improper for a lady to drink before supper."

Gil grinned and gave her his most charming smile. "I am, as ever, the soul of discretion. As for this lout..."

Robert harrumphed. "It's hardly my business. But what's got your face looking like you found a tuppence and lost a quid?"

"A tuppence and three pennies, as a matter of fact," Gil said. If there was a list of people Gil wanted to share his troubles with, not only was his brother's name at the very bottom of it, but his name had been torn off the list entirely and tossed on the fire for good measure. "I assisted with some unpleasantness today and it's put me in a low mood."

"Aye, the fellow who got his head bashed in, you mean?"

"Robert!" Gil hissed, looking pointedly at Catriona.

She smiled, but it was strained. "It's quite all right. If you two would care to discuss it, I can leave."

"The only thing I want less than discussing the matter further is for you to rob us of your presence," said Gil immediately. He gave his brother another look, but Robert only shrugged and poured himself another glass, his first having already been emptied. How fortunate Robert had the foresight to bring the bottle to the settee with him for just such a purpose.

"It doesn't matter anyway," said Robert. "I hear they've already arrested the killer. He's one of the other servants at that earl's house you work at, isn't he?"

Gil bristled, but held his tongue. He was Lord Crawford's estate manager and general overseer. Hardly a servant, but that distinction mattered little to Robert who preferred a life of noble idleness. It wasn't the genteel thing to actually earn a living. Far better to leech off the hard work of others, raking in the profits from those toiling on your estates. Not that Robert had any estates. Nor did their father, come to it. What their father did have was a brother for a baron and these days, that seemed close enough.

It hadn't always been that way. Bernard Charleton had been the estate manager at Balcarres for decades under the previous earl and never had a word to say against it. To the contrary, he'd often set Robert and Gil toiling on some project or the other, confident the hard work would improve their characters.

Considering one of his sons had turned out to be a drunkard and the other a molly, Gil wasn't certain it'd worked out as his father had hoped. Still, Gil now knew how to replace a roof in either thatch or slate, and what a beam looks like when it needs replacing immediately and when it can last another season. One couldn't learn that at university. He'd also learned how to manage the books and even ways to invest any surplus to increase profits. Those lessons in particular were ones he'd taken to heart and now found himself in possession of quite a nice little nest egg that no one in his family knew anything about.

But then cousin Patrick had died, Charles' older brother and the assumed heir to the barony. Seeing Charles become next in line seemed to have triggered something in Gil's father as a second son himself. Suddenly, the title didn't seem quite so out of reach and he'd begun to act accordingly. Within a fortnight, Gil had gone from having a father willing to walk the length of a stone wall with him to see what needed fixing to one who refused to tie his own cravat in his valet's absence.

At least Robert had been consistent in his detestation of hard work since childhood, happily letting his younger brother inherit the job of overseer from their father. And so the Charleton family lived on, sleeping in this house that was actually his uncle's, eating food paid for by his coin, and spending lavishly on clothes and furnishings to look the part, all using his name as credit.

On the settee, Catriona shifted, rearranging her skirts to fall more pleasingly. She, Robert, and the rest of the Charletons always dressed in the height of fashion, even for a family dinner with no guests. Gil looked down at his own clothes. They were perfectly serviceable, if a few years old. Besides, he needed a sturdy pair of boots more than he needed dancing slippers. They all might look down on him for working, but he'd rather have money to build his investments than rely on the charity of a barony that would never be his.

"Gil?" Catriona looked worried. "I'm sure Robert meant nothing by it. Is that what's distressing you? Is that servant a friend of yours?"

Jarrett? A friend? God no. Perhaps Gil might have once liked him to have been, but he'd clearly been blinded by a pretty face. Now that he knew how much of a danger Jarrett was to himself and others, Gil wouldn't even want to be in the same room as him. But that didn't mean he wanted to see the silly sod hang.

"Nothing like that," Gil reassured her. "I barely know the fellow. Still, it all seemed very quick to me. One moment we're stumbling over a bloo—the deceased, and before I could blink the magistrate is having Jarrett hauled off."

Catriona nodded sympathetically. "Aye, I can see why that would be upsetting. You can never be sure you really know a person, can you?"

She leaned over to pat his hand. "I'm sure Magistrate Carnbee knows what he's doing. After all, he's been the magistrate for as long as anyone can remember."

"Perhaps that's the problem," said Robert, pouring his third glass. "He's been at it so long he's too sure of his own opinions. Not that I don't know anyone else in this room like that. Still, if you think the matter needs more investigating, why don't you take it up with Uncle? I'm sure the word of a baron might cause a mere magistrate to reconsider."

Gil hadn't thought of that, but now that Robert said it, it was obvious. While in principle he might be against his uncle using his title to sway the course of justice, in this case it would be to save the life of an innocent man. Surely, that made it all right.

"Thank you, Robert," he said with sincerity. "That was unexpectedly helpful of you."

His brother's words were smug and only slightly slurred. "Think nothing of it. After all, you servants have to band together. Speaking of, can you go tell Uncle and Charles that it's about time for supper? It'll save us from having to ring the bell."

Gil gritted his teeth, but considering Robert may have just saved Jarrett's life, he let him have this round.

"Uncle Andrew? Charles? Are you about ready for dinner?"

The two men were huddled over the desk in his father's study, several account books and loose papers scattered in front of them. Gil's fingers itched with the urge to organise them properly, but the few times he'd offered his assistance, his uncle had scoffed at the idea. After all, Gil would never inherit, so the running of the barony was hardly his business. Never mind that

Gil already did exactly the same work, and for an earl, no less. Compared to the complexities of handling an earldom, a meagre barony would be child's play.

Still, he'd offered his help and had it rejected. Hopefully, the answer wouldn't be the same when he *asked* for help instead. He was just relieved his father wasn't in the study with them. These days, if he saw a chance to look better in his brother's eyes, he'd throw anyone else to the wolves, even his own son. Gil wasn't willing to let his father scupper this idea just because it was Gil's. Well, Robert's, but that was probably worse.

Charles smiled up at him, tucking a small pair of reading spectacles away. Gil watched with some envy, and adjusted his own ever-present pair. "Ah Gil, we were just finishing up. Say, you don't know a good supplier of granite by any chance?"

Decorative or structural? Gil wanted to ask, but his uncle cut him off before he had the opportunity.

"That's none of Gilleasbuig's concern," said the baron, closing the book in front of him with finality. "Thank you, we'll be down for supper in just a moment."

"Might I have a quick word with you before then, Uncle?" Gil glanced at Charles, who took the hint.

"I'd best see where that wife of mine has wandered off to."

"You might try the library," offered Gil, seeing no reason why Catriona's drink in the drawing room should be interrupted.

"That is the most likely place." Charles patted Gil on the shoulder as he passed, but considering his height advantage, Gil was just happy it wasn't a pat on the head.

"What is it you wanted, Gilleasbuig?" asked the baron once Charles had left.

"You heard about the murdered man they found today?"

"Only what the magistrate had to say this morning. I believe I sent you along to be of assistance. Carnbee is a fine man, I'd hate to think you represented our family poorly in his company."

Gil was too tired to try and parse whether his uncle meant anything particularly damning by that or if he was just being his usual self.

"I found some things that might prove useful to the investigation," Gil admitted.

"Oh dear Lord, you didn't actually get involved, did you?"

Gil gave up. There was no winning here. "Uncle. Sir. While I have naught but the utmost respect for Magistrate Carnbee, there are a few aspects of the investigation that I believe merit further examination."

Like finding a way to prove Jarrett had been elsewhere at the time without actually having to prove where he'd been.

"As such, I was hoping you might be willing to speak to the magistrate. I would, of course, never ask you to do anything that might be perceived as—"

Uncle Andrew rubbed the bridge of his nose. "As we speak, there is a fine meal being served with an even finer vintage. You are keeping me from that. State what it is you want so we can both have our suppers."

Gil hadn't noticed it before, but hunched over his papers by the light of a single lamp, his uncle looked older than his years and worn in a way that Gil could hardly put into words. It was unnerving to see on such a normally energetic man. Surely, it was just a trick of the light.

"What I'd like, Uncle, is for you to intervene. I believe an arrest was made with undue haste and would like you to strongly encourage the magistrate to examine other possibilities."

The baron rose from the desk. "I am far too busy to handle such trivial concerns. If it's that important to you, you may do as you wish. Tell Magistrate Carnbee that you have both my authority and my blessing. Will that suffice?"

At his uncle's words, a weight lifted from Gil's shoulders. He could breathe for the first time since Jarrett's shouts had faded into the distance as the cart trundled away. It wasn't enough yet to save Jarrett, but it was enough of a buoy to keep him afloat a while longer.

"Thank you, sir. Thank you!" Gil shook his uncle's hand a little too tightly.

The baron had a pleased twinkle in his eye. "Yes, well. I see no harm letting you indulge in this frivolity, as long as you conduct yourself in the proper manner and don't cause any offence to the magistrate. Now let's see if that brother of yours has gotten to the bottle yet or if there's any left for the rest of us!"

Even though he was exhausted, Gil found it impossible to sleep that night. After hours of tossing and turning, he finally gave up. Stoking the fire in the grate to cut some of the night's chill, he sat on the rug before it, a banyan draped over his shoulders.

Would Jarrett's cell have a fireplace? No, and the night would be bitterly cold without one. Hopefully, they'd been generous with the blankets, but Gil rather doubted it. He was restless, but wasn't foolhardy enough to tromp across the heath in the dead of night. He'd be lucky to only turn an ankle.

He'd wanted to dash off to the magistrate's home immediately, but his uncle had forbade it, forcing Gil to sit through the interminable meal and post-prandial conversation. By that time, it'd been far too late to go calling. He'd have to wait until morning.

He got up and began to pace. There had to be something he could do now. His eyes landed on the small desk he kept in his room. Perhaps some nice, boring estate paperwork would take his mind off Jarrett and let him rest.

It wasn't until he was halfway through a letter to an Edinburgh merchant that Gil realised that instead of the inquiry into a shipment of candles he'd meant to write, he was describing the dead man instead and asking if the merchant was familiar with him or knew anyone who might be. He finished the letter, then reached for another sheet of paper, addressing this one to a solicitor in St. Andrews. Then a clerk in Aberdeen.

It was likely a waste of time, but it was something he could do. Tomorrow, he'd inform the magistrate of his uncle's wishes, then ride to Crail to speak to Jarrett. Perhaps one of the men he'd been with at The Cross Keys was more than just a casual acquaintance. A lover might be willing to risk his life for Jarrett or at least come up with a convincing lie.

The thought sat poorly with him, even if it was the easiest solution. Best not to dwell on it. He was overtired and likely to think all sorts of strange things this time of night.

Climbing back into bed, he spared a last thought for poor Jarrett. Whatever cot and blankets they had for him wouldn't be anywhere near as comfortable as Gil's own. Still, Jarrett was a servant; he'd be used to rougher quarters. Tonight would be rougher than most, but he'd be fine. One night wouldn't hurt him. After all, it was just a tolbooth, not a prison. How awful could it be?

CHAPTER 7

J arrett awoke the next morning in the most awful place he'd
ever been.

He groaned. In truth, to say he awoke was a lie, as that
suggested he'd gotten any sleep at all. He *became slightly more
aware* the next morning in the most awful place he'd ever
been. Add to that, he only knew it was morning by the plate
of *something* his gaoler brought him. The cells were in the
basement of the tolbooth proper, and after they'd taken away
the lantern the day before, it was too dark to see his hand in
front of his face. At least it meant no one could see him cry.

He'd had his cell to himself that night, a small mercy, as it
meant no one could hear him crying either. Or his gasps when
the darkness closed around him, tighter and tighter, the air too
thin to breathe. *Oh God, they'd forgotten him down here they'd
forgotten him and he couldn't get out he couldn't—*

He shook his head, fighting back the panic. This wasn't
like that. He wasn't forgotten. They'd brought him breakfast,
hadn't they? And he'd only actually been alone a few hours.
There were a pair of drunkards in the cell across the way when
he'd arrived, but they'd been taken away shortly afterwards.
Thank Christ, because if he'd had to listen to their caterwauling
all night, he might actually have become a murderer.

The very thought made his eyes burn although he had no
tears left to shed.

Murderer.

He wasn't. He could never do anything so awful. But they weren't going to take his word for it. And the only way he could prove otherwise would keep him in this god-awful cell. If not somewhere worse.

He nudged the breakfast plate away with his bare foot, before tucking it back under his meagre blanket. It was likely teeming with fleas, but he'd take whatever small comforts he could get.

They'd taken his shoes before throwing him in, as well as his socks, which seemed unnecessarily cruel. They'd forced him to empty his pockets of his coins and keys as well, which had at least given him hope he'd be allowed to keep his coat, but that wasn't to be either.

So here he sat, a cold, hunched miserable creature with no coat, no shoes, and no hope of rescue. If he'd been allowed to keep the coin he'd been carrying, he might've been able to bribe someone to send a message to Lord Crawford on his behalf, but the earl would be halfway to London by now. Besides, while a lord might be able to use his power to get himself out of a murder charge, the same couldn't be said for his lowly servant. And there'd still be the question of where Jarrett had actually been if he wasn't out murdering folks, and pushing too hard for that answer would just land him right back where he was.

Better not to waste the earl's time with something he couldn't fix. Although, it might be worth letting him know he'd need a new valet when he got back.

Jarrett wasn't sure whether the noise that came out of him then was a laugh or a sob. Afterwards, he sat in miserable silence for what felt like an eternity until the unrelenting darkness began to press in again, smothering him. He squeezed his eyes shut, telling himself that was the only reason it was so dark. He'd be able to see perfectly clearly if he opened his eyes, but he was choosing not to. The lie didn't work at holding off the terror.

Finally, just when it felt like he couldn't take any more, he heard the rattle of keys in the basement door, then the sound of footsteps—two sets of footsteps—descending the stairs to the cells. Even better, the footsteps brought with them the golden glow of lamplight.

He got to his feet, stepping on a corner of the blanket to protect them from the frigid stone floor.

"Here he is, sir. I can't let you in w'him, but I'll let you have your privacy. Give a shout if there's anything you need."

"Thank you. I'll be sure to let Magistrate Carnbee know how much I appreciate your assistance."

The first voice was that of the lantern-jawed gaoler who'd led him down the night before, but the other... Jarrett would recognise that gentle burr anywhere, but what would Gil Charleton be doing here?

He straightened, trying to make himself as respectable as possible, which was hard enough without shoes, but even harder when the lantern drew close and Jarrett found himself squinting into the light after so long without. While he blinked the spots out of his eyes, he saw the gaoler give a small nod before leaving. And then they were alone.

"Good morning, Jarrett," said Charleton. Or at least, it sounded like Charleton; he still couldn't see with that light in his eyes.

"I don't know that it's good and I'll have to trust you that it's morning. Would you lower that damned thing? I don't think blinding is part of my punishment."

Perhaps not the most politic thing to say to his only visitor, but Jarrett's nerves were too frayed for pleasantries.

"Blinding? Oh, the lantern. Wait, have you been down here without any light this whole time?"

The lantern was set on the floor and Jarrett's eyes finally adjusted. Christ, it really was Gil Charleton. Jarrett liked to look at him at the best of times, but now, he was just about the most gorgeous man he'd ever seen.

It wasn't just the cold, or fear, or loneliness making him think that either. Lit from below, the lantern threw his features into sharp relief, making the definition of his legs, clad for riding in tight buckskins, impossible to ignore. The light sparked off his spectacles, making them glow in the darkness and turned his eyes a rich amber, a colour not like the scotch Old Tanner made in his barn, but like the fine spirits the earl kept in crystal decanters. Charleton's long black hair blended into the shadows, making it impossible to tell where he ended and the darkness began.

It was like looking at a saint. Or a demon.

Either way, he was here and whether it was as a blessing or a damnation, Jarrett welcomed the company.

"Jarrett?"

"Ah, aye. Or no," Jarrett stammered. "I mean, he needed a light to see when he brought me down here, of course, and again for breakfast, but aside from that..."

He shrugged. Charleton was frowning now, and wrinkling his nose in a way that meant he was too polite to cover it. Jarrett wouldn't blame him. If he was down here twenty years he wouldn't get used to the stench. Oh God, please don't let him be down here for twenty years.

Tendrils of fear coiled around his heart.

"What can I do for you, Mr. Charleton?" The words came out of him in a rush.

"Feel free to call me 'Gil', if you'd like," said Charleton. "I think, considering our location, we can allow ourselves a little informality. Besides, I've been calling you 'Jarrett' for long enough, it's past time to extend the same courtesy. However, I would ask you to refrain from using my entire Christian name. I'm afraid hearing it would only further augment the current unpleasantness of our surroundings."

Now it was Jarrett's turn to frown. Charleton might be pretty to look at, but he was clearly mad, babbling with ten quid words about names. Didn't he know you could call servants by their given names, or even give them new ones if you wanted, but the same didn't go the other way? But madman or no, Charleton's was the first friendly face he'd seen since being carted from the pub and Jarrett was a firm believer in "any port in a storm."

"Aye, all right, Gil. Thank you."

Now that Jarrett had said his name out loud, it did feel rather nice. Not that he'd ever be on even footing with the nephew to a baron, but it made him feel less like an unwashed criminal speaking to a free man. Then the bizarreness of the situation struck him. Here they were, politely discussing forms of address as if they were in a drawing room with a teapot and plate of biscuits to hand, instead of a stinking basement gaol where one of them was being held for murder.

"You'll forgive me for not offering you a seat," Jarrett said, giving an absurd little bow. "I wouldn't recommend giving your coat to the footman either. You won't be getting it back pressed and cleaned, that's for sure."

Jarrett fought the urge to pull the blanket tighter around himself as Gil frowned and looked him over, as if just noticing for the first time that Jarrett wasn't in full court attire.

"They took your coat? And your shoes too. Why would they do that?"

Jarrett shrugged. "Because they think I'm a bloody murderer? Won't need 'em where I'm going, it'll be far to h-hot."

His voice broke on the last word, but by dint of clenching his jaw and focussing very hard, he managed to keep from crying. Again.

"But there hasn't even been an inquest yet, never mind a trial." Gil shook his head. The man couldn't be amazed at the injustice of the world. Jarrett had figured that out when he was five and the other stable lads threw horse shite at him for not having a dad. As if that was his fault.

He shrugged again. "Like the magistrate said, clothes fetch a pretty penny. Apparently enough to murder over, so suppose I should count myself lucky the gaolers only left me to rot down here. I had a sixpence in my pocket that I don't expect to see back either. A few keys too, but none of them open secret treasure chests, more fool them."

One of the keys had been to his shed. It wasn't a treasure to a gaoler who resorted to stealing prisoners' clothes, but it was to

Jarrett. He had a spare hidden in Balcarres House proper, but that didn't mean he liked the loss of it any less. Assuming he ever got to see Balcarres House or his little shed ever again.

It was that thought that finally broke him. He sat heavily, landing on the cot more by luck than aim. Oh God, they were really going to hang him for murder, weren't they? He'd never sleep in his own bed or ride Thistle across the heath or have any of Janie's terrible cooking ever again.

"Jarrett? Jarrett? *Jarrett!*"

He heard his name being called in an increasingly worried voice, but what did it matter? Then something warm and soft struck him in the face.

He stared down at the scarf blankly, not fully understanding how it came to be there.

"For your feet."

He looked up at Gil who pantomimed wrapping his feet in the scarf. "Go on."

Not seeing what else he could do, Jarrett did as he was told. He wouldn't be able to do more than hobble with his feet tied up like that, but it wasn't as if he had anywhere to go. The scarf was warm from being wrapped around Gil's throat and Jarrett sighed as the heat sunk into his toes.

"That's better," said Gil. "I'll see what I can do about getting you your own things back, but you'd better take this too."

To Jarrett's shock, Gil then slipped off his overcoat and tossed it through the bars. He had a thinner, perfectly tailored coat on underneath, but it was clearly more decorative than anything else, as he immediately shivered and wrapped his arms around himself.

Jarrett couldn't bring himself to care, bracing himself against the cold for just as long as it took to pull the coat on, then draping the blanket back over top. The feeling was wonderful, unexpected warmth and comfort all in one.

The coat was a simple cut, plain brown wool with no unnecessary embellishments, but Jarrett would know it anywhere. He'd spotted it dozens of times from one of the upstairs windows of Balcarres House as Gil came and went on business. A good, practical coat for a good, practical man. There was a gentle scent rising from it, not enough to block out the stink of the cells, but enough to make it bearable. Lavender and something sharp, like citrus or pine. He wasn't certain which, but didn't want to frighten off his only visitor by taking an obvious sniff, especially not one who'd been so kind.

Handsome. Kind. If only the damn man had any interest in other men.

Unfortunately, that hope seemed even more unlikely than Jarrett ever being free again. From the gossip he'd heard, Gil had slept with half the county, but only the fairer half. Jarrett knew he was attractive, enticing even, to men who liked what he had, but if Gil was built to only enjoy a certain set of parts, there wasn't anything he could do about it. He'd tried to offer before, in one of their few, halting conversations. Seemed a shame now that he hadn't tried harder.

"Why are you doing this?" He asked. He shouldn't, but now that the words were out, he might as well say them all. "You barely know me. In fact, from the way you've acted around me in the past, I'm fairly certain you dislike me. Why are you here?"

"What? I—" Gil caught himself and took a deep breath. "I don't dislike you, Jarrett. I don't always know what to say around you, is all."

Before Jarrett could try to make sense of that, Gil continued.

"And I'm here because, well, you're right. I don't know you as well as I should, but I know you didn't do this. You're not capable of it."

"You believe me? But yesterday at the inn—"

"I behaved like a coward," Gil said fiercely. "I should have stopped them. I should have said something to keep it from getting this far, but I... I didn't. But I'm here now, and I'm going to do everything in my power to make this right. Do you hear me, Jarrett?"

If he said anything, he was going to break down again, so Jarrett just nodded.

Gil nodded back. "Good. I spoke to the magistrate before coming here. The coroner's inquest will be in a week, so you'll have to stay here until then, but it's only a week. And that gives me time to look into things on your behalf. If we can get this all sorted by then, you'll be free to go and won't have to worry about a trial or anything else."

Or hanging for a murder you didn't commit, was what he meant, but Jarrett appreciated him not saying the words out loud. That would make them far too real.

"Thank you," he whispered. "You're a good man."

Gil waved the words away. "Not quite. But I'm the man you've got, I'm afraid. Now, is there any way to prove to the coroner you didn't do this? Perhaps, anyone who saw you during the time the man was murdered? Anyone who would be willing to vouch for that? Or multiple people even? That might be better, if you knew them well enough?"

Oh aye, there were plenty of men who'd seen Jarrett that night, and quite a bit of him, but even if they'd be willing to join Jarrett in the cells, he didn't know their names to give. And no way of finding them either. Men came to The Cross Keys from all over Scotland, but only as frequently as they could get away with. He'd ridden for hours to get to the pub but no doubt some of the men there that night were from even further afield, and by the time they returned again, Jarrett's fate would have already been tried, sentenced, and executed.

He swallowed around a hard lump in his throat. "No one. After I left the inn, I borrowed one of His Lordship's horses, went for a ride, then came back and went to sleep."

"You went for a ride. Did anyone see you?"

Jarrett tried to think. If someone outside of the patrons of The Cross Keys had seen him in Kirkcaldy, he might be able to come up with an excuse for being there, or even say he just got carried away and hadn't noticed how far he'd gone, but the pub was outside of town and the road had been quiet. He'd passed a few people, but hadn't had a conversation with any of them. And by the time he'd ridden home, the weather had been so foul he wouldn't have seen his own mother if she'd been standing on the side of the road.

"No one," he said again.

"You're sure of that? Even one person who cared enough to help might be enough." Gil said each word slowly and his face was intense, as if there was some other question he was asking, but Jarrett didn't know what it was. No, there was no one who could help him. No one except Gil.

"There's no one. I went for a ride then came home. Weather was proper *drookit*, so no one saw me."

Gil sighed heavily and Jarrett couldn't help but feel he'd failed him somehow.

"Right. What about the other servants at Balcarres? Surely if you were out," Gil cleared his throat, "riding all night, you were in a state when you came in. Might they attest to that?"

"Or they might say I was in a state because I'd been out half the night killing someone," Jarrett pointed out. "Doesn't matter though, none of them saw me until breakfast, so they wouldn't know when I came in."

Gil pushed his spectacles further up his nose. Even in the midst of all this, Jarrett couldn't help but find the gesture endearing. "Mr. Howe didn't come to check when he heard the door open in the wee hours?"

"He wouldn't have. I slept in my shed."

That seemed to baffle Gil. "You what?"

"I have a shed, just between the stables and the gardens. His Lordship knows about it. I'm not somewhere I oughtn't. It's just a wee space I can call my own, that only I have the key to. Or did. It was in my coat, so them upstairs have it now. I sleep there some nights, and I didn't want to wake the household when I came in, so I slept there that night too."

It was the only part of his story that was completely true, but it sounded like a lie. What man would sleep in a garden shed when he had a room in a grand house like Balcarres?

"It's nice," he added, trying to get Gil to believe him, but he feared he was only making it worse. "It has a proper bed, a good one with a frame even! And there's a table and a chair. I even put in curtains..."

He trailed off. It *was* nice, even if he was the only one who thought so.

Gil gave him a gentle smile. "It sounds lovely."

He was lovely. Too lovely for this place, but Jarrett was glad he got to see him again, even if it was for the final time.

"It's not enough, is it?" Jarrett asked.

"It might be." Gil's smile wavered, but didn't fall. "And I've made other inquiries as well. Once we find out who the victim was, I expect it'll all fall into place. A bad business deal or perhaps he cheated the wrong man at cards. One week, Jarrett, then this will all be sorted at the inquest."

Jarrett found himself almost believing him. One week, then everything would be all right. He wanted to believe him. He *had* to believe him. Then Gil bent to pick up the lantern, and all that belief shattered under the force of renewed panic.

"You're leaving?" He jumped up from the cot and rushed towards the bars, hoping to somehow stop Gil from leaving him alone in the dark. But he'd forgotten about the scarf wrapped around his feet. He tripped, slamming into the bars with a clang that rattled throughout the cells.

He toppled back, unable to catch himself from where he was still wrapped in the blanket. Suddenly, he felt himself pulled against the bars as strong arms wrapped around him, holding him up.

"Jarrett?" Gil's face was close to his, his forehead pressed to the bars even as his arms were thrust awkwardly between them to keep Jarrett from falling. He was strong, and his spectacles were slightly askew, and Jarrett let himself be held, desperately needing the comfort, even if Gil didn't mean to be offering it.

I want to kiss him.

Kiss, and even more than that, he wanted Gil to stay, to keep holding him and telling him it would be all right. Perhaps that was why he did what he did next.

Content Jarrett wasn't in imminent danger of cracking his skull open, Gil let him go and slowly started to pull away. Jarrett shot his hands outs, freeing them from the blanket just in time to grab Gil and pull him back the lapels. Gil let out a loud "Oof" as he hit the bars.

"Please," Jarrett pleaded. "Please don't leave."

He was half-mad with fear. If Gil left, he might never come back. No one would, not even to hang him. They'd leave Jarrett in the cold and dark forever, until the moss grew over his bones and he'd long been forgotten.

"Please," he pleaded again. There was only one way he knew to get the things he wanted.

He licked his lips. Unclenching his hands, he let go of Gil's lapels, and flattened his palms against his chest. Gil gave a sharp inhale. His eyes were wide as Jarrett slowly slid his hands down, revelling in the feel of a strong male chest under his hands, even if it was through layers of fabric. Jarrett was doomed already, so he closed the distance between them.

The moment his lips touched Gil's, it was like a bolt of electricity lighting up the entire tolbooth in a single flash of brilliance. Gil froze, but didn't pull away, so Jarrett went further, licking his way into Gil's mouth. The feel of him was heavenly, even as Jarrett's nose kept bumping against both the cell's bars and Gil's spectacles. Then Gil turned his head just enough, and Christ, Jarrett didn't think it was possible to get better, but those smiling lips were moving against his and for a moment, everything was perfect.

Gil's coat was cut short at the waist and Jarrett didn't stop his hands, sliding them still lower, one curving around to caress Gil's hip, the other continuing straight down, pressing against his placket until Jarrett was cupping the hot length of him in his palm. With a groan, Jarrett pulled back from the kiss, revelling in the perfect temptation that was Gil's cock.

"Please stay," he whispered again, giving Gil a practised look through his eyelashes, his mouth slightly parted. "Please. I'll do anything you want."

Jarrett punctuated his words with a gentle squeeze and leaned in to kiss Gil again. The next thing he knew he was sprawled flat on his arse.

It took him a moment to realise what had happened. He lay in the middle of the cell where he'd fallen when Gil pushed him away. Gil, who was still standing at the bars, a look of shocked horror on his face. Then he turned and fled.

Oh Christ, what have I done!

Jarrett scrambled to get to his feet only to fall to his knees as he tangled in the scarf.

"Gil!" he cried out. "Gi—*Charleton*, I'm sorry! I didn't—It wasn't—Please don't go!"

But the footsteps pounding up the stairs never slowed and a moment later Jarrett heard the heavy door at the top slam closed.

He slumped against the bars. *Reckless, feckless idiot!* He'd just scared off the only person who'd been willing to help him! What in Christ's name had he been thinking?

Banging his head against the metal didn't undo the last few minutes, but the pain was enough to drive out the last dregs of his panic. But with the panic gone he was hollowed out, beyond the reach of tears or anger or even terror.

At least in his haste to flee, Gil had left the lantern behind. That was something.

Jarrett wrapped the scarf around his feet more tightly and buried his face in the collar of Gil's coat. Lavender and citrus, definitely. Perhaps orange oil. Aye, that was it. Lavender and orange oil. He draped the blanket back over himself and breathed in the comforting scent, watching the lantern flame flicker for hours until it went out and he was alone in the dark again.

CHAPTER 8

B y the time Gil arrived at the Kinneuchar Inn, all of the chairs were already occupied, and the crowd of standing onlookers was already several layers deep. The solemnity of a coroner's inquest had been lost on Marta, who was using the occasion to her advantage, pouring pint after pint for the thirsty audience. She'd even press-ganged two boys from the village into service, sending them diving into the hoard to pass out drinks and collect money.

Gil elbowed his way through with murmured apologies until he found a place where he could actually see. A semblance of a courtroom had been set up in front of the fireplace, with the only empty seat directly in front of it. To the left, Doctor Mills was seated with a man who must be the coroner, their heads bowed together in intense discussion. To the right, two rows of chairs had been arranged for the coroner's jury. The men in the front row had their arms slung over the backs to chat with the men behind them, all glowing with pride at being so important to the proceedings. Every juror had a drink either in his hand or under his seat. Some men had one of each.

Gil tugged his coat to straighten it. He'd worn all black, assuming this was going to be a decorous affair. He might as well have braided May ribbons into his hair. What an absolute disgrace. They were here to determine how a man had met his end, and everyone was treating the whole thing like a festival.

He looked over the crowd, unsurprised when he recognised almost everyone in attendance. He knew most everyone in this corner of the county, but the cows must have stopped milking and the bread be baking itself for them all to have taken the day off at once.

He wasn't surprised to see Robert taking up residence in one of the few chairs, but he couldn't believe who was sitting next to him.

"Catriona!" he hissed.

Somehow his voice cut through the din, because she turned his way, waving when she spotted him. She poked Robert, pointing at Gil, and his brother raised his tankard in Gil's direction.

Gil threw up his hands, hoping his face conveyed, *What in God's name are you thinking, bringing a future baroness to this?*

His message was only partly received, because Catriona cupped her hands around her mouth and called out in a most un-ladylike manner, "Charles was busy with his father! Robert was kind enough to be my escort!"

That made it sound like this whole ill-begotten idea was hers. In a perfect world, Robert would've had the sense to refuse, but in a perfect world... Well, a lot of things would be different.

He didn't have time to deal with his idiot brother now, the cacophony rose to a crescendo and then hushed as Magistrate Carnbee walked out of a back room and made his way to the seat before the fire. He was in full magisterial dress with robes and powdered wig.

"Silence!" he shouted, and to Gil's surprise, the throng obeyed.

"We will now begin the inquest into the death of an unknown man whose body was found on the sixth of March, year of our Lord 1819, in the chapel in the woods near Balcarres House, County Fife. Is the coroner, Mr. Boyd, in attendance?"

The man seated beside the doctor rose to his feet. "I am, your honour."

"Very well, I hand the proceedings over to you. You may call your first witness."

"Very good, sir. I call Doctor Mills to give evidence first."

From what Gil had heard, Mr. Boyd had come down all the way from Dundee to officiate the matter. There weren't enough suspicious deaths for County Fife to warrant having a coroner of its own, and all the ones in Edinburgh were too overrun with work to make the trip. He was a compact, sturdy man in his forties who had a mien of authority perfectly fitted to his job. A coroner's inquest was required before a case as serious as murder could be tried and at least this man looked like he knew what he was doing.

Gil had never been to an inquest before, but he didn't think the local magistrate usually had a role in one. However, knowing Carnbee, he wasn't surprised the man had found his way right into the middle of it.

As Doctor Mills went over the same evidence Gil already knew—stabbed in back, bashed in head—he looked out over the crowd again. He'd been summoned specifically to appear and give his testimony and could see the rest of the witnesses as well, the doctor and the magistrate, the men who'd carted the body, even young Davey. The lad had apparently found the body and was now perched on the end of the bar, kicking his feet back and forth and stuffing some sort of bun into his mouth as he awaited his turn. But there was one face that was noticeably absent.

Jarrett.

Gil hadn't gone back to the tolbooth since his first visit, but he hadn't stopped thinking about him either. How could he? He'd been shocked when he'd arrived and seen Jarrett in such an awful state. It'd been less than a day since he'd seen him last, but the man had looked as if he'd been to war.

It'd been rash of Gil to offer Jarrett use of his Christian name, but the man had seemed so beaten down that the idea of enforcing the barrier between servant and gentleman had seemed an unnecessary cruelty in light of what he'd already suffered.

Gil had known the tolbooth functioned as a gaol, but he'd envisioned one or two storerooms converted for the purpose, with a stove nearby and meals cooked by some watchman's wife. That miserable dungeon haunted his dreams. And the pettiness of taking a man's coat and shoes in such conditions was unforgivable. He hoped his scarf and coat were keeping Jarrett warm. In his rush to flee, he'd forgotten to demand the return of Jarrett's things. He'd written after, but had no way of knowing if his orders had been followed or just tossed on the fire. He could go back and check, but he couldn't. He *couldn't*.

Because the miserable conditions hadn't kept him away. It'd been that kiss. That kiss and the liberties which had followed.

And good God, what a kiss! Gil enjoyed kissing and had been fortunate enough to sample many men's kisses in many different styles: tender kisses, frenzied kisses, long, short, deep, fleeting, passionate, perfunctory, but Jarrett kissed like a force of nature. Kissing him was like being caught in a sudden storm: unexpected and wild, fierce and dangerous.

Gil had lost himself in it, completely forgetting where he was, and then, gloriously, there'd been a hand on his prick and he'd *wanted*. Looking into Jarrett's upturned face, seeing his lips, wet and pink and opened just enough for all the most sinful ideas to come rushing in, Gil had wanted Jarrett more than he'd ever wanted a man in his life.

"Please stay. Please. I'll do anything you want."

Those words had broken the spell and left Gil standing in the middle of the gaol, half-hard and horrified. What had possessed him to do such a dangerous thing as kiss another man in a public place, in the middle of a government building, no less? Aye, the basement had been empty except for them, but it could've very easily not been.

He'd like to place the blame solely on the narrow shoulders of a green-eyed tempter, but Gil had been a part of that kiss as much as Jarrett had. And that was the worst part of it. He'd taken advantage of Jarrett. There was no other way to look at it. Jarrett was a prisoner, for Christ's sake, without his freedom, his friends, or even his damned socks! He was scared and faced with a potential death sentence. Of course he'd offered up the one thing he had, himself, to the only person who'd come to check on him. Jarrett probably would've done the same to Magistrate Carnbee.

That was what had sent Gil running. Because even once he realised why Jarrett was kissing him, touching him, Gil still wanted him. Even though doing so would mean taking advantage of a man with no other options. And so he'd fled, to protect Jarrett as much as to protect himself, because if he stood there a minute longer, he was going to take what Jarrett was offering.

He'd only gone to the tolbooth to make sure Jarrett was all right and to work out if there was anyone who might be willing to give him an alibi. A stranger would've been ideal, but a discreet word to Jarrett's lover might also have done the trick. But either Jarrett was too loyal to whomever he'd been with at The Cross Keys to give up his name, or their intimacies didn't include that level of trust.

But instead of finding out anything useful, Gil had behaved disgustingly.

He was suddenly aware of a quiet in the pub and all eyes staring at him. Oh God, did they know what he'd done? How?

"Gilleasbuig Charleton," intoned Magistrate Carnebee.

Gil's voice was a croak. "Yes?"

"I've called you twice now to come give testimony."

A handful of quickly hushed titters broke out amongst the crowd. Someone nudged him forward.

"Right. Of course. The inquest." Gil said, fighting to regain some semblance of composure. Damn Jarrett. It was bad enough that Gil got flustered and said the wrong thing when the man was around, but now it seemed even thinking of him was enough to do the trick.

He bought himself a moment by wiping his spectacles on his handkerchief, then fixed on a smile for the coroner.

Most of his answers must have been a repetition of the doctor's only without the gory details, as the crowd grew restless at his description of hearing about the discovery of the body and going out to see it.

"...at which point I helped Doctor Mills roll the body over. We couldn't see the tattoo yet underneath all the blood, but we discovered the wound on his back, also that the grass beneath the victim was dry."

Mr. Boyd cocked his head at this in clear interest. "And why do you mention the grass, Mr. Charleton?"

"Because it rained that night. So, the victim had to have been killed before then, for his body to have protected the grass underneath it from becoming soaked. This means the man currently being held for his murder couldn't have committed it as he was out riding elsewhere until long after the rain had started."

The murmurs from the crowd grew louder and less restless.

"Order," Carnbee suggested rather than demanded. "Mr. Charleton, please stick to what you witnessed, not what you were told by others."

Gil couldn't hold back any longer. "Respectfully, why isn't Jarrett here to give his statement? Everyone here knows he's being held for this murder."

"We haven't established this is a murder yet," said the coroner firmly. "That is, in fact, what we are here to determine."

"Yes, but then why isn't Jarrett here? Surely the testimony of a man accused of murder should be important to whether or not a murder actually occurred!"

"Mr. Charleton!" Carnbee shouted to be heard over the crowd. "As Mr. Welch would only lie, his testimony was deemed unnecessary to these proceedings."

"Unnec—"

"If Mr. Boyd determines a crime has been committed, young Mr. Welch will have his chance to speak at his trial. Until then, there are plenty of other, more reputable witnesses who can attest to the events surrounding this man's death. Is that understood?"

Gil gritted his teeth.

You fucking forgot, didn't you? You lazy old bastard. You fucking forgot to have Jarrett sent here from the tolbooth. I'll bet you forgot he was even in there. Out of sight, out of mind? What a fucking disgrace.

"I understand perfectly, your honour. Thank you for clarifying. How fortunate we all are to have your guidance in such serious matters."

Before his sarcasm could penetrate the magistrate's thick skull, Gil added, "Mr. Boyd, as it has now been made clear to me that my purpose in this inquest is simply to relate what I have witnessed, you should be made aware that when I interviewed him from his imprisonment at the tolbooth, I *witnessed* Jarrett Welch say he'd been out riding, returning only in the very early hours and thoroughly drenched. He has the key to an outbuilding on the earl's property and spent the remainder of the night there so as not to wake the rest of the household. If you doubt the accuracy of my statement, I am certain that Magistrate Carnbee received the same information when he went to the tolbooth himself to conduct his own interview."

Gil's wager that he'd done no such thing was proved right when Carnbee's face went bright red.

"Furthermore," Gil added. "I *witnessed* Marta, the woman whose establishment this is, attest to the fact that Jarrett Welch left this inn several hours before the victim himself after having only the very briefest of conversations. Also, as the victim's identity may prove key to determining who wanted him dead, inquiries are also being made to determine who the man was. Inquiries independent of those doubtlessly being carried out by the magistrate's office, naturally."

"That is quite enough, Mr. Charleton!" bellowed Carnbee. "No further questions!"

"Actually," said Mr. Boyd, "I would like to—"

"No. Further. Questions."

The coroner hesitated, then shrugged. "Very well. If I may have the next witness."

The crowd parted as Gil made his way through the inn, save for one brave soul who patted him on the shoulder with a whispered, "Well done, lad." The rest seemed uncertain whether to say nothing for fear of Carnbee's wrath, congratulate him for standing up to the magistrate, or spit on him for defending a murderer.

He briefly glanced over at Catriona and Robert as he made his way past them. His brother was redder than Carnbee was. No doubt that was partially due to the alcohol, but Gil resigned himself to yet another lecture from his father when he got home about proper behaviour, the dignity of the family name, etcetera, etcetera, etcetera. He wondered if Robert would be getting a lecture on not taking another man's wife to a public inn to hear the details of a brutal slaying, but he doubted it. Catriona merely raised an eyebrow at him as he passed.

Snarling, Gil snatched a tankard out of Marta's hand as she made her way up to testify. Its intended recipient took one look at his face and decided not to protest.

Gil sat at the bar, nursing his ale as the testimony continued. It didn't matter. Marta testified, describing a large man in bright pants who'd only been in the once until he'd showed up on her bar again dead the next morning. Next was Carnbee, who seemed to have solved the crime all on his own and possibly even foreseen it happening, he was just that good. Then young Davey, who had little to add other than enthusiasm and gruesome details.

Gil knew what they were all going to say and none of it was worth a damn. The magistrate had clearly decided Jarrett was guilty and was treating all of this as a pointless but required necessity to bring the matter before the circuit court, which itself was only another required necessity to bring it before the hangman. If there was one blessing, it was that Carnbee lacked the authority himself to try Jarrett for murder and would have to wait on others to do the dirty work for him.

But Jarrett was innocent, God damn it! Innocent of being anything more than a fucking idiot with bad luck.

He stewed over his drink, waiting for the inevitable conclusion, so it was a surprise to hear one more witness called.

"Will a Mrs. Randall please step forward?"

An old woman hobbled forward. Her hair was tied up in a rag that had once been blue and she was so hunched over that her shoulders were barely higher than her hips. But her gaze peering out over her cane was sharp.

Gil knew her, not well, but in the way all people who lived in a place their whole lives knew each other. And no one had lived here longer than Mrs. Randall. The woman was the local Methuselah and had seen generations born and die while she still carried on. For every bairn that Doctor Mills helped bring into the world, she had brought in a dozen more, including Gil himself. As such, she was well-respected across the county and her word was as good as law.

"Mrs. Randall," Mr. Boyd said gently. "Could you tell us what you know of this unknown man's death?"

"Aye, he were murdered."

Overall, Gil wasn't sure if it was possible for the inquest to be going any worse. From the look on the coroner's face, it appeared he wasn't the only one.

Mr. Boyd tried again. "That's what we're here to determine. If you would please tell us exactly what you saw?"

"Well, I were out that night on account of it being a full moon, leastwise before the rain kicked up, but that is to be expected, and indeed I had expected it, so safe at home was I before it started."

That seemed to be the end of her statement.

"So, you didn't witness anything at all?"

Mrs. Randall harrumphed. "Well, o'course I did. I wouldn't be wasting my time coming up here otherwise, would I? No all that happened before the rain. I'd been out gathering my herbs.

Best gathered at night you know, and with the moon being full that's even—"

"And what did you see while gathering herbs?" interrupted the coroner, sparing them all.

"I saw a man come running. Up by the chapel this was, and him fleeing as if the Devil himself were on his coattails."

There was some muttering amongst the more astute in the audience who'd made the connection between the presence of a cunning woman picking herbs by the light of a full moon and the many plants that had overrun the chapel's small graveyard. She likely should have expected the Devil to appear. The more superstitious might even think that was her desired outcome. But she'd healed generations of families who couldn't afford the likes of Doctor Mills, so even if she was a witch, Gil doubted it would hurt her reputation much.

"Did you get a good look at the man?" Mr. Boyd asked.

She shook her head. "Too startled I was, and him bowling me over without so much as a glance back to see he hadn't done in two folks that night! Cracked my leg hard against one of those tombstones so bad I decided that were enough herb picking for one night and took myself off home to make a poultice."

The coroner looked down at his notes. "I see. And about what time was this?"

She hummed, "Oh, midnight or thereabouts. It had to be that late, 'cause that's when the herbs be at the most potent."

"Of course," said Mr. Boyd. "And you have no idea as to the identity of the man who knocked you over? Not even a general description?"

"I thought he were the *ghaist* of Bertram de Shotts come back for another victim until he knocked me arse over tea kettle, so I can't say as I know more than that."

That got a laugh from the assembled crowd, including the coroner, and Gil wondered if he was the only man there who actually cared that Jarrett's life hung in the balance. Apparently not, if testimony about the perpetrator being the ghost of a murderous giant was going to be admitted.

"Thank you for your candour, Mrs. Randall. And one final question, is there anyone who can corroborate your story? 'Corroborate' means—"

"I know what it means," Mrs. Randall snapped. "You think I'm a liar? Next you'll be saying I was the one done the poor fellow in!"

And wouldn't that neatly solve all of Gil's problems. Unfortunately, even as desperate as he was for someone else to spontaneously admit to committing the murder, he'd seen what had been done to the dead man's head, and it would've been impossible for a frail old woman like Mrs. Randall to have lifted the stone that had done it. Unless the ghost of Bertram de Shotts helped her.

Or she really is a witch.

Gil shook the thought away. That sort of thinking wasn't helpful.

Mr. Boyd was spluttering, "I meant nothing of the sort, ma'am. I meant, was there anyone with you at the time who can confirm this version of events?"

"The bruise he caused running me over is still healing. Quite a sight it is too." At this, Mrs. Randall lifted her skirt, flashing the injury in question to the coroner as well as a great deal else.

The inn descended into pandemonium.

In the end, the verdict of the coroner's jury was hardly surprising. Mr. Boyd read their decision aloud. The identity of the dead man remained unknown, but there was no doubt he'd been stabbed to death, then finished off with the rock. It was ruled a murder.

"And who has the jury decided was responsible for this murder?" Carnbee asked.

Gil fought the urge to bury his head in his hands. He knew what the answer was going to be.

To his surprise, the coroner hesitated.

"I'm afraid I disagree with the opinion of the jury and must take the rare step of issuing my own ruling in this regard. Due to a lack of definite evidence and considering the absence of a key witness," Gil didn't miss Mr. Boyd's pointed look at Carnbee, "I have decided to issue a verdict of murder by person or persons unknown."

Gil pounded his fist on the bar in triumph. It wasn't as good as Jarrett being declared innocent, but it did mean the magistrate would actually have to do some work to prove Jarrett had done it before taking him to trial. Gil had already been calculating how many of his investments he'd have to liquidate to afford a proper barrister for Jarrett. Between that and the ruling, he might just stand a chance.

He gave in and buried his face in his hands, but in relief. The crowd flowed around him as he collected himself. Some headed home now that the entertainment was over, others just needing another drink. A heavy hand fell on his shoulder.

"Well, well, well," slurred Robert. "That was more of a show than I expected."

"It really was quite thrilling," exclaimed Catriona.

Gil turned to face them both. Catriona's face was flushed with excitement. Robert's was just flushed.

"And you," Robert waved a finger in Gil's face.

"Oh, you were marvellous," Catriona said as Gil batted his brother's hand away. "Standing up for the poor absent Mr. Welch. It was like something out of a novel! Is he really imprisoned? Is it dreadful?"

Soft lips against his own, a warm hand on his prick.

"It is. Most dreadful. They've locked him up in the dark with no cause and taken everything from his boots to the last farthing in his pockets."

Catriona gasped, but it was tinged with delight. "Good gracious. And do you really think he's innocent?"

Gil nodded. "I do."

"How splendid! I'm so glad I convinced Robert to bring me. Charles will be so sorry he missed your moment of glory, but never fear," Catriona tapped a small book Gil hadn't noticed before. "I wrote everything down. I didn't want the rest of the family to have to rely on gossip when they could have an account straight from the horse's mouth."

Gil winced. That was just what he needed, his entire family knowing exactly how he behaved today.

He reaffixed his usual charm and tried to control the damage. "Surely, you're not calling yourself a horse, ma'am. Your hooves are far too dainty. And your horse blankets far too fashionable for stables such as these."

She pulled her shawl tighter around her shoulders. "Isn't it lovely? Charles ordered it from Edinburgh as an apology for our not going there this year. I've been waiting for a chance to wear it."

Gil gave Catriona an even more winsome smile. In truth, the shawl's stripes of violet and pale blue did little for her complexion, but he hadn't gotten a reputation as a charmer of women by being honest. "Its vibrancy suits you, even as it is entirely unnecessary, as you need no assistance in that regard."

Robert made a harrumphing noise, sounding rather like a horse himself. Gil ignored him. It was inevitable that the rest of his family was going to hear about his actions today, but Gil would rather they hear a more discreetly edited version from him, rather than Catriona's breathless retelling or Robert's drunken slander.

"Now," Gil continued, "if *I'm* the horse you were referring to before, you may have the right of it. In which case this lumbering brute would request the chance to tell the family myself. You know how my father can be, and I'd hate for Mother to be distressed by any undue accuracy."

Her face fell so he added, "But as my memory may not be perfect, I would very much appreciate your assistance in the retelling. Perhaps between my memory and your notes, we could regale them after dinner tonight?"

Catriona nodded, but couldn't get a word in before Robert said, "I wouldn't be worried about Mother and Father if I was you. It's Uncle Andrew. You made a right fool of Carnbee today.

I'm not saying it's more than he deserves, but Uncle won't like it. 'My boy, think of the family name!'"

Even drunk, Robert's impression of their uncle was uncanny. What was worse was that he was right yet again. Their uncle was going to be livid. He and the magistrate were good friends.

"I suppose I should go apologise," Gil sighed. "Try to undo the damage. That might take some time, so you two had best go back without me. I'll walk."

As he'd expected, Robert looked ready to protest and get himself another drink, but Catriona nodded.

"We should be getting back. We'll see you for supper. Don't spend too long apologising or I'll have to tell the whole story myself!"

Gil waved them out, then went to face the magistrate. Carnbee was in the midst of a heated discussion with Mr. Boyd. Both of them looked up at Gil's approach.

"Magistrate Carnbee," Gil said, reaching out his hand. In his experience, men of Carnbee's position would automatically shake an offered hand before their minds could catch up enough to give a cut instead.

He was proven right when Carnbee stuck his hand in his, then scowled a second later. Gil then offered his hand to the coroner.

"Mr. Boyd, I congratulate you on your handling of the inquest today. I apologise if I was somewhat adversarial during my questioning."

"Not at all," said the coroner. "I appreciated your candour."

Mr. Boyd looked pleased, but now that his job was done, it didn't really matter how he felt. He could head back to Dundee proud of a task, if not well done, at least finished, and put the lot of them behind him. It was Magistrate Carnbee whose injured pride could make life difficult. Gil was opposed to grovelling as a rule, but he would if keeping the peace meant an easier life for himself. And for Jarrett.

"Magistrate," Gil said, trying to put as much undue respect into his tone as possible. "I must apologise to you as well. I've had time to reflect on my words, and I see they may have been construed as an attack on your handling of the situation. I want to be clear that was not at all what I had intended."

It was exactly what he had intended, but the old bull was only snorting smoke now, not actual flames.

"Your words were indeed ill-thought, Mr. Charleton." Carnbee huffed. "Fortunately, as a magistrate it is my duty to keep a cool head during such outbursts and conduct myself impartially."

You can go soak your cool head. Gil thought, but aloud he said, "That is most gracious of you. I can only apologise again."

"Your apology is noted. Fortunately, there was no real harm done. We now have confirmation it was a murder and the killer remains in custody."

Both Gil and Mr. Boyd frowned.

"I believe my ruling was that of 'person or persons unknown'," said the coroner.

"Indeed it was," Carnbee replied. "But as you yourself stated, not all the evidence or testimony was available today. As such the main, nay only, suspect shall remain in custody until the trial. Fortunately again, this murder was a well-timed one. The circuit judge is due to arrive in just under a month. Until then, the public must be protected from this Jarrett. The safety of the people of this county is of the gravest importance."

One month. That's all Jarrett has.

"You can't mean to keep him locked up!" Gil shouted, undoing his hard work. But he couldn't shake the image of how Jarrett had looked in that cell after a single night. It'd now been a week. Would there even be anything left of him to try after a month?

Magistrate Carnbee stroked his moustache, making himself look every inch the villain. He didn't care a whit about the inquest, he'd made his decision and to hell with justice.

"Indeed I do." Carnbee's smile was cruel. "In fact, Mr. Charleton, since you were so kind to point out that you've already been to see the prisoner, perhaps you should be the one to tell him."

CHAPTER 9

The sight of Jarrett in his cell was every bit as bad as Gil had feared. He lay on his cot, wrapped in the blanket and didn't bother to rise at Gil's arrival. Like this, it was almost impossible to see the man who'd kissed him with such fierce abandon the week before. Jarrett had always had a fire to him that called to Gil like a hound to the hunt, but after only a week that flame was nearly extinguished.

"Jarrett?"

Are you all right? Are you alive? What is it about this place that affects you so badly?

Two of the other cells were occupied this time, but Gil ignored the jeers of the other prisoners.

"Hello, Mr. Charleton." Jarrett didn't speak the words so much as sigh them.

"I thought we agreed on 'Gil'?"

"Did we?" Jarrett asked with indifference. "I thought that was a dream."

The gaoler hadn't left this time, likely wanting to witness Jarrett's continued misery when Gil told him he wasn't getting out. "He's been like this all week. You'd've thought he was a prince of Persia the way he's been moping about a little cold and damp."

This was far beyond moping. Gil steeled himself for what he had to say next.

"Jarrett, I... That is, the inquest was today, and..."

He couldn't do it.

"Oh for God's sake, get him out of there."

The gaoler's eyes widened. "Sir?"

"Just do it!"

The keys were hardly in the lock before Gil was pushing the cell door open. Getting his arms around Jarrett, he tried not to remember the last time they'd been this close, the taste of those plush lips, the careful strength in his grip as he'd caressed Gil through his breeches.

Then he helped Jarrett to his feet and all those thoughts were rushed away in a flood of anger when he saw Jarrett's bare feet.

"Where in the blazes are his shoes! I instructed his things be returned to him a week ago!"

The gaoler paled. "I wasn't on duty then, sir. I didn't know."

"Fetch them now! We'll meet you upstairs!"

The gaoler looked like he had more to say, but one look from Gil was enough to send the man scurrying.

Jarrett murmured something unintelligible.

"What was that?"

"I said, I needed your scarf for my hands today."

Jarrett held out his hands, which were wrapped in Gil's scarf like a muff. From beneath the blanket, the sleeve of Gil's best overcoat poked out. His heart softened at the sight of it keeping Jarrett warm.

"Right," he said, removing the filthy blanket from Jarrett's shoulders. "You won't need this once you have your own coat back."

The short climb up the stairs took all remaining energy out of Jarrett and Gil had to haul him up the last few steps. Gil couldn't have done that with most men, but Jarrett was an inch or two shorter and had been slighter than himself even before the week of gaol rations. Still, by the time they reached the top, they were both panting.

There was only a pair of socks waiting for them, no shoes, no coat.

"Everything was turned over to the magistrate, sir," the gaoler said before Gil could ask. "All additional possessions. The socks might be someone else's but he can have them."

"I had a sixpence too," muttered Jarrett.

Gil raised an eyebrow at the gaoler who only stammered, "A-all additional possessions were given to the magistrate."

Gil snatched up the socks. Better for Jarrett to dry his feet in the carriage before putting them on than get soaked socks walking out to it. Gil had been driven out rather than deal with another ride in the rain. He felt sorry for his driver, but had never been more thankful for his own selfishness. There were several thick, woollen blankets kept in the carriage for the coldest of days, and he was going to wrap Jarrett in every single one of them.

"Very well, when I next see Magistrate Carnbee, I'll be sure to check that all items were delivered to him. Including the sixpence."

With that, Gil began to lead Jarrett outside.

"Sir? Sir!" the gaoler called out. "That man is a prisoner!"

Gil pulled up every inch of lordliness it was possible for the second son of a second son to possess.

"I have the authority and blessing of my uncle, Lord Charleton, to handle the matter of this prisoner as I see fit. And just today, I was told by Magistrate Carnbee himself that the safety of the people of this county is of the gravest importance. *All* people, including prisoners. And as you have been unable to keep this one safe from your own thievery, I am taking matters into my own hands."

With that, he pulled open the outer door, letting in the fresh smell of rain. He wrapped his arm tighter around Jarrett's back to lead him out.

"Come along, Jarrett. You're my problem now."

CHAPTER 10

*J*arrett could hear laughter coming from the rooms above him,
  then all around him, but no one was there. He was alone. Or
was he? In the dark, it was impossible to tell.

*He reached out and his hand struck a wall, the cold stone wet
against his fingertips. He ran his hands along it until he reached
a corner, looking for the entrance to his cell. There had been bars,
hadn't there? But his hands only met another stone wall, then
another, and another.*

*That wasn't right. Perhaps he'd been wrong and there weren't
bars, but there had to at least be a door. He went around again.*

Four walls. All stone. No bars. No doors.

*His heart began to beat more quickly. The laughter came
again, but more muted this time, further away. They hadn't
forgotten him, had they? He walked around again. Was he
imagining it or did it take less time to walk the length of each
wall. He counted five paces. Then four. Then three.*

*Something bumped the top of his head. The roof of his cell
pressing down, lower and lower. He pushed against it with all his
might, fingernails breaking as he fought against it but it was too
heavy.*

*"Let me out!" he screamed, but no one could hear him over the
laughter.*

A particularly rough jolt of the carriage bolted him from
sleep. Jarrett bit his lip to keep from crying out so the other
prisoners wouldn't hear. But he didn't remember the tolbooth

having velvet upholstery. Blinking, it took him a long moment to remember where he was. Then his eyes settled on Gil's worried face.

"Jarrett?"

"I'm all right, just groggy. How long was I asleep?" Jarrett rolled his neck. It would take more than a nap in a moving carriage to undo a week in a cell, the aches in his muscles as familiar now as the nightmare had always been.

"A little over an hour. We'll be back at—We'll be back soon."

Jarrett might be rattled in more ways than one, but he couldn't miss such an obvious deflection.

"Back where?"

"Well, that's something we need to discuss. There's quite a lot we need to discuss in fact."

Like me groping you. Or that kiss. Or the fact they gaoled me for murder and left me there to rot but then you came and fought to get me out and now I have no idea whether I'm free or you're taking me somewhere worse.

They should probably start with that last one.

"Are you taking me to be hanged?"

Gil's eyes went wide. He'd taken his long hair out of its ribbon while Jarrett slept, likely so he could lean back against the seat fully without it twisting his head to one side or the other. It streamed down the sides of his face, long enough to brush his lapels and looking softer than the velvet surrounding it. Jarrett wanted to sink his hands into that hair and never let go.

If he was to have an executioner, it was nice of them to provide such a pleasant one to look at.

"Christ, Jarrett, no!" The words exploded out of Gil and it was about all Jarrett could do to stay upright in his seat at the force of them.

Gil took a deep breath and regained some of his composure. "A lot has happened in the last week."

As they trundled along, Gil caught him up on the inquest, the magistrate, and everything else he'd missed. It was more than Jarrett could take in at once.

"So, I'm still to be tried, but not today."

Gil nodded. "That's right. Carnbee doesn't have the authority to try such a serious crime, but the circuit judge will be making his rounds within the month."

A month. That wasn't any time at all.

"I didn't do it," Jarrett whispered.

"I know," said Gil. "That is, you're not the sort to kill, are you?"

No. Jarrett wasn't. He'd learned that years ago. And he'd had far better reason back then than just a stranger turning him down for a tupping. Something hot and tight caught in his throat, but he forced the words past it. Gil deserved to hear them.

"I'm not, but I didn't expect anyone to believe me. Thank you. I can't tell you how much it means that you do."

"Aye, well. Of course." Like any good Scotsman, it seemed that Gil didn't know how to handle sincere gratitude. His cheeks were decidedly pink as he took off his spectacles and gave them a wiping they didn't need.

Jarrett realised he hadn't tried to flirt with the man even once since they'd set foot in the carriage. In fairness, he'd first been too focused on being out of the dark and then falling into exhausted sleep. After that, it'd seemed slightly more important to learn about how things were progressing with his *murder charge*, but still, it wasn't like him to spend this much time around a beautiful man and not say *something*. Yet the fact he was even thinking about it was mad. It would be a terrible idea, especially after that disastrous kiss a week ago, but terrible ideas had never stopped him before. Besides, if he only had a month...

But Gil hadn't mentioned the kiss. Hadn't mentioned it and had still come to free Jarrett despite it. That meant he shouldn't bring it up either. It would be foolish to even mention it. Idiotic even.

"I'm sorry I kissed you." Jarrett had never been one to do the smart thing. If he had, even once in his life, he likely wouldn't have ended up wanted for murder.

"And the rest of it," he added, making a groping motion with his hands because, *Oh hell,* why not make things as bad as possible. Really, he should save Gil the trouble and ask the driver to turn back to the tolbooth himself.

Gil fumbled his spectacles, dropping them on the bench beside him. He spent longer searching for them than seemed necessary as they were right there. When he finally retrieved them, his words sounded rehearsed.

"You were scared, confused, and not fully responsible for your actions. No one saw, and I have not spoken of it to anyone, nor will I. Let us just put the matter behind us and not speak of it again."

You kissed me too, Jarrett wanted to say, but had just enough self-preservation to hold his tongue for once. "Thank you."

Gil nodded, not meeting Jarrett's eyes, then returned to cleaning his spectacles.

After a few minutes of this, Jarrett settled back in his seat and wondered if he had time to take another nap.

"It's funny," he said drowsily, "that they let you take me."

Gil resettled his spectacles. "About that. They may not have 'let' me take you, so much as I... creatively interpreted certain statements. In fairness, no one said I *couldn't,* but I doubt the magistrate will see it that way, never mind my uncle. Which—please open your eyes, this is important—which means that I'm in quite a lot of trouble, I suspect. Or I certainly will be once we get to Balcarres."

That was enough to startle Jarrett into full wakefulness. "We're going home? I thought you were just taking me to another gaol in a fancy coach rather than a cart!"

"Why would I—never mind, that actually makes more sense than what I'm actually doing," said Gil. "No, I decided that since you haven't actually been convicted of a crime, especially a crime which we both agree you didn't commit, it would be cruel to continue to keep you imprisoned."

"Again, thank you. But Balcarres?"

"Well, I can hardly take you home to Mother," Gil snapped. It was only now that Jarrett began to see how tense he really was.

Gil removed his spectacles as if he was intending to wipe them again, then shook his head and pushed them back up his face.

"Jarrett, I made the decision to free you, but I think I need to be clear about the limitations of such freedom and the consequences should they be broken. The consequences to myself in particular. I have freed a man who is to be tried for murder. Some would argue that this was done unlawfully. Fortunately, due to my family connections, I see no likely repercussions for this, assuming you show up for court as expected. However, should you fail to make an appearance, I suspect the penalty shall fall heavily on me for providing you assistance. I recognise that I made this decision myself, but I would appreciate some assurance that this won't be the case."

Christ, the man could string a lot of words together when he wanted to. It took Jarrett a moment to parse his meaning. "You're saying that if I stay put, I go to trial for murder. But if I run off, you go to prison for helping me escape."

Gil nodded. "Precisely. Although I'm hoping that it won't come to a trial if we can find enough evidence to convince the magistrate of your innocence."

Jarrett didn't think that a decree of innocence brought down by the Angel Gabriel himself would be enough to convince Carnbee once he'd made up his mind. Likely the man would just be offended that God sent a messenger and didn't grant him an audience Himself, but Jarrett didn't want to ruin the hopes of the one person who believed in him.

"And you want me to prove I'm not going to run off. How can I do that?"

That halted Gil, but only for a moment. "I'd accept a gentleman's agreement."

Jarrett waved a hand at himself. "I'm hardly a gentleman."

Gil grinned. "You're a valet, a gentleman's gentleman. Linguistically speaking, that makes you twice the gentleman I am."

Despite himself and the entire absurd awfulness of his situation, Jarrett had to laugh. "You should've become a barrister, arguing like that. Any birds you want to convince to swim or fish to fly?"

"You agree then, on your word as a gentleman's gentleman?" Gil stuck out his hand.

Jarrett took it. Gil's hand was warm and his grip was strong. Jarrett was surprised by the roughness of his palm. Surely a gentleman, even a second son's second son should have soft hands, but he preferred this much more. He looked into Gil's eyes, and for a moment the easy confidence there faltered, as if he too was remembering the last time Jarrett touched him.

"I promise," Jarrett lied.

Gil might have lovely hands and an even lovelier face, but Jarrett wasn't going to let himself be hanged for them. He'd go along with whatever scheme Gil had to prove his innocence for now, but if they hadn't cleared his name before the day of the trial came, Jarrett was going to do what he did best.

Run.

It wasn't Jarrett's fault Gil had put himself in this position. None of it was. And a gentleman's punishment for assisting an escape was going to be far less than a valet's punishment for murder. He'd feel bad knowing Gil was suffering, especially now that he had a taste of it himself, but he'd be alive to feel bad. That was what mattered.

"Excellent," said Gil and slowly withdrew his hand. Jarrett already missed the feel of it in his. "Please don't take this the wrong way, but while I accept your word as your bond, I doubt the rest of the county will be so obliging."

More words. "You think Mrs. Finley is going to expect me to murder her in her bed."

"I would be more worried about Graham coming after you with a pitchfork, but aye. It might help the situation somewhat if I explain to them that you are under my supervision for the duration."

So Jarrett would have a gaoler but not a gaol. He could live with that. It was a lot easier to escape from one man than it would be to escape from the tolbooth. Especially if that one man was as damnably honourable as Gil. He probably wouldn't even think to lock Jarrett up while he slept and Jarrett certainly wasn't going to put ideas into his head.

"That sounds fair. One request."

Gil looked perplexed. "Yes?"

Jarrett grinned. "I want to be there when you tell them."

The show was exactly as entertaining as Jarrett had hoped. Janie screamed at the sight of him and Mrs. Finley had crossed herself in a decidedly papist way. Only Mr. Howe was a disappointment, maintaining the aloof calm which proved he was born to be a butler, only suggesting that perhaps Jarrett would like to freshen up before supper.

"You want to supervise this too?" Jarrett asked, just to see Gil's cheeks turn deliciously pink again. He peeled off Gil's coat and handed it over, already missing its familiar warmth.

"I think you can be trusted not to drown yourself," Gil replied, folding the coat over his arm and brushing away a bit of tolbooth dirt. "But I'll help you haul water so Janie isn't distracted from her cooking."

Jarrett doubted Janie's distraction would make the food any worse, but he could hardly argue the results. He didn't have the patience to wait for the water to grow truly hot, but he had a tub of warm water in half the time it would've taken him alone, and a locked door between himself and any prying eyes. A door he'd locked himself and could open at any time. He lit another lamp then stripped off, sinking into the water with a sigh. The tub wasn't large, but if he folded himself up, he could get most of his body in it at once. He crossed his arms over his knees and laid his head on them, enjoying the peace. He kept his eyes open, watching the steady flame of the lamp.

He was out. He wasn't free of this mess by a long shot, but he was out of the darkness. For now at least, he was safe, warm, and had Gil on his side. That thought made him feel even warmer. Gil said he hadn't told anyone about the kiss. It would've been easy enough for him to have the magistrate add attempted gross indecency to Jarrett's list of crimes. It meant something that he hadn't, didn't it?

And he'd kissed back, damn it. At least, Jarrett thought he had. Was certain he had. Was pretty sure he had. Gil was right, he hadn't exactly been in his right mind at the time, too filled with pure animal panic at being trapped in a cage and clawing at anything that came close. They'd agreed to put it behind them, so Jarrett wouldn't push. Not for now, at least. He'd just have to wait and see if Gil brought it up again. Perhaps after they'd found the real killer and Jarrett was truly free.

He smiled at the thought. It was a pleasant one, but in his experience, those who deserved justice rarely got it. Still, it was nice to dream. He reached for the soap and let himself think about what it would be like when his name was cleared.

Perhaps it would start with a parade in their honour. They'd be carried down the lane as heroes for stopping a vicious murderer before he could strike again. No, even better, they'd both ride down the streets on fine horses, pure white steeds like the knights of legend. As they rode by, one by one, everyone would doff their caps and apologise for ever thinking so poorly of Jarrett.

He lathered up a rag and started scrubbing his shoulders. Hell, it was his dream, Carnbee would be grovelling in the dirt, begging for forgiveness and offering to be locked up himself to prove how sorry he was. Jarrett wouldn't even glance at the man, just ride past. This would make Gil laugh and they'd spur their horses on, galloping until they came to somewhere quiet and, even more importantly, secluded.

He dipped the rag back into the warm water and ran it slowly over his skin. The wind would've pulled the ribbon from Gil's hair and his cheeks would be flushed with exertion. Lord, he'd been beautiful like that in the carriage. Why hadn't Jarrett done anything then? Exhaustion was no excuse when he had something like that so close and no one around to see.

He wouldn't waste the chance if he got Gil that way again. He'd pull Gil inside wherever they were. For this fantasy it could be Jarrett's shed, but an even nicer version, with room for more than one chair, and a bed with blankets so thick that when he pushed Gil down, he disappeared for a moment in their plushness. Or no, even better, the hay loft above the stables. They could bring the blankets from the other fantasy to protect themselves from any sharp pokes in unwanted places. Aye, that would be perfect, Gil spread out before him, inviting endless possibilities, the earthy scents of hay and horse and leather rising up from below.

Jarrett dropped the rag in the water and let it float to the surface, wrapping one hand around his cock. He was already half-hard. It had been all he could do to keep his wits in the cell; thoughts of taking his own pleasure hadn't even crossed his mind.

But he wasn't going to think about the cell now. Now, he was already naked and in his dream, so was Gil, skipping the fuss of undressing to get to the best parts. Or no, not entirely naked. Gil would still have his spectacles on. Even in his own fantasy, Jarrett wouldn't deprive Gil of the ability to see just for a bit of fun. Besides, the man was absolutely stunning in them. Spectacles lent most men a bookish, refined air that could be enticing in its own way, but on Gil they had the opposite effect, somehow enhancing his roguish charms. Their delicacy emphasised his firm jaw, the bright gold making his dark hair look even darker, especially when wisps escaped his ribbon and he tucked them back behind his ear, pinning them under the gold stems. Instead of looking less like a dashing highwayman, the spectacles made him look *more*—more handsome, more charming, more *Jarrett's*.

At least in his dreams.

Jarrett stroked himself, starting slowly, then once he was fully hard, faster and faster. Water splashed out of the tub onto the floor. In the hayloft, he was straddling Gil, leaning over him and feeding that ever-grinning mouth his prick, inch by inch. Not grinning now, those lips too busy wrapped around Jarrett, sucking him deeper.

"You all right in there?"

Jarrett gasped. The sound of Gil's voice—the real Gil, not his fantasy version—enough to tip him over the edge. His back arched as he came, all the fears and frustrations of the last week leaving his body on a wave of aching pleasure. He slumped back against the tub, his entire body limp, and watched his spend dissolve into nothingness in the water.

"Jarrett?" Gil's voice filtered through the door again, this time accompanied by the rattling of the knob.

"I'm fine!"

He was better than fine now and he could hear it in his own voice. Gil must have heard it too, because the doorknob stopped rattling and the silence from the other side of the door stretched into awkwardness.

"Supper is ready. I'll see you in the kitchen."

The faint sound of boots disappearing down the corridor followed Gil's clipped announcement. Jarrett sighed and reached for the rag again.

The secret to enjoying Janie's cooking turned out to be a week in gaol.

Jarrett snatched up another burnt roll, tearing it in half and viciously stuffing one piece into his mouth while he ran the other around his bowl to get out the last traces of her tripe and kidney soup, a recipe of her own creation. The noises he was making were more obscene than the ones he'd made in the bath.

"Christ, this is good. Where's Janie? She needs to be thanked."

"I think she and Mrs. Finley have locked themselves in their quarters with a number of kitchen knives." Gil said, pushing his untouched bowl across the table to Jarrett.

Jarrett nodded in thanks. "Sensible women."

"You're not offended?"

Jarrett shrugged. "Knowing village gossip, they've had a week to hear increasingly lurid tales of my murderous deeds. Then you walk in with the monster neither tied nor fettered."

Gil's brows drew together. "But they know you. Surely, they wouldn't have believed that nonsense. Well, Janie would, aye. But Mrs. Finley should know better."

There was only one more roll in the basket. Jarrett took his time with this one, dipping it into Gil's bowl of soup and watching the steam rise. "Even if she does, it's one thing for you to believe me. If you're wrong, you still stand a good chance if I came at you. Not so for an old woman."

He winced. The last thing he needed was to convince the one person who believed in him of his guilt. Risking a quick glance up at Gil, he found the man watching him back.

"Well," said Gil, "you were right about Mrs. Finley thinking you were going to murder her in her bed. I did explain the situation to them in more detail while you were bathing, but I don't expect we'll see much of either of them until this is cleared up."

Jarrett tried not to show how much their reactions stung. At least Gil believed him.

"Why you?" Jarrett asked, grabbing the sleeping dog by the tail and shaking, rather than letting it lie.

Gil blinked at him. "Beg pardon?"

"Of all the people to believe me, why you?"

Gil's face flickered through a series of emotions too quickly for Jarrett to read.

"I..." Gil shook his head. "I think the more important question is, 'How do we get everyone else to believe you too?'"

Jarrett popped the last bit of roll into his mouth and sucked a few wayward drops of soup off his fingers. "In the carriage, didn't you say something about a woman at the inquest who said she saw me do it? I didn't, so finding out why she's lying might be a good start."

Gil pinched the bridge of his nose and groaned.

"All right," said Jarrett, offended. "Let's hear your brilliant ideas then."

"It's not that," Gil said. "It's actually an excellent idea. I just realised I missed supper with my family. My cousin's wife was at the inquest and will have told them all about it. I meant to be there to keep her from recounting some of the more *vivid* details, but now, Lord knows what she told them. Whatever it was, I'm sure I'll be blamed for being involved. Never mind that Uncle Andrew ordered me to assist the magistrate with the body. Or that Catriona wouldn't have even been at the inquest if my damned brother hadn't taken her. Or if Charles kept a better eye on his wife!"

Gil let out a heavy breath. "I'm sorry, I know none of that's your concern at the best of times, never mind now. It's just... family."

Jarrett wouldn't know. He only ever had his ma, and hadn't seen much of her since he was old enough to hold a grooming brush, despite them both working for the same household. Still, he could certainly understand how it felt to be blamed for something that wasn't your fault.

"How well do you know Mrs. Randall?" Gil said finally.

"Is that the woman who said she saw me?" Gil nodded and Jarrett sat back in his chair, plucking up a few lost crumbs with a fingertip. "She's the one in the village over who makes tonics and the like? I'd know her to see her, but we've never spoken."

Gil smiled. "I forget sometimes you haven't lived here your whole life. I doubt there's a person within twenty miles I could say that about. The anonymity must be freeing."

Jarrett didn't know what that word meant, but before he could ask, Gil went on. "I'm not sure getting Mrs. Randall to recant alone will be enough to change the magistrate's mind. She is something of a known eccentric, so her changing her word is to be expected."

"But her word in the first place is good enough to get me hanged?" Jarrett said bitterly.

"No." Gil's voice was fierce. Then to Jarrett's shock, he reached across the table and put one of his hands over Jarrett's. His palm was warm and his fingers curled gently around Jarrett's wrist.

"You're not going to be hanged, Jarrett. We'll figure this out, I promise."

Looking into Gil's solemn eyes, there was nothing Jarrett wanted more than to believe him. The moment seemed to stretch into hours, the two of them joined by just that blazing touch, then Gil pulled away. Jarrett felt cold all over.

"Mrs. Randall alone won't be enough," Gil said. "But I've sent out some letters, trying to determine the identity of the victim. I'm convinced that who he was is the key to discovering who killed him. Why would a stranger no one has ever seen before find his way to the chapel in the middle of the night just to be murdered? How would he even know how to get there unless someone he already knew told him? We solve who he is and who that other person was; we solve the rest of it."

Jarrett's response was cut off by a jaw cracking yawn that took him by surprise. Now that he thought about it, his eyelids were rather heavy.

"Another excellent suggestion." Gil sounded amused. "To bed?"

That idea was enough to wake Jarrett right up. He knew Gil didn't mean it the way it sounded, but God, he wished he did. His session in the bath had barely taken the edge off. Still, even if he couldn't have what he wanted, he'd soon be in his own bed, in his own room, and free to have another go round with fantasy Gil, even if the real one was down the hall, out of reach.

"I'm sure Mrs. Finley made up one of the guest rooms for you before she barricaded herself in," Jarrett said, now very much looking forward to the solitude. "She'll probably be happier if I'm not under the same roof tonight. I'll be in my shed if there's anything you need."

Gil openly laughed at him. "Like hell you will. I need to keep an eye on you and I'm not sleeping out in some draughty old shed. Don't be offended, I trust your word that you won't escape, but I doubt they do. Consider it the first step in rebuilding their confidence. They'll sleep better knowing you're watched and when they see me in the morning without my throat slit, they might return enough knives to the kitchen to actually cook a proper breakfast."

Oh God, what new torment was this? Sharing a room with Gil but not sharing a bed with him was just cruel. Hadn't he suffered enough?

Jarrett licked his lips. "My quarters don't have enough room for one of us to sleep on the floor."

"A draughty old attic isn't any better than a draughty old shed. I already settled this with Mrs. Finley."

Gil got up from the table, and strode towards the door. All Jarrett could do was blink at him.

"Come along," Gil said, and when he turned back to Jarrett his grin was blinding. "Bedtime."

Which was how Jarrett found himself in one of the guest rooms, running his hands over a coverlet that would've cost him a year's wages.

The rest of the room was just as lavish. Paintings hung in gilt frames on every wall and a fire burned low in a hearth large enough for Jarrett to walk into upright. Like everything else in Balcarres, the luxury showed signs of long neglect, the bed drapes faded with age and the books crumbling on the bookshelves. It was still beautiful. And not meant for the likes of him.

"Don't tell me His Lordship only sleeps on old sacking," Gil said. "You see finer goods than a dusty old bedspread every day."

He was sitting on the other bed in the room, struggling to get his boots off. Jarrett's fingers itched to help, but he could only imagine how that action would be taken. It was a marvel that Gil was willing to share a room with him at all after the way he'd behaved in the cell. Most men would be begging Mrs. Finley to let them in behind the barricade. Gil's continued easy confidence around a man he knew to be unnatural was admirable.

He was making it damned hard not to think about that kiss though.

Jarrett kept his eyes on the coverlet while he listened to the maddening sounds of Gil undressing and climbing into bed.

"I *see* them every day. I don't get to sleep on them."

Jarrett risked a glance upward. Gil was in bed, his top half covered by his shirt and his lower half covered by the bed linens. It took all his willpower not to look at the neat stack of clothes Gil had left on a chair. If he did, he might be able to tell if Gil was wearing anything besides the shirt. But seeing Gil's drawers stacked neatly on top of his trousers might kill Jarrett, or make him do something he'd regret.

Fortunately, he was distracted by Gil being utterly bizarre about his pillows. There were several stacked on his bed and Gil was going through them one at a time, reaching his hand inside the slips to feel around before setting each aside and reaching for the next one. One of the pillows was an embroidered decorative one without a cover, and Jarrett watched on in utter confusion as Gil twisted it beneath his hands. His movements were sharp, like the pillow was an animal whose neck he was failing to break.

Eventually he realised he was being observed and gave Jarrett a sheepish smile.

"Habit," he explained, although that didn't explain anything at all.

Jarrett was at something of a loss. He offered, "A man's bedroom habits are his own business. I'm sure I've done stranger."

Once again, he'd said the wrong thing and knew it. He shouldn't be reminding a man who was now sharing a room with of his strange bedroom habits. Especially not one he'd fondled against his will. Christ, why couldn't he stop himself from saying such things? He wasn't even trying to flirt with Gil. It might be better if he was, at least that way some of things out of his mouth might not be utterly embarrassing.

Gil's smile fixed itself for a moment, but he once again gracefully ignored Jarrett's lack of subtlety.

"The servants at Charleton house tuck lavender into the linens to keep them smelling fresh," Gil explained. "The thought is a good one, but I'm afraid they're rather overzealous in their application. I got in the habit to avoid sleeping with a face full of twigs. Watch, I'll be turning my pockets inside out and my boots over in the morning too."

Jarrett chuckled and the tension of the moment eased. He turned away to get undressed and got himself ready for bed as quickly as he could, keeping both shirt and drawers on so he wouldn't get any ill-fated late-night ideas. Since it seemed he was also going to be denied the pleasure of his own hand as well, it was better to have a barrier to temptation.

As if anything could be more tempting than the man in the bed opposite. Gil had pulled the ribbon from his hair. A lock of it slipped over his lips as he leaned forward to set his spectacles on the night table. Jarrett found himself in the ridiculous position of being jealous of hair, even more so when Gil absently tucked the lock behind his ear and ran his fingers through the strands, fingers catching on a tangle before tugging it loose.

Jarrett bit his lip to keep from groaning aloud. He slipped into bed to hide the evidence of the way Gil's actions affected him. He would never be able to sleep with this torment. Then Gil reached towards the lamp.

"Leave it on." Jarrett's voice sounded closer to pleading than he intended. "Please."

Gil blinked towards him, but not quite *at* him and Jarrett wondered how bad his eyesight really was.

"Strange bedroom habits?" Gil asked, his voice teasing.

Jarrett nodded. Then realising Gil might not be able to see that, said, "One of my strangest."

Gil huffed out a laugh and lay down in bed, leaving the lamp burning. He didn't complain about the waste or ask any more questions, simply did it because Jarrett asked him to. It gave Jarrett a strange feeling in his gut, almost queasy but in a way that was strangely pleasurable. He'd never felt anything quite like it.

Or perhaps it was Janie's tripe and kidney soup.

Gil rolled over, turning his back on both Jarrett and the lamp's light with a muttered, "Goodnight, Jarrett."

"Goodnight."

Jarrett settled down, watching the flickers of lamplight making the shadows dance where the black of Gil's hair met the white of the pillows. He wanted to enjoy the luxury of both the bed itself and sharing a room with a beautiful man for as long as he could, but between one breath and the next, he was asleep.

CHAPTER 11

Gil slipped from the room just after dawn. He'd awoken, looked across the gap between the beds to see Jarrett sleeping peacefully, and realised he needed to leave before he did something rash.

The lamp had long since gone out, its reservoir dry, but enough light peeked around the curtains for him to see Jarrett asleep on his side, facing Gil's bed. Jarrett's sharp features were softened in the dim light. The cut of his cheekbones that had more than once made Gil's breath catch in his throat was no less beautiful for being half buried in pillows, but was even more inviting to touch. His lush lips were slightly parted, and long eyelashes swept down over his cheeks, hiding the dark circles that would take more than a single night of freedom to erase. In short, Jarrett safe, comfortable, and asleep was nothing less than stunning, even if his hair looked like a rat had made a nest in it while he slept.

No, curse it, the dishevelment actually made his allure far worse. As did the way one of his hands was curled beside his face, palm up. As Gil watched in hopeless fascination, his fingers twitched, the way a dog's leg would when it dreamed of hunting rabbits. It was a silly, ridiculous little motion, and Gil found himself utterly enamoured.

Which was why he was now sneaking from the room with his boots in his hands like an illicit lover escaping a cuckold.

Although that was perhaps not the analogy he should be thinking of as he tried to will his errant body under control.

He weighed wearing day-old clothes against the uproar that would follow the Balcarres household discovering he'd left a blood-thirsty murderer in their midst to run home and change. Never mind the fact they'd known Jarrett as long as he had. Besides, if Jarrett did decide to come after them all with a knife, there wouldn't be much Gil could do about it. He'd had a total of three fencing classes as a boy before giving up in inelegant disgrace and his one hunting outing had been even worse. He might be able to bore Jarrett to death by discussing the latest changes in import duties or how to build the most cost-effective stile depending on the type of fencing material available and breed of livestock to be kept in or out, but as a prison guard he was woefully inept. The best he could do was hope Jarrett honoured his word as a gentleman's gentleman, and that they found the real killer before anyone else realised how poorly guarded he was and sought some justice of their own.

That worrying thought carried him through a breakfast of eggs boiled to the point they could be effectively used as grapeshot, slightly-warm bread that only the most generous would call "toast", and passable ham, all supervised by a glowering Mr. Howe. When Jarrett came down to join him, reinforcements followed in the form of Graham, the stablemaster.

Fortunately, Jarrett seemed as uninclined towards their presence as they were to his, so after stuffing some eggs and bread into a handkerchief, he and Gil were on their way.

"How much further?" Jarrett asked, brushing crumbs from his fingers.

Gil looked down the road ahead of them. It was a beautiful day for walking, the bright sun warming the stone walls along the road, and the clear skies letting them see all the way to the cliffs and the glittering sea beyond.

"Only another mile or so. Mrs. Randall lives just the other side of Drumeldrie."

"Far enough to ride," Jarrett muttered.

Gil couldn't help but smile. "Yes, but by the time we convinced Graham to let you anywhere near the horses and got them saddled, we wouldn't have saved any time. Besides, I doubt it would endear her any if one of the beasts started eating her vegetable garden."

"I suppose not. Is that what we're trying to do? Endear her?"

Gil took a moment to think about that as Jarrett unpeeled an egg and began to gnaw on it. "I suppose we're here to get a better understanding of what she actually saw the night of the murder. I'll take her word that *someone* knocked her over, even if it's just to keep her from showing off that bruise again, but it certainly wasn't you and I'd like to know why she thought it was."

"I'd like to know that myself," Jarrett muttered. He gave up on the egg and tossed it over the wall. Hopefully, it wouldn't break a plough blade come planting. "She's not going to run screaming when she sees me?"

"She might. However, I couldn't exactly leave you back at Balcarres if I'm meant to be guarding you."

Jarrett hummed. "She might take it as a threat to keep her mouth shut, me showing up at her door. That said, I don't mind, if it keeps her from testifying against me."

Gil hadn't thought about that. Now that he had, he couldn't be entirely certain he was unopposed to that outcome.

"Wouldn't you rather she tell the full truth?" he asked, as much to himself as to Jarrett.

"I rather her not say anything that will get me hanged."

There wasn't anything Gil could say to that. Fortunately, they were just rounding the curve into Drumeldrie, and soon they were making their way up to a small cottage on the other side of the village. The cottage was tiny but in good condition, although the thatch on the roof had patches that looked thin. He added it to his list of repairs for the earl to approve upon his return.

A small figure stood in front of the cottage, tending to the garden. It was too early for any vegetables to actually be growing, so perhaps they could've brought horses, but there were a number of small bushes with berries he didn't recognise, and dried stalks bearing strange husks, so perhaps it was just as well they hadn't, for the animals' sakes.

He raised a hand in greeting.

"Good morning, Mrs. Randall."

Mrs. Randall squinted in their direction. "Is that young Charleton? And who's that with ye?"

Jarrett had fallen back a few steps and didn't seem inclined to answer for himself.

"Aye, it's me. This is Jarrett, ma'am," Gil said, smiling a little wider so she could see it. "From up at Balcarres House? We were wondering if we could ask you a few questions."

"The boy that did the murder?" She snorted. "I thought you were taller. Seemed that way, when you were bowling me over like skittles! Though I suppose even a sprig like you can run down an old woman when you've got the Devil in you. I still haven't got my apology."

"Apology?" asked Jarrett.

"For knocking me down! Whatever your business was with him you done in is none of mine, but you can't just be running folk down and showing up on their doorstep without a 'sorry'. I've still got the bruise—" she reached for her skirt.

"That's what we've come to talk to you about!" Gil interrupted before her hem rose any further. "It wasn't Jarrett that ran you down."

"Was it not?" she squinted at Jarrett again. "Well, I says it was. But I can't be making a Hand of Glory from you 'til they cut you down, so I suppose there's no harm in talking in the meantime."

It'd been nearly a century since the Witchcraft Act had been repealed, but she still shouldn't be talking about occult items like Hands of Glory quite so openly. It was rude, if nothing else. Worrying about being hanged must be terrible enough, Jarrett didn't need to add "then being chopped up for arcane trinkets" to his list of concerns. Not that one made from his hand would even work, since he wasn't actually a murderer, but that could hardly be much consolation.

"I want to know what you saw that night. As you know, I wasn't at the inquest," Jarrett said bitterly.

Mrs. Randall wiped her hands on her skirt, but mercifully let it fall.

"You've no one to blame but yourself." She sniffed, then launched into a retelling of her story from the inquest.

Unfortunately, it hadn't miraculously changed overnight.

"... so that left me limping all the way home. I got off better than that poor soul you done in the chapel, but I still haven't had an apology from you."

To his credit, Jarrett looked far less outraged than Gil would at being called a murderer to his face, but he'd had a week to get used to it. Instead, he was raptly focused on every word.

"Which way did he run?" Jarrett asked, in lieu of her expected apology.

For the first time since they'd arrived, Mrs. Randall looked perplexed.

"Who?"

"The man you think was me. Did you see which way he ran after he knocked you over?"

"Down the path, of course. He—*you* didn't stick around to help me back up."

Gil watched Jarrett's mouth form around the words, *Down the path*. He had no idea why he was so insistent on this point of all others, but it wasn't his life on the line, so if Jarrett thought it was important, Gil wasn't going to interrupt.

Jarrett continued his questioning. "Were you in front of the chapel or behind it when he ran into you?"

"In front. Too many trees 'round the back. The tansy doesn't grow."

Jarrett nodded quickly. "So, you were in front of the chapel, doing your harvesting, then a man came out the front, knocked you over, and took off down the path. The one from the *front* of the chapel back down to the main road. You'd swear to it?"

"Aye, that's what I said."

"And that's exactly what you're going to say in court?"

Mrs. Randall narrowed her eyes. "If I didn't know better, I'd think you might be suggesting it would be worth my time to say something else."

"Of course not!" Gil spluttered, just as Jarrett said, "How much?"

"Jarrett!"

Jarrett rounded on him. "What? I didn't do it. Easiest way out is if she says as much."

"We are not bribing a witness," Gil hissed. He couldn't believe he even had to say this. "It is both dishonourable and illegal."

"Fuck illegal," Jarrett spat. "And fuck dishonourable. You think my honour is worth more than my life?"

It wasn't. Nothing was. But Gil didn't know how to say that and also explain that it still didn't make it right.

Jarrett took his silence for either defeat or agreement, because he turned back to Mrs. Randall. The old woman was leaning on her garden wall now, watching the exchange as if it was the most excitement that had come to her doorstep in years.

"Sorry, ma'am," Jarrett said, his chest rising and falling with emotion. "That's an apology for the swearing I just did, not for knocking you over, which I didn't do."

"Aye, so you've said," she looked over at Gil. "You're not the first ones to offer to pay me for my story. A man came here, day before the inquest. Asked what I saw, then asked more questions, on who it was that ran me down. He said it was Jarrett here that done it. If he said so, I said. He offered me a good sum to say I was sure it was. So I told him what I'm telling you now: I didn't get a good look at the man, and no amount of blunt will change that.

"He says it was you, fine. I want my apology. You say it wasn't, so be it. I see why you won't apologise. But *I* say I don't know for certain. I only saw what I saw, and I'll say that in front of him, you, the court, and God with a clear conscience. You understand?"

"Yes, ma'am," said Gil meekly. Jarrett looked like he was fighting the urge to bow.

She nodded and picked up a rake that had been leaning against the wall. "Now that's settled. Away with you both. You're keeping me from my gardening."

Gil glanced over at Jarrett. It seemed their interview was over. They mumbled their farewells and turned back the way they came.

"A moment."

Gil turned and Mrs. Randall beckoned him back with a crooked finger, looking more like a witch than ever before.

"You were a good bairn, Gilleasbuig Charleton," she said as he reached the wall. "Didn't give your mother hardly any trouble coming out. You've turned into a good man too and sometimes good men don't know how to handle trouble when they first come across it."

She pointed her bony finger at Jarrett. "That one is trouble. You watch out for him."

Gil didn't need her warning, but he appreciated it anyway. He knew Jarrett was trouble and if Gil didn't watch out, he'd find himself in trouble too. He was already halfway there, having broken him out of the tolbooth. If they were lucky, they could find their way out together, but if not...

"Thank you, Mrs. Randall. I'll keep an eye on him." He walked back towards Jarrett, who was watching them both, his face unreadable. Gil couldn't tell how much of their conversation he'd heard, if any at all. However, he couldn't have missed Mrs. Randall quite literally pointing the finger at him.

The thought made Gil turn around. "Mrs. Randall? Who was it that tried to bribe you into putting the blame on Jarrett?"

She snorted. "Who else? It was that piss-proud arse, Magistrate Carnbee."

CHAPTER 12

The road to Balcarres from Mrs. Randall's cottage felt longer on the way back. As they walked through Drumeldrie in silence, a few faces popped out of doorways as they passed and one farmer nearly ran his cart off the road openly gawking. Jarrett ignored them all and Gil decided it would be best to do the same. It wasn't until they were on the other side of the village with nothing but empty road in either direction that he broke the silence.

"So. Carnbee."

"Carnbee," Jarrett agreed.

That seemed to be all he had to say on the matter, so Gil tried again. He'd been accused more than once of being able to carry both sides of the conversation without help, but sometimes he had no other option.

"So. Carnbee. I suppose the question we need to ask ourselves is whether this makes him a suspect or not. Frankly, while I might be willing to believe he'd kill under the right circumstances, I find it harder to believe he'd rouse himself in the middle of the night to troop out to the chapel to do it. That said, I would've also found it hard to believe he'd go down to Drumeldrie himself to badger a witness. Seems more the thing to strong arm a constable into doing."

At Jarrett's continued silence, Gil went on. "You're right, of course, it is a delicate operation. If he is the killer, the fewer people involved, the better. But if he isn't the killer, why be so insistent that she say she saw you specifically? You didn't spill wine on him back when you were a footman did you?"

That at least got him a shake of the head. There might even be the ghost of a smile on his lips if Gil looked closely, which he was trying to keep himself from doing.

"Very well. If it wasn't the wine, could it have been another infraction? Step on his foot with your boot heel? Cause his horse to bolt? Run over his dog? Bed his wife?"

The smile, that had been growing more present with each suggestion, vanished at the final one.

Blast. Of course Jarrett had no designs on Madam Carnbee. Gil had seen—and felt—the proof of that himself. He knew there were some men who enjoyed both men and women, but while they might kiss a man in hopes he would get them out of gaol, they wouldn't ride fifteen miles each way just for the chance to swive. There were plenty of other pubs between Balcarres House and The Cross Keys where Jarrett could've found feminine companionship if all he'd wanted was to get his end away. No reason to take the journey or the risk of seeking out men unless he felt as little attraction to women as Gil did himself.

Hell, it would probably be safer to bed Madam Carnbee. Easier too, if the woman's low necklines and blatant flirtations were anything to go by. Gil had never been interested in finding out, despite the many, many opportunities she'd offered him over the years.

"He might have done it on behalf of someone else," Jarrett offered quietly. "He's a toad-eating bootlick. Carnbee might not move his arse to protect himself, but he'd do it if he thought it'd curry favour for someone with power."

Jarrett spat out the last few words, making Gil hesitate to offer the first name that came to mind. The Earl of Crawford was the most powerful man in the county. But he was also Jarrett's employer, as well as Gil's friend. Surely he couldn't mean him?

"Lord Crawford?"

That startled a laugh out of Jarrett. "Good God, no. Can you imagine? I doubt the earl has ever even had to swat his own flies, never mind commit his own killings. Now, Dominick on the other hand..."

Gil had once witnessed the earl's companion lift the injured earl into his arms and carry him without breaking a sweat. He probably wouldn't even need a rock to bash a man's head in, he could just do it with his fists.

"For the right reasons, he could," Gil hazarded. "But they'd already left for London, hadn't they?"

Jarrett nodded. "The day before."

"Could it have been a trick? For everyone to think they were gone so they wouldn't be suspected?" Gil couldn't believe he was even suggesting such a thing, but if they were going to save Jarrett's life, they had to examine every possibility, even the ones that made him feel like a Judas even considering them.

"No," Jarrett shook his head. "Graham drove them down to Edinburgh himself. And before you say anything, he took Davey with him. He wouldn't have brought his son if it was all just a ruse."

That was a relief. Although now that he thought about it, perhaps they were missing an entirely different solution to their problem.

"Do you think he could help?" said Gil. "The earl, I mean. If Carnbee is willing to have you declared guilty on a powerful man's say-so, might he have you declared innocent for an even more powerful man? I could at least write to him and ask."

Jarrett didn't answer immediately. Instead he kicked a pebble down the lane, then once they'd caught up with it, kicked it again for good measure. He got in another two kicks before the pebble bounced off the road to join its brethren gathered at the foot of the stone wall.

"Don't write," Jarrett said finally. "It's less than a month, you said, until the circuit judge arrives? Assuming the earl reacts well to finding out his valet is accused of murder, by the time the letter finds him in London, even if he acts immediately, everything will be over before he even sends word back. If we clear my name by then, we'll have bothered him for nothing. And if we don't... Well, if we don't, there will be damned all he can do about it."

Despite the hopelessness of his words, Jarrett's tone was light. As if he was only discussing whether or not to send an invitation for a picnic. He'd been that way ever since they left the gaol, Gil realised. As if none of this really mattered, but he was willing to tag along for the adventure. Even now, he was plucking an acorn out of the road and twisting off its cap to make a whistle, the way small boys did. The high shriek it made was enough to raise the hairs on the back of his neck, reminding him of tales of the *caoineag*, the spirit of a woman who wailed for those who were soon to die.

He didn't want Jarrett to die.

Eventually, Jarrett let the acorn cap tumble from his fingers.

"Can do better without it," Jarrett said breezily, then demonstrated, putting two fingers in his mouth and letting out a whistle so loud, a distant flock of sheep took off in bleating alarm.

"Forgive my saying so," Gil hazarded, "but you seem to be taking this all rather well."

Jarrett gave a choked laugh at that. A laugh that led to another and another until he was hysterical with it and Gil couldn't be sure if he was still laughing or crying. He was like a man possessed and suddenly the road seemed far longer and emptier. It was terrifying to witness, yet when Jarrett bent over double, Gil still found himself reaching for him so he wouldn't lose his balance. His hand was caught in a fierce grip, as strong as it had been that day in the cells.

"I. Am. Not. Handling. Anything." Jarrett gasped out between laughs that had now become closer to whimpers. Impossibly, his grip tightened even further. "It's all so fucking impossible I can't even think about it properly and when I do, I fall to pieces."

Jarrett motioned with his free hand at his current position, but remained where he was. Gil desperately wished he could see his face.

He spoke as softly as he could. "I'm sorry. Lord, I know that's not enough, but for what it's worth, Jarrett, I'm sorry."

But not sorry enough that you won't serve him right back up to Carnbee at the end of the month. Not sorry enough that you'd let him escape and go to prison in his stead. If you were, you'd have done it already.

Gil shook his head angrily. No. No one was going to prison or worse. They'd find the real killer and everything would be fine. He said as much to Jarrett. He said it again now, hoping it would make the words true.

"It'll all work out."

"You really believe that, don't you?"

Gil didn't let himself hesitate. "I do."

Jarrett sniffed and pulled a handkerchief from his coat, wiping his face before he straightened. His eyes were red, but for a man who'd been halfway to bedlam a minute before, he was remarkably composed. He was, however, still holding Gil's hand.

"You got me out of the dark, Gil Charleton," said Jarrett with a watery smile. "If any man can get me out of the noose too, it's you."

The force of Jarrett's trust knocked the wind from Gil's lungs. What could he even say to something like that? More importantly, how did he make sure Jarrett's belief in him wasn't misplaced?

"It'll all work out," he said again. "We'll make sure of it."

"And we can't do that if we're standing in a lane falling to pieces." Jarrett chuckled, but it sounded genuine this time, not the madness-tinged sound from before. He shook out his shoulders and seemed somehow taller, as if a weight that had been crushing him had been lifted. Gil found himself feeling lighter too.

It *would* work out. Jarrett was innocent, they just had to prove it. Put that way, it was just another problem to solve, and a far more straightforward one than many he'd had to deal with as an estate manager. The stakes were high, but the problem was simple. Still, Jarrett was right, they weren't going to solve it standing in the middle of the road.

He began walking, fully expecting Jarrett to drop his hand as soon as he felt the tug, but Jarrett only gave a few jogging steps to catch up, then fell into pace still holding his hand.

Gil glanced at him out of the corner of his eye. Jarrett had his lips pressed tightly together, but when he caught Gil's look, his eyes glinted with mischief. It seemed Jarrett was back to his usual bright, bold self. Very well, two could play at that game.

"Mrs. Randall was a most pleasant woman, I thought." Gil swung their hands back and forth as they walked.

Jarrett's hand was warm despite the chill of the day, and rough in a way that Gil recognised from his own. Jarrett hadn't always known a life of relative ease as a gentleman's gentleman for an eccentric earl. These hands had known work. His grip was strong, but not as crushing as it had been. In fact it felt just right. He'd been startled at their strength the first time Jarrett had grabbed him. The man looked as if a stiff breeze would be enough to carry him off, but there must be some hidden muscle. Pity Gil had fled The Cross Keys so quickly, if he'd stayed longer he might have been able to see. Or touch.

"That is—" Gil tried to remember what he'd been in the middle of saying, "—pleasant in her own way."

"Aye, for a witch."

"Jarrett!" Gil admonished, but since he was grinning, he doubted Jarrett took it to heart.

"You were thinking it too! And of course you thought she was pleasant. I heard her. I'm trouble but you're a good bairn."

Gil groaned. "Please don't remind me."

"She was helpful though," admitted Jarrett. "At least she said I wasn't the one who ran into her."

Gil furrowed his brow. He would've remembered that. "She didn't?"

"Sure, she did. She said the one that scuttled her headed off down the main path. She swore it. Couldn't have been me then. Shortest path to Balcarres is a wee track from the back. I doubt many more than myself use it, but it's there. Get that circuit judge to walk it and he'll see it saves at least five minutes from the main path.

"I've walked it enough at night going up to the chapel to stargaze, I could probably do it blindfolded. I bet a jury would see a show like that and let me go on the spot. Murderer or no, no man who knows a path blindfolded is going to go the other way, knocking over witches left and right as he does."

"She's not a witch," Gil said absently. What Jarrett was saying made sense, but he doubted it would be enough. Still, he didn't want to lose this light, hopeful Jarrett by giving dire predictions. He gave his hand a soft squeeze.

"That's good. That's really good, Jarrett. But I think we should still keep looking for more evidence."

"Are you mad? Of course we should! My God, Carnbee barely knows his right from his left, imagine if this circuit judge doesn't know his front from his back."

Jarrett winked. "It's a start though."

"It is at that."

They walked a little further, still hand in hand, neither acknowledging it. Jarrett had to be the boldest man Gil had ever met. As far as Jarrett knew, Gil was completely free from unnatural desires, yet Jarrett had kissed him, fondled him, and now, after putting that behind them, was walking down a county lane, holding Gil's hand like a courting lover and *winking* at him. Bold didn't even begin to cover it.

Reckless, he reminded himself. *Reckless and dangerous. Never forget that.*

He hadn't. He wouldn't. So why was Gil holding his hand right back?

Jarrett let out a long groan, fully distracting Gil from his thoughts.

Reckless.

"I'm parched and my feet are about to fall off my ankles. Why do you insist on walking when there's a stable full of lovely horses right there at Balcarres? We could already be back choking down whatever hell Janie's cooked up for luncheon."

"It's only a few miles!" Gil protested. "Surely you can walk that far."

"I can. I can ride it too. Leave the walking to a creature with iron shoes. Why do you walk everywhere anyway? I'd think, being a *grieve* and having to go all over to care for the earl's property, you'd want to spare your feet as much as you can."

"I don't mind riding," Gil replied. "But when you're out walking, it's just you. You're not responsible for anyone or anything else. You're not having to watch for mole holes or darting rabbits. Or that is, you can watch for those things, but you get to enjoy them. I could roam for hours, never having to think about my steps even, just enjoying the wee beauties I'd miss if I was speeding by them. If I walk far enough, I'm not even myself anymore, just a part of all this."

He swept his free hand around, trying to encompass everything he couldn't put into words in a single motion. The distant sea, the sun-warmed stone, even the pebbles in the path and the acorn tops that made fine whistles. It was his home and he loved every inch of it.

Jarrett was watching him with wide eyes and the back of Gil's neck began to burn with embarrassment. "Aye, well. I'm not a poet. I just like walking is all."

"I know what you mean," Jarrett whispered. "It's like that when I ride. Especially if it's on the right horse. Thistle is my horse. Well, she's His Lordship's, but she's the one I feel that way with most. When I take her out, when I really get to go, it's me doing it, not Thistle. Or it's both of us, one and the same. Up and down, forward and back, same rhythm, same steps. She moves, I move. She flies, I *fly*."

They'd stopped while Jarrett was talking. Just as well, because for all Gil's words about not having to think about his steps, he'd trip all over himself if he tried to move now, too caught up in the look on Jarrett's face to remember how to walk. Jarrett was staring at something in the far distance, that horizon he was riding towards in his mind. His lips were parted, breathing deep and measured, matching the pace of a far larger animal. Gil could envision it, could see Jarrett flying.

Reckless. He reminded himself. *Reckless. Dangerous. Bold. Passionate. Bright. Funny. Brave. Strong. Beautiful.*

He shouldn't be thinking that, but it was true. Jarrett had always been gorgeous to behold, all sharp lines and inviting curves, but seeing him transported like this just by talking about something he loved? He was so radiant it hurt to look at him.

Gil swayed in, reaching for his spectacles to pull them out of the way, but instead of his own fingers, the back of a warm, rough hand not his own brushed his cheek.

The touch was enough to shock him to his senses. How could he have possibly forgotten he was holding Jarrett's hand?

He dropped it as if it was a burning coal. His own hand certainly felt like it was on fire. His cheek too, just from that slight touch. Good Lord, what had he been thinking? He'd been about to kiss Jarrett. Kiss him in the middle of the road like he had any right.

And it was the furthest thing from right he could possibly do. Never mind that Jarrett was depending on him. Or that he was acting as Jarrett's gaoler. Or that he'd seen Jarrett cutting a swath through The Cross Keys but Jarrett didn't even know he liked men. Or that Jarrett was reckless and bold and all sorts of other wonderful things that Gil wasn't.

It was that despite everything, Jarrett was freer than Gil ever would be.

Jarrett wasn't a gentleman; despite their agreement, his word was not his bond. If he ran, he could go anywhere and Gil would be duty bound to take his punishment or risk besmirching both his own name and his entire family's. Even if everything went right and they cleared his name, Jarrett wouldn't stay in a place where so many people had been so cruel to him. He wouldn't stay, and Gil wouldn't leave. Servants could leave anytime things went wrong, but even though Gil was only the second son of a second son, caring for lands that he would never own, this was his home. He cared for the land, the people, all of it.

He cared for Jarrett. And that was too reckless and dangerous to bear.

"D-do you mind if we make a short detour?" he stammered. And just like that, things were back to the way they always were, with Gil unable to string a proper sentence together around Jarrett.

Jarrett, who was wearing a look of utter confusion.

Please don't have noticed. Gil prayed. *Please don't have noticed that I nearly kissed you. Again.*

After an eon, Jarrett asked, "Detour?"

"Yes, um, I'd like to go by Charleton House. Pick up some fresh clothes, perhaps pack some necessities as it looks like I'll be with yo—I'll be staying at Balcarres House for the foreseeable future. Might be prudent."

The wait for Jarrett to respond was unbearable, but he finally did, breaking into a low, slow smile that made the fluttering in Gil's gut that much worse.

"You just want to walk more, don't you?"

Gil laughed nervously. "Yes, that's it. This way, I know a shortcut."

Gil splashed more water on his face and glared at his dripping reflection in the mirror.

"Pull yourself together, Charlêton," he told himself firmly.

He'd left Jarrett tucked away in one of the many salons downstairs. Neither of them had really wanted to bring Jarrett inside at all, but he couldn't be left standing in the lane unguarded, lest word hadn't quite spread yet that he was out of his cell and under Gil's watch. And Gil certainly hadn't wanted to bring Jarrett up to his bedroom either. Or rather, he very much wanted that, which was the whole problem. So they'd settled on the salon, with orders for Jarrett to stay quiet while Gil collected his things as quickly as possible.

He'd been fortunate enough to make it to his room without any of the staff seeing him. He'd nearly collapsed when they'd snuck in through the kitchen and he'd thought the entire array of servants had lined up to confront them, but it was just the line of overcoats hung by the door.

He'd felt more than heard Jarrett's soft chuckles against his shoulder, and tried very hard not to think about that as he'd thrown several days' worth of fresh clothes and necessary toiletries into a valise. After catching a glimpse of himself in the mirror, he'd stopped only long enough to brush his hair back into a proper tail, and splash some water on his face. And to admonish himself for being so foolhardy.

All that accomplished, he looked about the room, making sure there was nothing he'd forgotten.

His eyes landed on the desk. There was an unopened letter on top, and his heart began to thud. Could it be a response to one of the many letters he'd sent out about the victim? Or simply a business matter? Either way, he couldn't leave it here. He gathered it up, along with several other papers and ledgers. Best if he took as much of his work as he could. He'd need something to do when they weren't out hunting murderers and some boring, normal property business might help keep him grounded when the world was constantly shifting under his feet.

If he was going to do that though, he'd need to bring some more sealing wax as well. The earl wouldn't mind him using his, but it was never good to make free with one's employer's supplies, especially something as dear as sealing wax. He opened his desk and scowled. All of his was gone. Robert no doubt.

He drummed his fingers against the desk. It was a risk, but his father's study was on the way back to where he'd left Jarrett anyway; it would be worth a stop to collect more.

He'd just retrieved several sticks of wax from his father's desk and was wondering how housebreakers were always getting caught doing something so easy when he heard the shouting. Well, less "shouting" and more "bellowing".

Grimacing, he swiped his papers from where he'd placed them on the desk and shoved them and the wax into his valise. He wished he could pack them more neatly, but he'd wasted too much time already. He'd recognise that bellow anywhere. His brother.

And Gil had a pretty good idea what he was bellowing about.

CHAPTER 13

Gil poked his roast beef with his fork and wondered if he was in Hell.

It wasn't the beef's fault. Unlike Janie, the cook at Charleton house was exemplary. The roast was tender and the accompanying mushroom sauce wonderfully flavourful. It paired perfectly with the wine he'd been served and was preceded by an excellent smoked haddock soup. The meal would soon be capped by ratafia cakes, his favourite. If only the company was equally as pleasant.

Robert's discovery of Jarrett in the salon had gone exactly as poorly as Gil had feared. A shouting match between the two brothers had ensued, with poor Jarrett doing his best to sink into the settee and disappear. The commotion had alerted the rest of the household, and while his father hadn't actually ordered Jarrett to be dragged out and shot, it was enough of an unspoken possibility that his speedy retreat to Balcarres seemed prudent. Unfortunately, Gil's exit with him came with his uncle's order to, "Secure that wretch and then return to discuss your behaviour with the family."

Which was where Gil found himself now, in Hell.

The only thing making the meal bearable was the continued excellence of the Charleton House staff, as he had barely set his empty wine glass on the table before a footman was there to refill it, and not for the first time. He shouldn't be drinking so much, after all, there was still port to come, but his father had been lecturing on the esteem of the Charleton name since the first course and Gil wasn't facing that sober. He was hardly the only one. Robert had matched every glass of Gil's with two of his own so far and showed no sign of slowing.

He spent a moment envying Jarrett and whatever horrific concoction of Janie's he was eating at the moment. He'd been quiet on their walk back to Balcarres House aside from an offer to carry Gil's valise for him, as he was a valet. He'd remained subdued during the furious discussion amongst the staff of where he should be imprisoned during Gil's absence. Ultimately, Gil had rejected Mrs. Finley's suggestion of "down the well", Mr. Howe's "in irons", as well as Jarrett's own request to be housed in the wine cellar with a screw, a wheel of cheese, two lamps, and a deck of cards. As a compromise, Jarrett was locked into their shared room with a single bottle of wine, supper, plenty of lamp oil, and a deck of cards. A rotating guard of Mr. Howe and Graham was set to bring him his supper and ensure he stayed put until Gil's return.

As far as gaols went, it was certainly a step up from the tolbooth.

"...which is only the beginning of the ways your association with a common criminal—no, worse than that, a foul *murderer*—has brought this family shame."

"He's not," said Gil tiredly. He'd made the same protest twice so far and his father hadn't even slowed his diatribe. Gil had come by his reputation as a talker honestly, but he wasn't entirely sure his father had even stopped to take a breath.

"He's a thief as well," Robert muttered. "Should have searched him before we let him leave. Tell them, Catriona."

Catriona hesitated. "I couldn't find my new shawl when we returned this evening."

Oh Lord, every hen that refused to lay was now going to be blamed on Jarrett.

"I'm sure you just misplaced it, dear." Charles said, taking his wife's hand and gently kissing her knuckles. At least Gil had one ally.

Then Charles added. "After all, why would he steal your shawl when he could so easily have been pocketing your jewels? Have those been checked?"

Gil's mother seized the opportunity to join the fray. "And you let this murdering jewel thief into our home! Thank heavens Madam Carnbee invited Catriona over for tea. If I hadn't joined them—No, I dare not think it!"

From Catriona's thin-lipped smile, Gil doubted either she or the surprisingly young Madam Carnbee had actually wanted his mother to join them, but that was hardly his greatest concern at the moment. Neither was the fact that Jarrett was the safest intruder a woman could hope to have. Some impish impulse pleaded with him to set that cat amongst the pigeons and to share exactly how he knew, but the momentary satisfaction would hardly be worth it.

Instead he tried another tack. His uncle had been uncharacteristically quiet during the haranguing, especially since as Lord Charleton, it was both his name and title that Gil was dragging through the mud with his low associations.

"Uncle Andrew, I assume this discussion means you haven't informed the rest of the family of your instructions regarding this matter?"

His uncle frowned, but both his parents were blessedly silent as they awaited his answer, which was more than Gil could have hoped.

"My instructions?"

"Yes, when I came to you with my concerns regarding the haste with which Jar-Mr. Welch was branded the guilty party and my concern that the real killer might still be out there. If I recall correctly, your exact words were something to the effect of, 'I'm too busy for such trivial concerns. If it's that important, you have my full blessing to do as you wish.' You then gave me your full authority and bid me pass that along to the magistrate. While I admit to perhaps not handling that last part in the best manner, I've followed the rest to the letter."

Beside him, his cousin laughed. "My God, I'd thought you'd gone mad. You're saying you actually think this fellow is innocent? I'm not sure which is worse. Well, at least you got Father's blessing to free a killer. Pardon me, a killer *possibilis*."

"He is innocent," Gil muttered.

Charles patted his hand. Gil snatched it back. His cousin likely meant well, but that didn't make the gesture any less patronising.

The baron ignored his son's interruption. "I believe I also instructed you to conduct yourself in a proper manner. Is that what you would call parading this man across the county and humiliating Magistrate Carnbee, who is, I remind you, not only a servant of the law but also a family friend?"

"Oh Father, be fair," Charles interrupted before Gil could answer. "I think Gilleasbuig's solution is an admirable one. Don't you see? He feared the real murderer was still loose, now he has ensured that Carnbee is in agreement. Surely, this will only bring our families closer."

"You're not helping," Gil hissed.

"Am I not?" Charles' eyes twinkled. "Perhaps I should peruse the selection of criminals still available and see if any are interested in touring Charleton House. That seems to be your preferred solution. Oh Father, please say I can. Please? Gil has a murderer! I want one too!"

Charles had his hands clasped and a look of such desperate woe on his face that were he on stage, even those in the cheapest seats would think he was laying it on a bit thick, but to Gil's everlasting surprise, his uncle chuckled.

Charles winked at him and mouthed the words, "Not helping?"

"Gilleasbuig," said the baron, "I cannot say I'm pleased with the manner in which you've handled this matter, nor with how you've twisted my own words to suit your ends."

He raised a hand to cut off Gil's protest. "I will not have you playing the barrister at my own dining table. However, I will accept some of the blame is mine for not being clearer in my speech. Still, I think I speak for the entire family when I say that I am deeply disappointed in you."

Gil didn't have to look around the table to see the nods. He did anyway.

Disappointed. How could they not be disappointed with him? He was a second son's second son. The spare's spare. He had no purpose other than as an ornament to the barony or perhaps trapping some poor girl of even higher birth into an advantageous marriage for his family. And now, the first time he'd tried to find a different purpose, tried to use his station to do a bit of good, he was a disappointment. Bad enough he worked to fill his pockets rather than leech off his uncle or that he'd taken over this work from his father when he'd decided it was beneath him. Never mind that for years he'd been solely responsible for keeping the earl's properties running and his tenants happy when his own family wouldn't so much as let him look at the books.

Unused, unneeded, and unappreciated. He'd been a disappointment all along, it just took a murder to make him see it.

And his family was all in agreement. That much was clear. At least Catriona looked uncomfortable in her agreement. That was something, even if all those related to him by blood, even Charles, wore expressions ranging from saddened schoolmaster to furious minister. Robert was the most livid.

"Is that all you have to say?" his brother bellowed. "After all the harm he's caused this family?"

"Here, here!" his father chimed in, rapping on the table.

The baron shrugged. "No harm yet that can't be undone. I'm sure once he's rectified the situation regarding the prisoner, and given a suitable apology to Carnbee for his impudence, all will be forgiven, if not immediately forgotten."

Gil opened his mouth to protest, then paused. It was clear that by, "rectified the situation regarding the prisoner," his uncle meant for him to return Jarrett to the tolbooth. However, he hadn't actually said that, had he? Just as he hadn't said Gil couldn't take him out in the first place.

If pressed later, Gil could claim that he'd rectified the situation by proving Jarrett was innocent. It was exactly the sort of lawyering his uncle had just chastised him for, but he was finding it harder and harder to give a damn. As long as he could end this conversation before his uncle clarified his meaning further, he might just get away with it without being disowned.

"Thank you, Uncle Andrew, you've given me a great deal to think about," Gil said over his brother's splutters. "If you'll excuse me, I should begin tending to this matter at once. Please, if you see Carnbee before I do, pass along that I'm working on my apology. I wouldn't want to rush it and have him think me insincere."

Having brought his errant nephew to heel, the baron looked quite pleased with himself. "Very good. I'm afraid Charles and I have to skip dessert as well. We still have matters to look over before I retire."

Charles looked even more disappointed in that than he had in Gil. For the first time however, Gil didn't find the offer to help leaping to his tongue.

He said his good nights, mourning the ratafia cake that Robert would be all too happy to eat on his behalf, and headed towards the door.

As he collected his coat, he was surprised to hear his father's voice behind him.

"Gilleasbuig. A word?"

Gil eyed the front door longingly, but found himself following his father into a little-used music room instead.

"I will be blunt," Bernard Charleton said.

He stood between Gil and the room's fireplace, blocking not only the heat but also any chance Gil had of reading his expression, as it was thrown into shadow by the blaze. "I respect my brother's word as baron, but as your father, I cannot forgive your actions so easily."

Gil was tired. Tired of being reprimanded. Tired of putting on a brave face for Jarrett. Tired of trying to ignore the attraction between them. Tired of fighting for a cause he wasn't sure he could win. Just tired.

He sighed. "What else would you have me do, Father? You heard Uncle Andrew, I'm already to set everything to right as soon as I'm able. Would you prefer I grovel for forgiveness?"

"I would prefer you act with the sense due your station!" his father shouted.

Despite everything, Gil was still taken aback at the anger in his father's voice.

"You belong to a noble family and for too long I have overlooked your ignoble actions. That ends now."

Gil was too tired to fight the hysterical laughter that bubbled out of his throat. "Ignoble actions? And what pray tell, are ignoble actions for such a lauded station as the nephew of a mere baron? Should I be taking my cues from Robert instead? Whoring and drinking and gambling my way through half the county? Or Mother, frittering the barony's funds on expensive nothings? I wouldn't know how expensive, of course, because I'm too ignoble to ever be allowed to look at the books, despite handling my own investments and well as those for a sodding earl! Or you, who used to do exactly the same work I do, but decided it was too ignoble to get off your arse and earn an honest living?"

Because his father was in shadow, Gil never saw the slap coming.

He clutched his stinging cheek, all effrontery knocked out of him by blow.

His father's words were low, a thread of danger running through them that Gil had never heard before.

"You will do as your uncle bids and repair your reputation as much as is possible. Afterwards, you will accompany me to either Edinburgh or London. The season begins within the month. I expect you to make amends by doing your duty to your family."

"Doing my..." His father couldn't be serious. There was only one duty that was expected of noble sons and daughters during the season. "Robert is older than me, put him on the bloody marriage mart!"

"This isn't about your brother. This is about you. I know you were out the night of the murder."

Icy dread closed its fingers around Gil's throat.

"H-how?" he stuttered out.

He immediately realised his mistake as his father went deathly still. He hadn't known for sure, but Gil had just confirmed it.

"The stable boy was complaining about being awoken to deal with your horse. Gossip spreads quickly through houses like these."

Thank God, his father didn't know about The Cross Keys at least. That was a small blessing. Gil could explain his way out of simply returning a horse. An early morning ride, too early to wake the boy to prepare the horse perhaps, or a simple misunderstanding.

But he didn't get the chance.

"In light of the manner in which you've behaved, it occurs to me that Mr. Welch may have had an accomplice."

It took a moment for Gil to realise what his father was accusing him of. His blood turned to ice.

"No one has suggested such to the magistrate yet, but..." His father paused. "While you consider whether it's worth doing everything in your power to elevate the very family whose name you've disgraced, it's something to keep in mind. Family only protects family, after all."

The walk back to Balcarres was a blur.

Mr. Howe leapt to his feet when he saw him, pressing the room's key into his hand and exclaiming about catching a chill. Was it cold? Gil supposed it was. Now that he thought about it, it was raining too. His clothes were stuck to his skin and he could hear his teeth chattering.

He honestly hadn't noticed. His father's threat—because that's what it was, plain and simple, a threat—was still ringing in his ears. Grovel, marry, and be a part of the family. Or do none of those things and be named an accomplice to murder. All just for trying to do the right thing. For taking pity on an innocent man and trying to help. How was that fair?

Just because he wasn't willing to go along with what was easiest for everyone, his family was willing to turn their backs on him?

He wiped his spectacles with his handkerchief, but it was equally sodden, leaving wet blurs across his vision. No, his family had been angry, but willing to forgive. His father was just trying to scare him back into line, the same way he's told legends about the redcaps who would snatch away children to keep a young Gil from wandering too far from home. It hadn't worked then and it wouldn't work now. He was tired of being treated like a child and tired of his family ordering him around.

Whatever platitudes he gave Mr. Howe worked well enough that he went away without protest, leaving Gil in the hallway alone. His hand trembled as he fit the key in the lock. He wasn't just tired, he was exhausted.

As the door opened, he found himself stepping into such blissful light and warmth that for a delirious second, he wondered if the redcaps had gotten him after all and he was entering the world of the fair folk. Surely the creature sitting on the rug before the fire was too beautiful to be human.

Jarrett laid down another card then smiled up at him. "Oh good, you're back. I'm sick of playing patience. There's still some wine left. Pour yourself a glass and I'll lay out the cards for—Christ, did you walk back or swim?"

Jarrett clambered to his feet. He'd been sitting close enough to the fire that his skin was flushed and the hair at his temples were darkened by beads of sweat. He'd stripped down to shirtsleeves and as he walked towards Gil, the firelight behind him outlined his trim body through the translucent fabric.

"Now then," Jarrett said when he was only a few steps away, "I'm the valet here, let me help you with that wet coat."

He was still smiling that damned puckish, irresistible smile. Gil couldn't help it. He grabbed Jarrett by his shirt and kissed him.

CHAPTER 14

J arrett had to be dreaming.

He'd barely been able to breathe when Gil stepped into the room drenched from the rain, his clothes clinging to him obscenely, highlighting the strong muscles of his thighs that made Jarrett's mouth water. Thick locks of his long dark hair had pulled free from the tie and clung to his cheeks, his chin, his jaw—all places Jarrett wanted to touch, to taste. He'd looked like a dashing pirate come home from the sea or a rakish highwayman rode in on the storm.

Then Gil had kissed him and it became even harder to breathe. Jarrett had been too desperate in the tolbooth to really enjoy their first kiss. He wasn't going to make that mistake again.

He grabbed Gil's face in his hands, pulling him in even closer. His spectacles bumped Jarrett's nose; how fortunate he had the perfect grip to reposition them. He twisted his fingers into Gil's hair and directed the angle of his head until it was perfect, better than perfect. His hair was like wet silk, even softer than Jarrett had dreamed, the heavy strands flowing between his fingers. Gil groaned as Jarrett raked his scalp, so he did it again, then took advantage of the distraction to slip his tongue between Gil's parted lips.

When he'd dreamed of this, he'd imagined he'd be the master. After all, he'd been with plenty of men in the past, all that experience had to count for something. But Gil met him immediately, his tongue stroking against Jarrett's and sending waves of pleasure rolling through him with every caress. He was the one to break away first, unable to bear the sensations and dizzy with lack of air.

Gil chuckled as Jarrett panted against his shoulder, the bastard, until Jarrett realised he was in the perfect position to bring some of his fantasies to life. He kissed the hinge of Gil's jaw, gentle once, then with teeth, feeling the delicious scrape of stubble against his lips, the tiny pinpricks of sensation promising reminders of their touch tomorrow. He pressed his tongue against the delicate underside of Gil's throat, feeling the pulse of it as Gil swallowed heavily, then Jarrett pressed his teeth against it, not biting down, but just because he could, feeling the shivers that ran through Gil. His chin received the same treatment, kissing and tasting, then his cheek, but Gil's mouth was too much of a prize to be ignored for long.

Gil's hands tightened on his shirt as they kissed, twisting the fabric tighter and tighter. Jarrett hoped it tore, hoped Gil ripped the damn thing right off him. Hoping to encourage such an action, he slid a thigh between Gil's, only to be left hissing as those powerful muscles clenched around his leg, trapping him there.

Christ, if his thighs could do that...

His hips bucked at the thought, forcing him to realise he was hard, as hard as he'd ever been, and only from a bit of kissing. Gil hadn't even touched him properly, and Jarrett was rutting against him like the shameless wanton he was. It would be embarrassing if it wasn't so arousing. But he hadn't spent in his trousers since he was an untrained adolescent and he wasn't going to start again now.

He pulled away, unable to tear his eyes from the strand of spittle that connected their mouths for a brief second before snapping. His entire front was damp from Gil's clothes, clearly they had to go—both his clothes and Gil's.

He'd never be this rough in his duties at a valet, but dressing an earl for supper was nowhere near as important as getting Gil naked immediately.

"Off. Off now." He yanked at Gil's coat. The angle was poor with Gil still clinging to him, but he was determined. It would be a shame to ruin such a nice coat, boring brown thing that it was. He appreciated that it had kept him so warm in the cells, but it needed to be gone immediately.

Then Gil opened his eyes. Jarrett didn't even know when Gil had closed them, but the beauty of them made him forget what he'd been doing. Even foggy lenses couldn't hide the lust that darkened the hazel, making the lighter flecks shine like bits of fire.

"God, you're lovely," he breathed. Then he remembered what he'd been doing and gave Gil's coat another yank. "Off. Now. No wet clothes in bed. No clothes in bed."

Gil's shoulders dropped back and Jarrett was able to wrestle the coat down his arms. Unfortunately, the moment he was in reach, Gil kissed him, completely distracting him once more.

"We can't," Gil said when they finally pulled apart.

"Of course, we can. I'm certainly going to."

Gil laughed softly, his hot breath curling under Jarrett's collar. "Not in the house, there's too many people around."

"That doesn't stop the earl and Dominick," Jarrett sniped. As soon as the words were out of his mouth, he wanted to snatch them back. Oh fuck, that wasn't his secret to tell. Gil's interest in him didn't necessarily make him safe, as much as Jarrett might desperately hope otherwise, and a secret like that could ruin everything.

But Gil just laughed.

"Oh, I'm sure it doesn't. They're not nearly as subtle as they think they are, are they?" He dropped another kiss against Jarrett's lips, this one light and painfully brief. "But I doubt they have to worry about Mr. Howe listening at the keyhole to make sure one of them hasn't murdered the other. The poor man is nervy enough as it is, I don't want to be responsible for giving him apoplexy."

He gave Jarrett another kiss, stepping back when he tried to chase after it. "Besides, we're not earls. We need to be cautious. Discreet."

Jarrett wanted to tell him he could stick his discretion up his shapely arse, but that might impact his chances of getting his cock up there instead. Besides, a request for caution wasn't a "no" and Jarrett did have a perfectly discreet place they could go.

"Aye, not in the house. How about a spot just outside it?" But his spirits fell immediately. "Ah Christ!"

"What is it?"

"My keys," said Jarrett. "They were taken off me at the tolbooth along with my coin. Bastards never gave them back."

Gil's brow furrowed adorably and Jarrett wanted to kiss the little wrinkle that made just above the bridge of his spectacles. Which was not a thought he'd had about another man before. There wasn't much adorable about trying to get your prick sucked quickly then going your separate ways. Assuming you could even see the fellow or his adorable wrinkles at all in the dark of an alley.

This wasn't any different than those other times. It *wasn't*. And the fact he hadn't thought twice about taking Gil to his shed meant nothing. They couldn't go at it in the house and it was raining; the shed was the only sensible option. They'd get off, get dressed, and that would be it.

"Why do we need keys?" asked Gil.

"For, um, for the shed. My shed." Jarrett corrected. It *was* the only sensible option, nothing more. "There's a spare, but it's hidden."

Whatever worries he had faded in the brightness of Gil's smile. "Lead on then!"

They snuck their way downstairs, shushing each other and giggling like schoolboys. Jarrett exchanged the lamp he carried for a small lantern at the first opportunity. He could likely find his way through Balcarres House in the dark and Gil knew the place even better than he did, but even shuttered as tightly as he dared, the small beam of light was a comfort, turning their sneaking into an adventure.

"Won't poor Mr. Howe be surprised after he shoots us for being burglars," whispered Gil, then he snorted.

"What?" Jarrett whispered.

"My family already thinks you're a jewel thief. Catriona can't find her shawl, clearly you mistook it for a golden necklace dripping with rubies and diamonds."

"Shh," Jarrett said, fighting back the urge to giggle. "We're almost there."

He reached back, taking Gil's hand in his because he could, and dragged him into the library. There he made straight for his hiding place.

"What's that?" asked Gil as Jarrett pulled the book from the shelf. Then he read the cover. "*The Book of Common Prayer and the Administration of the Sacraments for the Use of the Church of Scotland*?"

Jarrett opened it and plucked his spare key from within. "If you say so. It was the dustiest of a dusty lot."

"What if someone wants to read it?"

Jarrett raised an eyebrow at him. "With a title like that in a house like this? Now shush, we've got more sneaking to do."

They successfully snuck their way out through the kitchen without being caught. The front doors were too heavy to open without creaking and most of the other entrances were so disused they were even worse. Besides, the kitchen afforded them the opportunity to grab a pair of overcoats from the hooks beside the door on their way out. Gil might already be soaked, but Jarrett saw no reason he should be as well.

It was bitterly cold, so much so that he didn't hesitate as he unlocked the door to the shed, the desire to have four walls protecting him from the wind overriding any doubts he might have had about bringing another person here. About bringing Gil here.

It was only after he ushered Gil inside, making sure the door was firmly locked behind them, that he began to worry. But Gil was already making his way over to the table. Without a fireplace, it was still chilly inside, but the quilt was warm and the shed was so small that two warm bodies, especially two active bodies, should warm it up in no time.

Gil didn't say anything but touched the small carving that sat on the table. It was of a running horse, its mane streaming out behind it and its mouth open in a whinny. Jarrett had bought it just because he liked it.

"It's not much," Jarrett said. "But it's not the house. And it's discreet, like you asked. The door locks and we can go back to the room after. Or the household will just think we were up early if we want to spend the night here instead."

He wasn't sure why he added that last part.

"This is all yours?" Gil asked, tracing his finger down the horse's back.

"Aye."

Gil smiled. "It's lovely."

Tension Jarrett hadn't even realised he'd been carrying unwound. "Oh. Aye, well. It'll do." Now that the worry was gone, he felt suddenly wrong-footed. By the time things got to this point, he'd never needed more words than, "Mouth or arse?" before and wasn't sure what to say now. He couldn't ask Gil something as coarse as that. Or he could, but he found he didn't want to.

"I'll, um, I'll light the lamp, so we have more than just the lantern. If that's all right." He wasn't sure what he'd do if Gil wanted it dark instead. He barrelled on so he wouldn't have time to answer. "If you'll check the curtains are closed tight and there's ah, oil. In the chest. If that's something you think we'll need?"

"Jarrett." Gil's smile was different from all his others. Jarrett could barely make it out in the gloom, but it was softer, almost tender. "The oil is something we will *definitely* need."

Jarrett hoped his blush wasn't visible. This wasn't like him at all. He put on his most sultry smile and tilted his head so he could look up at Gil through his eyelashes. "I didn't want to presume."

Gil laughed and shook his head, but didn't say anything else. Instead he busied himself with the curtains so Jarrett turned his attention to lighting the lamp. It was easier having the lantern to work from and within a few moments the shed was filled with cheerful light. He widened the shutter on the lantern for good measure.

Blinking in the sudden light after so long without, he heard the familiar creak of the chest opening. He turned to tell Gil to look under the spare clothes he kept in there, but he was distracted by something wrong with the bed.

He hadn't been in here since the day of his arrest, but he could've sworn he'd made the bed and pulled the quilt all the way up to the pillows. But now there was something light at the top of the bed, as if the sheets had been pulled down, and they looked dirty. As his eyes adjusted, he could see they weren't sheets at all, but a white shirt crumpled on top of a pair of plaid trousers. Both were stained the colour of old blood.

"Jarrett?"

Not knowing what else to do, Jarrett turned to look at Gil. His heart caught in his throat.

Gil was standing at the foot of the bed, one hand resting on the open lid of the chest. In his other hand, he held a knife.

CHAPTER 15

G il stared down at the knife in his hand and tried to ignore the sickening dark smears along the blade.

He knew Jarrett was innocent. He'd seen him at The Cross Keys with his own eyes. It was absolutely impossible for him to have committed the murder. But for one terrible second, doubt crept in.

"Ah fuck! Ah fuck! Ah Christ! These weren't—I didn't—Christ! Gil, I swear, I don't know how these got here."

It wasn't Jarrett's words, but the absolute terror on his face that whisked away Gil's shred of doubt. "I know, I know. It's all right."

"It damn well isn't!"

Jarrett's voice was strangled with panic. Gil dropped the knife back into the chest and held up both his hands to show they were empty.

"You're right, it isn't all right. But I know you didn't kill anyone. Take a deep breath."

Jarrett visibly made a show of breathing in and out heavily, then did it again. Gil hadn't actually expected it to help, it was just something people said in stressful situations, but to his surprise Jarrett actually seemed calmer even if his voice wavered.

"You know I didn't do it?"

"I believe you when you say you didn't," answered Gil evasively. He wasn't sure why he was still hiding the fact he'd been at The Cross Keys; his actions in their room made his interest in men abundantly clear. Perhaps because The Cross Keys was his place of safety and whatever this was with Jarrett—this wild, irresistible, dangerous thing—it certainly wasn't safe. Besides, this was hardly the right time to tell him, not when there was a bloody knife to deal with first.

At least he was no longer exhausted. If that kiss hadn't revitalised him, finding a murder weapon certainly had.

Jarrett was staring at something on the bed.

"Are those?" Gil asked.

Jarrett nodded.

A bloody knife and bloody clothes as well. Wonderful. "I don't suppose it's too much to hope this is some kind of cruel joke?"

Jarrett shook his head. "I recognise the trousers. They're the same ones the dead man was wearing. You don't forget trousers that ugly."

No, Gil supposed you didn't. Even before they were stained in blood, they would've been a memorable sight. For a moment, the pattern almost seemed familiar. Likely one of the more voguish wallpapers his mother had considered. After her redecorating, they already had a few rooms now too hideous to use.

"He's been here, hasn't he?" Jarrett whispered. "The killer, I mean."

Gil nodded. "I think we have to assume that."

Jarrett pulled the key from his pocket. "The door was locked. Just now, it was locked and I'd swear before God I locked it when I left that morning. The bastard stole my key! Christ, now we know who did it! One of those damned gaolers at the tolbooth! One of them must have killed the stranger, then stolen my key to leave the bloody proof here so I'd swing instead! We just need to find out which one and we've got him!"

The anger and elation warring across Jarrett's features was painful to watch, even more so because Gil was certain he was wrong.

"That's one possibility," he said diplomatically. "I think you're right that these... *items* were left here deliberately, and it certainly couldn't hurt to find out who was on duty that night, but how would a guard know the key went to the shed? *Your* shed, more specifically, that only you had the key to? Who else knows about this place?"

"No one!" Jarrett yelled. Then he pinched the bridge of his nose and took another deep breath. "Dominick. He's the one who gave me use of it. His Lordship too, I'd wager, since I doubt there's anything one of them knows he doesn't immediately tell the other."

"But they're both in London by now and couldn't have done it anyway," Gil said glumly. Not that he wanted two men he considered friends to be murderers, he just wished there was someone more suspicious than Jarrett. "What about the staff here?"

"I haven't made a secret of it," admitted Jarrett. "None of them can understand why I'd want to sleep rough when I have my own room in the house. They've never shown much interest otherwise, but aye, I suppose they all know. But that's all. No one else. That means it's one of them, isn't it?"

A cold realisation weighed heavy in Gil's gut, crushing the last embers of arousal that had been stirred by their kissing.

"That's not all," he said, more reluctant with every word. "I think this might be my fault. You told me in the tolbooth about this place, and the key, and I may have brought it up at the inquest."

Jarrett stared at him. "You what?"

When Gil was eight, Robert had told him, with all the wisdom of an elder brother, that filling his shoes with nettles would make him run faster. Charles had found him in the woods by the sound of his sobbing and Gil hadn't been able to walk for three days.

He felt even stupider now than he had then.

"I'm sorry. It was an inquest. I didn't even think about it. If it means anything, I was trying to defend you. No, don't say anything, it doesn't help, I know. Lord, just about the entire county was there. It could have been any one of them."

Jarrett moved as if to sit on the bed, then thought better of it and sat heavily on the only chair instead. He drummed his fingers on the table, making the carved horse wobble.

"Carnbee was there, wasn't he?" he said at last.

"At the inquest? Of course." He saw where Jarrett was heading. A month ago he would've thought it was impossible, but he'd have said the same thing about ever acting on his attraction to Jarrett and here they were. "The gaoler said the magistrate had all the things they took from you. That would include your keys. You think he was worried there wasn't enough to convict you and planted the bloody clothes here?"

"Someone did," Jarrett replied. "Someone wanted to make sure I swung instead of them. Carnbee makes sense."

"But you saw him by the body. He wouldn't go near it. Whoever did this stripped bloody clothes off a corpse and kept them for over a week before hiding them here. The knife too." Gil wasn't willing to discount the magistrate quite yet, but he couldn't envision the priggish man doing such a thing.

Jarrett waved a hand towards the bed. "Someone did though. And they meant for them to be found. And not by us, I'd wager."

Suddenly Jarrett leapt to his feet, knocking into the table in his haste and toppling the horse. "They'll come looking! We need to get out of here now!"

"Calm down!" Gil shouted. When Jarrett showed no signs of doing any such thing, Gil grabbed him, holding him in place with one hand on his shoulder and the other pressed to the centre of his chest. He could feel Jarrett's rabbiting heartbeat against his palm. "Calm down, deep breaths remember? In and out, let me feel it."

He could, he could feel every push of breath in and out of Jarrett's lungs.

"That's good," he said softly. "That's very good. Keep breathing, just like that. We've got time. No one is coming tonight. You think Magistrate Carnbee is coming out now? He wouldn't get out of bed on a night like this if he knew you were out here strangling Walter Scott himself."

"You're right," Jarrett said on a rush of breath. "We've got time."

He leaned forward and dropped his head against Gil's shoulder. For some reason, that felt more intimate than anything they'd done so far. It was a strange feeling, standing there, with his hand on Jarrett's heart and Jarrett's head on his shoulder, but that didn't stop Gil from gently laying his cheek against his hair and closing his eyes. They were standing in a frigid shed with a murder weapon and a dead man's clothes, but he didn't think he'd ever been more comfortable.

Eventually Jarrett stepped away. He wouldn't look Gil in the eye, but his cheeks were pink. Some tiny, hopeful part of Gil wondered if he'd felt the same thing.

"You're cold," said Jarrett, still not looking at him. "Your clothes are, I mean. I brought you here to get you out of those. I didn't do a very good job."

It was a weak jest, but it did the trick of dispelling the strange tension from the room, so Gil returned one of his own. "I don't much care for the replacements you found."

Jarrett huffed. "Well, clearly I'm not a very good valet."

"Clearly." Gil sighed. "I hope you're better at hiding things. I doubt these will fit in a prayer book."

"We should just burn them."

The idea was tempting. "We'd still need to hide the knife. That won't burn. And the clothes might be important, although I don't have the faintest idea how. It's up to you though."

Jarrett sighed heavily. "I know a place to hide them. If nothing else, so I can drop them on the killer's bed when we find him. See how he likes it."

"Perhaps he left his own house key in a pocket to make it even," Gil suggested. They should check the clothes for clues to the dead man's identity if nothing else, but neither of them made a move towards the bed.

Then Jarrett straightened his shoulders and gingerly picked up the trousers, turning them this way and that. Held up to the light, the stains were even worse, dried the colour of tea at the edges, but darkening towards the centre of each stain. The blood had soaked deep into the fabric, blurring the colours of the plaid to a solid reddish black.

Gil's stomach turned, but he wasn't going to let Jarrett face this alone, so he picked up the shirt with two fingers. If anything, it was even worse, the white fabric a starker and more horrible contrast. The entire back of the shirt was a single stain, emanating from a jagged tear in the centre.

"There wasn't a hole in his overcoat, was there? That's strange. No hole in the coat, but a hole in the shirt. He was still wearing this when he died."

Jarrett dropped the trousers on the floor and picked up what looked like a waistcoat. He grimaced as he ran a finger into each small pocket.

"Nothing in here," he said. "And nothing else I can see with pockets. His overcoat will still be with him in Marta's cellar, if you want to check, but I'm sending you in to get it. I don't need her knocking me over the head with that cudgel."

Jarrett looked over the pile of clothes again, but his disgust now appeared tinged with genuine interest. He pointed at the pile.

"Socks look homemade, but the boots are good quality. Not stylish, but sturdy. And his cravat was just in a mail coach knot, I do remember that. If this is all of it, it looks like he didn't have a proper coat underneath that overcoat. Not a fancy sort then, but I could have told you that from looking at him. But these aren't worn enough to be a beggar's either."

Gil smiled. "For not being a very good valet, you certainly seem to know your clothes."

Jarrett looked pleased, if a little embarrassed. It suited him; he should look that way more often. Then he stuck his fingers through the back of the waistcoat and waggled them.

"Hole in this one too."

Now it was Gil's turn to be disgusted. He laid the shirt down on top of the trousers, not wanting to touch it any more. "It was a cold night. I wonder why he took his coat off."

"Ah, I, uh, might have an idea about that," Jarrett said, setting the waistcoat down on the shirt. "This is based on my own experience, mind you, but that night, I asked him up to the chapel to go stargazing."

Gil snorted. Whatever he was expecting, it wasn't that. "I take it you meant something else entirely."

"It may have been a code, aye." Jarrett ducked his head. "He wasn't having it either way, told me to steer clear of the chapel. So I wonder, since he'd taken the coat off at least, if he turned me down because he already had plans to *stargaze* up there with someone else."

That certainly would explain a few things. Although it opened up even more possibilities. Gil left Jarrett to gather up the rest of the clothes while he retrieved the knife. It fit well in his hand, but looked more like something taken from a kitchen than one designed for gutting an animal after a hunt or a man in a back-alley brawl.

"Our killer could be a woman," he said as he laid the knife down on top of the clothes, watching as Jarrett rolled the whole mess into a tight bundle. "She'd have to be strong to lift that rock, even if he was already on the ground after being stabbed. But a woman like Marta could do it. It doesn't explain why she would take his clothes though. She'd have to know they'd be soaked in blood."

Jarrett added, "Or why, if she was going to take them off him anyway, that she'd have him take the coat off, but stab him before he got to the rest. It'd have been a lot easier for him to do the whole job for her."

Jarrett had somehow managed to roll everything together in a way that left the outer layer unbloody. Anyone who saw them carrying it wouldn't think twice. At least not about the bundle itself. Them skulking around in the middle of the night with mysterious objects was another story.

"Look around and make sure there's nothing we've missed," said Jarrett.

Fortunately, nothing else turned up. Their killer must have wanted to make sure even Carnbee couldn't miss the clues. His searching did turn up a number of other things though. The oil they hadn't gotten a chance to use, for one. But also a small collection of treasures on the windowsill, feathers with an iridescent sheen, rocks in interesting shapes, small sea shells and even a piece of glass worn smooth by the sea.

By the time Gil turned his collar up to brave the rain again, he was dismayed to find he was more than a wee bit charmed by Jarrett. The man might have a tendency to panic, but he'd been brave enough to handle the clothes before Gil could, and his insights showed real intelligence. All traits Jarrett had shown already, but it was like he was really seeing them now. Even more charming was the way he'd put care in turning his little shed into somewhere to do more than *stargaze*. It was a place that felt homey and he'd decorated it with small and beautiful things.

He's a small and beautiful thing.

No. Gil wasn't going to start thinking that way. It was one thing to want to bugger Jarrett, Lord, who could look at Jarrett and *not* want to bugger him? Especially with those looks he gave, and those teasing smiles, and the way that when he blushed, it ran in a straight line from ear to ear, as if his cheekbones were a clifftop with a perfect trail at the top for the colour to walk across... And those cheekbones!

He'd rather lost where he was going. But yes, it was one thing to want Jarrett for his body. He clearly had no qualms about giving that. But Gil was starting to suspect he wanted more from him. More that Jarrett might not be so willing to give.

It was a terrible idea anyway. He shouldn't want Jarrett at all, especially not while he was under Gil's protection. But not even counting that, Jarrett was too reckless to have any place in Gil's carefully protected life. After all, the reason he couldn't defend himself from a hanging offence was because he'd been too busy committing other hanging offences at the time. Even one night together was far too dangerous to be worth the risk.

But then Jarrett looked up at him again through that forest of eyelashes, the move so practised it should be ridiculous and not send all of Gil's blood rushing to his cock. Jarrett puckered those sinful lips and blew out the lamp, leaving only the lantern to light the wicked grin that stole over his face. He tucked the bundle under his arm and headed towards the door, turning to look back at Gil over his shoulder in a way that put entirely too much of his long, delicate neck on display.

"Coming?" Jarrett breathed.

Well. Perhaps just *one* night.

CHAPTER 16

S neaking back into the main house was nowhere near as fun as sneaking out of it had been. The thought of getting caught carrying the murder weapon was enough to have Jarrett startling at every shadow. He'd fully intended on seducing Gil the moment they made it back to their room, but by the time they'd stashed the bloody bundle under the cushions of a crumbling settee covered by a moth-eaten dust cloth in one of the countless unused rooms in the east wing, his nerves had been worn to the point of exhaustion and he collapsed facedown on his bed without even bothering to remove his shoes.

He heard a chuckle from behind him, then hands still chilled from the night air were working off one shoe, then the other.

"I'm the valet," Jarrett muttered into his pillow.

"I know," said Gil. "But you looked like you needed some help."

Jarrett blindly waved an arm behind him. It wasn't much of an attack, but it got Gil to leave his socks alone.

"You're cold," Jarrett told the pillow. "Take care of your own clothes then get in bed and warm up."

For a long moment there was silence. He wondered if Gil had even heard him, but turning his head to check seemed like far too much effort. After a moment, he heard Gil step away, then the click of the valise he'd brought from Charleton house and the rustle of fabric. The chance to watch Gil change into a nightshirt was almost enough to entice him to lift his head, but he used that energy instead to struggle out of his own clothes until he was down to just his shirt and drawers.

He wasn't entirely sure how he was going to get underneath the coverlet on his own, but that seemed less important than sleeping right this instant, so he was barely awake when it was dragged from underneath him and helpfully draped over his body. The comfort was so exquisite that it took him a moment to realise he wasn't alone.

That was enough to wake him at least enough to turn his head. When he opened his eyes, it was to see Gil's face inches from his own.

Well then.

He'd meant Gil should get into his own bed and get warm, but he was hardly going to correct him now. Neither of them were large men, and the bed was more than big enough for two. Even if it hadn't been, Jarrett wouldn't have said anything, especially not after a tentative hand—still cold, but who gave a damn—rested on his hip.

"Is this all right?" Gil asked. He looked different somehow, and it took Jarrett a moment to work out why. He wasn't wearing his spectacles. Gil didn't look better or worse without them, just different. If the way his eyes kept darting over Jarrett's face was any indication, he didn't have any difficulty seeing him at this range. As a test, Jarrett licked his lips, and to his satisfaction and delight, Gil's eyes immediately snapped to follow the movement. He'd freed his hair too, and it tumbled over his shoulder in long, dark waves.

"More than all right," Jarrett said. Then after a moment he added. "What the hell are you doing?"

The motion under the pillows stopped suddenly, and Gil sheepishly pulled his hand out from underneath.

"Sorry," he whispered. "Strange bedroom habits."

Jarrett snorted, remembering what Gil had said that morning. Christ, had it only been that morning? Between their conversations in the tolbooth and everything that had happened since Gil freed him, he'd grown closer to Gil in just a few days than he had in all the months they'd known each other before.

He grinned at himself. Of course they were closer. There wasn't much closer they could be and still have clothes on.

"You won't find any dried lavender here," he said. "Perhaps a dead mouse. Considering the state she's in, I wouldn't put it past Mrs. Finley to express herself in about that subtle a manner."

Gil wrinkled his nose in disgust. It shouldn't have been a fetching look at all, but Jarrett found it made him desperately want to kiss him. Then he remembered he could, and did.

"What was that for?" Gil asked when they pulled apart.

Jarrett shook his head, burying himself back into the pillows, but he could still watch Gil with one eye. Over Gil's shoulder, he noticed the lantern they'd carried with them was sitting on the night table. Beside it sat Gil's spectacles and the bottle of lamp oil. The sight made Jarrett's heart swell with an emotion he hadn't felt before.

"No reason," he said, swallowing thickly. "You refilled the lantern?"

Gil shrugged, lifting the coverlet. "Strange bedroom habits. I knew you'd want it left burning. And I certainly don't mind being able to look at you all night. You're easily the most beautiful man I've ever had in my bed."

Christ. It'd been hard enough to watch the Charleton Charm at work on others. Jarrett took back every unkind thought he'd ever had about women tittering just because Gil had given them a compliment and a wink. He felt like tittering himself and he hadn't even gotten the wink.

"You're the only man I've ever had in mine," he admitted.

Gil frowned and raised up on an elbow. "You don't have to lie. I saw you—that is, I've seen the way you act. And you certainly don't kiss like a blushing virgin. That's not a complaint, mind you, quite the opposite."

Jarrett yawned. "Not a lie. It's just that not many alleys have feather mattresses in them. The chapel certainly doesn't."

"But your shed?"

"I'd been hoping to christen it tonight." Jarrett was still sore that plan had been scuppered. He added another tally against the killer for ruining his night. It wasn't as dark a tally as framing Jarrett for murder, but it was still there.

"Never had a space of my own I could use that way before. And you know how it is when you find someone and your blood's up; wherever's dark and nearby will do. Besides, it's Scotland. Most of the time it's too fucking cold to even get your trousers properly out of the way! One time, after we were done, I was keeping close because it was coming down rain and ice both and the roof only went out so far, and without noticing I accidently buttoned my fall to the other fellow's waistcoat! It's a good thing you never have to see them again, eh?"

He laughed at the memory and expected Gil to do the same—it hadn't been very funny at the time, when they'd both ended up falling in the mud, but it certainly was now. But Gil was silent, his brow furrowed again. One of the fingers on Jarrett's hip started tapping, but from the faraway look on his face, he didn't think Gil realised he was doing it.

"One question," said Gil. "No, several questions, but this one first. You're saying you've never had sex with a man in a bed."

"Not with a woman either, if that's your next question. Haven't done anything with them at all. Done just about everything I can think of with men though."

Perhaps that was it. He supposed he could see why Gil might not want to hear about Jarrett's other exploits, funny as they were. Even without knowing anything about them, Jarrett was jealous of any men Gil had already fucked.

Gil nodded slowly. "And all that you've done, you've done... outside?"

"Of course not, milord. I've got an entire manor I use just for swiving. Don't you?"

All the questions were starting to make Jarrett uncomfortable. He might not be accustomed to the fineries the nephew of a baron had, but he didn't feel ashamed for keeping his simple pleasures simple.

Gil squeezed his hip then, and Jarrett was willing to forgive him a little. He'd be able to forgive him a lot if he moved that hand from over the shirt to under it. If Gil wanted to keep going past his drawers as well, Jarrett wasn't going to stop him.

"Sorry," said Gil. "I'm not judging. I just prefer to find a room in a discreet place with a door that locks. Aren't you worried about getting caught?"

"No more than I'd worry about someone breaking down that door. Easier to run if you're in the open, even if you are holding up your trousers one-handed. Besides, who has the time to bother?"

He wondered if Gil knew about The Cross Keys. For all his talk about discretion and locked doors, he'd probably enjoy it. He'd have to take him sometime, once they sorted this all out.

Because they *would* sort it all out. He wasn't going to let himself think otherwise, especially not now, snuggled up warm and cosy with a handsome man. He was starting to see the appeal of this sort of thing. At least if that handsome man was Gil.

This was too damned nice. He had the sneaking suspicion Gil was ruining him for sharing a bed with anyone else. And after the murder, stargazing at the chapel didn't hold the appeal it used to either. Ah well, as long as alleys had walls, he'd be able to find a man interested in pushing him up against one. Shame it didn't sound like that would be Gil.

That thought struck him harder than he'd expected. Of course, it wouldn't be Gil. Jarrett was never with the same man more than once. It was better that way for everyone. And he certainly didn't spend the night with them in some discreet room with a locked door.

Except wasn't that what he was doing now? They'd only kissed, but lying here with Gil, he felt closer to him than he had with any of the others. And they'd already spent one night together, even if it was in separate beds.

And I want to spend many more nights with him, perhaps even all of them.

He was so jarred by the thought, he missed what Gil said next.

"What?"

Gil looked sheepish. "It's not my place to ask. It's just you mentioned not seeing them again and I just wondered if there was anyone... that is, what's the longest you've been with someone?"

"About half an hour."

"No, I meant—wait, what?"

"What? That's a perfectly respectable amount of time. It's not like I'm done in a single pump."

Gil was staring at him. "I meant how long *of a relationship* have you had?"

"Oh. Same answer then. About half an hour. What about you? Have you got some decades-long romance I should be jealous of?"

Why the fuck had he said that? It was none of his business what or who Gil did.

"Never mind," he added quickly, since he didn't really want to know the answer. "Forget I asked."

"I have *friends*," Gil said softly. "Who I see from time to time. But no. No one special."

Jarrett tried to squash the wee bubble of happiness that gave him, but try as he might, he couldn't get it to burst.

"Ah. I suppose that makes two of us," he said, willing himself not to smile and failing miserably.

Gil smiled back. "I suppose it does."

They lay there, smiling at each other like fools. Outside, the rain was beating on the windows and the county was full of people who wanted him dead, but in here, in this bed, he was more content than he'd ever been.

"You know," Jarrett said at last. "I've still never had a *naked* man in my bed."

He plucked at Gil's nightshirt and Gil's smile turned devilish.

"Well, I think we can f—" A jaw-cracking yawn interrupted Gil's words and Jarrett couldn't help but laugh at the shocked look on his face.

"Jarrett, I'm so sorry. No, stop laughing. Lord, what time is it? It must be nearly two in the morning."

At that exact moment, the hall clock struck the hour. Three.

Gil groaned. "Please don't think this is lack of desire on my part, but I'm afraid I'd put up a rather poor showing. I'm too tired to do any of the things I want to do with you."

Jarrett wanted to know what each and every one of those things was. If it was anything like the list he had of things to do with Gil, he might, *just might*, see the appeal in being with the same man more than once. After all, he wouldn't even be able to get through the first page of his list in just one night. However, there were advantages to doing things his way as well.

He licked his lips again, just to watch Gil watch him. "I know something we can do, and you'll barely have to move at all."

Gil raised an eyebrow. "Oh?"

"Aye. Won't take too long either, at least, not for me. Then you can have all the beauty rest you need."

Jarrett wouldn't admit it now, but he was even more tired than he'd been when Gil took his shoes off for him. Still, he wasn't going to spend his first night in bed with a handsome man just sleeping.

At Gil's nod, Jarrett took charge of the hand on his hip, leading it where he'd wanted it minutes ago—months ago—moving it under his shirt, under the hem of his drawers, and around his cock.

Gil gasped, his hand tightening deliciously. The angle was awkward, and Jarrett struggled blindly to get his drawers out of the way. He'd never been more thankful for his bony hips than when his drawers slid down without needing to be unfastened. He kicked them off just as Gil adjusted his grip, and it was Jarrett's turn to gasp. Those calloused palms that were so unbecoming of a nobleman were perfect for caressing the sensitive skin of Jarrett's cock, especially when Gil ran his thumb over the head, collecting the moisture that was already beading there.

Gil's hands were still slightly cool and the difference against Jarrett's overheated skin made him want to squirm. He'd been half-hard since the moment he'd realised it was his bed Gil was getting into instead of his own, and Gil's hand on his hip had been a maddening distraction throughout their entire conversation. He wasn't going to be breaking his thirty-minute record tonight. Christ, if he didn't act soon, he'd spend without even getting his hands on Gil and that was a more unspeakable crime than any he'd actually committed.

Jarrett rarely minded being able to see so little of the men he fucked. In some cases, he actually preferred it. But he regretted not being able to see Gil. The lamp was low and behind him, throwing much of his face into shadow, and the coverlet was drawn up tight to his shoulders to keep out the cold. Here he was in Jarrett's bed in only a shirt and drawers, yet Jarrett could see more of his body on any given day as Gil went about his business, his practical brown coat perfectly framing his shoulders, boots curving along the line of his calves and tight buckskins hugging his thighs.

Still, even if he couldn't see him, at least he could feel him. And reached out and made a wonderful discovery. His delight turned into a groan of pure pleasure as Gil stroked him again, twisting a little as he did.

"F-forward, aren't we?" Jarrett gasped, pushing up Gil's shirt and running his fingers through the thatch of hair at the base of his cock with no drawers at all to get in his way.

"You did invite me into your bed," Gil replied, his voice strangled.

Jarrett hadn't been going to argue that before and he certainly wasn't now, not when he could be finally scratching off at least one item on his list. Gil was as hard as he was, and his skin was like silk beneath Jarrett's fingers. Christ, he wished he could see him. He'd wager Gil had a prick as lovely as the rest of him. Tracing the vein that ran along the underside made Gil shudder and let out a strange noise halfway between a croak and a hiccup. It made Jarrett want to do it again, just to see what other sounds he could wring from him, but he could already feel himself drawing closer and closer to his own climax, Gil's hand never stopping its wicked work. Perhaps, if they did this again, he could find out then.

He threw his leg over Gil's hip and pulled him close. Without breaking his rhythm, Gil shifted his hand to wrap around both their cocks, their fingers interlacing.

If Gil's cock had felt good in his hand, it felt amazing pressed against his own, wetness smearing between them and over their fingers.

Gil's eyes were closed, his mouth open and brow furrowed in either pain or unbearable pleasure. Jarrett didn't know which he was feeling himself.

"Fuck, that's good." He hissed.

"Mmm," agreed Gil. "And that's just with our hands. Think about what we'll be able to do next time."

Next time.

The thought of it now, with Gil here, real, touching him, was too much. Jarrett dropped his head, muffling his cry against Gil's shoulder as he came. Immediately he was enveloped in the rich scent of lavender and orange oil that he remembered from Gil's coat in the tolbooth. The smell that meant safety.

Gil stroked him through it, their cocks growing wetter with every pulse. Until he stilled, stiffening all over and Jarrett felt the hot splash of Gil's spend joining his own between their bodies. As the last few bolts of pleasure faded, he wished that he could have seen it.

The exhaustion Jarrett had been pushing back hit him all at once. He was filthy and completely tangled in Gil. At the very least, he should move his leg so Gil could go clean himself properly and retire to a nice clean bed. The both could, in fact. All they had to do was get up, scrub off, change out of their shirts, and climb into the other bed. It would take all of two minutes.

Or they could deal with the discomfort and dirty linens in the morning.

As he drifted off, he felt Gil's hand settle back on his hip. "You deserve to be worshipped properly."

Jarrett hummed. "And you deserved to be fucked in a dark alley. But I'll settle for this."

Then he fell asleep, dreaming of cool hands and warm promises.

CHAPTER 17

Gil spread his arms and took in a great lungful of the morning air. An easterly *haar* was blowing in off the sea, the cold wind bringing with it a thick fog that crawled under the collar and clung to the skin. Ahead, the road disappeared as the fog hid anything on either side of the hedges save for the occasional ghostly outline of a dead tree. The crunch of his boots echoed in the unnatural stillness.

It was a beautiful day to be alive.

"For Christ's sake, will you slow down!" The reason for his good cheer then swore heavily. "I knew we should've ridden."

Gil grinned. "Nonsense, it's perfectly fine weather for a walk. Besides, you would've felt guilty taking the horses out of their nice warm stables in this *dreich*. Admit it."

"So, it's perfectly fine for us, but too awful for horses." Jarrett said. His shadow in the fog solidified as he drew nearer. "Shows what you think of me."

As a matter of fact, Gil thought a great deal of Jarrett, and even more so after last night.

Lord, last night. Last night had been bliss. At least after they'd dealt with the bloody clothes and murder weapon. That had been terrifying. He hadn't wanted to say as much at the time, but their discovery of the clothes removed any chance that the murderer had done his vile deed and fled. Not only that, but now he was coming after Jarrett.

That worry only stirred up all the others, but Gil kept it all to himself. Jarrett had enough to be afraid of already. Instead he'd just held Jarrett a little closer while they slept. He hadn't wanted to get out of bed at all this morning, their room, their bed, that was all that felt safe anymore. But as much as he might want to tell himself that appointing himself Jarrett's guard also meant he could protect him, he knew Jarrett wouldn't truly be safe until the real killer was where he belonged. And the sooner they could make that happen, the better.

Still, vague fears of confronting an unknown future were poor motivation to get out of bed compared to watching Jarrett blink awake in the grey morning light, seeing the moment he realised Gil was in bed with him, and watching that wicked, kiss-bruised mouth curl into the softest smile. Even when that smile had turned into a scowl and Jarrett had begun cursing the dried, itchy mess they'd left behind, Gil still wanted to stay where they were and let the world handle its own problems for once.

Unfortunately, it was his experience that the world wasn't much good at that, so here they were, tromping through the foggy gloaming with differing levels of enjoyment, off to collect the last piece of the dead man's wardrobe and hope there was something to be learned from it.

"Quit your complaining," he said once Jarrett caught up. Gil bumped his shoulder playfully. "We're almost there. I'll wager that shadow just up a ways is the kirk. It'll only be a few steps from there and you can rest your poor feet in front of Marta's fire. I'll even buy you an oatcake if you'd like. Imagine that, a breakfast you can actually eat. What a novelty that will be!"

"You're a damned cheerful bugger in the mornings."

"Only when I'm graced with such amiable company."

Jarrett rolled his eyes, but the blush on his cheeks betrayed him. Good. Now that Gil was free to turn his charm on Jarrett, he planned on abusing that gift as often as possible.

They walked on and sure enough, the churchyard soon came into view, first in one solitary tombstone, then another, but soon the square tower of the kirk itself was visible through the fog. As they approached, a collection of figures also came into view. At the sight, Jarrett fell a half step behind him, and when the features of the men standing in the yard became clear, both he and Gil swore.

After Sunday's sermon, Minister MacLennan had cornered his uncle to discuss matters he deemed of extreme importance and since the earl was absent, a baron and baron's heir would have to do. His uncle been able to foist the minister off for a few days. Apparently, the time had come. The question of whether or not the kirk needed new pews and who was going to pay for them was so trivial, Gil had completely forgotten about it.

Had he slowed down like Jarrett had asked, his uncle, cousin, and the minister might have already gone inside the kirk and been avoided completely. After the battle at supper last night, he certainly didn't want to run into any of his family now, but the identity of the fourth figure in the group made it even worse.

"Well, well, well," said Magistrate Carnbee.

Gil inclined his head the barest fraction that could still be passed off as polite. "Good morning to you all. We'll not keep you from your business. Enjoy your day."

"And where are you both headed off to?" asked his uncle, his sneer heavy on the word "both".

Because the sensible thing to do would be to keep his mouth shut, Jarrett replied, "What's it matter to you?"

The look of shock on his uncle's face was almost worth it. He'd likely never been spoken to so directly before in his life and certainly not by a mere servant.

Even if the rest of his family despised him, there still might be some decency left in Charles, because he cleared his throat of what sounded suspiciously like a choked laugh and said, "Here now, there's no reason for any of us to be uncivil. Surely there's something about that in the Bible, Minister?"

Minister MacLennan was happy to regale them all with a few verses he found pertinent, pouring oil on troubled waters, at least for the moment.

"...but I think it's best said in Romans, 'Let us therefore make every effort to do what leads to peace and to mutual edification.'"

"Very edifying, indeed. Thank you, Minister." Gil did his best to make their exit then, but was pulled up short by Magistrate Carnbee.

"I'm sure your uncle is only concerned with your wellbeing, Mr. Charleton. Considering the company you have decided to keep, I'd say we're all concerned. Good that it won't be for much longer."

Jarrett gave a sharp intake of breath, inaudible to anyone else, but it made Gil want to knock the moustache from Carnbee's smug face. Instead he painted his smile even wider.

"Indeed? You're close to catching the real killer then?"

Carnbee's answering smile was vicious. "I'd say I'm close enough to touch him. He's not nearly as smart as he thinks he is, despite his ability to pull the wool over some people's eyes. It's as well you're out and about. I've dispatched several constables to search for further evidence and would hate for you to be inconvenienced."

Even knowing there was no way the constables would find the clothes in their new hiding place, a frisson of fear ran down Gil's spine. If they hadn't gone out to the shed last night...

But they had. That was what mattered. Carnbee's men would find nothing.

"Very civil of you to be so concerned, Magistrate," Jarrett said, and from the looks on the other's faces, Gil wasn't the only one who wanted to throttle him. How had he forgotten even for a moment how damned reckless Jarrett was?

Lighting the oil on those troubled waters, Jarrett added, "And what a clever idea. Was it given to you or did you come up with it yourself?"

"I will not be discussing any information pertinent to this crime with the man suspected of it," Carnbee huffed. "Nor any of his proponents."

"Which reminds me," Gil interrupted, before Jarrett said anything worse. "Some of Mr. Welch's personal items were not returned to him at the tolbooth. We were told they may have been sent on to you. Would there be a good time to collect them? As you say, he is only suspected of the crime and those items are rightfully his."

That seemed to catch Carnbee off guard. "What items?"

"Mere trinkets, a few coins and the like," said Gil, hoping Jarrett wasn't going to openly accuse the magistrate of stealing his money. "Nothing of real value, but his property nonetheless."

"I'd hardly bother myself with such things. If they're anywhere, they'd be with the body and the rest of the evidence. You're free to look, since you've taken so many other liberties already."

Lord, how had a man so stupid risen to such an important position? If Jarrett was the killer, Carnbee had all but invited them to go ahead and do away with any inconvenient evidence. Granted, they were already planning on doing something very similar by taking the coat, but he hadn't expected to be *invited* to do it.

"The poor man hasn't yet received a proper burial?" Minister MacLennan cried.

"Mr. Boyd assured me that the storeroom at the inn is sufficiently cold to keep him preserved for some time. There is no rush to bury him when an identification might still be made and family found to cover funeral costs."

Charles laughed. "I'm sure old Marta loves that. You think she's charging a penny a peep? I'll bet she is and I'll go double or nothing that Robert's already been."

"Charles," rebuked Uncle Andrew. "We do not discuss such vile things and we certainly do not stoop to placing such crass wagers."

"Does that mean you don't want me to cover your penny, Father? I see no reason to pretend the entire Charleton House isn't interested in the case." Charles inclined his head towards Gil. "Some more than others."

"Charles!" The baron snapped again. "Cease this. And Gilleasbuig, isn't there something you wish to say to Magistrate Carnbee?"

His uncle's order to apologise to the magistrate mingled with his father's threats of what would happen if he didn't. Gil's cheek tingled from the memory of the slap. It would be the sensible thing to do, even if he had no intention of following it up by forcing Jarrett to go anywhere near the tolbooth again. A few pretty words to smooth things and they could be on their way.

Jarrett's fingers brushed against his, the touch too small to have been noticed by the others, but it must have infected Gil with some of his recklessness, because Gil found himself much more inclined to consign that pompous arse to the Devil, standing on sacred ground or not.

Instead, he found a compromise.

"I do apologise, Magistrate Carnbee. It seems we have taken up valuable time best spent on more important matters. The issue of the new pews is a most serious one. We'll leave you to your work, taxing though it must be."

With that, he grabbed Jarrett by the arm and pulled him away. "Good day, gentlemen!"

As soon as they stepped into the Kinneuchar Inn, Marta went for her cudgel.

Gil raised his hands, for all the good it would do. Marta wasn't a woman known for her mercy. If it came to a fight, Gil wouldn't come away with anything other than a pair of broken arms.

"It's all right, Marta. I'll vouch for him."

That made Marta pause, although she still had a hand below the bar.

"And I'll buy a round for everyone?" Gil tried.

That seemed to please her well enough, although she still scowled at Jarrett before turning to her task.

Much to Gil's relief, the inn was nearly empty, save for a couple of old farmers sitting in the corner and considering the early hour, they were only drinking small beer. He startled at a touch to his back.

Jarrett whispered in his ear, just barely enough distance between them to be decent. "Would it be better if I just stayed at Balcarres? I can see I'm more than a bit of trouble to take out."

Gil gave him an incredulous look. "You have a wonderful gift of understatement."

He hadn't meant it as a compliment, but Jarrett still looked pleased. "I can, though, if it's too much bother. Our room's far better than a cell, and as long as Mr. Howe is willing to crack the door every few hours to drop off a fresh bottle and take the empty, I can amuse myself well enough until you return."

And once Gil returned, they had a whole new set of options for amusements.

"No, it's fine," Gil replied. "Everyone already knows what I've done, so I doubt they'd treat me much better whether you're here or not."

It probably wasn't true. There was no denying the way, well, everyone had reacted to Jarrett's presence since his arrest. Despite that, the idea of swapping one cell for another, even one in a house as grand as Balcarres, didn't sit well with him. Besides, surely it was safer for Jarrett to be where Gil could keep an eye on him, for his own safety more than any else's.

Gil leaned back into Jarrett's touch. Hell, he was giving himself too much credit. He wanted Jarrett around because Gil liked being around *him*. The sooner he admitted that fact, the better.

"Go warm yourself by the fire," he said. "I'll see if Marta is willing to let us down to the cellar."

Jarrett nodded. "Be careful. The inquest was in her inn, remember? She heard everything you said. And if my key was here, it wouldn't have taken her two seconds to go get it."

That wasn't worrying at all, and exactly the sort of thing Gil needed to be thinking about as he set out to charm the dragon queen.

He squared his shoulders and armed himself with his most powerful weapon for the battle ahead, flattery.

"You haven't made up any oatcakes today, have you, Marta? I passed on breakfast solely on the blind hope you might. They say one oatcake's as good as any other, but I'd swear yours are the best I've ever had. You put something extra in them, don't you? Go on, you can tell me. It'll be our secret."

She was still scowling, but not nearly as much as before. That was a start.

"Allow me," he said, taking a tray loaded with small beers from her hands and delivering it to the men in the corner. By the time he returned, there was a plate of oatcakes and a jar of potted cheese sitting ready. Only enough for him and not Jarrett, but one step at a time.

"It's got a bit of Old Tanner's brew in it," she said, nodding towards the cheese. "Gives it flavour. What's in the oatcakes is my business."

It wasn't difficult to wax lyrical over the breakfast, even as he felt Jarrett's glare from across the room. By the time he'd made his way through a second oatcake, Marta had her elbows on the bar and was gossiping gaily.

"...and I'm sure you know what I said to that! Aye, but it is hard finding good lodgers to be sure. She shouldn't be blaming herself. There's a lot worse she could do." This was said with a pointed look in Jarrett's direction.

"Speaking of which, how's your lodger?" asked Gil, tilting his head towards the cellar door.

Marta grinned. "Quieter than most, and that's a relief. Keeps to himself mostly and doesn't hassle the cleaning girl. I wish more men were like him. But he still gives me a start every time

I go down there. He's still fresh enough or I'd be telling that Carnbee to keep the damn thing in his cupboard and see how he likes it. Unnatural it is, to keep a body around like that."

Gil leaned in conspiratorially. "Ah, but does he pay his rent?"

Marta leaned in as well. "He does indeed. I asked Carnbee to cover some of it, but the old miser said it was my duty to put the poor sod up, free of charge. That said, I couldn't tell you the last time we had a murder here, and there's plenty willing to pay for a look. He's certainly a popular fellow. There's not a man in the county who's had more callers!"

Gil laughed. "How much do I owe you then? For the breakfast, the beers, and... paying a call?"

"Can't do the last I'm afraid. All calls must be chaperoned by myself and I've no one else in to man the bar this morning. That's my stock down there too, and I can't be having any callers throwing their own parties! Not that I'm saying you would, but you know I can't show favourites."

Marta pursed her lips and tapped the top of the bar directly above where the cudgel was stored. "You give an inch with this lot... I even had one aim to get around the visiting price! Tried to sneak in after hours. Didn't get a look at him, but if my legs were just a wee bit longer he'd have tasted my cudgel. And before I started paying close attention, folks were chipping bits for themselves off that rock that done the man in. Now what are you going to do with a bit of bloody rock?"

"Myself? Absolutely nothing. But an enterprising woman of business? I'd say at least a sixpence an ounce."

She snorted, and tallied up his bill. As he counted out the coins, she added, "Ach, go on then. It'll be a penny to pay your respects."

He handed her two.

She pursed her lips and looked from Gil to Jarrett, expression souring even further. He was worried he'd overplayed his hand, but eventually she relented. "Go on then. I suppose he can't kill the poor sod twice!"

Neither Gil nor Jarrett wanted to spend any more time with the body than was necessary, especially as it wasn't nearly as fresh as Marta implied. If they didn't discover the man's identity within a day or two, Gil might need to bend the minister's ear, or failing him, the doctor.

The body was laid out on boards across two large barrels, one of them worryingly tapped and Gil was glad he'd forgone a drink. Then he saw that the shelf the dead man's feet were propped on was lined with familiar looking jars of potted cheese.

He pressed a hand to his now churning stomach. "Are any of your things down here?"

"No," Jarrett replied immediately. He was digging through a crate by the victim's head. "Not a shilling. Fucking Carnbee."

"We don't know he was the one to take them," Gil offered, but Jarrett sneered.

"No fucking key either, but we knew that already. Let's go."

"But what about the coat, is there a hole in it or not? There should be, since there's one in the shirt, but I'd have sworn there wasn't."

"I don't know!" Jarrett snapped. "And it's too damn dark down here to see. Can we go?"

Too dark. The walls of the cellar were packed earth and little light came down from the inn above. Marta had given them a single candle to light their way, but it was of cheap tallow, only lighting a few feet in any direction, the flame sputtering and smoking and ready to go out any minute, leaving them in darkness. Jarrett had left lamps burning both nights they'd been together. Gil considered himself reasonably intelligent, but he'd failed to consider that perhaps a man who was clearly uncomfortable in the dark might not want to venture down into a cellar containing a dead body with only a single, unreliable source of light.

In the dark, Jarrett's eyes were large. "Please?"

"Right, of course. Let's—no, wait a moment. Just a moment, I swear."

Gil grabbed the balled-up mess of a coat, flattening it as best he could. "Your coat's looser than mine. Can you?"

Within a few seconds, they'd tucked the dead man's coat down the back of Jarrett's own. It was reasonably well hidden, even if Jarrett now looked more hunchbacked than he had when they'd arrived.

"It'll have to do," Gil decided, noticing the way Jarrett was shifting restlessly from foot to foot, his eyes locked on the patch of light at the top of the stairs. "Just try to leave as quickly as you can without drawing attention. I'll keep Marta distracted."

"Aye, you're good at that. Too good."

Before Gil could ask what that meant, Jarrett was tearing up the stairs.

So much for not drawing attention.

CHAPTER 18

G etting the coat out of the inn without anyone noticing was easier than Jarrett expected. Or perhaps it hadn't been, perhaps Gil fought their way out with his bare hands. Jarrett wouldn't have noticed, he was too focused on just getting out of the cellar before the walls closed in around him, trapping him in the dark with a corpse.

But now they were back outside, with the inn and cellar both lost in the fog behind them, and the dead man's coat an awkward lump against his spine. The fog was still just as thick as it'd been before, but he could feel a breeze against his face. It was an even chance whether that meant the fog would be lifting soon, or blowing in even thicker.

"So, where now?" he asked, chewing one of the oatcakes Gil had snuck into his pocket for him. It was plain, but considering all the months of Janie's cooking, it was easily the best breakfast he'd had in a long time.

"I'd like to get a look at it where there won't be anyone around."

Well, obviously. Jarrett wasn't about to waft out their stolen evidence in the middle of a county lane, fog or no fog. "Not Balcarres then. Unless you want me to hand it right over to Carnbee's men and myself alongside it."

"No."

Jarrett didn't want to think about what would happen if the constables actually managed to find where they'd ended up hiding the bloody knife and clothes after moving them from the shed. But even that bastard Carnbee would hesitate to command his way into an earl's home without a solid reason. Besides, even if he did, Balcarres was vast. Jarrett still got lost in it sometimes and even Gil, who'd been in and out of it their whole lives, might have trouble finding that exact room again, and he knew where to look.

"Not Charleton House either," mused Jarrett. "Your brother said something about a horse whip last time. I don't want to find out if he meant it."

Gil sighed. "I almost hate to mention it, but there is one place we know is secluded…"

"You can't be serious."

Half an hour later, Jarrett found himself climbing a familiar path through the woods, the fog slowly parting to reveal the ruins of the chapel.

"Do you think it's safe?" he asked.

Gil shrugged, but he had a look Jarrett recognised from horses. He wasn't quite about to bolt, but he was certainly putting on a show of being more at ease than he was. An unwary rider could easily get thrown if they weren't paying attention.

"It hasn't fallen down yet. I doubt it will today. Or do you mean from spirits? If the dead man's ghost is here, surely he'll see we're trying to help him and leave us to our business."

If ever there was a day for spirits to roam, it was a day like today. Jarrett tried not to think of ghostly figures in the fog.

"I meant, is it safe not to be at Balcarres while the magistrate's men are there?"

"They won't find the clothes." Gil said firmly. Jarrett envisioned a horse nervously sidestepping as he said it.

A sudden thought chilled him in a way that had nothing to do with the weather. "But what if they find something else? We didn't search our room, what if there's something in there?"

"I don't think that's likely," Gil said with far less conviction. "Anyone with the stolen key could have gotten in the shed without being seen, but Mr. Howe has the house itself locked up tight. We know the best ways to sneak in because we belong there, but there's no way an outsider could find their way in without the alarm being raised."

An icy touch curled under Jarrett's collar and he had to tell himself it was only the fog. "An outsider couldn't, aye, but what if the killer belongs too?"

The idea there was a murderer running free was bad enough, but to think they'd been sleeping in the same house as him—or her—was enough to raise the hairs on his neck.

"I... don't know," Gil said haltingly. "I'd like to think not but... But all right, let's say it is. Who do you have in mind?"

Jarrett shook his head. "I haven't been there long enough to say for certain. Davey found the body, but he'd been gone with his father. Besides, he's far too wee to lift a stone like that. I'd say the same for Janie, but I wouldn't be willing to wager on it."

"Her method of murder would be poisoning, not stabbing." It was a poor jest and they both knew it. Gil raised a hand before Jarrett could protest. "My apologies. I will say though, that if she is the killer, the stage lost a rare talent. I'd certainly believe she's terrified.

"So, as Davey and his father were gone the night of the murder, that rules Graham out as well. What about Mr. Howe?"

Jarrett pursed his lips. "I wouldn't want to think it. He's always been kind to me. Before all this I mean. Mrs. Finley either. But..."

"But."

They were both silent after that. A month ago, Jarrett would have said the woman was far too gentle to do anything of the sort, a true embrace-all-with-open-arms sort. Now it seemed you could never really tell with anyone, no matter how long you'd known them.

He hadn't been back to the chapel since the day they'd found the body. How could he have been? He'd spent most of that time locked away underground. Looking around now, it didn't look any different. Rain had washed away any traces of the blood, and the grass under the body had sprung back into shape. There was no sign anything terrible had ever happened. It didn't seem right. There should be some sign that things had changed forever.

Gil took off his spectacles and wiped them.

"If it's any comfort," Gil said finally. "If one of the household is the killer and has left something for the constables to find, it's unlikely we'd be able to find it first even if we were there."

"That's very comforting, thank you," Jarrett said drily. "What about Marta?"

Gil frowned. "How could she—Oh, I see. I suppose I wouldn't put a murder past her. I've never seen her cudgel in action but—"

"I have," Jarrett interrupted. "It would've been hard to get away from the inn without being missed long enough to do it, but she's certainly strong enough. Might not have used the rock at all, could have brought the cudgel along and left the rock behind so we wouldn't think it was her."

Gil added, "And she had access to your key."

Jarrett nodded. It made a frightening amount of sense. "And the inquest was at her pub, so we know she heard everything, including about my shed. You shouldn't have rushed so quick to get her to let us in the cellar. A few more minutes of offering yourself up like that and you could've got a hand up her skirt. I bet she'd admit to all sorts of crimes then."

Gil spluttered. "I'm not sure who should be more offended, Marta or myself. And I wasn't offering myself up, like some persons I might name, I was being charming. There's a difference."

Jarrett shrugged. He couldn't be offended by Gil's words, likely because they were true. And he'd started it. Seeing Gil charm Marta so easily had bothered him though. Likely just because things always came so easily for people like Gil and went so poorly for people like Jarrett.

"If you say so. At least I follow through on my promises." Jarrett shook his shoulders. "Christ, this thing is damned heavy. This coat better have the name of the victim stitched into the collar and the killer's initials on the sleeves."

He began to wriggle then, the movement so undignified, especially considering the circumstances, that Gil began to chuckle.

"Fuck you, it's too cold to unbutton," Jarrett laughed. "Come help me."

"The valet can't handle his own coat?" Gil replied, but came over to help anyway.

As soon as Gil got his hands under his coat, however, Jarrett couldn't help but remember the feel of those same hands on him the night before. The firmness of Gil's touch as he stroked him, the surety of his hand on Jarrett's hip as if it belonged there.

He leaned into Gil's touch shamelessly.

"Stop that," Gil hissed.

Jarrett rolled his eyes, but pushed his shoulders back in a way that loosened his own coat just enough for Gil to yank the victim's coat out from underneath.

"It's not like anyone is going to see. Who'd be daft enough to come up to the chapel on a day like today besides us?"

"That's not the point," Gil chided. "You're a damned distraction."

They had more immediate concerns, but Gil was clearly flustered just by getting his hands up another man's coat out-of-doors. How strange to see the difference a locked door made. Jarrett couldn't resist giving Gil a coy look through his lashes, snickering when Gil pointedly forced his attention back to the coat. He held it at arm's length while Jarrett got himself back to rights.

After turning it this way and that, Gil said, "We were right. No hole in the coat. No blood either. Or, a bit on the sleeve but that's all."

"He took it off before being stabbed then. Another point against Marta. Or Janie or Mrs. Finley, I suppose. There's only one reason a man comes up here to the chapel and starts taking off his clothes when it's that cold."

Gil raised an eyebrow at him. "Bring a lot of *women* up here then, do you? Just because he didn't want to come up here with you doesn't mean he didn't come up here with another man."

Jarrett was offended.

"He wouldn't have gotten better," he sniffed. "And look where he ended up. Should have known a good thing when he saw it."

Gil didn't respond to that. He was too busy raising and lowering the coat like he was weighing it.

Now that he thought about it, it had been heavier than Jarrett would've expected. Bulkier too. Not that a full woollen greatcoat was ever going to be small or light. If the overcoat he'd grabbed off the peg in the kitchen at Balcarres hadn't been sized to fit the likes of Graham as well as himself they'd never have been able to smuggle it out of the inn.

Gil paused with his weighing, head cocked as something on the inside of the coat caught his eye. As Jarrett watched, he stuck a finger into a small tear in the seam and began to fish around inside.

"What have you got there?" Jarrett asked, coming to stand at his shoulder.

Gil tore the seam a little more and was able to get a second finger in and grasp something between them. When he pulled it out, it shone with the unmistakable lustre of new gold.

"Christ, is that a sovereign?" Jarrett ran a finger over the coin reverently. "I've never seen one before."

"Me neither." Gil swallowed. "They only started minting them, what, a year ago? Two? You can only get them at banks."

"They certainly aren't being used to purchase sheep. Not around here at least. Are there any more?"

Gil tore the lining even more. This time when he reached in, he pulled out a sheaf of bank notes. They were folded sharply, crisp in a way that meant they hadn't yet passed through many hands. He unfolded them and jerked his head back, nearly causing his spectacles to tumble from his head.

"What is it?" Jarrett asked. "How much are they worth?"

Gil told him.

Jarrett whistled, the sound echoing eerily off the bare stone of the chapel. "Well. I think we know why he was murdered."

Gil dug out another sovereign coin and handed it over. Then another.

Jarrett held one out admiringly. Balcarres House was filled with all sorts of overwrought bits of finery, but there was something about a solid gold coin that made it seem especially valuable. Perhaps the way it could be slipped into a pocket so easily.

Just one of these coins would give him a good head start if he had to run. And it was starting to look more and more like he would. He'd wait a little longer just to see if they really could catch the real murderer, and he'd like to get in another round with Gil before he left, but it couldn't hurt to be prepared. Perhaps he should go ahead and get started now...

The hand holding the coin twitched towards his waistcoat pocket, but then he stopped. Gil was an overseer. He counted money for a living. No doubt he'd been tallying every sovereign in his head as it came out. He'd notice immediately if one was missing. Better to wait.

Jarrett held the coin out again. Then he frowned. "He went to the bother of making the dead man strip off his coat before stabbing him. Why leave a coat full of money and take the bloody clothes?"

"That's a damned good question. Perhaps the killer didn't know the money was in there."

"Then why kill him?"

Gil didn't seem to have an answer for him. He just continued to pull money from the hole in the lining. In the end, he pulled out eight more sovereigns, each wadded between several bank notes. He handed them over to Jarrett as he counted.

"Well? What's the total?" Jarrett asked.

"Between paper and coin, just over two hundred pounds."

Jarrett choked and his hands clenched tightly around the money.

"We're going to have to return them when we return the coat," Gil said warningly. "They're evidence."

"All of them?" Jarrett breathed. At Gil's look he sighed. "Fine. All of them. It's a damned shame though. We both know Carnbee's only going to keep them for himself."

"You're probably right, but still, it's the right thing to do."

The Devil with that. I'm not letting Carnbee get away with stealing my sixpence. You think I'm going to let him steal two hundred pounds?

But since Gil was the only one who believed he wasn't a murderer, he probably shouldn't let him wonder if Jarrett was planning on being a thief instead, never mind that it was Gil who had the idea to steal the coat. So Jarrett just forced a laugh and said, "Better if you hold onto them for now then. But it'll be worth it to see the look on the face of the murderer when we catch him. Imagine stealing all those bloody clothes and not knowing this was sitting right beside them all along!"

Gil handed the coat over to Jarrett, then started wrapping the coins in his handkerchief. The dead man was smart to wrap them in the bills to keep them from rattling.

"I don't know what else there is to learn," Gil said. "Although the sovereigns might be a clue. They certainly didn't come from here. I'll write again to my contacts in Edinburgh, St. Andrews, even Dundee. Have them go to the banks and see if anyone who looked like the victim took out a great deal of money, partially in gold sovereigns. I'm sure that's the sort of thing even the most jaded bank teller would remember."

For the first time, Jarrett began to wonder if this plan to catch the real killer might actually work. All they'd need was one gossipy clerk and they'd have the stranger's name. And with a name, they could find out so much more. There was no lawful reason a man needed to be carrying around that sort of money. That meant he was involved in the sorts of things that could make a man enemies. Enemies who could be willing to kill. All they needed was a name and they could find their killer. Or at least, find enough to put doubt into the mind of a jury.

He'd been trying to push down his hope. From the start, he'd known it'd be hard to prove he was innocent of murder without proving he was guilty of other things. Once they found the clothes hidden in his shed, he'd been terrified it might be impossible.

He wasn't going to let down his guard; the moment it looked like anyone was even thinking of taking him back to that fucking gaol he was gone. Better to live looking over your shoulder than dead from a stretched neck.

"Jarrett, this is good," Gil said, tucking the coins away. "This is really, really good. With any luck we'll have our answer within the fortnight. Long before the judge is due. Perhaps even within the week if he was an Edinburgh man!"

Gil began sorting the banknotes, Jarrett assumed by value, smoothing out creased corners and tapping their edges so they lined up neatly.

While he did, Jarrett examined the coat again, more carefully now. It might be the very thing that saved him, it should be treated with care.

"I found some lost buttons and lace when I came up here on my own," Gil said. "Any belong to our dead man?"

Jarrett looked it over. No missing buttons that he could see, but he wasn't going to take anything for granted. Carnbee had missed two hundred fucking pounds in this coat, he wouldn't be surprised if he'd missed a confession from the killer stuck into the sleeve.

No such luck.

He checked the pockets. No sixpences or keys to be stolen, or anything useful. A twig seemed to have gotten in one when it'd been lying on the ground, draped over the body. Jarrett tugged on it to toss it out. Part of it crumbled in his hand, and all his hopes came crashing down.

He'd been wrong. He'd been terribly, terribly wrong. And he was going to hang for it.

"Jarrett?"

Gil's worried voice came to him. He was closer now than he'd been a moment ago. When had he moved? His eyes shone with worry from only a few feet away and he was reaching out, almost touching Jarrett, but not quite, as if he wasn't sure if Jarrett was going to run or kick. Jarrett wasn't sure himself.

Jarrett swallowed heavily. "I was wrong. It's a common style, every house in Scotland must have one, but I was certain. Of course, I was. It was there when we found him."

"I don't know what you're talking about." Gil said softly. He reached out again, one hand resting gently on Jarrett's arm.

"I thought this was his coat," said Jarrett. "The dead man's. But it's not. It's his murderer's."

Gil's eyes widened. "How can you be certain?"

Jarrett's mouth was dry.

"Because I know where it came from."

Then he pulled his hand out of the pocket. The twig was from a common plant, one that he recognised less by touch than by smell. Gil would recognise it too. He'd have found similar ones dozens of times before, in his boots, under his pillows, in his own coat pockets.

Jarrett closed his fist around the dried sprig of lavender, and the smell that rose from it was the smell of Charleton House, Gil's home, and Gil's family.

CHAPTER 19

The sight of the lavender had Gil reaching for his own pockets. How many times had he been jabbed under the nail by a sharp stem or plucked dozens of the tiny blooms out of his clothing?

The sprigs turning up unexpectedly had been a lifelong annoyance. This one was far worse.

"Steady," Jarrett said, in the same tone he likely used on his damned horses. "This mightn't mean what you think it does."

"I don't know what I'm thinking." Gil's words were lies, but so were Jarrett's. He knew exactly what he was thinking and despite what Jarrett said, he knew there was no chance he was wrong.

The coat was the murderer's, not the victim's. It was the only thing that made sense. And that same coat had hundreds of pounds hidden in its lining and a sprig of lavender tucked into a pocket to keep it fresh. The coat, *the killer's coat*, had come from Charleton House. As much as he might want the murderer to be Carnbee, or Mr. Howe, or even bloody Marta, it was someone much closer.

"M-my family," he stuttered out.

He felt warm hands closing around his elbows, then found himself being walked backwards and seated on a hunk of rock, likely a broken tombstone for one so long dead that time had erased their name from the stone.

"Steady," murmured Jarrett again. "It might not be one of them. Could be a servant. You know what we're like. Can't trust a one of us."

The jest was weak, but Jarrett carried on, his grip on Gil's elbows more comforting than it should have been. "It could be a servant. You remember that Carnbee thought I stole the dead man's clothes to sell? It happens more often than you'd think. Perhaps the old *gowk* had the right reasons, but the wrong man. You think anyone in your family would know the first thing about washing blood out of clothes or mending knife holes? That's servant's work. I doubt you'd see your mother trying to sell second-hand clothes down the pawnbrokers. See? It's bad, but not so bad as you think it is."

A vision of his mother appeared before him like Lady MacBeth rubbing at spots of blood that wouldn't come out, and a dagger only she could see.

He pulled off his spectacles and wiped them, dispelling the vision. Jarrett released him and stepped back, giving him room. When Gil slid the spectacles back on, no cleaner than they were before, he saw several tiny flowers clinging to his coat where Jarrett had held him, left there by the crushed sprig still in his hand.

He knocked them from his sleeve like they were hot embers that could burn him if left a moment more.

"It's not a servant," he said at last. "Where would a servant get two hundred pounds? Those sovereigns could only have come from a bank. A proper one, not some box club or something run by the grocer. You think Cook has an account at Coutts?"

Jarrett didn't have a response to that and Gil didn't know what else to say. Someone in his family had killed a man. Lured him to the chapel, stabbed him in the back, and crushed his skull with a rock. Then they'd sat at the breakfast table with Gil the next day as if nothing had happened.

He watched dully as Jarrett tucked what was left of the lavender back into the coat and folded it neatly.

Perhaps it was a coincidence. Perhaps half the households in Scotland were overrun with lavender turning up in pockets and pillows. Perhaps it had nothing to do with his family at all. Never mind that the killer had to be someone close enough to get the key from the inn and hide the clothes in Jarrett's shed.

He dropped his head into his hands. It wasn't a coincidence.

He didn't know how long he stayed that way, wallowing in the fear, betrayal, and misery of their discovery before Jarrett cleared his throat.

"You can say 'no'," Jarrett started, which was rarely a good sign. "But seeing as it's best we don't go back to my shed for a bit, or Balcarres at all, for that matter, and certainly not Charleton House, and seeing how no one else is going to be traipsing about in this fog, I wonder if you might want to take advantage of the weather and do a bit of stargazing?"

Gil looked at him blankly, then pointedly turned his face upwards to where the noon sun was only a dull blur of brightness in the thick fog.

"No, *stargazing*," Jarrett said pointedly. "I told you before, when I didn't have any better options, I'd invite men up here to *stargaze*. I can't—I'm sorry. I only knew my mam, and we haven't spoken since I left. But I can't imagine how I'd feel if I thought she'd done something like this. I can't fix what you're feeling now about your family, but... I can take your mind off it for a while?"

Jarrett was watching him with something so earnest in his expression that Gil wasn't sure he'd seen it before. It didn't quite suit his sharp features, but neither did the nervousness that had him shifting from foot to foot. It was that, more than anything else, that finally made him realise what the hell Jarrett was talking about.

Stargazing.

The act—or acts—that Jarrett did in dark alleys with strangers and Gil did in private rooms with men he considered friends. What they'd been about to do in the shed, and what Jarrett had done with him in their shared bed, his hand firm and his lips so soft against Gil's own. There was a lyrical quality to the euphemism, a beauty that belied what Jarrett was offering now: a hard fuck against a decaying wall. Rough, meaningless, and out in the open where God and any untimely passerby could see.

Gil would never do anything so reckless. It was a terrible idea. Not the least because Jarrett preferred his fucks anonymous, men he'd never have to see again. Apparently, he didn't count hands alone as sex, since he hadn't tried to run from Gil after last night, but Gil only had sex with men he liked, and God help him, he liked Jarrett. Liked him more with every minute he spent in the man's company. Liked him so much, he wasn't sure that if he had Jarrett once, he'd be able to face never having him again.

Perhaps he might've when Jarrett had invited him to the shed, somewhere soft and safe that they could be together. But what he was proposing now? It was bold, foolhardy, and without any thought to the possible consequences in the face of immediate pleasure.

It was, in a word, Jarrett.

"All right."

Jarrett looked as surprised by his agreement as Gil was. "All right?"

"Aye, all right." Gil said again. "You've done this here before, where do you want me? Under a chapel window or bent over a tombstone?"

Jarrett wrinkled his nose. "I usually go around the back, outside against the wall. I know it's not still a chapel really, but I'd rather not do anything inside and be wrathfully struck down with my trousers around my ankles. Truly, you want to?"

Gil answered that by getting to his feet, grasping Jarrett's face in his hands, and kissing him until all doubts vanished. He hadn't actually known how much he wanted this until Jarrett's mouth opened under his with a soft sigh. As Gil deepened the kiss, losing himself in the sensation of Jarrett's tongue sinuously stroking his, he had the thought that his family could go to the Devil. Then there were no more thoughts, only need.

Finally, the need for air overcame all others and they broke apart. Jarrett looked dazed, but he still gave Gil that fox-like grin, the one that made his teeth a bit too sharp, then took him by the hand and dragged him out of the chapel and around to the back.

He nearly lost his footing in a tangle of weeds, but Jarrett caught him, laughing. Then they reached the back of the chapel. There were fewer graves back here, only a pair of broken columns side-by-side, and woods crept closer than they did to the front. It made the space feel less illicit somehow, more right, with the sheltering leaves reaching over them, and the fog softening all the edges. It was still a fuck against a wall though, nothing could change that.

Reaching the wall in question, he suddenly felt awkward. "How do you usually—"

Jarrett put a finger against his lips. "You think too much."

Then he pushed him back against the wall, following with his body. Gil had had to focus to keep from cracking his skull against the stone. He was usually shorter than the men he was with, not that it mattered much when they were both in a bed, so it was a novelty to angle his head down to kiss, seeing the jut of Jarrett's jaw as he leaned up to meet him. His body fit perfectly against Gil's too, slim body stretching as he reached up to wrap his arms around Gil's shoulders, greatcoat too large for his body and billowing around them, cocooning Gil in their shared warmth, making this feel safer than it was.

But he didn't *want* safe. He wanted Jarrett.

He bit down on one of those plump lips to hear Jarrett gasp, then sucked it hard, hoping it would bruise. It should bruise. It would be fair punishment for all the times he'd made Gil stutter and lose his train of thought just by using those damned lips to speak to him! How dare he. Months of questions about the weather, or would he like tea, or no, the earl wasn't in but he could wait in the study if he'd like. All with those damned distracting lips.

Jarrett responded by threading his fingers into Gil's hair and twisting, sending sparks skittering down Gil's spine. That felt too good. Gil said he kept his hair long because it was just easier that way, but in truth he loved nothing more than the feel of someone running their fingers through it. Gently or roughly, both sensations were exquisite. Jarrett seemed to have chosen "roughly", yanking the tie from Gil's hair and tugging again, pulling the groan out of Gil.

He felt the grin of those sharp teeth against his lips.

"Like that, aye?" Jarrett whispered, and tugged again. He followed that up by raking his nails down Gil's scalp. "Well?"

"Don't—Ah!—Expect an answer if you're going to be a damned distraction."

Jarrett chuckled, sliding a leg between Gil's own. His cock pressed against Gil's thigh, and even through two layers of buckskins, Gil could tell he was hard.

So was he. With some men it would be whole evenings of foreplay and kisses, before Gil was ready to move on. No one had ever affected him the way Jarrett did. Lord, he'd been hard since Jarrett led him around the wall. No, before that, since he'd realised what Jarrett meant by "stargazing". And if Jarrett kept rolling his hips against his in that dangerous way, this would be over embarrassingly quickly. He put his hands on Jarrett's waist, meaning to push him back so he could get distance enough to *think*, but was immediately distracted by how far his hands wrapped around. His calluses caught on Jarrett's waistcoat as he squeezed, trying to see if he could stretch his fingers just a little bit further...

Jarrett took advantage of his distraction—of course, he did—and wedged his thigh more firmly between Gil's own, shifting the angle so their pricks rubbed against each other. The fabric against his sensitive skin was hell. It was bliss.

Jarrett wrapped his fingers in Gil's hair, pulling as he rose up on his tiptoes to press his lips to Gil's ear. The move was more for show than anything, Gil wasn't *that* much taller than he was, but God, what a show.

His whole body rose up against Gil's, a tight wall of pure sin to his front to match the crumbling wall of the chapel to his back. Jarrett's nose bumped against the stem of his spectacles, knocking them askew.

"How would you like it?" Jarrett whispered. Gil had to bite his lip to keep from keening as Jarrett's hot breath tickled against his ear. Then Jarrett, damn him, nipped his ear lobe. Gil keened.

"We can keep going like this," Jarrett continued. "Or we can use hands, like last night. Or," he nipped again, "I can use my mouth."

Lord, the thought of that was almost enough to end things then and there. The thought of Jarrett on his knees at Gil's feet, looking up at him with those lush lips wrapped around Gil's cock, his throat hot and tight as Gil thrust in again and again.

His hips bucked and he clawed himself back from the brink only by thinking how many men had already gotten to see that, had gotten to have what he hadn't and hadn't fucking *appreciated* it.

He let out a long unsteady breath.

"Well?" Jarrett asked.

Gil didn't care how many men had been with Jarrett before, he was the one with him *now*.

"I want you to fuck me."

Jarrett tugged his hair, playfully this time. "I know, sweetheart. I'm asking how."

"No, that's how. I want you to fuck me."

Jarrett stilled. Finally he said, "Perhaps in your locked rooms you can take your time and spit's enough, but like this, it isn't. Trust me. Anything else you want though."

Gil could feel his cheeks turning red. He just hoped Jarrett was too close to see it. "I have oil."

Jarrett, who'd begun kissing his way along Gil's jaw, stilled again. "You what?"

"I have oil. In my pocket. I—All right, damn it, when we were emptying the clothes from your shed, I removed it because I was afraid it was incriminating. And then I kept it because, well, because I was hopeful."

Jarrett was silent a long while.

"I didn't even think about the oil," he whispered. Then he shook himself. "You were hopeful?"

Gil reluctantly released Jarrett's waist and fumbled for his pocket, pulling out the small bottle.

Jarrett laughed, the sound loud in his ear, then put his palms against Gil's chest for leverage and pushed himself back, snatching the bottle as he went. "Hope should be rewarded."

With that, he began to unfasten his breeches. As much as he wanted to, and he desperately wanted to, Gil couldn't watch. They'd spent too long out here already; it was far too dangerous to risk another round. Once he spent, he was done. And if that happened before he got Jarrett's cock in him, he'd never forgive himself.

He turned to face the wall, unbuttoning his trousers with shaking fingers, and cursing when he then had to deal with drawers as well. Glancing left and right one final time to make sure no one was around, he lowered them slightly, only to feel the material of his coat in the way. Usually so practical, the damn thing was now a decided inconvenience. He tried flicking it to the side, but it didn't work.

"This is more complicated than you made it sound," he grumbled.

Jarrett only laughed.

With one hand at a time on his breeches, Gil shrugged his coat off, hearing it land somewhere in the grass. He lowered his breeches again, just a few inches, his skin immediately pebbling in the cold air.

He shivered. "Is this enough? Or do you need more?" He pushed them down a little further. Obviously, he knew the mechanics of the act, but that didn't mean he wanted to have breeches sliding down around his ankles if he could help it.

He heard a sharp inhale from behind him and risked a glance over his shoulder. Jarrett had undone his fall and was gripping his cock in his hand tightly, too tightly, the shining head almost painfully red where it peeked from its sheath.

"Christ Gil, you're going to kill me. Stop thinking so much. Rest your arms against the wall and spread your legs. They'll stay up naturally."

Gil did as he was told. For a moment, nothing happened and the anticipation heightened his arousal even further. How must he look? Breeches down, shirt pushed up around his waist, arse bare, and a man standing somewhere behind him, waiting to fuck him. And nothing but the fog and the solitude of the place to keep them from being seen.

He heard the pop of the cork being removed from the bottle and dropped his head against the wall. When Jarrett finally touched him, Gil flinched. He'd expected Jarrett's cock against his entrance, forcing its way in so they could hurry and be done. Instead, an oiled finger traced along the curve of his arse, first one cheek, then the other.

"Has anyone told you that you have the most magnificent arse in the world?" Jarrett asked breathlessly.

Gil huffed out a laugh.

"Aye, it's true," Jarrett said. "Absolutely glorious."

Then that finger was pressing against him, sinking in. When he was in a room, Gil could take as long as he wanted with this part, but Jarrett knew only how much time he absolutely had to take, adding another finger before Gil was truly ready for it, but still able to take it. He worked his way up to three fingers faster than Gil thought possible, his fingers stretching, expanding, but purely practical, never reaching deep enough to hit that perfect spot.

Then Jarrett removed his fingers and Gil felt something larger, blunter against his entrance. Jarrett leaned in, pressing up against him, their clothes an unwelcome barrier between their bodies.

"Ready?" Jarrett breathed.

"You've no idea," growled Gil.

The Jarrett thrust, his cock immediately striking the spot his fingers had missed. Gil gasped, closing his eyes to block out anything but the feel of Jarrett filling him. He bit down hard on the sleeve of his coat to keep from crying out when Jarrett thrust again, rutting into him hard and fast.

It was rough, wild, and unlike anything Gil had ever done before. Dizzy with sensation, he breathed in deeply and was hit with the smell of lavender. Opening his eyes, he saw a few blooms still clinging to his sleeve from where Jarrett had grabbed him before. No, he needed his distraction.

"Jarrett," he begged. "Jarrett, please. Harder."

Jarrett swore, then did as he was told, his fingers gripping Gil's hips achingly tight as he increased the strength of each stroke.

Gil barely had time to wrap a hand around himself before he was coming, his whole body going taut and his vision darkening even as white lights danced through it, setting off sparks of pleasure with every pulse of his cock.

He panted, his blood racing and heartbeat pounding in his ears, then before he could recover, he was hit with a keen sense of loss as Jarrett pulled out. Gil turned just in time to see Jarrett stumbling a few paces back, hand rapidly working his cock even as his eyes were glued to Gil's arse. Then he looked up and as their eyes met, Jarrett came, his mouth opening in a silent "O" even as his eyes rolled up in his head. His spend splattered the grass at his feet and he swayed, barely catching himself in time.

He was beautiful.

Gil's heart beat even louder.

They were both quiet as they walked back towards Balcarres House. It wasn't the pensive silence of earlier, but something that had Gil smiling softly each time he spotted Jarrett out of the corner of his eye. He could still feel Jarrett on him, *in him*, and the ghostly trails of that touch seemed to seep into the surrounding air. The fog wasn't as cold, the day wasn't as gloomy, and the wind didn't carry the final bite of winter, but the first breath of spring.

They stopped to hide the coat under a fallen log and toss Jarrett's ruined handkerchief into a small stream. It wasn't safe to have either in their possession when they returned to Balcarres in case Carnbee was still there. They would need to return the coat before the trial, but Gil didn't want his family knowing where it was before then. If the killer stole it, their strongest proof that Jarrett was innocent would be gone forever.

That thought was enough to bring some of the chill creeping back in. So much so that when Jarrett gasped, Gil thought he must be thinking the same thing.

Then he saw it.

They'd made their way back to the grounds of Balcarres and were nearly to the house itself, but there hadn't been laundry strewn everywhere when they'd left this morning. And surely Mrs. Finley would hang the washing up rather than leave it on the dirty ground. Gil toed a bit of fabric with his boot before he realised what it was. It was a curtain, one just barely large enough to cover a tiny window, like those in the shed.

A few feet further brought more fabric: the blanket that had been on the bed. Jarrett knelt, gathering it up and brushing mud from it. His mouth was fixed in a flat line.

When they reached the shed, the damage was even worse. The door was hanging off one remaining hinge. Apparently, whoever told Carnbee he'd find the bloody clothes and murder weapon in Jarrett's shed hadn't also provided him with the key. Straw was everywhere, the mattress ripped open and its contents strewn about. The chest was on its side, a large crack running down the back.

Carnbee's men hadn't found what they were looking for, thank Christ, but it hurt Gil to see the damage they'd done in their search for evidence. Assuming this was just from them searching and not them destroying Jarrett's things out of sheer malice. And if it hurt him, he couldn't imagine the agony Jarrett must be feeling. He'd only hinted at how much the shed meant to him, but Gil had seen how proud of it he'd been, how much he loved it.

"Jarrett?"

Jarrett shook his head. He set the blanket down on the single chair, which had miraculously remained upright, then stooped to pick something from the floor. When Gil saw what it was, his heart clenched with sorrow. Someone in his family had done this, had brought unimaginable pain to a man Gil cared for so much that he was beginning to suspect there might be an even stronger word for the way he felt. And if he and Jarrett hadn't found the clothes last night, it would have been so much worse.

Without thinking, he wrapped his arms around Jarrett's waist, pulling him in so his back was to Gil's chest and Gil could feel the rise and fall of his breaths. When those breaths turned to sobs, Gil held him even tighter, pressing kisses against his shoulder and promising him it would all be all right. Promises he knew he couldn't keep.

And in his hands, Jarrett cradled his little wooden horse, all four of its legs broken.

CHAPTER 20

J arrett checked his horse's speed with a click of his tongue and the barest pressure on the reins. Pepper, the grey gelding he'd chosen for today's ride, tossed his head but slowed to a stop. As they waited for Gil to catch up, Pepper snorted impatiently and even danced a little when his rider refused to let him have his way. Jarrett made a note to mention this behaviour to Graham. A bit more exercise was likely all Pepper needed; too much time in a stall without fresh air would get to anyone. He shied away from the thought that if they didn't find the real killer, he'd be the one trapped somewhere far worse than a horse stall.

The rest of the day before had been spent cleaning out what remained of his shed. Gil had been an unexpected support, although Jarrett wasn't sure why he'd been so surprised Gil was willing to help. Surely, after breaking Jarrett out of gaol, a little sweeping and mopping was nothing. He still wasn't entirely sure why Gil was willing to do these things for him, but he didn't know how to ask without sounding ungrateful.

The first thing Gil had done was head into the house to check the clothes and knife were still in their hiding spot. When he'd returned with a bucket of water and some rags, Jarrett had already gotten out most of his tears in the ruins of the one place that felt like home. Any later tears he was able to blame on the dust stirred up by the "work" of Carnbee's men. If Gil noticed, he didn't say anything, yet another kindness.

They'd sorted the things that could be mended and hauled away the things that couldn't. It'd been Gil who'd added the horse figurine to the mending pile, even though they never found one of its legs. He'd also been the one to re-hang the door, telling Jarrett all about his father's days as overseer, sending Gil out with the labourers to learn an appreciation of the work that was more than just giving orders. He hadn't once complained, even though he had to be sore from what they'd done at the chapel. And when the sun had finally gone down and they returned to their room, he'd slipped into Jarrett's bed with an easy smile even though neither of them had the energy to do more than sleep.

It was *nice* to have Gil there, not just in his bed, but for all the events of the day, both the ground-shakingly good and the earth-shatteringly bad. Why Jarrett enjoyed his company during the good was obvious, the man had a mouth made for sin and an arse that ought to be more illegal than it already was. But why Jarrett felt better with him there during the awful parts, realising one of Gil's family was the killer and the destruction of his shed, was more of a mystery. Sure, an extra pair of hands made for lighter work, but there was more to it than that.

Despite his exhaustion, Jarrett had lain awake in Gil's sleeping arms pondering the riddle. And he was still pondering it now.

Turning in the saddle, he looked back to see how far Gil had fallen behind. Gil wasn't as bad a rider as he'd made himself sound with his endless speeches about the joys of going about on foot, but he still wasn't a match for Jarrett. What he lacked in grace however, he made up for in style. As Jarrett watched, Gil crested the hillock. The wind had kept pulling wisps of his long dark hair from its tie, until Gil had given up and let his hair hang loose around his shoulders. It streamed behind him as he rode, like that of some pagan king riding into battle astride his war horse, the black stallion beneath him matching him in conquering spirit. The sight was breathtaking and Jarrett couldn't help indulging in a brief fantasy of being dragged back to this warlord's tent, his blood high from victory in battle.

As he pulled up alongside Jarrett, the fierce chieftain wiped a bit of mud from his spectacles and loosened the reins on his mighty stallion so Liquorice could nibble at a patch of early blooming primrose.

"What are you grinning at?" asked Gil.

"Riding suits you," Jarrett replied. It was true, but Gil didn't need to know just how much. At least, not right now. Even if Gil might be more amenable to an open-air encounter after their time in the chapel, there wasn't anywhere suitable to tie up the horses and he couldn't risk them running off.

God, Gil really had been magnificent with his arms folded against the crumbling stone, the arch of his back a graceful curve that Jarrett wanted to trace again and again until he could draw it from memory. And the sounds he'd made, those beautiful half-broken cries, so intoxicating that Jarrett didn't just want to hear them again, he *needed* to. Needed to know what they sounded like when they weren't muffled by Gil's sleeve, what it took to make them louder, or deeper, or what Gil could do to get Jarrett to make those noises instead.

Nothing they'd done had been anything Jarrett hadn't done a dozen times before, but he hadn't been able to stop thinking about it. That was unusual, as he generally forgot all but the most important details by the next morning—like whether they'd both gotten their end away or if the other bugger had left Jarrett wanting—but he found himself wanting to remember every moment of his time with Gil. Perhaps it wasn't so strange; Gil was attractive, and responsive, and a joy to kiss. Of course Jarrett would be thinking about him, especially as the man was always *right there*.

What *was* strange, was that even more than the sex, Jarrett found himself thinking about the way Gil had held him last night, giving Jarrett the comfort he desperately needed while asking nothing in return. Or the set look he got when he was determined to do something rash, be that free a man from gaol or kiss him senseless. Or the way he was constantly tucking loose strands of hair behind his ears, only for them to come free again the moment he adjusted his spectacles. Why these thoughts would affect him even more than the memory of Gil's glorious arse around his cock made no sense, but affect him they did.

He shifted in the saddle and willed his body to calm down. Riding with even a partial stand was a misery he wasn't looking to repeat. Gil threw him a worried glance, no doubt noting Jarrett's discomfort, even if he was entirely wrong about the cause. He'd been throwing Jarrett the same look ever since they'd found his shed in shambles. Jarrett knew, because he'd been looking at Gil the same way since they'd realised the killer had to be one of his family. If throwing his cautions to the wind and himself at Jarrett in the chapel hadn't been signs enough that Gil wasn't taking the news well, there was a tightness around his eyes that hadn't been there before.

"How are you?" Jarrett asked.

Gil looked surprised at his bluntness. "Well enough, I suppose. A bit sore still from yesterday, but not so much that it's the reason I'm such a poor rider, that's all natural ability."

Jarrett shook his head. "That's not what I meant. And you ride well enough, although you need to put your heels down more. And sit further forward in the saddle. And loosen your grip, Liquorice is a gentle soul, she doesn't need much prodding. Aside from that, I mean, you're well?"

"Jarrett, I should be asking that of you. With everything—"

"I know." Jarrett cut him off. He didn't need the full list of terrible things he was facing reeled off again. Shame, ruin, imprisonment, hanging, he knew them all. He could hardly tell Gil that he had no plans to be around for the worst of it. Especially not now they knew the killer was part of Gil's family. It wasn't that he didn't trust Gil's desire to do the right thing, but he didn't like his odds when it came time for Gil to choose between, say, his mother or a man he'd fucked once.

From the moment he'd stepped out of that gaol, he'd sworn he'd never go back and he certainly wasn't about to let anyone hang him. He'd actually believed for a moment that they'd be able to clear his name, but now? There were plenty of men finding new lives in the colonies, and it wasn't like there was anything tying him to Balcarres. That Gil would likely be imprisoned for some time for letting him escape was unfortunate. But when it came for Jarrett to choose between his life or a man he'd fucked once? The decision was an easy one.

He'd been too hopeful that it wouldn't come to that, but knowing now that Gil's family was involved, Hell, that the family of *a baron* was involved, he'd need to start making plans to leave and the sooner, the better. The only advantage he had was that Gil hadn't seemed to realise yet how this changed things. That gave him some time.

Pepper had wandered over to steal some of Liquorice's primroses, so Jarrett gave a tug on the reins, directing the horse away from his prize. Their beasts were so close that his knee brushed Gil's buckskin-clad thigh as he wheeled Pepper around. Christ, those bloody boots and buckskins were sinful enough when Gil was on his own two feet, but stretched taut over muscle as he sat astride his mount, they were downright obscene. He allowed himself a lingering look. At Gil's raised eyebrow he merely clicked his tongue, signalling Pepper to begin a gentle walk down the other side of the hillock.

"You shouldn't have let me talk you into riding if you were sore," Jarrett said when Liquorice's hoofbeats fell into step beside him.

"Fishing for compliments?" Gil asked. "It's not that bad. Besides, it was something you wanted to do and I—Well, I could hardly let you go out alone. They take even more offence to horse stealing around here than they do to murder."

That was a good point. Jarrett would have to remember that when it was time to make his escape. He gave Pepper an absent pat on the neck. He would miss the horses when he ran. The earl had the beginnings of a fine stable, even if he didn't seem to know it.

"Is that one your favourite?" Gil asked. "I'll be honest, I'm not sure I know enough about horses to know what makes one better than the other, but he seems... good?"

Jarrett smiled. "Pepper's not my favourite, but he's a sight more than good. Graham, damn him, won't give me his full lineage, guards it closer than Mr. Howe does the silver, but I'd wager there's a champion somewhere in the line. Just look at him; you can tell there has to be. Pepper could outrun the Devil if he put his mind to it, but only over short distances. He's a sprinter who could race or pull a curricle if His Lordship takes a mind to join the Corinthians.

"But pretty as he is, he'd never make a good carriage horse. No stamina for distance. And he's still young, a bit hot headed. Not like your Liquorice there. I'd happily put my nan holding her best crockery on her and feel safe they'd all make it to the kirk fete in one piece."

"And here I thought I was improving," Gil muttered. "No, I don't need your pity. Which of the other creatures is it then? The spotty one? Or perhaps the big yellow one?"

Jarrett hoped the man was teasing. It would be embarrassing to discover he was fond of someone that clueless about horseflesh.

"Thistle. She's the bay mare. The lass with the brown coat and black feet, if you need it in those words. No fancy breeding from the looks of her, but despite what they might say at Tattersalls, breeding's not all. She's a lighter touch than Pepper but more spirited than Liquorice. Best of all, she can run farther than any horse I've ever seen. I think if she had her head, she'd run all the way down to Dover without breaking a sweat, then keep going straight across the channel to France. She's not the most fashionable horse in the stables, but she's a rare beauty."

When Gil didn't respond, Jarrett glanced over. Gil was watching him again, but the worry had been replaced by something softer.

"You really do care for them, don't you? My uncle has a kennel of hounds at his main estate, but I doubt he could tell you a single dog's name. His only care is the prestige their breeding brings him. I thought that was how you felt about horses, but you actually care, don't you?"

"How could I not?" Jarrett patted Pepper's neck again. "Why's your uncle here, anyway? The hounds run him out of that other estate?"

"He's the baron. Usually he'd be in Edinburgh with my aunt this time of year, but Charleton House is part of the barony. Therefore, he owns it. Therefore, he can come and go as he pleases."

"Aye, but it's your home. The earl owns damn near everything around here that your uncle doesn't, but I'd still wonder what he was doing there if I found him in my bed. I wouldn't complain, mind you, but I would wonder."

Gil snorted. "Is the second son of the younger brother to a baron not prestigious enough for you?"

In truth, Jarrett still couldn't quite believe that someone like Gil would want to be in his bed either. Well, no, he couldn't believe that the second to the youngest to the nephew to the uncle or whatever-he-was to Lord Charleton would. But Gil the man was a different story. Now that Jarrett had gotten the chance to know him, the clever, funny, kind man behind the family name, well, he still couldn't believe it. Especially not now it was clear Gil wasn't just keeping an eye on him while he was out of gaol, but enjoyed Jarrett's company right back. After all, sharing a bed with a man was hardly required to keep him on parole.

He clasped a hand to his heart and fluttered his eyelashes. "You should be honoured! I rarely bed anyone below a viscount!"

Gil shook his head fondly. "Oh? Lot of viscounts at The Cross Keys, are there?"

The moment the words were past his lips, Gil looked stricken and froze in his saddle. Liquorice, sensing the change in his rider, came to a stop with much stamping of hooves, but Jarrett barely noticed Pepper halting as well. Gil knowing of the pub and the sort of patrons it catered to wasn't much of a surprise, even though neither of them had brought it up before. But the way he'd said it so casually, as if he knew for a fact Jarrett would be familiar, and then his stricken look afterwards...

The terrible truth clicked into place and he realised what Gil had been hiding from him.

"You saw me there," Jarrett whispered. "That's... In the cells, you weren't surprised when I kissed you. Because you knew. You'd seen me at The Cross Keys before. I never saw you. If I had—"

Jarrett stopped. The reminder of that first, desperate kiss in the gaol brought up other memories. Things Gil had said to him that didn't make sense at the time. They way he'd pushed so hard to know if there was anyone who'd be willing to vouch for him. He'd really been asking if any of the men Jarrett had been with the night of the murder cared enough to come forward. Clearly not. But it couldn't have just been a lucky guess that Jarrett was at The Cross Keys that night of all nights.

"You were there that night too."

The look on Gil's face was all the answer he needed.

Something twinged painfully behind Jarrett's breastbone then spread in a hollow ache. It was followed swiftly by that instinctive fear at being discovered.

Run! He knows what you are. Run!

The fear was ridiculous; Gil was safe. But he couldn't shake it away. And the other sensation, the one that felt so very much like betrayal, only grew stronger. All this time he'd thought Gil believed him, believed *in* him. For all the taunts and threats and terror, he'd been able to face them because Gil believed Jarrett over everyone else. He'd thought Gil had seen something in him, something that Jarrett wasn't even sure he had some days, something worthwhile and that was why he'd stood up for Jarrett, rescued him, and was trying to save his life.

But Gil hadn't believed him. He hadn't needed to, because he'd known for a fact there was no way Jarrett could be the killer.

Gil had seen him at The Cross Keys while the murder was being committed. Seen him—Oh God—seen him doing what?

"Why didn't you say anything?"

"I was going to," Gil said quickly. He reached up but had to take the reins in both hands again as Liquorice began to wander.

Jarrett knew what he'd been about to do. Gil wanted to adjust his spectacles, the way he always did when he was uneasy. He'd follow that by tucking his long hair back under the stems. When had Jarrett started to notice things like that? He didn't even know the names of most of the men he'd had and here he was, despite everything, feeling warmth at knowing such a small detail about Gil.

Gil continued. "There was just never a good time. At first, I couldn't, because admitting I knew you were there meant you would know about me and I didn't know you well enough to risk it. Especially since—"

Gil's jaw shut over the end of his sentence with an audible snap.

"Since? Since what? Christ, Gil, you owe me that much!"

Gil sighed. Getting Liquorice under control had caused him to turn, his back now half to Jarrett so he couldn't see his face. This wasn't a conversation for horseback, but Jarrett wouldn't be the first to dismount and have Gil look down on him.

"Since I knew what you were like, Jarrett. The way you've always been so careless with your gazes and your words that I knew you fancied men long before we'd ever even had a real conversation. I couldn't trust my secret to someone so *reckless*. And seeing you in The Cross Keys that night, the way you acted right out in the open? My God, it was only a matter of time before you were dragged in on a hanging offence. I was just shocked it was for the one crime you hadn't committed that night!"

His words were a slap across the face.

"Don't you dare." Jarrett hissed. "You were there that night, same as me. Same reasons too. Don't make out like you're better than me because you've decided all your rules about when and where and who. At least I'm honest in what I want. You flatter women you've no intention of bedding just to have a lie to hide behind while you skulk off to your 'discreet rooms' and lock yourself away. Who was it that night?"

"It doesn't matter."

A memory of the day they'd found the body came then. Gil had been calm and capable right up until the point Doctor Mills had noted a tattoo.

"He's tattooed, isn't he?" Jarrett asked, knowing he was right when Gil winced. "You thought the dead man was him."

"Only for a moment. The build was similar and I was afraid he'd followed me somehow and something had happened."

The hollow ache deepened, a pit that Jarrett didn't know how to fill. Whoever this tattooed man was, he meant enough that Gil had trusted him, had thought he might be willing to ride hours in the rain to come to him.

Jarrett wasn't that man. He'd thrown himself at Gil the first chance he had, near-prostituted himself for the chance to get out of that cell. That Gil knew all along made it even more humiliating. No wonder he didn't trust Jarrett with his secret until that night in their room with thick stone walls and a locked door behind him. Jarrett wasn't the sort you worried over. He was just a quick fuck in a dark place.

It shouldn't hurt. It wasn't fair that it hurt. What did it matter that Gil hadn't actually believed it him? He'd known Jarrett was guilty of being a trollop, but still helped him because he knew he was innocent of murder. It was Jarrett who'd put more meaning onto things than he should.

Stupid, stupid, stupid! This was why he never saw men again after he fucked them. He pretended it was easier that way, but the truth was that it was safer. Safer, because if he saw them again, spoke with them again, shared his worries and listened to their own, found out who they really were behind their charming smiles and gentle humour, he might start to have feelings for them.

Feelings like he had for Gil.

He hadn't wanted to admit it, not even to himself, but there was no reason to lie now. Not when everything he'd believed their... relationship was based on turned out to be a lie. It wasn't as if it changed things. He'd never be the sort to ride through the night to get to his lover, he only ever ran away. And despite his hurt at Gil keeping the truth from him, Gil had still rescued him and stood by him, even in the face of the law and his own family. He was a good man and he deserved more than Jarrett had to give.

Gil made a second attempt at his spectacles, scowling when Liquorice thwarted him again. "It's not like that with me and Daniel, he's not—It's beside the point. The point is I saw you there and knew you were innocent. Carnbee made up his mind you were guilty with no evidence. It was so clear he was wrong, just picking the easiest target out of laziness. Anyone could see that. I couldn't give him your alibi or we'd both swing, but I couldn't just leave you to rot."

"And if you hadn't seen me?" Jarrett asked, knowing he was only poking a bruise, making the pain flare again. "If you hadn't seen me at The Cross Keys that night, would you have believed me when I said I didn't do it?"

"Jare—"

"Would you have believed me?"

Gil exhaled heavily. "Now, of course. We have proof it was someone in my family."

Jarrett nodded. "But not back then. So I'd still be down there in the dark. And we never would've gotten to now, would we? No evidence, no hope, no nothing."

Gil was staring down at the reins in his hands even though Liquorice was finally still. A muscle in his jaw jumped, but Jarrett couldn't see enough of his face to read his expression. At last he whispered, "I couldn't have taken the risk."

"Fuck you," Jarrett snarled. Then he kicked Pepper in the sides.

It was harder than he deserved and he gave a startled whinny before bounding away, speeding into a full gallop without

Jarrett having to prompt him again. Behind him came Gil's shouts and a moment later the sound of hoofbeats echoed the roar of Pepper's own.

Jarrett didn't have to look back to know Gil was following. In a fair contest, Liquorice was the better horse for a chase with longer legs and a deeper chest, but Gil wasn't half the horseman Jarrett was. They both knew the terrain equally well, so he knew why he heard Gil shout again as Jarrett raced closer to the edge of the earl's land and the stone wall that surrounded it.

He heard his name called one last time as leaned forward, gripping Pepper's mane and rising in the saddle as Pepper soared into the air. They cleared the wall, Pepper landing gracefully and continuing on without breaking stride. A volley of curses replaced the second set of hoofbeats behind them, either Gil or Liquorice having the good sense not to attempt the wall themselves.

The air tasted of salt blown off the sea as Jarrett galloped across the heath, free but alone.

CHAPTER 21

G il looked out the window for the fifth time in as many minutes.

He generally considered himself a man of above-average intelligence, but also one who could admit when he'd been an idiot. And by God, had he been an idiot.

He looked out the window again. The view from the earl's study at Balcarres covered the long expanse of heath that stretched all the way to the coast. If the day was clearer, the view would be a lovely one with the sun sparkling off the sea. Instead, the only brightness came from the gorse bushes that dotted the landscape, their bright yellow blooms hiding the wicked thorns beneath.

There were more picturesque views from other windows, but he'd been neglecting his duties for too long and the study contained the earl's account books, so it was the logical place to work. Never mind that the study looked out over the best land for walking or riding. That it overlooked the stables as well was also mere coincidence. He'd be able to see anyone approaching the house on horseback from miles away. But so far, he'd seen no one.

With a sigh, he dragged his attention back to the ledger in front of him, but it was impossible to concentrate on the columns of numbers when he was too busy berating himself for being a damned fool.

Aye, perhaps next time don't anger a man with every reason to run. If he's an excellent rider, it might be best to ensure he's not on an extremely valuable horse at the time either. And if he's also a wanted man, you could also try to make sure not you're the one who goes to prison if he runs.

That final image of Jarrett leaping the wall, man and beast flowing like water where Gil would've been dashed against the stones, came to him, as did the sound of fading hoofbeats as Jarrett disappeared amongst the hillocks and headed towards the trees. He kept telling himself Jarrett was going for a ride to cool his head and would be back when Pepper grew tired. But each time he looked out the window to see only empty land, he worried a little more that Jarrett might be gone for good.

He'd been a fool not to say anything about The Cross Keys earlier, but at the time it'd seemed sensible not to risk it. And the other things he'd said had been the truth, but that didn't make them any less cruel. In all honesty, as angry as he was at himself for letting Jarrett escape, he didn't blame Jarrett at all. The man was facing a murder charge with the odds stacked against him and had nearly as much fear of imprisonment as the gallows. The only thing keeping him from running had been the slimmest thread of his trust in Gil and now that had snapped. It wasn't surprising he'd run. The real question was why hadn't he done so sooner?

Gil scribbled a few sums at the bottom of the page, hoping they were right.

Why had Jarrett stayed for so long when any sane man would have been on a ship to the colonies with a sack of the earl's silver the first time Gil fell asleep?

If Gil allowed himself to indulge, he might wonder if it had anything to with warm skin, hot breaths against the back of his neck whispering praise and curses both into his hair, long walks punctuated by laughter, slow smiles over lamplight, and the comfort of reaching out in the dark and knowing you'd find someone there.

He'd told Jarrett that knowing him now, he'd believe him and he would, just as he would believe any of his friends. But now that he had a moment to think without either Jarrett or his family around to distract him, he began to wonder if there might be more. He liked most of the men he'd slept with, and would be happy to share a pint as much as bed them, but spending a day hauling out their broken furniture or holding them as they cried? He'd never done either of those before and he wouldn't want to. It suggested a level of intimacy that wasn't safe.

He'd wanted to do those things for Jarrett and he wanted the chance to do them again, safe be damned.

He should have known he was doomed the moment he'd freed Jarrett in the cell. Hell, earlier even. The man had been working at Balcarres for months, and Gil had barely been able to string a sentence together to say to him the entire time. He prided himself on being charming, but he'd never been able to charm Jarrett. And Jarrett's flirtations had never charmed him either. It was the real man underneath who he cared for.

Who he loved.

The realisation was like a blow to his skull. He'd never had these sorts of feelings for another man before, but that didn't mean he didn't know what it meant when you worried for someone else's safety more than your own, put their comfort ahead of yours, their happiness. He'd stood up to his family for Jarrett. *Jarrett*, sly and saucy, brazen and gentle, unapologetic, dangerous, and above all things, kind.

And if Jarrett was truly gone?

If he was lucky, Gil would never see him again. The horse would be sold off in Dundee or Aberdeen for the price of admission aboard a ship headed anywhere else.

If he was unlucky, the next time Gil saw him would be in the back of a thief catcher's cart on the way to trial. Or their paths might cross again in gaol itself. After all, Gil had given his parole, and now his prisoner had escaped. After his father's words, he had no doubt the man would be willing to see charges pressed against his own child. Gil didn't know off the top of his head what the sentence for aiding a fugitive from justice was, but he knew it would be harsh, especially for the second son to a second son who was used to soft beds and open skies.

With that in mind, he closed the ledger with a snap. If he was to be gaoled for letting Jarrett escape, it hardly mattered if the earl's accounts were slightly out of date before he went to prison. So the best thing Gil could do now was to figure out who in his family was a filthy murderer. At least if he was going to gaol, he'd have company.

If only he knew which member of his family would be sharing a cell with him. If it was Robert, they'd only need to pay the hangman for a single execution. He hoped it wasn't his mother. Not that she could be the killer herself, it would be impossible for even strange old bird like Mrs. Randall to mistake his mother for a large man, even in the dark and taken unawares. Besides, his mother would be too concerned about staining the hem of her skirt with blood to commit such a vicious murder. But if she knew who the killer was and was protecting him, the law would not look on her favourably.

What an awful mess. He'd loved his family once, loved them still in their better moments, and didn't want to be the one to bring them harm, especially not harm as awful as this. But Jarrett was innocent and as ridiculous as it was, he loved Jarrett too.

He briefly entertained the thought of going back to Charleton House and taking out his frustrations there. Knocking over some furniture and cursing them all to the Devil would make him feel better for at least a few minutes. But it would hardly help in the long run. Worse, letting the killer know how close they were to discovering the truth would only put Jarrett in further danger.

If he ever comes back, that is.

He looked out the window again.

Enough. His spinning thoughts were taking him nowhere. If the earl's accounts weren't interesting enough to distract him, perhaps dealing with his own problems would be. He grabbed another stack of papers, the ones he'd stuffed into his valise during their rapid departure from Charleton House, his brother's shouts ringing in his ears.

Smoothing out the top page, he began to read. When he reached the bottom of the first page of a lengthy letter from an old school friend, he reached for the next, only to find a dressmaker's bill in his hand instead.

He frowned. The friend had been getting around to asking him to invest in some sort of mining operation. Either that or he was asking for courtship advice, it was hard to tell, and without the next page when he finally got to the point, it would be impossible to know for certain. Gil flipped through the stack, hoping the papers had only become disorganised in transit and he hadn't somehow lost the rest of the letter.

The next paper was from his banker in Edinburgh, then one from his banker in London. Then another bill, this time from a hat shop. As Gil hadn't bought any ostrich feather bonnets lately, nor any dresses he could recall either, clearly he'd grabbed more than just his own papers off the desk. Wonderful. Returning the rest of the stack to Charleton House would no doubt be a simple, civilised affair, and not get him accused of thievery at all.

He set the letter from his friend on one side of the desk and set to the task of sorting the papers into his and theirs. He eventually found the second page of his letter, the friend was indeed asking Gil for advice about a young lady rather than mining equipment, but the further he delved into the stack, the more confused he became. His friend's request aside, his papers were largely all business related, as would be expected. But the rest of the pages didn't make any sense. The only time he'd set his papers down at Charleton House was on the desk in his father's study, so the additional ones he'd inadvertently picked up had to have come from there, but why were repair requests from tenants and his mother's bills mixed in with invitations to balls in Edinburgh and clippings of racing results from several newspapers?

It was highly improper to go through barony documents without their permission, but time and again, he'd offered to help his uncle and his cousin when they sequestered themselves in the study, and each time he'd been rebuffed. Really, they only had themselves to blame for his curiosity.

An hour later, he sat back heavily in his chair and pulled off his spectacles, setting them on the papers he'd now gone through half a dozen times. None of it made any sense.

He rubbed his temples, trying to ease the building headache. The tea he'd brought in with him had long since gone cold, but he drank it anyway before deciding he needed something stronger. Normally, he'd never take such a liberty as pouring himself some of the earl's best whisky, but given the circumstances, the earl would have to forgive him.

Returning from the sideboard with a glass of the amber liquid, he stared down at the papers on the desk again. Without his spectacles, the words on them were no more than a blur of illegible squiggles, but what they actually said was just as hard to understand.

The barony was bankrupt.

He couldn't be completely certain without seeing everything, but from the increasingly concerned letters from bank managers and promissory notes well past their deadlines, it was the only logical conclusion he could draw. Logical, but still unbelievable. Before his uncle's arrival, Gil had all but taken over the accounts for Charleton House and their surrounding lands. He knew how much they earned each year and how much they spent. Their income might not be as impressive as the earl's, but they'd been comfortably affording all their expenses with more than enough to spare for his mother's interminable redecorating.

Now, it looked as if they might not even have the funds to pay the servants their next quarterly wages, and that was with the money held not just in Charleton House, but across the entire barony.

Deep in thought, he barely noticed as he pulled out his handkerchief and began cleaning his spectacles. Rubbing the lenses with slow, habitual movements, he wondered how in God's name this had happened. His fingers twitched briefly, itching with the desire to get his hands on the rest of the barony accounts. One of the banker's letters had made oblique reference to several large sums of money having been withdrawn, but how much? And more importantly, by whom?

The only paper he hadn't touched was a letter from his aunt in Edinburgh to his uncle, and that was only because the letter was unopened and he wasn't sure he'd be able to open it without damaging the sealing wafer.

Pushing his spectacles back up his nose, he mulled over what it could all mean. He was beginning to see the rough shape of things, but he still didn't have the full picture. If only he had someone to discuss it with.

With a start, he glanced out the window. He'd been so focused on the papers, he hadn't noticed the already grey sky growing darker with the coming night. He could still make out the landscape, the gorse bushes now patches of darkness in the twilight, their bright blooms dimmed, but in another hour all would be dark. Yet he still didn't see any rider making his way home to Balcarres House. If Jarrett hadn't come home while he'd been distracted... But surely Gil would have heard him return or Jarrett would have sought him out when he got back. He hoped so at least.

He wanted to spring up out of his chair and go check the stables, but forced himself to remain sitting. If Jarrett was back, that meant he didn't want to see Gil just yet, and if he wasn't, he would soon be out alone in the dark, with no money, no food, and a horse he'd already admitted was not the best for distance riding, not to mention too obviously well-bred to belong to man in Jarrett's clothes. Gil hoped he was smart enough to realise all that and come back, almost as much as he hoped Jarrett was smart enough to run while he still had the chance.

The very thought of never seeing him again made his chest ache in a way that another glass of the earl's whisky wouldn't heal, but it was still worth a try. The idea that their last words together were spoken in anger made him add an extra finger of liquor to the glass. He'd never gotten a chance to tell Jarrett he loved him and if he didn't come back, he never would.

But someone in his family was already out for Jarrett, and now, knowing the true depth of his family's desperation, whoever it was was more dangerous than ever.

He looked out the window again and willed himself not to go tearing across the heath, calling out Jarrett's name as he stumbled through the dark like some ridiculous character in a melodrama. He'd wait until full dark, then go inspect the stables. If Jarrett wasn't back by then, Gil had his answer.

Knowing the minutes would crawl by at a tortuous pace, he turned back to his own papers, unable to look at his family's mess any longer. The first few were even duller than his friend's letter, and did nothing to keep Gil from glancing at the darkening skies every other minute, but then he came across something unexpected.

It was a piece of correspondence about an investment opportunity. There was nothing unexpected in that, but the author was writing as if they were in the middle of a longer discussion of which Gil had no memory. The name at the bottom of the page was vaguely familiar, as was the letterhead, but it wasn't until he read the letterhead that he placed it.

Sinclair and Sons
Drapers and Merchant Tailors

He remembered now.

Several months before, he'd been contacted about investing in a proposed trading opportunity, fine Scottish wool sent to the Orient to be sold at a great profit, which would be used to purchase silks to bring back to Scotland to sell for even greater profit. On the surface, the idea had merit, but the guaranteed returns on investment were comically high, the sort that would have inexperienced investors salivating, but made more seasoned men like Gil wary.

He'd decided it was a scam even before he'd even looked at the sample fabrics they'd sent him, which were frankly garish. It was just as well he doubted the cloth would ever actually make its way onto a ship. Surely any silk merchant would think the Scots a race of blind madmen to wear clothes made of such material. But instead of confounding some poor trader across the sea, likely the money would simply be collected and after a period of several months to a year, all investors would receive a letter about the terrible loss of the ship, sunk rounding the Cape with all hands and cargo. No refunds. It was an obvious swindle, but a common one.

But remembering those awful fabrics, he realised he'd seen them again.

The chair caught in the rug in his rush to stand, striking the floor with such force that the sound echoed throughout the entire wing. He looked again at the letter, mouthing the signed name at the bottom.

Murdo Sinclair.

The name of the victim.

He read the letter again, holding it up to the lamp to ensure he caught every word, then folded it with great care, tucked it into his waistcoat, and downed the last of his glass.

He strode through the halls of Balcarres, set on his goal and seeing only a worried Mrs. Finley on his way.

"Mr. Charleton, are you quite all right? I heard a noise and was afraid..."

The look on his face was enough to make her stop there. She then gave a quick curtsey then promptly found somewhere else to be.

Reaching the hiding place, he pulled out the victim's clothes, stained and stiff with dried blood. The last light of the dying day barely filtered into the dusty room, but it was enough to see the pattern on the trousers. An unsightly plaid of greens and reds, shot through with a single strand of yellow that was as unmistakable as it was unforgettable. He'd been too distracted by all the blood and the terror of finding the bloody clothes and knife in Jarrett's shed, but now he knew where he'd seen that plaid before. It was one of the samples sent to him in the original letter.

But he'd never responded to that first letter, so why did this new one say things about it being "impossible to advance return on investments" but with "another package to follow in thanks for funds already given"?

Was someone trading in Gil's name? If so, who? The killer obviously, but why?

A cold shiver ran down his spine. Squinting against the darkness, he pulled the new letter from his pocket to make sure he remembered the wording correctly as he read the last lines again.

"Unfortunately an urgent matter has arisen that must be discussed in person. Please respond with a time and place where we may speak in private. I can come to you."

Another tactic he'd seen in swindles, and even been taken in by before he'd learned better, was to create a sense of urgency in the victim. Likely Sinclair had been prepared to spin a tale about more funds being needed immediately or all would be lost, expecting the investor to panic and hand over the funds without taking the time to think. It was a common trap, but this time, the swindler himself had been the one to walk into it.

And if anyone came looking for him, there was a trail of correspondence left behind with Gil's name on it.

That shiver of cold down his spine hardened, freezing him in place as he realised the awful truth. Someone he knew, *someone in his family*, had set Gil up to be blamed for a murder. But something had gone wrong with the killer's plan and Jarrett had been accused instead. And now, Jarrett was gone.

Gil was already going to gaol for allowing him to escape. If Jarrett didn't return to stand trial, how long before the killer reverted to the original plan and other letters with Gil's name on them addressed to the victim came to light? The killer would make certain of it, just to ensure someone was convicted so he wouldn't have to keep looking over his shoulder for the rest of his life.

What little proof they had would damn Gil as much as it might save Jarrett. The bloody clothes would have to stay hidden and the coat came from Charleton House. And now he knew he was the only Charleton who could easily line it with money.

Gil's throat went tight as if he could already feel the noose around it.

There was one piece of evidence that could prove Jarrett and Gil were both innocent, but they didn't have it and he had no idea where to look.

But if Jarrett came back and faced trial for the murder, Gil would be safe. He could present everything they'd found, even the letter itself. They still didn't have anything to directly tie the murderer to the crime, but they had a good story that also happened to be true. There was a chance Jarrett wouldn't be found guilty. But could Gil bet on the life of the man he loved to save his own?

The last gleam of twilight extinguished like a candle being snuffed out, leaving Gil sitting in pitch blackness, holding a set of bloody clothes in one hand and a letter that could save him or damn him in the other.

Now he just had to decide what to do next.

CHAPTER 22

Jarrett stared out across the sea, watching the afternoon sun try its best to shine off the waves, but do little more than give them a greenish glow. Behind him, Pepper was greedily devouring the scrubby grass that grew along the clifftop, raising his head every now and then to send him a baleful look. Jarrett had pushed him hard escaping from Gil, and it would take more than a few weeds to earn his forgiveness.

Taking one more look at the sea, he walked over to Pepper, untying his reins from the wind-twisted tree he'd used to keep him from wandering off the edge of the cliff in search of tasty morsels.

Pepper let out a complaining huff as Jarrett pulled himself into the saddle, but seemed to have recovered from his flight. It hadn't been more than an hour or two since they'd leapt the wall, and Jarrett had slowed them as soon as they made it to the woods and were safely out of sight, but Pepper had the heart of a racehorse, swift but delicate, and the last thing Jarrett wanted was to harm an innocent animal because of his own stupidity.

He knew he shouldn't blame Gil for not actually trusting him, but that didn't make it hurt any less. All along, Gil had known Jarrett was innocent. Known, and said nothing about it. He could've spoken up that first day and Jarrett would never have been imprisoned for murder at all. He'd come swanning in like some great saviour to deliver Jarrett from the darkness, when every single minute he'd spent in that cell had been Gil's own fault.

He directed Pepper off the coastal path when the road forked. Not really caring where they went, but he couldn't stop thinking about the whole mess, and a distracted rider on a headstrong horse along a cliff's edge was a recipe for disaster. He wasn't going to give Carnbee the satisfaction of thinking Jarrett had found his own way to escape the noose when he'd just been reckless.

Reckless.

Gil had called him that, and other things besides, for flirting and going after what he wanted.

Well, Gil's damned caution was going to get Jarrett hanged. That and the entire awful, murderous Charleton family. Jarrett didn't care which one of them it was, they'd all band together to protect the real murderer if it came down to it, putting the weight of their considerable family name against Jarrett and what? A dried flower? A coat filled with money that they were too rich to even notice was missing? If only Gil had spoken up first!

A flock of starlings erupted from a nearby bush with a clamour of whistling trills and flapping wings. Pepper danced sideways and by the time Jarrett got him settled, the birds had taken to the sky, wheeling high overhead as they searched for somewhere more peaceful to rest. He hadn't noticed the sky beginning to darken. If he was going to get back to Balcarres before nightfall, he'd better turn back soon.

If.

He considered it. He had no money, but a good head start and a horse well worth selling if Jarrett could find someone who wouldn't ask too many questions. If he rode all night, he could be in Edinburgh or Dundee before the alarm was raised, assuming Gil hadn't put out the call the moment Jarrett was out of his sight.

Gil. If Jarrett ran, Gil would be the one to take his place, locked away in the dark. His punishment wouldn't be nearly as severe as Jarrett's would be for murder, of course. But how long would he be left in the dark, unable to walk more than a few paces in any direction? Months? Years?

Well, it serves him right.

Even as he thought the words, Jarrett didn't believe them. He couldn't blame Gil for not speaking up in his defence, for the same reason Jarrett himself hadn't said anything. What good was an alibi if it got you hanged anyway? And if Gil had spoken up, it would've meant his neck too.

Jarrett wouldn't have expected him to risk everything for a man he barely knew. Even now, with everything they'd been through, everything they'd done, he wouldn't expect it. Gil was kind, and determined, and so bloody convinced that justice would be done to take that risk for the sort of man Jarrett was.

Christ, if he really had seen Jarrett in The Cross Keys that night, he knew exactly the sort of man Jarrett was.

That he'd begun to feel differently towards Gil than he felt about those men in the pub that night or any of the men before them meant nothing. Nor should it, not when Jarrett was still debating running and leaving both his feelings and Gil behind.

If he was going to run, he'd better start now. Pepper couldn't take him as far as Thistle might in a single night, so best to get as many miles behind him as possible.

And why shouldn't he run? All that was holding him back was his word to Gil, but why should he keep his word to someone who didn't trust him in the first place? That was, if Gil was even still willing to help him after their spat. Even if he did, they were swiftly running out of time and they still had no way to prove Jarrett was innocent of murder without getting him hanged for sodomy. Looking at it that way, it would be more reckless to stay.

But he couldn't forget the look on Gil's face, arms spread and face tilted towards the sky as he breathed in the fresh air. The way he'd looked was the same way Jarrett felt when Pepper leapt the wall, weightless and free. The idea of cutting Gil off from that feeling made something in him feel heavy and cold.

Rubbing his chest, he looked around, taking in his surroundings for the first time. It took a moment to realise where they were, until he spotted a particular bend in the stream crossed by a fallen oak tree. Pepper had more stamina than he let on, the spoiled creature, they weren't half a mile from Mrs. Randall's house at this point. Perhaps he'd just ride that far and make his decision then. Doubtless the daft old woman wouldn't be pleased to see him, but perhaps he could flirt a cup of tea out of her to warm him for the ride either onwards or back.

He snorted. *His* cup would likely be poisoned, but if he had Gil's charm, the old woman would pack him a full saddlebag of provisions and directions to a crooked horse trader to boot!

As he approached the cottage, he was surprised to see a horse tied to the gate out front. Not just any horse either, even at a distance it was clear she was a fine beast, proud head held high despite being tied, sharp ears twitching at their approach. The saddle looked strange and Jarrett couldn't help riding closer to get a better look. It took him a moment to place it, there not being any of that sort at Balcarres for obvious reasons. It was a sidesaddle and a well-made one at that.

He was busy marvelling over it when he heard the front door to the cottage open. The two women in the doorway stared at him. Mrs. Randall he knew, but like the saddle, it took him a moment to place its rider, and when he did, he cursed himself.

What other woman in this area could afford such a fine horse except a Charleton? He'd only seen this one once, standing fearfully in the open front door of Charleton House while that brute Robert Charleton screamed about having him horsewhipped. She must be the cousin's wife, come to visit with her husband and the baron, damn them all. Catriona, he thought her name was.

Neither of the two women moved, so he gave a quick bow, the best he could do from the saddle.

"Ma'am. Ma'am," he said, bowing to each woman in turn. Likely it wasn't the proper greeting to give, but what was the proper greeting to a woman who would testify against you, and another who might be the murderess herself?

"Taking up horse stealing as well as murder?" Mrs. Randall cackled.

Jarrett straightened, trying not to look like a man who'd been considering exactly that. "I was just riding by."

Catriona Charleton clutched her cloak tighter around herself as if Jarrett was liable to fling himself at her virtue at any moment. "Is Gil with you?" she asked fearfully.

Aye, that was a fair question. By all rights he should be.

"He's looking into other matters just now. Thought we should split our efforts, get twice as much done. I was to come out and see if Mrs. Randall had remembered anything more about that night the murderer ran into her. The murderer who wasn't me."

He directed the last bit towards Mrs. Charleton in what he hoped was a reassuring manner. If she was the killer, she would already know he was innocent, of course, but she looked more ready to bolt than he was.

"Nothing I haven't already said." Mrs. Randall crossed her arms. "Out picking herbs, a big fellow in a coat bowled me into a gravestone. You still haven't apologised for that, have ye?"

"That wasn't—" Jarrett caught himself. It wasn't worth arguing with her over. He wasn't going to convince her and attempting to would just sound like he was trying to intimidate her into changing her story.

"Nothing at all?" he floundered. "Nothing about the man that might give us a clue *if he wasn't me*?"

"You think I'm going to say I saw your face? I said before that I won't lie and say I did, if that's what you're worried about. The bruise you left is still there, though. The court will see that. Faded, but still all sorts of colours to shock a jury."

"Why were you even out there that night?"

"Gathering herbs, as I said."

This wasn't helping, but he'd just said that Gil sent him to gather information, so he had to at least pretend to do something of the sort. "What kind of herbs do you need from a graveyard?"

Mrs. Randall had a reputation as a cunning woman, so doubtless she collected all manner of strange things for her tonics and charms, but the thought of eating something that had grown from the bodies of the dead unsettled him.

"I hardly see what business that is of yours."

Jarrett was startled not by the words themselves, but who spoke them.

Catriona Charleton glared at him before continuing. "Mrs. Randall is not the one here who is on trial. I don't see what relevance any of this has, but doubtless if the court thinks it is important, she will be asked then. Until such a time, I would thank you not to trouble her any further with either your questions or your presence."

It suddenly occurred to Jarrett that he wasn't the only one who shouldn't be out riding without a male Charleton to chaperone.

He looked around uneasily, expecting to see her husband come charging at him from some unnoticed hiding place. Pepper sensed his unease and grew restless.

"Is your husband about?" he asked, tightening the reins. Even if she lied about where he was hiding, she might accidentally give some hint so Jarrett knew which direction to flee in to avoid a trap.

She hesitated and cast a worried look at Mrs. Randall. The older woman patted her arm.

"You think a woman needs an escort just to buy a wee headache powder? I suppose if she was having a tooth pulled, she'd have brought a whole garrison! These roads are safe enough," she glared at Jarrett, "for the most part."

Jarrett had been a valet long enough to know a dismissal when he heard one. He nodded and turned Pepper back towards Balcarres House. He could hardly ride off in the other direction now with them both watching.

"You don't need an escort back?" he asked. It was a ridiculous question under the circumstances, but it was the sort of thing a servant should ask a lady.

"I think not," Mrs. Charleton said icily.

Jarrett nodded. He didn't blame her. He wasn't the killer, but now, he didn't think she was either. Even in the dark, Mrs. Randall wouldn't mistake a small woman for a large man, which meant Catriona Charleton was sharing a house—or even a bed—with a murderer and might not know it.

"Be careful, Mrs. Charleton," he said. "I'm no harm to you, but others might be, even those you trust."

No matter what she thought of Jarrett, he now knew too well what it felt like to be deceived by a man you had feelings for. If she truly was innocent, he wouldn't want her to feel the same hurt.

He set his heels to Pepper before she could respond and rode back towards Balcarres. And Gil.

The sun had fully set by the time he made it back to the stables, but he'd ridden in the dark before and had no trouble finding the way back. As he approached, he glowered at the warm light spilling out the stable door. The last thing he needed at the end of today was another lecture from Graham about taking the earl's horses without permission.

To his surprise, it wasn't Graham running his hands over the horse tack hung up across from Thistle's stall, but Gil.

For a long moment, neither of them said anything. The light from the single lamp at Gil's feet threw the stables into deep shadow, but Jarrett could still see the slump in his shoulders even if he couldn't clearly make out the expression on his face. The light caught on Gil's spectacles, but behind them his eyes were dark and unreadable. He was in his shirtsleeves and waistcoat only, his practical brown coat nowhere in sight. He looked rumpled, his hair tousled and half-pulled from the tie, as if been running his fingers through it as he paced, too agitated to dress properly before storming out of the house.

"You came back." Gil's voice was only a whisper. "I'd hoped, but—"

"Aye," Jarrett interrupted. He wanted to apologise, wanted to curse Gil all over again, wanted to run, wanted to never leave.

Pepper butted his shoulder with his great head, so instead of doing any of those, Jarrett led him to his stall and began setting him to rights. Gil didn't say anything as Jarrett unbuckled the saddle and bridle, although he stepped aside so Jarrett could hang all of Pepper's tack on the racks set for him on the wall opposite his stall. It wasn't the way things had been stored at the last house Jarrett had worked at, but the earl had enough saddles for each horse to have its own and then some. It did make it quicker to get the animals ready, with each piece of gear already fitted to the particular animal's body and easily found.

He fetched a feed bag and brushes and let Pepper have a long-delayed supper while Jarrett brushed him and looked him over, giving particular attention to his legs and hooves after their long ride. As he squinted over a foreleg, the stall brightened. Gil held the lantern out and followed Jarrett from leg to leg, shining the light where he needed it most.

The quiet sounds of the other horses in their stalls, the crunching of oats as Pepper ate, the rasp of the brush as he worked, these were sounds he'd known as long as he could remember and they settled his nerves as he worked.

"I thought you might want a light if—when you returned," Gil said at last.

That small kindness was enough to form a knot in Jarrett's throat. His eyes stung, and he focused on his fingers as he worked them through Pepper's mane so he wouldn't be tempted to look at Gil instead.

"I was five when I was sent to work in the stables," Jarrett said quietly, picking through a tangle. "I loved the horses, but I was too small to do most of the work. The other boys bullied me for it. Nothing too terrible. I was too small to shovel horse shite so they made me carry it by hand, that sort of thing. The stablemaster would swat their heads if caught them at it during the day, and when he went to his cottage at night, we boys all slept in the hayloft together like a litter of puppies. It was the happiest I'd ever been.

"Then one night after the stablemaster had left, one of the older boys told us he'd made a discovery. We all filed out to one of the outbuildings, whispering and giggling like boys do. He and two of the other boys pulled up some boards on the floor that had begun to rot, and revealed a second floor beneath, this one with a great square in the middle, with a ring in it. We knew what trapdoors were from adventure stories when'd been told and it took all of us together pulling on the ring to lift it. Beneath was just darkness. We argued over who should go down first, but I was the smallest..."

The knot in Jarrett's throat tightened. He'd never spoken of this to anyone. Of how the space was smaller than they thought with barely room enough for him to stand. The white flash of pain as the door fell on his head followed by blackness. The terror that had overcome him trapped down there in the utter darkness, not knowing if he was blind or if it was just too dark to see. The laughter of the other boys, muted through the heavy wood, then drifting further away. His own screams were deafening in the tight space, until he couldn't scream anymore and he'd sobbed with what little voice he had left, curled on the cold earth in the dark.

He swallowed. "They let me out in the morning. Some said it was just a jest, others an accident. I don't know if I believe either. I'd broken all my fingernails trying to claw my way out."

"My God," Gil whispered.

Jarrett nodded, resting his hands on Pepper's warm back. There was nothing else he needed to do, but he didn't want to see pity on Gil's face.

"I don't know if locking me down there or being punished for it was what made things change, but their bullying became crueler and I was terrified one night they'd shut me down there again. So I started doing whatever I could to make them like me, doing their chores for them, giving them the best parts of my food, learning funny songs and dances. Later, when I was older, I found there were other ways to make other boys like me. I didn't mind so much, because I liked it too. It started to become a game for me. And it meant I was never shut in the dark again."

There came a rustle from the far end of the stables. A small shape moved in the shadows, trotting closer in an uneven gait. Eventually the lantern light revealed it to be one of the barn cats, the wee three-legged one that was the cherished pet of the stablemaster's son Davey. Where the kitten was, Davey was never far behind.

"Perhaps we should continue this conversation elsewhere," Gil said.

Jarrett spent a few moments putting the empty feedbag away and checking on the other horses, rubbing Thistle's soft nose and smiling as she lipped his hands looking for treats.

"She's the one you were talking about earlier, isn't she?" Gil asked. "Your favourite who could run all day?"

"Aye," Jarrett answered. "Although Pepper did himself credit today. Gil, I—"

"Elsewhere," Gil said firmly.

Jarrett wasn't surprised when instead of leading him back to the house, Gil made his way towards the shed instead. The door was back on its hinges and locked again, but despite the lack of coat, it seemed Gil was prepared, pulling the key from his pocket and letting them in.

As Gil locked the door behind them, Jarrett took another look at the ruin the magistrate's men had caused. The shed was all but empty now, most of the furniture fit for little more than kindling. At least the mattress had been salvageable. Carnbee's men had cut it down the centre and torn out the hay, but it had been easy enough to re-stuff and flip over to hide the damage. God knew when he'd be able to buy a proper frame, but perhaps the earl would let him drag one out of the attic. His little horse carving lay on a windowsill alongside three of its four legs.

"I'm sorry," Gil said. He was using a piece of misplaced mattress hay as a taper, using the flame from the lantern to light several candles that had been placed on the floor where the table once stood.

Jarrett shrugged. "I should be the one apologising to you, I think. I was angry, but I understand. You couldn't have said how you knew I was innocent, not even to me. If I'd been me, I wouldn't have trusted you with my secret either."

"You trusted me now, with why you don't like the dark."

"Now is different," Jarrett said, and how true that was. Now, he actually knew Gil as more than just the pretty overseer, had spoken more than just a few stuttered sentences to him when his years of practised flirtations failed in the man's presence. Gil had pulled him from the dark, fought for him, kissed him more gently than Jarrett deserved. What were a few childhood terrors compared to that?

"Dogs," said Gil when the silence between them stretched too long. "That's my fear. Dogs. My uncle took me on a fox hunt when I was far too young for it. I enjoyed playing with his hounds in the kennels and he wanted to show me just what they could do.

"I still hear the screams of the fox when the hounds cornered it and the carnage that happened after. I never went near the kennels again. Even now, it affects me if some widow's lapdog yaps at me and I'm not prepared for it. Silly I know, for a grown man to be afraid of dogs."

"No sillier than a grown man afraid of the dark."

Gil gave him a small smile. "I never went back to my uncle's house either after that trip, but that was his choice. I'd embarrassed him in front of the other hunters. But now he's here and trouble has followed after."

Gil removed his spectacles and wiped the lenses in his familiar gesture.

Jarrett hadn't known anyone well enough before to recognise familiar gestures and know what they meant. But his enjoyment of that feeling of connection was ruined, because he did know what Gil cleaning his spectacles meant, and it was nothing good.

"It was one of my family," Gil said, giving the spectacles another wipe for good measure. "I know we suspected that, but I found some documents today that have confirmed it. As well as some other documents that taken with everything else... I have strong suspicions of who in particular. And why.

"But nothing we have is enough to prove murder on its own, not in a court of law, especially not if it's the rest of my family's word against yours and mine. But I was thinking; since we have his coat, he must have taken the victim's coat when he took the rest of his bloody clothing. But he didn't leave the coat here for the constables to find. Perhaps he's holding onto it in case something goes wrong or perhaps he doesn't realise it's the wrong coat yet. If we knew where he stashed it... But lacking that or some sort of confession, my family won't see—"

Gil's voice broke on the last word. Jarrett had known before that it was his life or one of the Charletons', but he hadn't fully realised what it must be costing Gil to help him. The only way to save Jarrett's neck from the noose was to put a member of his family's neck in there instead. Someone he'd grown up with, perhaps even loved. It was an impossible choice.

"I have funds," Gil said. He lifted his chin as he spoke and Jarrett wanted to brush back the strands of dark hair that clung to his firm jaw.

"I swear, Jarrett, whatever it costs, I'll get you out of this. I've already written to some of the best barristers in Scotland and there are investments I can sell if I need to hire more. And if it comes down to it, I'll say under oath that I saw you at The Cross Keys and what you were doing—what we were *both* doing that meant I kept quiet about it until now.

"I might as well, my father all but threatened to have me charged as an accomplice if I kept helping you. At least this way, with the right barrister, we have a chance at only getting transportation, perhaps even without incarceration once we reach Australia. It's not a guarantee, but it's the best I can do."

No.

The thought was so strong that Jarrett almost thought he'd spoken aloud. *No.* A conviction for murder was a guaranteed death sentence, a conviction for sodomy only a likely one. He wouldn't let Gil risk the ruin of his own life on the chance it might lessen Jarrett's sentence. Jarrett wouldn't put him through that. He couldn't.

He opened his mouth to ask—to beg—Gil to run away with him, but that would ruin Gil's life just as much. He'd be leaving behind his home, his money, his good name, all for a life of looking over his shoulder, never knowing a moment's peace. It was a worse fate even than transportation.

If Jarrett stayed, Gil would either see him hang, someone he loved hang, or have his life ruined forever.

If Jarrett ran, Gil would be imprisoned for helping him, Magistrate Carnbee would ensure it. The idea of leaving Gil behind to suffer tore at him, but at some point he would be freed. He'd be freed with no more damage to his name than being the poor fool taken in by that villainous Jarrett Welch. His soft heart at trying to help such an irredeemable character might even gain him sympathy. Gil could go back to his old life, with his long walks under open skies on land carrying his name and forget that Jarrett had been anything more than a bad dream. He would be safe, his family, awful as they were, would all be alive, and Jarrett would be free. And alone.

If Jarrett ran, he'd never see Gil again after tonight. Swallowing hard, he drank in the sight of him now.

By candlelight, Gil was so beautiful it hurt to look at him. His shirt was horrifically wrinkled and there were ink stains on the cuffs. A good valet would want to whisk them away to be cleaned before the stains and wrinkles could set, but Jarrett wasn't a very good valet and he wanted to remove them for entirely different reasons. Peel them off slowly, layer by layer, kissing each inch of skin as it was revealed. He'd seen Gil in his nightshirt, and flashes of muscular arse and thigh as he'd fucked him outside the chapel, but he wanted all of him. And not just for a quick fumble against a wall, but for a whole night, many nights, possibly all of the nights Jarrett had left in his life, however short that might be.

All the days too. He wanted to walk with Gil, ride with him, laugh and fight and argue. And like that, Jarrett finally knew the name for the strange feelings he got around Gil, the loss of words, the pounding heart. It wasn't just caring for him or even something as simple as lust. It was love.

And he wasn't going to ruin the man he loved.

But Gil, beautiful, kind, loveable Gil, wouldn't understand. For all his talk about only being the second son of a second son, he was more noble than all of them. He'd never understand a coward like Jarrett running from his problems.

But Jarrett wasn't just a coward, he was a selfish one. If he was only to have one more night with the man he loved, he would take it and keep the memory of it for all the other nights he couldn't have.

He let out a deep breath, letting his limbs go languid and loose. He dropped his gaze, looking up at Gil through his lashes. Old tricks, but ones that worked. He didn't miss the slight parting of Gil's lips, or his quick intake of breath. It was the easiest thing in the world to give a seductive grin and step closer to Gil, closing the distance between them. He ran his fingers slowly down the buttons of Gil's waistcoat.

"I-I wish I'd thought of it earlier," Gil stuttered.

"Hmm?"

"Saying I was the one with you at The Cross Keys. I could've been your alibi from the start, avoided all this mess."

Jarrett raised an eyebrow. "You'd have admitted to being with me when you weren't? I wish I'd seen you there that night. Perhaps then it wouldn't have been a lie, eh?"

Gil huffed. "I would've said we were playing cards, you idiot."

"Is that what you call it?" Jarrett dropped his grin from seductive to sincere. "I don't suppose you'd care to play a hand now?"

Gil closed his hands over Jarrett's own, trapping them against his chest.

"Jare, I'm serious."

Jarrett swallowed. "I am too," he admitted. "I want you to show me what I missed out on that night. What I've been missing all along when I was against alley walls with strangers while you were in real beds behind locked doors with someone you... trust. I've shown you my way. Will you show me yours?"

CHAPTER 23

G il tried to remind himself of all the reasons this was a terrible idea. Just the way Jarrett was looking at him should be reason enough. If Jarrett had been giving him a practised flutter of his eyelashes or another one of those coy gazes, Gil might have been able to resist. But instead he stared at Gil directly, his green eyes honest and more than a little vulnerable.

But if this was a terrible idea, they'd already done far worse.

"All right," he said. And that was enough.

Jarrett wanted to know what it was like to have a locked door, a discreet room, and a man to spend the whole night with. He'd already provided the first two for himself, Gil wasn't inclined to deny him the third.

"When I go to The Cross Keys, or other places where I can meet friends," Gil said slowly. "I like to think of the door locking being more than just the turning of the key, but sealing off the room from the rest of the world, shutting out all my concerns, my frustrations, my f-family, whatever bothers me, none of it can get past that barrier."

Jarrett looked at him a moment then nodded. He went over to the shed door and unlocked it. Then as Gil watched, he gave a long exhale and gave a strange shooing motion with his hands before slamming the door shut and turning the key with a flourish.

Gil tried to fight back the smile, but was afraid he was losing. "I didn't mean to be quite so theatrical."

Jarrett laughed. "It's a good idea though. All right, outside's outside. What's next? Remember, when it was my turn I already had your breeches down by now."

Gil rolled his eyes. "I thought you wanted to do this my way. We have the whole night. We can take our time. Is there anything you want to do?"

"Fuck."

"*Jarrett*. Anything in particular?" At Jarrett's confused look, Gil sighed. "Oh never mind, just come here."

In the small shed, "here" was only about two steps, so Gil had Jarret's lips on his almost immediately. Jarrett immediately tried to deepen the kiss, his tongue pressing against the seam of Gil's lips, his fingers gripping Gil's hair tightly. Gil cupped his hands around Jarrett's jaw, holding him gently but firmly, then leaned back.

"We're. In. No. Rush." He punctuated each word with a kiss so Jarrett wasn't completely bereft. Still, he hadn't realised before, it wasn't just at the chapel, when they'd kissed or brought each other off with their hands, every time Jarrett went straight for his goal. For a man who spent so much time flirting, there was no exploration, no play, only the act itself.

He leaned back further and felt a wicked grin steal over his face. Jarrett gave him a frustrated scowl, but didn't push against the hands on his face. Gil took the opportunity to rub his thumbs over Jarrett's cheekbones, almost afraid he'd cut himself. Jarrett was all angles, sharp nose, razor jaw, and cutting looks when he was in a mood. No wonder Gil had fought so hard against his attraction to him. He was dangerous.

All of him was sharp except his lips, Gil traced his thumbs over those next. They were soft, full, and even more dangerous than the rest of him.

"I hid the bottle under the mattress," said Jarrett. "The oil bottle you brought up to the chapel? When we were setting everything back to rights, I tucked it under there. 'Hopeful', as you said."

Dangerous.

"Good thinking." Gil swallowed. Then he said, "I'd like you to undress me. Slowly."

"Christ," Jarrett muttered.

At his nod, Gil dropped his hands. Jarrett gave himself a little shake and pulled his shoulders back, the proper gentleman's gentleman once more. Or as proper as he ever was.

He began unbuttoning Gil's waistcoat with practised efficiency, then stopped, before continuing more slowly. Two buttons later, he started trailing his fingers down the fabric as he worked, causing Gil's stomach to clench involuntarily.

"You're a quick study," he said.

Jarrett grinned. "And you're ticklish."

He continued on. When the waistcoat was undone, he slipped his hands under the fabric, running them up Gil's chest and over his shoulders. Stepping between Gil's toes as he pushed the waistcoat down his arms.

Gil rewarded him with another kiss. This time he let Jarrett's tongue in, stroking it slowly with his own.

Jarrett groaned. "All right, you may have a point about all this."

Gil narrowly avoided making a crude jest. "Cuffs next."

He held up one wrist, then the other. Jarrett removed the cufflinks from each, but the second time, held onto Gil's hand a moment longer. Then to Gil's surprise, he pulled Gil's palm to his face and kissed it.

Before Gil could respond, Jarrett dropped his hand, turning away to set the cufflinks on the windowsill beside the horse figurine, but Gil could swear his cheeks were flushed pink. He couldn't get a good look, because Jarrett made too-quick work of his cravat, tossing the linen aside with undue care, before attacking Gil's shirt buttons equally aggressively. There were only three of them, and then Jarrett was behind him, pulling his shirt from his breeches. His fingers traced around Gil's waistline, following the fabric as it was removed, and he flinched again.

"Ticklish," Jarrett huffed in his ear. And Gil certainly wasn't, but he also wasn't going to give the wee fox any ideas. Jarrett seemed to have plenty of ideas of his own though, wrapping his arms around Gil from behind, embracing him under the shirt. It was pleasant, more than pleasant, standing like this in Jarrett's embrace; it was the sort of thing he could get used to.

But before he could think about that, he felt clever fingers working at his fall.

"Aye!" He yelped, slapping at Jarrett's hand. "Slowly, I said. You haven't even got my shirt off yet."

"Christ, no wonder it takes you all night. I could have come three times already!"

Impatient creature. Fine, if Jarrett wanted to get to the "bed" part of "locked door and a bed," Gil could oblige.

"All right, all right, I'll get my own shirt. Get yourself naked then."

With a sigh, Gil pulled off his shirt, pausing to grab his cravat that had fallen a little too close to one of the candles on the floor for comfort. He then made his way over the single chair to work on his riding boots. It had survived the magistrate's men somehow and by the time he sat down, Jarrett was naked.

Gil opened his mouth to say something, but an undignified croak was all that emerged. If Jarrett clothed was beautiful, he didn't have words for what Jarrett naked and hard and stroking one hand up his cock while ran the other across his chest was. His skin was pale, far paler than Gil's, and he almost seemed to be glowing, lit from within with either holy light or hellfire, Gil didn't care.

He croaked again.

"What was that?" Jarrett teased.

Gil cleared his throat. He was the charming one, Goddamn it. And this was his night to be showing Jarrett, not the other way around. He looked Jarrett right in those wicked eyes and said, "Boots."

Then he spread his thighs.

Jarrett's eyes went wide.

"Boots." Gil said again. When Jarrett didn't move, he added, "Kneel."

Jarrett sank down, then crawled forward, his cock bobbing, and came to a stop between Gil's spread thighs. He ran his hands up the back of Gil's boot. Gil hadn't bothered to change after their ride earlier in the day, and the boot went nearly to his knee. He was a practical man, but the one place he made sure to have the finest quality was in his footwear. He had to, with all the time he spent walking. As such the boot was perfectly moulded to his calf and he could feel Jarrett's touch against it as if it was against his own skin.

The downside to this though, was that without a boot jack, they were a devil to get off, and from the look on Jarrett's face, he knew it. Of course he did, he was a professional, after all.

Gil raised an eyebrow. "Get to work."

Watching Jarrett struggle and curse was certainly entertaining, but Gil wasn't one to just sit back and watch. He reached for his fall, flicking open one button, then the next.

Jarrett groaned and rested his head against Gil's knee. Gil took the opportunity to run his fingers through Jarrett's hair. It was lovely. Neither too long nor too short, too light nor too dark. Just brown, just perfect.

He set back to work on his buttons. Just as he'd finished the last one, Jarrett gave a final pull and yanked his boot off with a triumphant cry. Then he looked back at Gil and the cry turned to a soft, "Oh."

"Hopeful." Gil shrugged.

Perhaps he had been a bit. What other excuse could he have for giving up on wearing drawers?

Now freed, his cock rose obscenely from his open breeches. Jarrett dived for it and everything in Gil screamed to let him have it, to get that mouth he'd dreamed about wrapped around himself at last. But there was a point to be made.

He pressed his still-booted foot against Jarrett's bare chest.

"You're a fucking bastard," Jarrett swore.

Gil tapped him with his toe.

He was surprised the leather survived Jarrett's assault. He considered dragging it out more—breeches, socks—but for all he was pretending otherwise, he was hanging onto his control by the barest thread. One more hate-filled look from *a naked Jarrett at his feet* and he was going to spend all over his face.

And that was the wrong thing to think of. Gil gripped himself tightly, wrapping his fingers painfully hard around the base of his cock and tugging down on his bollocks until he felt like it was safe to breathe again. Aye, they had all night, and he was only twenty-five. It wouldn't be the end of the world if he came now, he'd have another chance. But it would be incredibly embarrassing.

A firm tug had his second boot off and a very smug Jarrett grinning up at him. "Would you like some help with that?"

To Hell with resisting.

Gil leaned back and Jarrett took that for the invitation it was. He hovered over Gil's cock for just a second as if savouring the moment, then descended, swallowing Gil halfway down without warning.

Gil shouted and his hips flew off the chair. Jarrett made a choked noise, but didn't release him, pinning Gil down with his hands and pulling back so only the head of Gil's cock was held between his lips.

The string of apologies Gil had been repeating slurred into incoherence. Oh God, he'd thought at the chapel he wouldn't last a minute with Jarrett's mouth on him. In truth, he was going to be lucky to make it half that. Jarrett licked over the head and Gil gripped the seat of his chair with both hands, hearing the wood creak in his grip. His eyes wanted to shut against the unbearable pleasure, but he forced himself to watch.

Jarrett was looking up at him through his eyelashes again, this time sinking inch by inch down Gil's cock as he did. Those full lips were stretched taut around Gil's prick and his long, sinful lashes beaded with wetness. With a shaking hand, Gil wiped a drop from the corner of his eye. Then Jarrett swallowed around him, and there was no room left in Gil's body for tenderness, only sensation as Jarrett sucked and swallowed and then *hummed*.

The force of his climax slammed into Gil, knocking him back in the chair. He cried out, but Jarrett kept going, swallowing Gil's spend as if there was nothing else he'd rather be doing. Finally, it became too much, and Gil weakly batted him away. Jarrett didn't go anywhere, resting his head against Gil's knee again while he caught his breath.

"Lord," Gil panted finally. "I haven't even gotten you into bed yet."

Jarrett perked up. "You want to keep going?"

As if that wasn't the single stupidest question Gil had ever been asked. "Are you mad? Of course, I do. We have hours of night left and the door is still locked."

Jarrett laughed and Gil could have sworn he felt a lightning quick kiss against his knee before Jarrett was scrambling up and clambering over to the bed, such as it was. The frame had been destroyed, so for now it was just a mattress on the floor, but it would be comfortable enough, with sheets, pillows, and a sprawling, hard, and unsatisfied Jarrett, which was all really mattered.

Enticement like that was enough to get him out of the chair and his cock stirring again. He stripped off his breeches and socks quickly before swinging a leg over Jarrett, kneeling above him with one leg either side of his narrow waist, and surveyed his options. Then he surveyed Jarrett.

Beautiful. Small constellations of moles he hadn't noticed before dotted Jarrett's chest. Five? No, six. Perhaps more constellations on his back. He'd have to count when he got there. A scar even paler than the surrounding skin under his collar bone, shaped like a half-moon. Another that was a raised line on his shoulder.

"What are you doing?" Jarrett asked.

"Looking." Gil traced a finger over the half-moon scar. "Touching. I think I'm going to touch all of you tonight."

Jarrett stretched an arm up and a moment later a familiar glass bottle was being pressed against Gil's chest.

"You'll need this then."

Gil smiled and set the oil on the mattress beside him. Then he leaned over the scar and licked. Jarrett gasped, so Gil nuzzled into the sensitive skin of his collar, scraping his day-old beard over delicate skin and licked again. Jarrett jerked underneath him, hands coming up to grip Gil's forearms.

"Christ, that's good."

Gil hummed in agreement and continued his explorations, teasing gasps and sighs out of Jarrett until he got to his nipple and Jarrett yelped.

Gil looked up. Jarrett's eyes were blown wide with amazement.

"Has no one ever done that to you before?"

A dazed Jarrett just shook his head.

What a pack of utter fools, to miss out on this.

Gil took advantage of others' stupidity, licking and biting in turn, moving to the other nipple when the first grew too sensitive. While Jarrett was distracted, Gil used a great deal of previous experience to get the bottle open one handed, coating his fingers in the oil. He shifted, moving down as if to get a better angle on Jarrett's chest, but instead moving between those slim thighs. Jarrett's legs came up around him as if of their own accord and at the same time Gil blew across a nipple, he slid a finger in.

Jarrett keened, the sound filling the small room. His nails dug into Gil's skin, leaving half-moons of their own. Gil continued like this for some time, alternating between strokes of his finger and teasing Jarrett's chest, but he was after more.

He sat up, and Jarrett dropped his head back against the pillow, but he'd only survived the first onslaught. Gil shifted, moving Jarrett's legs higher up his thighs, and pressed into him again, reaching deeper and deeper until Jarrett threw his head back in a silent shout.

There.

"You can reach that with just fingers?" Jarrett's voice was hoarse.

Gil chuckled and reached it again, this time with two.

Gil had been with men who were loud in bed, men who were quiet, some with simple wants and others with perverse needs, but he'd never been with anyone who fell apart under his hands like Jarrett. Jarrett came undone as if it was an art that only he had mastered. By the time he replaced his fingers with his cock Gil could barely stand to look at him he was so lovely, splayed across the sheets like a wanton. But not content to passively take, with every thrust his hips rose to meet Gil's.

"God, Jare," Gil panted. By some miracle his spectacles had managed to stay on, but the damp heat of their bodies was filling the room. It was just as well, because he wouldn't be able to take the sight of Jarrett beneath him much longer.

"Gil, Gil, Gil!"

Hearing that desperate voice pleading his name was too much. Gil dropped down onto his elbows. He was afraid he'd crush Jarrett underneath him, but Jarrett's legs were wrapped around his waist and he was half off the bed. With what little sense he had left, he shifted his weight to one arm, using his hand still slick with oil to stroke Jarrett in time with his thrusts.

He didn't know if his climax sparked Jarrett's or Jarrett's sparked his, but at the same time he groaned, Jarrett *wailed* and hot spend spread over his fingers as he filled Jarrett again and again.

Through the haze of his spectacles, Jarrett looked like something out of a dream. Gil dropped his head onto his shoulder, careful to keep the gold frames from digging into his skin.

I love you.

He said the words silently. Mouthing them against Jarrett's shoulder, his scar, wherever he could reach.

Jarrett, I love you. I love you. I love you.
And he still had the constellations on his back to discover.

When he awoke the next morning, the broken horse figurine lay on the pillow beside him and Jarrett was gone.

CHAPTER 24

J arrett rode as he'd never ridden before. Mile after mile, taking roads where he could and cutting through fields when they drew too close to villages. Thistle leapt hedges and streams with equal ease, her hoofbeats a steady cadence never slowing in their rhythm. But they both had to rest eventually.

The sun never quite rose, only lightening in shades of grey, but around what Jarrett believed to be midday, the road turned towards the woods and Jarrett slowed Thistle to a walk and led her into the trees. Her sides were heaving and her coat darkened with sweat, but she still pulled at the reins, driving them forward.

Jarrett let her have her head and not long after, the sound of running water reached his ears. He slithered gracelessly off the saddle, kneeling down beside Thistle as they both drank deep gulps from the stream she'd found.

Thirst finally sated, Jarrett got to his feet with a groan. Even he wasn't used to being in the saddle from before sun up until midday, especially not at such a pace, without breaks, *and* following a full day of riding yesterday as well. He'd worried, when he first pulled Gil into bed, that he might not be able to ride today at all. He'd been with men like that, but the risk had seemed worth the reward. But Gil had been so cautious, so heartbreakingly gentle with him. At least with the way he'd touched Jarrett, that had been gentle. His words, on the other hand, and his *looks*, those made Jarrett shiver even now.

Lying together afterwards, he'd feigned sleep as he watched Gil's eyes grow heavier and heavier. Climbing out of bed while Gil slept was the second hardest thing Jarrett had ever done, following only closing the shed door behind him.

He shook his head. Enough. Climbing the gallows would have been a good deal harder if he'd stayed, all the more so if Gil was there to watch. Now, he would live and things would be easier for Gil. Even if he was imprisoned for a bit and hated Jarrett forever. Gil was so kind, surely he'd prefer that to Jarrett being dead?

He kicked at a pebble with his boot, watching it bounce along the ground before dropping into the stream with a small splash. If Gil felt about Jarrett the same way Jarrett felt about him, he would. But he'd been too uncertain. Far better to sneak out in the night and make the decision himself, even if he did feel like an utter cad.

Well, there was nothing to be done about it now. He would live. Gil would hate him. And Jarrett would spend the rest of his life missing him. It wasn't fair, but so little in life was.

But he wouldn't live if he got caught, and there were still many miles to Dundee and from there to... who knew? But neither he nor Thistle was going to get there on an empty stomach. He'd had to saddle her in the dark, unwilling to risk a light that would bring either Graham or Davey investigating, but perhaps there was some logic to Graham's system after all, as he'd been able to get her tack off her spot on the wall and onto her by feel alone. He'd even thrown a few handfuls of oats into the saddlebags for her and a loaf of blackened bread nicked from the kitchen for himself.

Thistle had found a patch of clover and was doing her best to ensure not a single leaf was left, so he could save her oats for later or for himself if Janie's bread proved inedible. He gave Thistle's mane a fond scratch when he made his way back over to her. He'd miss her too. Perhaps just selling her tack would be enough to book him passage on a ship. He could have a letter sent to the earl before he set sail, saying where she could be collected. It would be risky, but he didn't like the idea of both of them losing their homes because of his foolishness. Perhaps he could even include a message for Gil, if he could think of anything better to say than, "I'm sorry."

His stomach interrupted these mawkish thoughts with a loud grumble. Making his way to the saddlebags, he stopped before opening the first one. He hadn't been able to see them in the dark, but they looked fuller than they should for the meagre breakfast he'd packed. He'd been tempted to prove Mr. Howe right and pocket the silverware on his way out, but hadn't. Graham wasn't in the habit of using the bags for storage when not in use, so what could possibly be inside?

Unlatching the strap, he saw the bread he'd taken, with loose oats scattered around it, but underneath, there was something soft and brown filling most of the bag. Holding the bread in his teeth, he pulled the bundle out. Shaking it out sent oats flying and he had to step back as Thistle moved to get them.

It was a coat. His heart stopped, for a moment thinking he'd accidentally stolen the one good piece of evidence they had in the murderer's coat, but that one had been black. The one the victim had been wearing was also black, so this wasn't his either, planted like the bloody clothes to frame him.

Looking back into the saddlebag revealed nothing else, so Jarrett carefully stepped around Thistle to inspect the bag on the other side. This one revealed another bundle, but despite being smaller, when Jarrett pulled it out it was heavy for its size.

Something splashed the back of his neck. Jarrett looked up just in time to get a drop of rain in his eye, then another as a steady drizzle began to fall. He stopped to drape the second coat over his own before retreating to the shelter of a wide oak to examine the bundle. He unfurled it slowly, revealing a stained and dirty scarf.

His hands began to shake. He knew this scarf. It was the one Gil had given him in the cell to wrap around his bare feet. He continued unrolling it and something clinked from within. A few more tugs, and the centre was revealed. The wind caught at the paper within, and Jarrett had to clamp his hands tight to keep the bank notes from fluttering free. He couldn't read how much they were worth, but there were a lot of them, and if Jarrett had to guess, he'd wager that along with the bright gold sovereigns that peeked between his fingers, they were worth about two hundred pounds.

The ground didn't seem to want to stay where it should and Jarrett thunked back against the oak as he waited for the world to right itself.

Two hundred pounds.

The money from the murderer's coat, it had to be. But what was it doing in Thistle's saddlebags?

Two hundred pounds was more than enough to buy him passage on a ship, it was enough to buy him an entirely new life, and a good one at that. Instead of scraping a living in whatever foreign port he found himself, he could set himself up wherever he chose, perhaps training horses in Australia, or starting his own herd of mustangs in the Americas. It was more than just money, it was freedom.

He looked again, just to make sure he wasn't dreaming. Carefully, so as not to let the wind snatch them away, he peeked again. Banknotes and gold and something else, which he gently pulled free. It was a sprig of lavender.

Gil.

Gil had done this. He'd been in the stables when Jarrett had returned with Pepper yesterday, his hand on the Thistle's saddlebag when Jarrett came in. He'd even asked earlier which horse was Jarrett's favourite. How long had he been planning this?

Because this meant Gil knew. If he'd just been using the saddlebags to hide the money, he wouldn't have packed the coat. But he'd packed it, along with the scarf because he knew Jarrett was going to run, and he wanted him to be warm. And he'd packed the lavender so Jarrett would know it was him. As if there would ever be anyone else.

Jarrett buried his face in the collar of the practical brown coat and was struck with the scent of lavender and orange oil. He took another deep breath. It was the smell of hair like spilled ink and golden spectacles hiding even more golden eyes.

He wanted to cry. Gil had ensured that Jarrett would be warm and provided for and in exchange Jarrett had left him to be shackled in the dark where he couldn't walk, couldn't roam free across the open spaces he loved.

He crammed the money back into the saddlebag. The scarf he wrapped around his neck before tucking the sprig of lavender into his waistcoat, just above his heart. It was a little bulky, squeezing his arms into another coat, but the rain was picking up in earnest and they had another half day's ride ahead of them.

Another coat.

Oh Christ. They'd been so blind.

He pulled himself up into the saddle and allowed himself just enough time to take another deep breath of Gil's scent before touching his heels to Thistle's sides. Clever animal that she was, she started walking in the direction they'd been heading towards Dundee.

Jarrett wheeled her head around. Thistle nickered, sounding for all the world like a question.

"Sorry, lass. We have to go back."

She snorted, and Jarrett took that as agreement.

"I know, but it wasn't all for naught. I think I know where to find the proof we need. And if I'm wrong, well. I've run enough. I can't leave him to face all that alone, can I?"

Thistle didn't respond, but as he eased her up to a trot, she broke into a canter instead. Jarrett tucked his face into the scarf to protect against the rain, the cloth enveloping his smile. They were going home.

CHAPTER 25

G il had walked this same road so many times, his boots could carry him to his destination on their own. It was just as well he didn't have to think about where he was going as he was far too preoccupied with what a terrible idea it was to go there. More than terrible, it was foolhardy. Rash. Dangerous.

Reckless.

Despite everything, the word made him smile.

From the moment he'd reached out in bed to feel nothing but cool sheets, the day had been miserable. Even before he'd opened his eyes and seen the little broken horse, he'd known Jarrett was gone for good this time. He hadn't needed to go to the stables to know Thistle would be missing either. Jarrett's favourite, who could run all day. He could have gone into the house and found out whether Mrs. Finely was in hysterics about the larder being broken into or Mr. Howe was in an uproar about missing silver, but he didn't. Instead he pulled the torn quilt further up around his shoulders and tried to pretend he could still feel some of Jarrett's warmth. How could he already miss the feel of Jarrett beside him in bed?

He'd already known the answers to all of the questions except that one. Thistle would be gone, but the silver and larder would be untouched. For all Jarrett's *Jarrettness*, he had a good heart, no matter how desperately he tried to hide the fact. He would've felt guilty enough about taking Thistle, he wouldn't have touched anything else.

Gil ought to feel betrayed or even used. Perhaps he would tomorrow. Today, he'd told Graham he'd given Jarrett permission to exercise Thistle and Janie that they were meeting for breakfast at the pub and not to worry about supper either. Tomorrow, no doubt one of the servants would alert Magistrate Carnbee, but he could give Jarrett today.

He'd spent the day out walking, going to all his favourite spots. After tomorrow, it might be some time before he saw them again. There was only one place his walk could end, however.

Staring up at the grey stone of Charleton House, the slate of the roof high above merging with the slate of darkening sky, he hoped that wherever he ended up, Jarrett would be happy there.

Then Gil pushed the great door open and entered his childhood home for the final time.

Either the servants had not yet been expressly ordered to bar his entrance or the butler and two footmen he encountered took one look at his expression and decided discretion was the better part of valour, because he wasn't stopped as he stalked through the house.

He had to go by his office first, then, after finding something expected and something else unexpected, he checked the dining room. But his family kept country hours and the room was empty save for a lone maid clearing the last of the plates who was clearly shocked to see him. Only one other place they could be. As he approached the drawing room, the sound of voices told him he'd been correct. The door had been left open, so no one noticed when he stepped inside.

The room was dark, the fire in the grate being the main source of light with the older generation of Charletons seated close to it. Gil's father and Uncle Andrew were seated in two large chairs before the fire and his mother was on the settee nearby, squinting down at her embroidery. In the dimness beyond, Gil could see a bowl of blue flame, Catriona and Charles laughing and taking turns plucking chestnuts from the flaming bowl, playing snapdragons as if it was Christmas

Eve and not mid-March. Robert, unsurprisingly, was at the cellarette pouring himself a drink, likely lamenting the waste of good brandy being set alight.

Good, they were all here. If Gil was going to destroy his relationship with his family, he might as well do it entirely. He took in the scene a little longer, one last moment of peace.

"Murdo Sinclair."

All faces turned towards him at the name of the murdered man, but only one looked stricken. It was all he needed to know he'd been right about which one of them was the killer. The confirmation settled his roil of emotions into a cold dread and he had to fight back the urge to cry. There would be time for tears later.

"Gilleasbuig!" his father bellowed. "What are you doing here? I made myself very clear what would happen if you brought that villain back to this house!"

"Jarrett isn't here." Gil said through gritted teeth. "I came alone."

His mother gasped. "You mean you've left a murderer to run loose? Think of what might happen! What people will say!"

It was almost funny. She hadn't once objected to her son putting himself in danger by being in the presence of a supposed killer, but now that people might *talk*...

"Don't worry, Mother. You don't have to worry about a murderer roaming the countryside. He's right here in this room."

His mother jerked her head frantically around, as if expecting Jarrett to leap out from behind a curtain with a knife clenched between his teeth.

The last of the blue brandy flames spluttered out, leaving the fire as the only illumination. The atmosphere was a little too gothic for his tastes, so Gil walked over and placed another log on it, stirring the embers until it caught and blazed almost cheerfully.

"I say, Gil, aren't we being a bit overdramatic?" asked his brother, of all people. "Pour yourself a glass and settle down, you're scaring the women."

Robert was right about their mother but Catriona hardly looked frightened. Her mouth was a grim line and she met Gil's gaze coolly.

"I considered it might be you, at first," Gil admitted to her. "You're a more impressive woman than we give you credit for. And women often have secrets their husbands know nothing about."

"I say!" Charles laughed. "You know I'm fond of a game, Gil, but this one's in poor taste. And you're coming damned close to insulting my wife."

"Do be quiet," Catriona said softly. She didn't look at her husband, but kept her eyes on Gil, her eyes darting over his features as if he was an open book and she was reading him to see what he contained. After a long moment, she gave him a slight nod, then deliberately looked at Robert.

He'd been right about that too then. What she saw in his drunkard of a brother, Gil had no idea, but that wasn't his secret to tell. On the list of crimes committed by his family, adultery was hardly the worst.

Gil gave her a brief nod back, then continued. "But while I don't doubt your ability if pressed, the rock used to crush Mr. Sinclair's skull was impressively heavy. And even if you could lift it, neither you nor my mother would be mistaken for a tall man by Mrs. Randall, not even in the dark.

"No, the Charleton women have been content to keep their felonies to theft, although even in that, I'm not entirely sure you can be blamed. You studied law when you were at Oxford, didn't you, Uncle Andrew? Is it still a crime if you don't know you're committing one?"

"Gilleasbuig Ailean Charleton!"

His father got to his feet. In the low light his anger-flushed face made him look like some Roman god, equal parts rage and bluster. Gil raised the poker he still held to his father's chest, leaving a dark spot of soot on his pale green waistcoat. That was enough to at least make his father pause. Gil didn't think he could actually bring himself to strike him, even after all the things his father had said, but Bernard Charleton looked far less certain.

Good. Let someone else be frightened for a change. Gil was weary of the feeling.

"Really, Gil. Theft as well as murder? This is too much." His uncle sounded distant as ever as he spoke, as if Gil accusing his family of multiple crimes was hardly more vexing than a slow walking companion who couldn't keep the pace, or a line of numbers that didn't quite add up.

"Perhaps it isn't theft," Gil admitted. "I'm afraid I'm not certain of the legal term for purchasing dresses on credit when you have no money to pay them off. Fraud, perhaps? Speaking of which, just how in debt *is* the barony, Uncle?"

That set them all off at once. For just a moment, Gil let himself enjoy the squabbling. One way or the other, it would likely be his last time hearing it. He might know who the killer was, but if he walked out of this room alive, proving it would be another matter. And if the rest of the family chose to close ranks around the killer, it would be almost impossible to take to trial. But for Jarrett's sake, he had to try.

He raised the poker again, like a maestro settling an orchestra before the final performance.

"I apologise, Mother, I doubt you realised you were spending money we didn't have. If it means anything, you were hardly the only one bankrupting us. Had I been allowed to look at the finances for the barony, I would have questioned whether the second morning room really needed repapering, but I'm neither the baron nor his heir, so my advice was not sought. Was yours, Father?"

He didn't have to look at his father to know it wasn't. It was a cruel jab, but hardly more than he deserved.

"That's unfortunate," Gil continued. "Until you decided you preferred the life of a country gentleman, you were an excellent estate manager. Without the skills you taught me, I might not have worked it out. I'll always appreciate that."

Gil cleared his throat and forced away memories of happier times, running after his father in boots he'd yet to grow into as his father inspected a tenant's farm, pointing out repairs that would need to be made, and knowing down to the penny how much they'd cost.

"Uncle Andrew, does Aunt Anne have any idea about the debt? Every single year you all go to Edinburgh after Christmas to wait out the rest of winter in the city, but not this year. I did wonder if that was why she went to Edinburgh alone rather than coming here with you and Charles, but then I realised it was the other way around. It wasn't that she didn't want to come here, but you didn't want to go the city. Too much temptation there perhaps? Gambling hells on every corner and horse races in every paper? But you must have been in Edinburgh for at least a little while. Where else would you have gotten these?"

From his pocket, Gil pulled one of the gold sovereigns. It glowed in the firelight, just the sort of beautiful temptation a man would kill for. The entire Charleton clan seemed to have forgotten it was their crimes he was revealing and were transfixed, either by Gil's telling or by the gold itself. He rather suspected it was the latter.

"Where did you get that?" Charles rasped.

"From the coat that was found with the body. Sewn into the lining was just over two hundred pounds."

"Two hundred pounds!" the baron cried.

"Where's the rest of it?" snapped Gil's father.

Gil smiled and knew from the way they recoiled there was no trace of charm in it. It was the sharp grin of a fox.

"Somewhere much better than lining a killer's pockets, literally or figuratively."

"Surely," interjected Charles, the first of the group to recover, "it was lining the *victim's* pockets, if we are to believe you based on a single coin, and this coat of riches was found with the body."

"That's true," Robert piped up. "After all, why would a killer take that much money with him to commit his crime? And he certainly wouldn't leave all that behind. Not that I would know!" He added when the rest of the family turned to look at him.

Gil was impressed. It wasn't like Robert to put that much thought into, well, anything.

"The coat, which I have stored somewhere safe rather than bringing tonight for reasons that should be obvious, is undoubtedly the killer's and not the unfortunate Mr. Sinclair's. There is neither blood on it nor a knife hole in the back."

Gil let the poker rest loosely on the floor, but held up his free hand to forestall the inevitable questions.

"Aye, the victim was seen wearing a similar coat and may have removed it before being murdered, but it would be a damned coincidence if the maids in the Sinclair house were as fond of tucking lavender into pockets as they are here. I'd wager, if I took that coat down to the kitchen right now, I would find a dozen identical ones hanging by the door. Minus the money in the lining, of course. I'd also wager that if I were to ask Cook if there was a knife missing, I'd know the answer. I did mean to ask before I came up here, but I'm afraid I was rather impatient."

It would have been the logical, careful thing to do, to make sure he had as much evidence as he could before confronting his family, but Jarrett had clearly been rubbing off on him in more ways than one.

He let himself be distracted by the memory of Jarrett in their shared bed the night before, sated and happy. Gil could almost feel those clever fingers tracing over his face, gentle and reverent before Gil captured them to kiss one by one. He fought the urge to adjust his spectacles, the heavy iron of the poker in his hand bringing him out of that pleasant remembrance and back into the awful present.

"It was not the murderer's intention to leave his coat behind. He chose the chapel for his crime, so he wouldn't be interrupted in his foul work. So the sounds of someone in the graveyard must have been especially startling. I can only imagine the look on the murderer's face when he realised that in his haste to flee, he had carried off the victim's coat and not his own."

His father scoffed. "And who told you all this, Mr. Welch? I wonder how it is he knows so much?"

The others murmured in agreement.

"I determined it, as a matter of fact," Gil fought to keep his voice level. "After retrieving the coat from Marta's cellar and examining it more thoroughly. If Magistrate Carnbee had taken the time to do the same, Mr. Welch, an innocent man, would never have been blamed for this crime."

Charles leaned back in his chair and crossed his arms. If he thought this was a game before, he clearly didn't now. "What do you mean, you 'retrieved' it?"

"I stole it," Gil said frankly. "The same way the killer attempted to, by paying Marta to view the body. A coat isn't an easy thing to slip out, but I succeeded where he failed. No doubt this was why he tried to break into her cellar in the night, only to fail again."

Gil hesitated. He was starting to enter the realm of conjecture, rather than known fact, but he was certain he was right. If they were very lucky, Marta might even recall who she'd given a tour to in the day or so before the break in attempt. It was likely half the county, but she had a good memory, and a Charleton, *any Charleton*, was the sort of personage you remembered.

He wasn't being completely honest about how he'd acquired the coat, but bringing Jarrett into it would do no good. For the same reason, he didn't bring up that while the killer was unsuccessful in making off with Murdo Sinclair's coat, Jarrett's possessions had been held in the same cellar and the key to Jarrett's shed would have been much easier to pocket.

It'd never been Carnbee who'd taken it. Why would he have bothered with something so worthless? Besides, if he had, the fool wouldn't have bothered to hide it by knocking the shed door off its hinges when his men came searching; he'd have just told them to go get the key back from the killer and then waltzed right on in to find the bloody clothes.

No, the shed key had been slipped into the killer's pocket from Marta's storeroom after Gil had been stupid enough to mention it at the inquest. But he saw no reason to bring up the key now. After all, trying to explain why Jarrett had a room full of the victim's bloody clothes wrapped around the murder weapon was unlikely to convince anyone of his innocence. However, if the killer wanted to bring up the key, the clothes, or *how he knew about them*, Gil was happy to let him do so. He paused, hoping the man would take the bait.

His father was still standing in front of his chair, looking like he'd crumple into it if Gil touched him with the poker again. Robert had abandoned his glass to drink straight from the bottle.

Both women were sitting bolt upright. He hadn't been sure if one of them knew more about the crime than she'd let on, however, they both looked as if their worlds were crumbling around them, albeit for slightly different reasons.

Charles was still sat opposite his wife at the table, his long legs kicked out in front of him, arms crossed, and brow furrowed. That left only Uncle Andrew.

The baron had his fingers steepled, his air of aloof appraisal returned once more, but to Gil's disappointment, neither he nor any of the other three men, one of them the killer, said anything.

To Gil's surprise, it was his mother that broke the silence.

"What nonsense!" She harrumphed. "You bring us this... this fairy story and expect us to believe it? I don't know which is worse, if you came up with drivel on your own or if that *valet*"—she said the word the way some would say "louse-infested vermin"—"came up with it and you're so gullible as to turn against your own family."

"She has a point," said Catriona, another surprise. "That is, I was at the inquest and while the case against Mr. Welch may not be perfect, I'm not sure this is any better. Everything you've said, well, they're all just assumptions, aren't they? And even if you did remove the coat from the cellar, how can you prove the one you have is the same one? Or that the lavender and money you speak of were there before you got hold of it? I don't mean to doubt you, Gil, but your accusations are serious and your association with Mr. Welch calls them into question. Do you have any real proof?"

Her voice was soft, gentle, but there was a note of urgency in it too, as if she was pleading with him.

"*Association.*" His father snarled. "I think we've all heard quite enough about Mr. Welch and your *association.*"

"Hear, hear!" Robert shouted, with only a slight slur. "You come in here calling us k-killers and-and thieves who can't pay our bills! I should have thrown you and that lying, murdering weasel both out on your arses!"

"Would you, please?" the baron asked dryly.

Robert lurched forward.

"Robert!" Catriona cried.

"He's right, my dear," said Charles. "I hate to say it, but these slanderous allegations have gone too far."

Robert took another step forward. A childhood of being tormented by his older, bigger brother had Gil raising the poker before he even realised he was doing it. It made a far better weapon than the wooden swords of his youth, but whether from anger or drink, Robert didn't stop. Their mother was shrieking, but Gil couldn't tell which son she was concerned for. The rest of them were yelling now too. Catriona's high pitched, "Stop! Stop!" rising above the shouts of the men all spurring Robert onward.

Christ. What had Gil been thinking? He hadn't, that was the problem. He'd been reckless and now his family had turned on him. Their casual displeasure of before was nothing compared to this. Even worse, he'd tipped his hand to the killer and had nothing to show for it.

He was so focused on Robert, he almost missed Charles drawing closer until he lunged. Gil darted out of the way at the last moment, but that only drove him deeper into the room. Now he was trapped.

Turning to face his attackers, his back struck the far wall. He kept the poker raised, waving it in front of him to ward off his brother and cousin. He still didn't know if he'd be able to bring himself to use it, but he didn't trust the gleam in their eyes.

What happened now? Either he fought his way out and ran, potentially injuring someone he once cared for, or he let them take him and then, what? Jarrett was gone and his family was against him. They'd make sure he was tried for Jarrett's escape, and likely anything else they could make stick.

But he couldn't think about that now. Robert was raising his fists and looked ready to leap at him, damn the consequences.

Then the air was split by an ear-splitting whistle.

The noise was so loud in the small room, that Gil nearly dropped the poker in surprise. Then he saw where the noise came from, and the poker clattered to the floor.

In the doorway of the drawing room stood Jarrett.

The firelight caressed his features, sharpening the angles of his face even further and making him look not-quite human. Despite the circumstances, he had that wicked grin on his face and his eyes glittered with mischief. In his arms, he held a bundle of something dark.

He gave Gil a quick wink, then turned to Catriona, who sat stunned, her hand to her mouth.

"It was proof you wanted, ma'am? Will this suffice?"

Jarrett then shook out the bundle and held it out in front of him. It was a coat, similar to the one they'd found by the body, black and heavy and so long Jarrett had to hold it above his head to keep it from brushing the floor. Even in the dim light, it was clear the dark fabric was covered in stains the same red-brown as on the clothes left in Jarrett's shed. He pushed his hand against the fabric. After a moment, his fingers poked through a large gash in the back of the coat, where the deadly knife had gone through.

After a moment to ensure they all saw, Jarrett tossed the coat at Catriona's feet. She recoiled.

The coat spread as landed, the great cape fluttering down like bat wings. Lying open on the floor, most of it was flat, but Gil noticed a bulge where something large had been crammed into a pocket too small to hold it. The fabric spilling out of the pocket was neither black nor bloody-brown, but striped in violet and pale blue.

"I found your missing shawl too, ma'am," Jarrett said to Catriona.

Gil cleared his throat. "You should have hidden it better, Charles."

CHAPTER 26

J arrett had never witnessed anything like the stunned silence of the Charleton clan after Gil said Charles' name.

Gil himself was at the back of the lot, pressed against the wall, poker at his feet and a look of relief on his face. Whether that was relief at seeing Jarrett, or if any rescuer would do, he didn't know and honestly, he didn't care. Charles might be the only one of these hounds who had actually had blood on his muzzle, but they were all vicious, and Jarrett was done running. He wasn't going to leave the man he loved to be torn apart by them.

The silence was broken by the elder Mrs. Charleton shrieking.

"Is that blood? Oh, the murderer has come to kill us all!"

"No, Mother," Gil said, with undeserved patience. "Well, aye. It is blood, but until a few minutes ago, the murderer was playing snapdragons with Robert and Catriona. If he'd wanted you dead, he could have done it then."

That didn't seem to help Mrs. Charleton's disposition any.

"What is the meaning of this?" bellowed Gil's father.

Jarrett shrugged. "I heard you as I was coming down the hall. You wanted proof that what Gil said was true. So I brought it to you. That's the victim's coat there, covered in his blood."

"And you, the killer, brought it to us," sneered Charles. "Why even bother with a trial?"

Jarrett grinned, sharp and vicious. "Because half your staff just saw me take that coat from the bottom of the ones hanging by your kitchen door. None of them tried to stop me after I asked if there was a knife missing from the kitchen as well." He kept his body facing Charles, but risked a quick glance at Gil. "You were right, by the way. Apparently, your cook made quite the fuss about that. I'm sure they all remember when it was discovered missing, and it was long before I ever set foot in this house."

"And my shawl?" Catriona Charleton said softly.

Jarrett gave Gil another glance. He'd just been guessing that part, but the dead man didn't seem like the sort to wear much purple and blue and Gil had mentioned him being blamed for a missing shawl belonging to Mrs. Charleton, so when he'd seen it in the pocket of the bloody coat, he'd assumed.

Gil understood the look at once and took over. "The victim, Murdo Sinclair, was a fabric trader. Or rather, he was a charlatan who made money by convincing people to invest in his trades, wildly inflating the value of sub-standard goods and coming up with excuses to keep their money. He sent me samples some time back, but I wasn't interested. Someone else responded in my name. The pattern on your shawl is the same as one of those samples. Fortunately, unlike some who burn all unwanted correspondence, I keep mine for reference. As you can see here."

Gil reached into his waistcoat and unfolded a piece of paper, affixed to which were several squares of fabric, each uglier than the last. Catriona Charleton had gotten off lightly with the blue and purple. But it was the fabric square next to the one matching her shawl that really caught Jarrett's eye.

"Is that—"

"Aye, the same pattern as the dead man's trousers. The swatches link the trousers to Sinclair, Sinclair to the killer, and the killer to the shawl."

"Mrs. Charleton," Jarrett asked gently. "Where did you get your shawl?" He already knew the answer.

Catriona Charleton could barely force the words out. "It was a gift from Charles."

Gil nodded. "No doubt, when you came back from the inquest and told everyone what happened, you mentioned that the victim's distinct trousers had been noted. He couldn't risk the two garments being linked. So he hid your shawl with the coat. I admit, I hadn't made the connection to your missing shawl until I retrieved this letter from my files just now. I only remembered seeing a swatch of fabric matching the description of the victim's clothing. Yours was a surprise."

"Aye," Jarrett chimed in. "And where better to hide a stained coat than with others that have been used for years? You couldn't hide it in the rest of the house, not with staff. We know where all the dirty laundry is. So you hid it in plain sight.

"You've more coats than staff, so it was unlikely anyone would find it. Even if they did, if you're only grabbing something to keep the rain off, you're not going to think it's blood. You'll say, 'That coat at the bottom is filthy. I'll grab another,' and not think twice about it. Wool makes an awful stink, or I'd imagine he'd have burned it already. And that's a damned big coat, greater chance to get caught smuggling it somewhere else to hide. Or he might have been waiting to see if he could plant it somewhere to make me look guilty. I'd like to know why me though."

"It was because his original plan didn't work." Gil said and Jarrett wondered if anyone else could hear the way the thin coating of calm hid the anger underneath.

Gil turned to the baron. "Uncle Andrew, let us be clear. I know you didn't come here for the sea air. You came here because you discovered Charles was gambling the family into ruin, so you brought him out here to keep an eye on him. I don't think you quite understood how thoroughly he'd already emptied the family coffers. As your heir, he had every right to do business in your name. But he'd taken the money and what little he hadn't squandered, he'd hidden. Sovereigns and crisp bills from the bank. Which account did he empty for that?

"That was why you two kept locking yourselves away to do the accounts. Uncle, you were trying to fix his mess, but

Charles just saw how completely broken it was. He was heir to a bankrupt barony and with entailments, he would be stuck with it. That is, unless he was murdered.

"Jarrett, you met Mr. Sinclair the night he died. How would you describe him?"

A great nasty brute who didn't even have the good taste to want what I was offering.

"Tall, broad. Ugly trousers and a face on him that might have been improved by getting smashed in."

The rest of the Charletons looked pained at the last part, but Gil only nodded. "Tall, broad. And how did Mrs. Randall describe the man who knocked into her?"

"She thought she remembered him being larger than Mr. Welch here," Catriona Charleton said. "I heard her say that to him, and at the inquest she also described him as like the ghost of Bertram de Shotts, the giant!"

Gil nodded. "Murdo Sinclair was a large man. Ja-Mr. Welch, is... slight of both frame and stature. Charles, however, is also a large man. He needed a new life, one not burdened by the responsibilities he'd squandered, and to do that, he needed a body that was like his, but not a local's who would be missed. So he lured Mr. Sinclair out here, killed him, and destroyed his face with the rock so he could not be recognised.

"His plan was then to swap his clothes with those of the corpse, so when the body was found, we would all believe that it was *Charles* who had been murdered. Swap all the clothes, that is, except for the coat lined with money. That would go with him. He'd even gone so far as to leave a trail of letters leading back to the 'real' killer—his black sheep of a cousin, me. And should the body's true identity ever come to light, those letters would make it look like I killed two men that night, but was much better about hiding Charles' body. That way, he was assured that no matter what, he'd be assumed dead and would be free to start his new life.

"However, Charles didn't count on two things, the victim having a tattoo, and Mrs. Randall. It's likely he missed the first in the dark as he was stripping the body, it was quite close to the stab wound and we didn't notice it at first ourselves through all the blood. But I have written for confirmation that Murdo Sinclair is both tattooed and missing. As soon as I receive that, this all goes from speculation to fact.

"As for Mrs. Randall, she interrupted him before he was finished. Charles had no choice but to flee. Panicked and in the dark, he took the victim's clothing with him, but left his own coat behind. Lucky for him that Magistrate Carnbee saw Jarrett as the guilty party and decided to look no further."

If Jarrett wasn't already in love with Gil, he would be now. Cornered, scorned, and still every word he said was even, reasoned, and laid out the events perfectly, leaving no room for doubt that what he said was the absolute truth.

So obviously Gil's father gave a derisive snort. "And who's to say Magistrate Carnbee was wrong?"

"And where would I get a coat full of gold sovereigns?" Jarrett snapped. From the man's son just a few hours ago, actually, but that was hardly the point.

"How dare you speak to your betters that way!" snapped the baron. "I order you to apologise immediately."

That was what warranted an apology?

Jarrett didn't hide his disgust. "I don't work for you. I work for an *earl*."

As one, the elder Charletons all gasped at his boldness. It was all the distraction Charles needed.

He charged, grabbing at Gil. He snatched the letter with the fabrics out of his hands and knocked him back. Then he leapt a side table, making straight for Jarrett. Jarrett, who was standing between a killer who was easily several hands taller and several stone heavier than he was and the only door. But he'd been dealing with massive brutes since he was a child, and been kicked by more than one horse, so he braced himself to stop him even as he heard Gil shout his name.

But at the last second, Charles ducked down, and scooped up the bloody coat and shawl, throwing them and the letter on the fire.

The room was plunged into darkness as the heavy wool smothered the flames. All Jarrett's childhood fears rushed back to him. He was trapped in the dark, but this time, the monster was not of his imaginings. It was real, and it was still coming for him. Jarrett braced his feet against the floor and waited in the dark.

Something heavy struck him, knocking him to the side, but Jarrett lashed out, his fingers catching on fine linen. He dug in, flinging himself at the invisible assailant. Fighting for his life and for the man he loved. He kicked, hearing a curse, and kicked again. Then he was falling, dragging the beast down on top of him. He tried to push him away but it was too late.

His head hit the stone floor, and the pain brought everything back. He was pinned, trapped in the dark. He couldn't get out! He couldn't see! He couldn't move! But still he held on. Punching and kicking, he held on. This wasn't then. He just had to hold on and keep fighting.

Then the monster gave a vicious howl. The choking smell of burning hair filled the air as the coat caught, going up in a rush that lit the room even brighter than before.

Jarrett scrabbled back and leapt to his feet. Charles lay on the floor where he'd been, back arched with pain, the hook on the end of the poker embedded in his shoulder. Gil stared down at him, clearly shocked at what he'd done.

"So much for your proof!" Charles howled. "I'll see you hanged! Both of you! I heard you in that shed! Filthy abominations!"

Gil went very still. He'd made it through everything else his family had done, everything else they'd said about him, but now he looked as if he was about to break. Jarrett knew how cautious he'd been, how careful for so many years and to have his secret revealed like that, in front of his entire family. And all because of Jarrett.

He wanted to run, but he'd come back for Gil and he wasn't going to leave him to suffer this alone with the echoes of Charles' words ringing in his ears.

"Wait," said Jarrett, "What were you doing by the shed? It wouldn't happen to have anything to do with those bloody clothes turning up? Not to mention the knife. Since you admit to being there, perhaps we should fetch it. Have your cook tell us if the knife's the one she's missing."

"The word of a cook and a valet against a Charleton," Charles sneered. "Against all the Charletons? Save, of course, the one you've got bent over for you? We'll see how that goes in court."

"Not all the Charletons," said a quiet voice.

Catriona Charleton stepped forward. Her chin raised, determined and unrepentant. Jarrett had seen that look on her face outside Mrs. Randall's cottage.

There were many uses for grave-gathered herbs, tansy, in particular. His mother had known many, and used them to help women who came to her, their eighth child in their arms, unable to afford the ones they already had and needing precautions against any more. Others who found themselves in a family way and for reasons of their own needed not to be.

He didn't know which Catriona Charleton was, nor did he care. Her husband was a brute. He didn't blame her for not wanting to bring his child into the world. And if he had been too busy running up debts to be with his wife and she'd found solace elsewhere, with the inevitable result, then she had every right to be terrified of him. Yet she stepped forward anyway.

"I'll testify," she said. The crackle of the flames seemed to hush to hear her. "It wasn't right what you did, Charles. Both the murder and then blaming an innocent man."

She addressed the baron, now ignoring her bleeding husband before her. "He's been acting strange since the night of the murder. I thought he'd been out gambling again, and I was afraid to tell you. When my shawl went missing, I assumed he'd lost it at the tables, trivial as it was. Then I began rereading my notes from the inquest and realised it was that same night. It's almost a relief to know.

"I'll testify to seeing the bloody coat, and the letter with the fabric that matched my shawl, and everything else that's happened here tonight... And to everything *else* he's done."

"Enough!" If the baron had any reaction to seeing his son bleeding on the floor before him, he didn't show it. Despite the anger in his voice, his face was unchanged.

Yet his eyes glinted with malice as he spoke. "There is no benefit to be gained by discussing this unpleasantness further. I will speak to Carnbee, and the charges against Mr. Welch will be dropped. Assuming he and my nephew do not continue their slanderous allegations against my son. This is a family matter and should be kept as such. No one need be disgraced over it."

The charges dropped, just like that. It was the sort of miracle Jarrett had been praying for since this entire nightmare happened.

"No."

Jarrett's heart sank. He looked around to see which Charleton wanted to destroy him. To his shock, it was Gil.

"No," Gil said again. "The dead man's family deserves justice, and Jarrett's name won't be fully cleared unless the guilty party is brought to court."

Charles growled. "You put me on the gallows and you and your catamite will be right there beside me."

Gil flinched, but continued. "Culpable homicide. Charles admits in court to killing Sinclair, but that it wasn't his intention. As your heir, he'll likely receive transportation to a penal colony rather than hard labour. The regent may have him removed from the line of inheritance, but you can send for him once he's served his sentence if you wish. I won't stand in your way.

"But if you threaten Jarrett again, not only will I tell the judge what a calculated killer Charles is, but I'll tell everyone who will listen how in debt the barony is. Not just in the county either. I'll write letters to every bank, creditor, and investment opportunity I know. You'll be socially ruined and you'll never dig yourself out of the hole he's dug for you.

"And if you try to discredit me," Gil grinned. "I'll be sure to mention I'm a Charleton as often as possible in the dock and stain the family name as much as I can before I swing."

Jarrett felt the bold, reckless, and utterly idiotic urge to kiss Gil right there in front of them all. He knew it was a terrible idea, but by God, Gil deserved it. He summoned what little self-control he had and forced himself to be still.

Everyone held their breath as Gil and his uncle stared at each other.

Finally, the baron nodded.

"I accept." He raised a finger, silencing his son's protests without bothering to look at him. "But, if the Prince Regent disinherits Charles, you're disinherited as well. You will not be recognised as or by any Charleton and you will never set foot in this home again."

Gil nodded back. "This isn't my home."

He took one last look at his family, then to Jarrett's shock, wrapped his arm around Jarrett's waist and led him out of Charleton House forever.

EPILOGUE

Gil awoke to warm sunlight coming in through his bedroom window. The old saying about April showers bringing May flowers had certainly proved true. Even overgrown as they were, the gardens of Balcarres House did not disappoint. If he got up and opened the window, he'd be able to smell the fragrance of a dozen different flowers in bloom, and hear the drone of fat bees as they bobbed lazily between them. He'd have to see about cutting a few stems to bring inside for decoration. Not lavender though, that was one flower he was content to leave outside where it belonged. It'd been two months since he'd been stabbed by sprigs of lavender in unexpected places, and he was only just beginning to let his guard down.

At the moment, however, getting up to open the window was impossible. Without his spectacles, the arm tossed over his waist was blurry, but the tousle of brown hair resting on his shoulder looked just about perfect. He leaned over and kissed Jarrett's head, earning himself a sleepy murmur and a tightening of the arm around his waist.

Gil chuckled. "Come on, lazy bones. Look at you. A proper valet should rise at the crack of dawn."

He didn't quite make out Jarrett's response to that, but that was probably for the best. Then Jarrett gave an enormous yawn and blinked himself awake. Morning breath or no, Gil couldn't help but reward his fox with another, more thorough kiss.

"I love you," he whispered some minutes later.

"I love you too," Jarrett responded. Gil hadn't yet grown tired of hearing him say it, and doubted he ever would.

If anything was better about the last two months than not being assaulted by lavender at every turn, it was waking every morning like this with Jarrett in his arms. They'd argued about the risk of it at first, until Jarrett had pointed out that since he seemed to have contracted Gil's habit of actually having sex in a bed, the least Gil could do was still be there in the morning. It'd been hard to argue with that logic, harder still when they'd actually gotten into bed and Jarrett proved that just because he was finally fucking indoors didn't mean for a moment that he was tamed.

And if Gil had returned the favour by laying Jarrett down in a hidden glen in the woods and making love to him there? Well, it turned out love was all about compromises.

Compromises like having a space that was theirs that didn't mean Gil had to sleep in a freezing shed without even a fireplace. Gil might have been disinherited, but he was still raised the second son of a second son to a barony and had some needs, like not freezing off all his important bits in winter. And he planned to spend many, many winters with Jarrett.

Fortunately, Balcarres had more bedrooms than generations of earls had known what to do with, and this bedroom, while it had all the amenities required of an occupant of his birth, was also off on its own, near the servant's stairwell closest to Jarrett's official room. The earl might be surprised to return and find his estate manager having taken up residence, but considering Gil knew for a fact there was a secret door connecting the earl's room to that of his "companion", Gil very much doubted he'd mind.

He nudged Jarrett again. "Up with you."

"Why?" Jarrett yawned. "Not much work for a valet without someone to valet."

"You can help me price the whitewash needed to repaint the McGregors' barn then."

Jarrett grumbled and tightened his hold.

"We can ride over."

That got at least an interested noise out of Jarrett, although it wasn't until sometime later that Jarrett finally rose to go clean himself at the washbasin, leaving Gil panting on the bed.

"I saw your brother yesterday," Jarrett said, as Gil was taking his own turn at the basin, using the mirror above to brush and tie back his hair.

"Aye?"

"Aye."

Jarrett pulled a set of clothes for each of them out of the wardrobe and laid them on the bed. It made more sense for him to emerge fully dressed from Gil's room than to risk returning to his own room in his night clothes. After all, it was only respectable for a valet to extend his services to the guest in the house.

"He didn't so much as look at me, but he was out picnicking with Catriona Charleton, who says hello. She told me to say that if you wished to write to her, you can address your letters to *Riona* Charleton."

"Really? Robert and Riona. Well, well. Another matched set of Charletons."

He turned and looked Jarrett up and down. "How is 'Jarrett' spelled anyway?"

Jarrett rolled his eyes. "I wouldn't know, but you start pronouncing it '*Garrett*' and I might actually be guilty of the next murder. With that hair of yours though, you'd make a lovely 'Jill'."

Gil didn't deign to give that a response. "Well, good for them. Picnicking, you say? They're braver than me. It's still too damned cold. You want to take me picnicking or *stargazing* at the chapel again, you're going to have to wait until July."

That was a blatant lie, as Gil had proven on several occasions, but instead of calling him out, Jarrett only tossed his shirt at him. Compromise.

"Does that mean he'll be the next baron then?" The sting of Jarrett's question was softened when he took the shirt from Gil's hands and pulled it over his head. Gil hardly needed the help of a valet, but the only thing more fetching than Jarrett dressing him was Jarrett undressing him.

"Possibly. With Charles on his way to Australia and about as thoroughly disinherited as it's possible to be, we'll have to wait a few months to be certain. If Ca-Riona is with child—" Gil stepped into the breeches Jarrett had chosen for him, good for riding, but rather tight across the thighs, which he suspected was the real reason he'd picked them. "—and it could be argued it's Charles' child, then it becomes less clear. But if she's not, first my father inherits, then Robert."

"And then you?" Jarrett asked, holding up two waistcoats before choosing the amber one. He handed Gil his cravat to tie himself. For some reason, despite being a valet, Jarrett had never developed the knack for them.

"Well, they'd have to dis-disinherit me first." And from the cut direct his mother had given him when Gil saw her in town the week before, that didn't seem likely. Although, as she'd been emerging from the pawnbrokers when he'd been on his way to see about investing in a new colliery, they might decide to welcome back the prodigal son with open arms if he was willing to open his bankbook.

"But if I'm reinstated and Robert doesn't drink himself into an early grave before providing a *legitimate* heir, then aye, perhaps, one day. But for now I'm just a disinherited second son of a second son and that barn needs painting."

Gil put on his spectacles, but before he could adjust them, Jarrett got there first, adjusting them himself, then tucking a few loose strands of Gil's hair back behind his ear.

Surveying his work, Jarrett grinned and said, "Good. You're exactly the way I want you."

As they walked towards the stables, they heard a crunching of gravel. Looking down the long drive, they made out a carriage slowly working its way closer.

"His Lordship isn't expected back yet, is he?" Jarrett asked.

Gil shook his head. "Not that he's written. No crest or anything on it, so it's nothing official either."

He felt more than saw Jarrett relax beside him. Despite Magistrate Carnbee personally giving him the closest thing to an apology the man had ever uttered, Gil knew the fear of the gallows that had hung over his lover still hadn't completely vanished.

Mrs. Randall had been right about one thing. Jarrett was trouble, and if Gil had to spend the rest of his life at Jarrett's side, watching out for him, then so be it. That was where he planned to spend it anyway. Jarrett had come back to him twice; if he had to run again, Gil would go with him, hand in hand.

Whoever was in the carriage and whatever challenges they might bring, Gil and Jarrett would face them together with just the right blend of recklessness and charm.

THE END

AUTHOR'S NOTE

J ust a brief note to thank Emily and Veruska as always for their absolutely incredible help on this book!

Also, on a very tangential historical note, young Davey may have been right when he said he saw the Prince Regent in Edinburgh. While George IV didn't officially visit Scotland until 1822, it was rumored he'd previously visited the city several times incognito when his exploits in London became a little too newsworthy.

ABOUT THE AUTHOR

SAMANTHA SORELLE

S amantha SoRelle grew up all over the world and finally settled in Georgia, USA where the humidity does all sorts of things to her hair.

When she's not writing, she's doing everything possible to keep from writing. This has led to some unusual pastimes including perfecting fake blood recipes, designing her own cross-stitch patterns, and wrapping presents for tigers.

She also enjoys collecting paintings of tall ships and has one pest of a cat who would love to sharpen his claws on them.

*Join her newsletter at **www.samanthasorelle.com** and receive a FREE short story in your inbox. Also be the first to know about new books, sales, freebies, and other goodies!*

BY SAMANTHA SORELLE

HIS LORDSHIP'S MYSTERIES
His Lordship's Secret
His Lordship's Master
His Lordship's Return
His Lordship's Blood
Lord Alfie of the Mud (Short Story)
His Lordship's Gift (Short Story)

HIS LORDSHIP'S REALM
The Gentleman's Gentleman

OTHER WORKS
Cairo Malachi and the Adventure of the Silver Whistle
Suspiciously Sweet
The Pantomime Prince
An Heiress for Christmas

HIS LORDSHIP'S SECRET

BOOK ONE OF HIS LORDSHIP'S MYSTERIES

*L*ondon 1818

Alfred Pennington, the Earl of Crawford, knows someone wants him dead. An illicit boxing match seems the perfect opportunity to hire a champion fighter to watch his back, but Alfie is shocked to recognize the beaten and bloody challenger as his childhood friend, Dominick, one of the few people who knows the truth about Alfie's past.

Life has been hard for Dominick, so he can't believe his luck when Alfie—now with fine manners and a fancy title—offers him a chance to escape the slums in order to catch a potential killer. That's difficult enough, but not falling in love with the refined, confident man his friend has become may prove trickier still.

The investigation draws the two men closer than ever, but it becomes clear that their years apart may prove too much to overcome. As the danger mounts, can they find their way through the past to a future together? Or will hidden secrets cost them their happiness... and their lives?

His Lordship's Secret is the first novel in the His Lordship's Mysteries series.

Available Now

CAIRO MALACHI AND THE

ADVENTURE OF THE SILVER WHISTLE

"The first time I met the love of my life, he died in my arms."

C airo Malachi, Conduit to the Spirits is a liar, a thief, and a fraud. He may be building a reputation as one of the most fashionable mediums in London, but he doesn't even believe in ghosts and has certainly never conjured one. Which is why, after he witnesses the brutal slaying of a handsome young constable, he's shocked when the man's spirit appears in his home, begging for his help.

Constable Noah Bell is everything Mal can never be—honest, funny, and kind. But it's ridiculous to be attracted to a man he can't even touch, especially when every step they take towards solving Noah's murder is one step closer to bringing him the justice he needs to move on—and out of Mal's life forever.

As their investigation brings unexpected enemies to light, the secrets they're keeping from each other may prove even more dangerous. Mal and Noah will have to work together... or risk a fate worse than death.

Available Now

Printed in the USA
CPSIA information can be obtained
at www.ICGtesting.com
LVHW091151070424
776686LV00028B/386

9 781952 789199